Also by K. Bromberg

Driven

BOOK ONE

K. BROMBERG

Cover art created by **Tugboat Design**
Copyediting by **Maxanne Dobson of The Polished Pen**
Copyediting by **Amy Tannenbaum**
Formatting by **Champagne Formats**

ISBN: 978-0-9894502-1-8

Dedication

To B, B & C-

May you always follow your dreams.
The path will never be easy and you might have to chase them for
years.
There will be obstacles to overcome and criticisms to ignore.
There will be periods of doubt and moments of insecurity.

But you will reach them.

And when you finally touch those dreams,
No matter how old you are or where life has taken you,
Hold on tight—savor that feeling of accomplishment—and never let go.

Ever.

Chapter One

I SIGH INTO THE WELCOMING silence, grateful for the chance to escape—even if only momentarily—from the mindsuck of meaningless conversations on the other side of the door. For all intents and purposes, the people holding these conversations are my guests, but that doesn't mean I have to like or even be comfortable around them. Fortunately, Dane was sympathetic enough to my need for a reprieve that he let me do this chore for him.

The clicking of my high heels is the only other sound accompanying my categorically scattered thoughts, as I navigate the vacant backstage corridors of the old theater that I've rented for tonight's event. I quickly reach the old dressing room and collect the lists that Dane forgot in our chaotic, pre-party rush to clean up. As I start to head back, I run over my mental checklist for tonight's highly anticipated date auction. The niggling in the back of my mind tells me that I'm forgetting something. Reflexively, I reach for my hip, where my cell phone with my always-compiled task list lives, but instead, I come up with a handful of my cocktail dress's copper-colored silk organza.

"Shit," I mutter to myself as I stop momentarily, trying to pinpoint what exactly it is that I'm overlooking. I sag against the wall, the ruched bodice of my dress hindering my ability to inhale a deep sigh of frustration. Even though it looks incredible, the damn dress should've come with a warning: breathing optional.

Think, Rylee, think! With my shoulder blades pressed against the wall, I shift inelegantly back and forth to try and alleviate the pressure on my toes, which are painfully crammed into my four-inch heels.

Auction paddles! I need the auction paddles. I smile widely at my brain's ability to remember, considering I've been so overwhelmed lately as the sole coordinator of tonight's event. Relieved, I push myself off of the wall and take about ten steps.

And that's when I hear them.

The flirty, feminine giggle floats through the air, followed by the deep timbre of a masculine moan. I freeze instantly, shocked at the audacity of our party's attendees, when I hear the unmistakable sound of a zipper, followed by a breathless but *familiar* feminine gasp of, *"Oh yes!"* in the darkened alcove a few feet in front of me. As my eyes adjust to the shadows, I become aware of a man's black dinner jacket lying carelessly across an old chair shoved askew and a pair of strappy heels haphazardly discarded on the floor beneath it.

You couldn't pay me enough money to do something like that in public. My thoughts are interrupted when I hear a hiss of breath followed by a masculine, exhaled, *"Sweet Jesus!"*

I squeeze my eyes shut in a moment of indecision. I really need the auction paddles that sit in the storage closet at the end of the intersecting hallway. Unfortunately, the only way to reach that hallway is to walk past Lover's Lane alcove. I have no choice but to go for it. I send up a silent yet ludicrous prayer, hoping that I can skate past unnoticed.

I scurry forward, keeping my blush-stained face angled to the wall opposite them while I walk on my toes to keep my heels from clicking on the hardwood floor. The last thing I need right now is to draw attention to myself and come face to face with someone I know. I breathe a silent sigh of relief when my clandestine tiptoe is successful.

I'm still trying to place the woman's voice when I reach the storage closet. I fumble clumsily with the handle, having to aggressively tug on it before finally yanking it open and flicking on the light. I spot the bag of auction paddles on the far shelf as I walk inside the closet, forgetting to prop the door open. As I grab the handles of the bag, the door at my back slams shut with such force that the cheap shelving units in the closet rattle. Startled, I whip around to reopen the door and notice that the arm on the self-closing hinge has disconnected.

I immediately drop the bag. The sound of the paddles hitting the concrete floor and spilling out causes an eruption of sound. When

I reach for the handle, it turns but the door doesn't budge an inch. Panic licks at my subconscious, but I suppress it as I push again on the door with all of my strength. *It does not move.*

"Shit!" I chastise myself. "Shit, shit, shit!" I take a deep breath and shake my head in frustration. I have so much to do before the auction starts. And of course I don't have my cell phone to call Dane to get me out of here either.

When I close my eyes, my nemesis suddenly makes its move. The long, all-consuming fingers of claustrophobia slowly begin to claw their way up my body and wrap themselves around my throat.

Squeezing. Tormenting. Stifling.

The walls of the small room seem to be gradually sliding closer to each other, closing in on me. Surrounding me. Suffocating me. I struggle to breathe.

My heart beats erratically as I push back the panic rising in my throat. My breath—shallow and rapid—echoes in my ears. Consuming me. Zapping my ability to suppress my haunted memories.

I pound on the door, fear overwhelming the small hold I have left on my control. On reality. A rivulet of sweat trickles down my back. The walls keep moving in on me. My need to escape is the only thing I can focus on. I pound on the door again, yelling frantically, hoping someone roaming these back corridors can hear me.

I lean my back against the wall, close my eyes, and try to catch my breath; it's not coming quickly enough and dizziness surfaces. Becoming nauseous, I start to slide down the wall and accidentally hit the light switch. I'm submerged in pitch-black darkness. I cry out, frantically searching for the switch with my trembling hands. I flick it on, relieved to have pushed the monsters back into hiding.

But when I look down, blood covers my hands. I blink to try and snap out of my reverie, but I can't shake it. I'm in a different place. A different time.

All around me, I smell the acrid stench of destruction. Of desperation. Of death.

In my ears, his thready breathing is agonizing. He's gasping. Dying.

I feel the intense, blazing pain that twists so deep in your soul, you fear you'll never escape it. Even in death. My screams shake me out of the memory, and I'm so disoriented that I'm not sure if they're from the past or the present.

Get a grip, Rylee! I rub the tears off my cheeks with the backs of my hands and think back to my previous year in therapy to try to keep my claustrophobia at bay. I concentrate on a mark on the wall across from me, try to regulate my breathing, and slowly count. I focus on pushing the walls out, pushing the unbearable memories away.

I count to ten, gaining a scrap of composure, yet desperation still clings to me. I know Dane will come looking for me shortly. He knows where I went, but the thought does nothing to alleviate my surmounting panic.

Finally, I surrender to my intense need to escape and start pounding on the door with the heels of my hands. Shouting loudly. Cursing sporadically. Begging for someone to hear me and open the door. *For someone to save me again.*

In my ragged state of mind, seconds feel like minutes and minutes feel like hours. I feel like I've been locked in this ever-shrinking closet forever. Feeling defeated, I yell out once more and rest my forearms on the door in front of me. Bracing my weight on my forearms, I lay my head on them and succumb to my tears. Large, ragged sobs shake violently through me.

And suddenly, I have the feeling of falling.

Falling forward as I stumble into the solid body of a man in my path. My arms encircle a firm torso while my legs lie awkwardly bent behind me. The man instinctively brings his arms up and wraps them around me, catching me, holding my weight and absorbing my impact.

I look up, quickly registering the shock of dark hair spiked haphazardly, bronzed skin, the slight shadow of stubble … and then I meet his eyes. A jolt of electricity—an almost palpable energy—crackles when I meet those guarded, translucent green irises. Surprise flashes through them fleetingly, but the intrigue and intensity with which he regards me is unnerving, despite my body's immediate reaction to him. Needs and desires long forgotten inundate me with this one, simple meeting of eyes.

How can this man I've never met make me forget the panic and desperation I felt only moments before?

I make the mistake of breaking eye contact and glancing down at his mouth. Full, sculpted lips purse as he studies me intently, and then very slowly, they spread into a lopsided, roguish grin.

Oh, how I want that mouth on me—anywhere and everywhere all at once. What in the hell am I thinking? This man is way out of my league. Like light years away out of my league.

I draw my gaze back up to see amusement in his eyes, as if he knows what I'm thinking. I can feel a flush slowly spread over my face as embarrassment for both my predicament and my salacious thoughts registers in my brain. I tighten my grip around muscular biceps as I lower my gaze to avoid his assessing eyes and try to regain my composure. Bringing my feet back under me, I accidentally stumble farther into him, my balance compromised by my inexperience with sky-high heels. I jump back from him as my breasts brush against his firm chest, setting my nerve endings ablaze. Tiny detonations of desire tickle deep in my belly.

"Oh ... um ... I'm so sorry." I hold my hands up in a flustered apology. The man is even more disarming now that I'm able to drink in the whole length of him. Imperfectly perfect and sexy as hell with a smirk suggesting arrogance and an air exuding trouble.

He raises an eyebrow, noticing my slow inspection of him. "No apologies needed," he responds in a cultured rasp with just a hint of edge. His voice evokes images of rebellion and sex. *"I'm used to women falling at my feet."*

My head snaps up. I can only hope he's joking, but his enigmatic expression gives nothing away. He watches my response, bemusement in his eyes, and that cocksure smile widening, causing a single dimple to deepen in his defined jaw.

Despite having taken a step back, *I am still close to him.* Too close for me to gather my wits, but close enough for me to feel his breath over my cheek. To smell the clean scent of soap mixed with his subtle, earthy cologne.

"Thanks. Thank you," I respond breathlessly. I see the muscle in his clenched jaw pulse as he watches me. Why is this man making me nervous and feeling like I have to justify my situation? "The-the door shut behind me. It jammed. I panicked—"

"Are you okay? Miss—?"

My response falters as his hand cups the back of my neck, pulling me closer and holding me still. He runs his free hand up and down my bare arm in what I assume is an attempt to make sure that I'm not physically harmed. My body registers the trail of sparks his fingertips blaze on my naked flesh while my mind becomes acutely aware that his sensuous mouth is only a whisper away from mine. My lips part and my breath hitches as he moves his hand up the line of my neck and then uses the back of it to run his knuckles softly down my cheek.

I have no time to register the confusion mingled with a heavy dose of desire that surges through me when I hear him mutter, "*Oh fuck it*," seconds before his mouth is on mine. I gasp in utter shock, my lips parting a fraction as his mouth absorbs the sound, giving him an opening to caress his tongue over my lips and dart slowly between them.

I push my hands against his chest, trying to resist the uninvited kiss from this stranger. Trying to do what logic tells me is right. Trying to deny what my body is telling me it wants. To abandon inhibition and let myself enjoy this one moment with him.

Common sense wins my internal feud between lust and prudence, and I manage to push him back a fraction. His mouth breaks from mine, our breaths panting over each other's faces. His eyes, wild with lust, hold steady to mine. I find it hard to ignore the seed of desire that's blooming deep in my belly. The vehement protest that's screaming in my mind dies silently on my lips as I succumb to the notion that I *want* this kiss. I want to *feel* what I have been so devoid of—what I have purposely denied myself. I want to act recklessly and have "that kiss"—the one that books are written about, love is found in, and virtue is lost with.

"Decide, sweetheart," he commands. "A man only has so much restraint."

His warning, the insane notion that *simple me* can make a man *like him* lose control, bewilders me, confusing my thoughts so that the denial on my tongue never crosses my lips. He takes advantage of my silence, a lascivious smile curling the corners of his mouth before tightening the hold he has on the nape of my neck. From one breath to the next, he crushes his mouth to mine. Probing. Tasting. Demanding.

My resistance is futile and lasts only seconds before I surrender to him. I instinctively move my hands over his unshaven jaw to the back of his neck and tug my fingers in the hair that curls over the top of his collar. A low moan comes from the back of his throat, bolstering my confidence, allowing me to part my lips and take more of him. My tongue entwines and dances intimately with his. A slow, seductive ballet highlighted with breathy moans and panted whimpers.

He tastes of whiskey. His confidence exudes rebellion. His body evokes a straight punch of lust to my sex. A heady combination hinting he's a bad boy that this good girl should stay clear of. His urgency and adept skill hint at what could come. Images flash through my mind of back-arching, toe-pointing, sheet-gripping sex that no doubt would be as dominating as his kiss.

Despite my submission, I know this is wrong. I can hear my conscience telling me to stop. That I don't do *these* kinds of things. That I'm not *that* kind of girl. That I'm betraying Max with each caress.

But God, it feels so incredibly good. I bury all rationality under the surmounting desire that rages through my every nerve. My every breath.

His fingers stroke the back of my neck while his other hand travels down to my hip, igniting sparks with every touch. He splays it on my lower back and presses me into him. Laying claim to me. I can feel his erection thickening against my midsection, sending an electric charge to my groin, making me damp with need and desire. His leg slightly shifts and presses between mine, adding pressure to the apex of my thighs and creating an intense ache of pleasure. I push farther into him, softly mewling as I crave more.

I am drowning in the sensation of him, and yet I'm not willing to come up for the air I so desperately need.

He nips my lower lip as his hand moves down to knead my backside, pleasure spiraling through me. My nails scrape the back of his neck in reaction as I stake my claim.

"Christ, I want you right now," his husky voice pants between kisses, intensifying the ache in the muscles coiling below my waist. He moves the hand from the back of my neck and traces it down my ribcage and over until it cups my breast. I cry out a soft moan at the sensation of his fingers rubbing over my hardened peak through the

K. BROMBERG

soft material of my dress.

My body is ready to consent to his request because I want this man too. I want to feel his weight on me, his bare skin sliding on mine, and his length moving rhythmically in me.

Our entangled bodies bump up against the small alcove in the hallway. He presses me against the wall, our bodies frantically grabbing, groping, and tasting. He skims his hand down to the hem of my cocktail dress, finding purchase when he touches the lace tops of my thigh-high stockings.

"Sweet Jesus," he murmurs against my mouth as he runs his hand at a painstakingly slow pace up my outer thigh to the small triangle of lace that serves more as decoration than as panties.

What? Those words. When they finally register, I recoil as if whiplashed and push on his chest trying to shove him away from me. Those are the same words that I'd heard earlier in the darkened alcove. They hit me like cold water to my libido. *What the hell? And what in the hell am I doing anyway, making out with some random guy?* And more importantly, why pick now to do this while I'm in the midst of one of my most important events of the year?

"No. No—I can't do this." Staggering back, I bring a trembling hand up to my mouth to cover my swollen lips. . His eyes snap up to mine, the emerald color darkened by desire. Anger flashes through them fleetingly.

"It's a little late, sweetheart. It looks as if you already have."

Fury flashes through me at his sardonic comment. I'm intelligent enough to infer that I've just become another in the line of his evening's conquests. I look back at him, and the smug look on his face makes me want to hurl insults at him.

"Who the hell do you think you are? Touching me like that? Taking advantage of me that way?" I spit at him, using anger to ward off the hurt I feel. I'm not sure if I'm more upset at myself for my willing submission or the fact that he took advantage of me in my frenetic state. Or is it that I feel ashamed because I succumbed to his mind blowing kiss and skilled fingers without even knowing his name?

He continues to observe me, his anger simmering, eyes glowering. "Really?" he scoffs at me, cocking his head to the side and rubbing a hand over his condescending smirk. I can hear the rasp of his

8

stubble as his hand chafes over it. "That's how you're going to play this? Were you not participating just now? Were you not just coming apart in my arms?" He laughs snidely. "Don't fool your *prim* little self into thinking that you didn't enjoy that. That you don't want more."

He takes a step closer to me, amusement and something darker blazing in the depths of his eyes. Raising a hand, he traces a finger down the line of my jaw. Despite flinching, the heat from his touch reignites the smoldering craving deep in my belly. I silently castigate my body for its betrayal. "Let's get one thing clear," he growls at me. "I. Do. Not. Take. What's. Not. Offered. And we both know, *sweetheart*, you offered." He smirks. "*Willingly.*"

I jerk my chin away from his fingertips, wishing that I were one of those people who can say all the right things at all the right times. But I'm not. Instead, I think of them hours later and only wish that I'd said them. I know that I'll be doing that later, for I can't think of a single way to rebuke this overconfident yet completely correct man. He has reduced me to a mass of overstimulated nerves craving him to touch me again.

"That poor defenseless crap may work with your boyfriend who treats you like china on a shelf, fragile and nice to look at. Rarely used..." he shrugs "...but admit it, sweetheart, that's boring."

"My boy—" I stutter, "I'm not fragile!"

"Really?" he chides, reaching up to hold my chin in place as he looks in my eyes. "You sure act that way."

"Screw you!" I jerk my chin from his grasp.

"Ooooh, you're a feisty little thing." His arrogant smirk is irritating. "*I like feisty, sweetheart.* It only makes me want you that much more."

Prick! I'm just about to make a retort about what a manwhore he obviously is. That I know about his "getting acquainted" with someone else down the hall not too long ago before moving onto me. I stare at him, the thought rattling around in the back of my head that he vaguely reminds me of someone, but I push it away. I'm flustered, that's all.

As I'm about to open my mouth, I hear Dane's voice calling my name. Relief floods me as I turn to see him standing at the end of the hallway, looking at me oddly. Most likely perplexed by my disheveled state.

"Rylee? I really need those lists. Did you get them?"

"I got sidetracked," I mumble. I glance back at Mr. Arrogant behind me. "I'm coming. I just … wait for me, okay?"

Dane nods at me as I turn to the open door of the storage closet and quickly grab the scattered paddles off of the floor as gracefully as possible and shove them in the bag. I exit the closet and avoid meeting *his* eyes as I start to walk toward Dane. I exhale silently, glad to be heading toward more familiar ground when I hear his voice behind me. "This conversation isn't over, *Rylee.*"

"Like hell it isn't, *A.C.E.,*" I toss over my shoulder, the thought at how perfect the acronym fits him passes through my mind before I continue hastily down the hall, keeping my shoulders squared and head held high in an attempt to keep my pride intact.

I quickly reach Dane, my closest confidant and friend at work. Concern etches his boyish face as I loop my arm through his, tugging him back toward the party. Once we're through the backstage door, I release the breath I didn't know I was holding and lean back against the wall.

"What the hell happened to you, Rylee? You look like a hot mess!" He eyes me up and down. "And does it have anything to do with that Adonis back there?"

It has everything to do with the Adonis, I want to confide but for some reason hold back. "Don't laugh," I say, eyeing him warily. "The closet door jammed shut, and I was stuck inside."

He stifles a laugh and looks toward the ceiling to contain it. "That would only happen to you!"

I playfully push his shoulder. "Really, it's not funny. I got panicked. Claustrophobic. The lights went out and it brought me back to the accident." Concern flashes in his eyes. "I freaked out, and that guy heard me yelling and let me out. That's all."

"That's all?" he questions with a raise of his eyebrow as if he doesn't believe me.

I nod. "Yes. I just really lost it for a minute." I hate lying to him, but for now it's my best course of action. The more adamant I am, the quicker he'll drop the subject.

"Well, that's too bad because *damn,* girl, he's fine." I laugh as he wraps his arm around me in a quick hug. "Go on and freshen up. Take a breather. Then we need you back out to mingle and schmooze. We're about thirty minutes out from the start of the date auction."

I stare at myself in the bathroom mirror. Dane's right. I look like hell. I've ruined the hair and makeup my roommate, Haddie, helped me with. I take a paper towel and try to blot at my makeup to repair the damage. The tears have left my amethyst eyes rimmed red, and I need not wonder why my lipstick is no longer perfectly lining my lips. Pieces of my chestnut color hair are falling out of its clip, and the seam of my dress is horribly askew.

I can hear the dull bass of the music on the other side of the wall. It plays background to the hundreds of voices—all potential donors. I take a deep breath and lean against the sink for a moment.

I can see why Dane questioned what had really happened and if Mr. Arrogant had anything to do with it. I look completely disheveled!

I shift my dress so its sweetheart neckline and my more-than-ample *girls* sit properly. I smooth my hands over my hips where the fabric clings to my curves. I start to put the wisps of hair that have escaped back into my clip but stop myself. The tendrils have returned to their naturally wavy state, and I decide that I like the softened effect the curls have on my overall look.

I reach into my purse, which Dane has brought me, and freshen up my make-up. I add some mascara to my naturally thick lashes and reapply my smudged eyeliner. My eyes look better. Not great—but better. I pucker my lips, tracing my lipstick over the full M shape of them, rub them together, and then blot.

Not as good as Haddie, but good enough. I'm ready to rejoin the festivities.

Chapter Two

JEWELS, DESIGNER GOWNS, AND NAME-DROPPING are prevalent among the celebrities, socialites, and philanthropists who fill the old theater. Tonight is the culmination of much of my efforts over the past year—an event to raise the majority of the funds needed to break ground on the new facilities.

And I am way out of my comfort zone.

Dane discreetly rolls his eyes at me from across the room; he knows I would much rather be back at The House with the boys in jeans and my hair pulled back into a ponytail. I allow a ghost of a smile to grace my lips as I nod my head, before taking a sip of champagne.

I am still trying to wrap my head around what I willingly allowed to happen backstage and the sting of knowing I wasn't the first person Mr. Arrogant had made his moves on tonight. I'm dumbfounded at both my uncharacteristic actions and confused by how hurt I feel. Surely, I can't expect a man looking for a quick romp to have any intention but to boost his already-inflated ego.

"There you are, Rylee," a voice interrupts my thoughts.

I turn to find my boss—a bear of a man standing close to six and half feet tall with a heart bigger than that of anyone I've ever met. Appropriately enough, he looks like a big teddy bear.

"Teddy," I say affectionately as I lean into the arm he's placed on my shoulders in a quick hug. "Looks like it's turning out well, don't you think?"

"Thanks to all your hard effort. From what I hear, the checks are coming in." His lips curve, the smile causing his eyebrows to wiggle.

"And even before the auction begins."

"Just because it's a successful way to raise money, doesn't mean I have to agree with it," I reluctantly admit, trying to not sound like a prude. It's a debate we've had countless times over the past couple of months. Even though it's for charity, I just don't understand why women are willing to sell themselves to the highest bidder. I can't help but think the bidders are going to want more than just a date in return for the fifteen-thousand dollar starting bid.

"It's not like we're running a brothel, Rylee," Teddy admonishes. He looks over my right shoulder as a guest catches his attention. "Oh, there's someone I want you to meet. This is a cause very near and dear to him. He's one of our chairpeople's sons who—" he stops his explanation as whoever it is approaches nearby. "Donavan! Good to see you," he says heartily as he shakes hands with the person at my back.

I turn around, willing to make a new acquaintance, but instead I meet the bemused eyes of Mr. Arrogant.

Well, shit! How is it that despite being twenty-six years old, I suddenly feel like a prepubescent, awkward teenager? The half an hour away from him has done nothing to dampen his scorching good looks or the forbidden pull he has on my libido. His six-foot-plus frame is covered in a perfectly tailored black tuxedo that screams affluence, and my knowledge that beneath the jacket lies an obviously toned torso makes me bite my lower lip in unwanted need. And yet despite his magnetism, I'm still furious.

I think again about how he looks familiar, how he resembles someone I know, but the shock of seeing him again overrides the thought.

He smirks at me, his mirth apparent, and all I can think about is how those lips felt on mine. How his fingers, holding a tumbler now, felt traveling over my bare skin. About the length of his body pressed against mine.

And how he had licentiously *acquainted himself* with another woman moments before moving on to debase me.

Plastering a fake smile on my face, my eyes glare at Donavan as an unaware Teddy addresses him. "There's someone I'd like you to meet. She's the driving force behind what you see tonight." Teddy turns to me, placing a hand on my lower back. "Rylee Thomas, please meet—"

"We've already met," I say, interrupting him, saccharine oozing from my words as I smile at them. Teddy looks at me oddly; it's rare for me to be insincere. "Thank you for the introduction, though," I continue, looking from Teddy to Donavan, reaching out to shake his hand as if he were just another potential benefactor.

Dragging his eyes from me and my abnormal behavior, Teddy focuses back on Mr. Arrogant. "Are you enjoying yourself?"

"Immensely," he muses, releasing his too-long hold on my hand. I have to refrain from derisively snorting. How can he not be enjoying himself? *Arrogant bastard.* Maybe I should get on the stage and take a schoolyard poll of women here tonight to see whom he has not debauched already.

"Were you able to get some food? Rylee was able to get one of the hottest chefs in Hollywood to donate his services," Teddy explains, always trying to be the consummate host.

Donavan looks at me, humor crinkling the corners of his eyes. "I had a little taste of something while I was wandering around backstage." I suck in my breath, catching his innuendo as he moves his eyes back to Teddy. "It was rather unexpected but quite exquisite," he murmurs. "Thank you."

I hear someone call Teddy's name, and he eyes me again with curiosity before apologizing. "If you'll excuse me, I'm needed elsewhere for a moment." He turns toward Donavan. "It's great seeing you again. Thank you for coming."

We both nod in assent as Teddy leaves. Scowling, I turn on my heel to walk away from Donavan. I want to erase him and his memory from my evening.

His hand hastily closes over my bare arm, tugging me so my backside lands against the steeled length of his body. My breath hitches in response. I glance around, glad that everyone seems to be so absorbed in their own conversations that we've not drawn their attention.

I can feel Donavan's chin brush against my shoulder as his mouth nears my ear. "Why are you so pissed, *Ms. Thomas*?" There is a biting chill to his voice that warns me he's not a man to be messed with. "Is it because you can't let go of your highbrow ways and admit that despite what your head says, your body wants more of this rebel from the wrong side of the tracks?" He releases a low, patronizing growl in my ear. "Or are you so practiced at being frigid that you always deprive yourself of what you want? What you need? *What you feel?*"

I bristle, trying unsuccessfully to pull my arm out of his firm grip. Talk about a wolf in sheep's clothing. I still as another couple walks past us, eyeing us closely. Trying to figure out the situation between us. Donavan releases my arm, and rubs his hand over it instead, giving the impression of a lover's touch. And despite my fury, or maybe because of it, his touch triggers a myriad of sensation everywhere his fingers trace. Goose bumps ripple in their wake.

I can feel his breath rake over my cheek again. "It's very arousing, Rylee, knowing that you're so *responsive* to my touch. Very intoxicating," he whispers as he trails a finger across my bare shoulder. "You know you want to explore why your body reacted the way it did to me. You think I didn't see you undressing me with your eyes, enjoy you fucking me with your mouth?"

I gasp as he puts his hand on my stomach and pulls me tightly back against him so I can feel the evidence of his arousal pressing into my lower back.

Despite my anger, it's a heady feeling to know that I can make this man react in such a way. But then again, he probably reacts this way to the numerous women who, without a doubt, throw themselves at his feet on a regular basis.

"You're lucky I don't drag you back in that storage closet I found you in and take what you offered. Make you cry out my name." He nips softly at my ear, and I have to stifle the uncontrollable moan of desire that threatens to escape. "To fuck you and get you out of my system. Then move on," he finishes.

I've never been spoken to this way—would never have thought I'd allow someone to—but his words, and the vigor with which he speaks them, unexpectedly turn me on.

I'm mad at my body for its unbidden reaction to this pompous man. He obviously knows the hold he can have over a woman's body, and unfortunately, it is mine at the moment.

I turn slowly to face him and narrow my eyes. My voice is cold as ice. "Presumptuous, aren't you, Ace? No doubt your typical MO is to fuck 'em and chuck 'em?" His eyes widen in response to my unexpected vulgarity. Or maybe he's just surprised that I have him figured out so quickly. I hold his stare, my body vibrating with anger. "How many woman have you tried to seduce tonight?" I raise my eyebrows in disgust as guilt flickers fleetingly across his face. "What? Didn't you know that I happened upon you and your first conquest of the evening in the little alcove backstage?" Donavan's eyes widen. I continue, enjoying the surprised look on his face. "Did she play you at your own game, Ace, and leave you wanting for more? Aching to prove what a *man* you are since you couldn't fulfill her? That you had to pick a frantic woman locked in a closet to take advantage of? I mean, really, how many women have you used your bullshit lines on tonight? How many have you tried to leave your mark on?"

"Jealous, sweetheart?" He raises his eyebrows as his grin flashes arrogantly. "We can always finish what we started, and you can mark me any way you'd like."

I gently shove my hand against his chest, pushing him back. I'd love to wipe that smirk off of his face. *Leave my mark that way.* "Sorry, I don't waste my time on misogynist jerks like you. Go find someone—"

"Careful, Rylee," he warns as he grips my wrist, looking every bit as dangerous as his voice threatens. "I don't take kindly to insults."

I try to yank my wrist away but his hold remains. To anyone in the room, it looks as if I'm laying my hand on his heart in affection. They can't feel the overpowering strength of his grip.

"Then hear this," I snap, tired of this game and my warring emotions. Anger takes hold. "You only want me because I'm the first female who's said no to your gorgeous face and come-fuck-me body. You're so used to every female falling at your feet, *pun intended*, that you see a challenge—someone immune to your charm—and you're unsure how to react."

Despite his nonchalant shrug, I can see his underlying irritation as he releases my wrist. "When I like what I see, I go after it," he states unapologetically.

Shaking my head, I roll my eyes. "No, you need to prove to yourself that you can, in fact, get any girl who crosses your path. Your ego's bruised. I understand," I patronize, patting his arm. "Well, don't sweat it, Ace, I forfeit this race."

He raises an eyebrow, a ghost of a smile appears on his lips. The muscle in his clenched jaw tics as he regards me momentarily. "Let's get something straight." He leans in, inches from my mouth, the gleam in his eyes warning me I've gone too far. "If I want you, I can and will have you, at anytime and in anyplace, sweetheart."

I snort in the most unladylike way, astonished at his audacity, yet trying to ignore the quickening of my pulse at the thought. "Don't bet on it," I sneer as I hastily try to skirt past.

His hand whips out and grabs hold of my arm again, spinning me back toward him, so I'm standing intimately close. I can see his pulse beat in the line beneath his jaw. I can feel the fabric of his jacket hit my arm as his chest rises and falls. I glance down at his hand on my arm and glare back at him in warning, yet his hold remains. He leans his face in to mine so I can feel his breath feather across my cheek. I angle my head up to his, not sure if I'm raising my chin in defiance or in anticipation of his kiss.

"Lucky you, I'm a gambling man, Rylee," his resonating voice is just a whisper. "I do, in fact, like a good challenge now and again," he provokes, a mischievous smile playing at the corners of his mouth. He releases my arm, but runs his finger lazily down the rest of it. The soft scrape of his finger on my exposed skin sends shivers down my back.

"So let's make a bet." He stops and nods at a passing acquaintance, bringing me to the here and now as I've forgotten that we're in a room full of people.

"Didn't your mother teach you when a lady says no, she really means no, Ace?" I raise my eyebrow, a look of disdain on my face.

That smarmy smirk of his is back in full force as he nods in acknowledgement at my comment. "She also taught me that when I want something, I need to keep after it until I get it."

Great, so now I've acquired a stalker. A handsome, sexy, very annoying stalker.

He reaches out and toys with a loose curl on the side of my neck. I try to remain impassive despite my urge to close my eyes and sink into the soft touch of his fingers across my skin. His smirk tells me that he knows exactly what his effect is on me. "So, like I said, Ryles, a bet?

I bristle at his proposition, or maybe his effect on me. "This is asinine—"

"I bet by the end of the night," he cuts me off, holding a hand up to stop me, "I have a date with you."

I laugh out loud, stepping back from him. "Not a chance in hell, Ace!"

He takes a long swallow of his drink, his expression guarded. "What are you scared of then? That you can't resist me?" He flashes a wicked grin when I roll my eyes. "Agree then. What do you have to lose?"

"So you get a date with me and your bruised ego is restored." I shrug indifferently, wanting no part of this contest. "What will I get out if it?"

"If you win—"

"You mean if I can resist your *dazzling* charm," I retort sarcastically.

"Let me rephrase. If you can resist my dazzling charm by the end of the night, then I'll donate." He flickers his fingers through the air in a gesture of irrelevance. "Let's say, twenty thousand dollars to your cause."

I catch my breath and look at him in bewilderment, for this I can agree to. I know that there's no way in hell I'll succumb to Donavan or his captivating wiles, the *arrogant bastard*. Agreed, I was caught in his tantalizing web for a few moments, but it was just because it's been so long since I've felt like that. Since I've been kissed like that. Been touched like that.

Come to think of it, I don't think that I have ever been made to feel like that. But then again, I know that a man has never kissed me while his lips were still warm from another woman's.

I regard him impassively, trying to figure out the catch. Maybe there isn't one. Maybe he's just so cocky that he really thinks he's that irresistible. All I know is that I'm going to increase our contribution total tonight by twenty thousand.

"Isn't this bet going to put a damper on your evening's pursuit of other possible bedside companions?" I pause, taking a survey of the room. "It's not looking too promising, Ace, considering you're oh for two right now."

"I think I'll manage." He laughs out loud. "Don't worry about me. I'm good at multitasking," he quips, trying to beat me at my own game. "Besides, the night's still young, and by my count the score is oh for one so far. The second score has yet to be settled." He arches his eyebrows at me. "Don't over think it, Rylee. It's a bet. Plain and simple."

I cross my arms over my chest. The decision is easy. *Anything for my boys.* "Better get your checkbook ready, Ace. There's nothing I like better than proving arrogant bastards like you wrong."

He takes another sip of his drink, his eyes never leaving mine. "You sure are certain of yourself."

"Let's just say that my self-control is something that I pride myself on."

Donavan steps closer to me again. "Self-control, huh?" he murmurs, challenge dancing in his eyes. "Seems we've already tested that theory, Rylee, and it didn't seem to hold true. I'd be glad to test it again, though ... "

The muscles in my core clench at the possible promise, the ache burning there, begging for relief. Why am I acting like a girl who has never felt a man's touch before? *Maybe because it has never been this man's touch.*

"Okay," I tell him, sticking out my hand to shake his, "It's a bet. But I'll warn you, I don't lose."

He reaches out to take my hand, a broad smile lighting up his features, eyes sparkling a bold emerald. "Neither do I, Rylee," he murmurs. "Neither do I."

"Rylee, sorry to interrupt but we need you right now," says a voice behind me.

I turn to find Stella, with a look of panic on her face. I look toward Donavan, "If you'll excuse me, I'm needed elsewhere." I feel awkward, unsure of what else I should say or do.

He nods his head at me. "We'll talk more later."

As I walk away, I realize I'm not sure if his response is a threat or a promise.

Chapter Three

I AM SITTING BACKSTAGE IN the chaotic aftermath of the auction, but my mind is still reeling from it. The last hour and a half has been a blur. A successful blur in fact, but one that has come at a very high cost—*my dignity*.

At the last minute, one of our "date" auction participants had become ill. With no one else willing to partake, and programs pre-printed with a set number of participants, I begged, bribed, and pleaded with every member of my staff to step in and fill the role. Of all of the available people who were not physically needed for the facilitation of the auction, those left were either married or seriously attached to someone.

Everyone that was, except for me.

I whined, cajoled, pleaded even, but in an ironic twist that many of the staff took pleasure in, I became auction block Item Number Twenty-Two. So I had to suck it up and take one for the team, all the while ignoring a hunch that something wasn't quite right, but I couldn't put my finger on it.

And believe me, I hated every fucking minute of it! From the beauty-pageant-style introduction, to the parading around on a stage like a trophy, to the whistling catcalls of the audience, to the vapid calling of bidders' dollar amounts by the announcer. The lights were so blinding I couldn't see the audience, just a vague outline of figures. My time in the spotlight was consumed by embarrassment, the sound of my heartbeat rushing in my ears, the fear that my sweating from the heat of the stage lights would leave dark marks on the underarms of my dress.

I'm sure if I'd been on the other side of the stage, I would have found the auctioneer's comments entertaining, the participation of the audience endearing, and the silly antics of some of the women on stage trying to increase their bids amusing. I would've watched the contribution total rise and would have been proud of my staff for the successful outcome.

Instead, I'm sitting in the backstage area, taking a deep breath, and wrapping my head around what the hell just happened.

"Way to go, Ry!" I hear Dane's amusement at my predicament as he makes his way backstage toward me through the twenty-four other women who were willing participants in the auction. They're all exiting off the stage, gathering their bags of swag that we provided to thank them for their participation.

I glare at him, my annoyance evident. He gives me a wide, toothy grin as he grabs me in an unreciprocated hug. I'm beyond grumpy. I'm downright bitchy. I mean what a fucking night! First locked in the closet, then playing unknown sloppy seconds on the conquest list of Mr. Arrogant, and then enduring the humiliation of being purchased like prime beef at a meat market.

I cannot believe the giddiness of the women around me. They are chatting animatedly about their moment in the spotlight and bragging at how much they went for. I'm grateful for their participation, ecstatic at the outcome, but just simply bewildered by their enthusiasm.

His earlier accusation of being prim comes back to my mind, and I shake it off.

"That was fucking horrible!" I whine, shaking my head in incredulity as he laughs sympathetically at me. "All I want is a large glass— no screw that, a bottle of wine, some form of chocolate, and to get this damn dress and heels off, in no particular order."

"If that's all it takes to get you naked, I'd have brought you wine and chocolate a long time ago."

I glare at him, finding no amusement in his comment. "Too bad I don't have the right equipment to keep you satisfied."

"Meow!" he responds, biting his lip to suppress his laugh. "Oh, sweetie, that had to have been horrible for you, Ms. Keep-me-out-of-the-spotlight-at-all-costs! Look at you ..." He sits in the chair next to me, putting his arm around my shoulder and pulling me to him. I rest my head on his shoulder, enjoying the comforting feeling of friendship. "At least you sold for above the asking price."

"You asshole!" I pull away from him as he laughs childishly at me, rubbing in what he knows is a sore spot. To be honest, I still have no idea what amount my 'winning bid' was because I was too busy listening to the frantic pounding of my heartbeat fill my head.

To say that my ego doesn't care how much I was auctioned for is a mild understatement. Even though I detested the process, what female wouldn't want to know that someone thinks she is worthy enough to be bid money on for a date? Especially after my experience earlier in the evening.

"What are friends for? I mean between the bidding war and the ensuing brawl over your potential suitor..." he blows out a large breath, humor in his eyes "...and the all-out melee that ensued—"

"Oh, be quiet will you!" I laugh, relaxing for the first time at his ribbing. "No really, how much did I raise?"

"Listen to you! Most women would first say 'How much did I go for?'" he mocks in a high-pitch, pretentious voice, making me giggle, "and then the next question would be 'How hot is my date?'"

I turn to him and arch my eyebrows in the manner that always has the boys at The House answering quickly—or taking cover. "Well?" When he doesn't respond, but rather stares at me in mock horror for wondering, I allow myself to become one of the whiney voiced women around me. "Dane, give me the details!"

"Well, my dear, you sold ... " I shiver in mock horror at his words. He continues, "Excuse me, your future date spent twenty-five thousand dollars for an evening with you."

What? Holy shit! I'm dumbfounded. I know the starting bid was fifteen thousand for all entrants, but someone actually paid ten thousand more than that? Pride and a feeling of worth soars within me, repairing part of the damage Donavan inflicted earlier.

I try to rationalize someone I don't know spending that kind of money on a date with me, and I can't. It had to have been one of the chair people who worked closely on the board with me. This was the only plausible explanation. Most of the other women on the stage had been part of the elite Hollywood charity circle—they had friends and family in the audience to bid on them. I didn't.

I sigh and relax a bit with the knowledge that I will probably have to go on a date with a widowed elderly gentleman or possibly none at all. Maybe the person just wants to donate to us and will let me off the hook. What a relief! I was worried about the date part. Some loser expecting something in return for his generous donation—ugh!

"So did you see who won the auction?"

"Sorry, sweetie," he says as he pats my knee. "The guy was off to the side. I was in the back. I couldn't see him."

"Oh—okay." Disappointment fills my voice as I begin to worry again.

"Don't worry. I'm sure it is one of the old guys from the board—" he stops, realizing he's just implied that those are the only men willing to bid on me. He continues cautiously, knowing full well that I'm in bitch-mode right now. "You know what I meant, Ry. They all love you! They'll do anything to support you." He eyes me carefully and realizes he should stop while he is ahead.

I sigh loudly, relaxing from the realization that I'm uber-sensitive right now. I take note that most of the participants have cleared out of the backstage area. "Well, my friend, I should be getting back to the soiree." I stand, smoothing my dress down and wincing as my feet bunch back down into my shoes. "I, for one, am more than done with my duties for the evening. I'm ready to go home and devour that chocolate and wine in the comfort of my fluffy robe and comfy couch."

"You don't want to wait and see what the tally is for the night?" he asks, rising from the seat to follow behind me.

We walk past the alcove that Donavan and I had occupied earlier, and I blush, keeping my head down so Dane won't question me. "I asked Stella to text me later when it's added up." I push open the door to enter the party again. "I don't need to be here for that—" I falter as I walk through the door and see Donavan leaning a shoulder casually against the wall, surveying the crowd.

He's a man who is obviously at ease with who he is, regardless of his surroundings. He exudes an aura of raw power mixed with something deeper, something darker that I can't seem to put my finger on. Rogue. Rebel. Reckless. All three descriptions fit him, and despite this man's refined look, he screams trouble.

Dane bumps into me from behind as I stop abruptly when Donavan's scanning eyes connect with mine. "Rylee—" Dane complains until he realizes why I've stopped. "*Well, shit,* if it isn't Mr. Brooding. What's going on here, Ry?"

I roll my eyes at the thought of Donavan's stupid bet. "Arrogance run amuck," I mutter to him. "I have to take care of something." I toss over my shoulder, "Be right back."

I stalk toward Donavan, more than aware that his eyes track my every movement and at the same time annoyed at having to deal with this now. Our banter has been an amusing way to pass the evening's time, but the night's over and I'm ready to go home. Game over. He pushes his shoulder off the wall, straightening the long length of his lean body as I walk toward him. The corners of his mouth turn up slightly as he attempts to gauge my mood.

I reach him and hold up a hand to stop him before he even begins to speak. "Look, Ace, I'm tired and in a really shitty mood right now. It's time for me to call it a night—"

"And just when I was going to offer to take you places you didn't even know existed before," he says dryly with just a ghost of a smile and an arch of an eyebrow. "You don't know what you're missing, sweetheart."

I snort loudly, all propriety out the window. "You're fucking kidding me, right? You actually get women with lines like that?"

"I'm wounded." He smirks, his eyes full of humor as he holds his hand to his heart in false pain. "*You'd be surprised what my mouth gets with those lines.*"

I just stare at him. The man has absolutely no humility. "I don't have time for your childish games right now. I just had to endure humiliation beyond my worst nightmare, and I'm more pissed off than you can imagine. I *especially* don't want to deal with *you* right now."

If he is shocked at my rant, he hides it well. His face remains impassive except for the muscle pulsing with his clenched jaw. "I do love a woman who tells it like it is," he murmurs quietly to himself.

I place my hands on my hips and continue, "So I'm going home in about ten minutes. Night's over. I win our idiotic bet, so you better get your check and fill it out because you're going home with lighter pockets tonight."

His lips quirk up in an amused smirk. "Twenty-five thousand lighter, in fact," he deadpans.

"No, we agreed on twen—" I stop as a smile spreads across his lips, realization slowly dawning on me. *Oh fuck!* He bid on me. Not only did he bid on me, but he bid on me and won. He *officially* has a date with me.

I grit my teeth and raise my head toward the ceiling, inhaling slowly, trying to calm myself. "No—uh-uh. This is bullshit and you know it!" I glare at him as he starts to speak. "That wasn't the deal. I didn't agree to this!" I'm flustered and exasperated, so furious that I'm beyond reason.

"A bet's a bet, Ryles."

"It's Rylee, you asshole!" I spit at him. Who the hell does he think he is? First he buys me and then he thinks he can give me a *nickname*? I know that the irrational female in me has reared her Medusa-like head, but I really don't care at this point.

"Last time I checked, sweetheart, my name wasn't *Ace*," he retorts with some justification. The rasp of his voice grates over me like sandpaper. He casually leans back against the wall, as if this is a conversation he has every day.

His nonchalance fuels my ire. "You cheated. You-you-aaarrgh!" My frustration is stifling my ability to form coherent thoughts.

"We never had time to outline any rules or stipulations." He raises his eyebrows and shrugs. "You were pulled away. That left everything as fair game." His smile is irritating. The humor in his intoxicating green eyes is infuriating.

Oh shit! I try to argue cleverly with him and I just end up looking like a guppy, opening and closing my mouth several times without a word falling from my lips.

He pushes off the wall and steps in closer to me. His signature scent envelops me. "I guess I just proved you do, in fact, lose sometimes, *Ryles*." He reaches up to move a tendril that has fallen over my face, his lone dimple deepening with his victorious smirk. I recoil at his touch but he holds my jaw firm in his hands. "I'm looking forward to our date, Rylee." He grazes a thumb over my cheek and angles his head to the side while he considers his next statement. "In fact, more than any other date I've had in a while."

I close my eyes momentarily, leaning my head back as "Oh God!" slips from my lips in a sigh. *What an unbelievable night*!

"So that's what it will sound like?"

I open my eyes, confused by his comment, to see him regarding me with a bemused look on his face. "What?" I bark, my response harsh like a curse.

"Those words, *Oh God*," he mimics me, reaching out and running a finger down the side of my face. "Now I know exactly how you'll sound when you say that while I'm buried deep inside of you."

I open my mouth in shock at his audacity, the overconfidence of his words astounding me. His haughty smile grates on my last nerve. *The arrogant prick.* Luckily I'm able to voice an articulate thought. "Wow! You sure think a lot of yourself, don't you, Ace?"

He slips his hands into his pockets, his smirk dominating his magnificent face. He leans in, a salacious look in his eyes and his voice a daunting whisper. "Oh, sweetheart, *there is definitely a lot of me to think about.*" His quiet laugh sends a chill up my spine. "I'll be in touch."

And with that, Mr. Arrogant turns on his heels and walks away without a backwards glance. I watch his broad shoulders until he disappears into the throng of people and finally exhale the breath I didn't know I was holding.

Screw him and his sexy mouth and his gorgeous green eyes framed with thick lashes and his dexterous hands and his … his … *just his everything*! Ugh! I'm shaking I'm so furious with him.

And at myself. Donavan is confident and sure of himself and more than comfortable with being the alpha male. For me, there is nothing more attractive in a man than that. But right now, I'm irritated with him. He's gotten under my skin. And I'm not sure if that's a good thing or not, but I know that places inside of me that died that horrific day two years ago showed some signs of life tonight.

Starting the moment he touched me.

I stand there trying to comprehend the night's unexpected events, and after a few moments, I'm certain of two things. First, there is absolutely no way I am honoring this agreement. And second, deep down, despite my staunch resolve, I know this will not be the last time I'll be seeing Donavan.

Chapter Four

I STRUM MY FINGERS ON my desk as I peruse our parent company's website. I have so many other things I need to be doing right now, but I find myself looking at pictures of all of the chairpersons on our board, as well as the members of the organizing committee.

I can't place which member's son is Donavan, and it's really starting to annoy me. I don't have his last name to help the puzzle pieces fit into place. I wish I hadn't told my staff that they could wait a few days on getting me the paperwork. I was just trying to be nice after all of the hard work they had put in. If I had it though, I'd have the answer. I know I could just call up Stella or Dane and ask the name of my future date, but then they'd know something is up because something like that wouldn't be important to me. And with those two gossipers, I don't want to open *that* floodgate.

More importantly, I'm irritated at myself for even caring who he is. "Manwhore," I grumble under my breath.

I rub my tired eyes and run my fingers through my hair, pulling it back off my shoulders. I exhale loudly. It's been a long, tiring weekend, and I'm exhausted.

I glance at the clock. I have fifteen minutes before I have to leave to get to The House for my twenty-four hour shift.

My computer pings and I click on my mailbox to see an incoming email. I don't recognize the address but can assume the person's identity. *Here we go again.* I click on it because the subject line has piqued my curiosity.

To: Rylee Thomas
From: Ace
Subject: Backstage Liaisons

Ryles—
**Would you have opened the email if the subject line simply
stated, "Date the Highest Bidder"?**
Didn't think so.
You owe me a date.
Let me know your availability so I can make plans.
You have twenty-four hours to respond. Or else.
—Ace

I sigh heavily in confused relief. I'm irritated at his ridiculous ultimatum. More so though, I'm irritated at myself. Why, even if I don't want to go out with him, do I feel like a giddy schoolgirl excited that he's emailed me? That the cool, popular kid has acknowledged the awkward, ordinary girl.

After he's made out with the head cheerleader behind the bleachers, that is. *God, he is annoying!* I check the clock to make sure that I have time for a response.

To: Ace
From: Rylee Thomas
Subject: Cat Got Your Tongue?

Ace—
Demanding, aren't we?
**You never addressed your subject line. Should I worry about
how many other emails you sent out with the same title to your
other conquests from Saturday night trying to get a follow-up
date?**
-Ryl-E-E

I smile as I hit send, picturing his face in my mind. His smile. His emerald eyes. The devastation he had over my control. It's only been two days since the auction, and yet I wonder if my memory is making Donavan out to be more than he really is. Making his transgressions seem less offensive than they really were. Before I can ponder it further, my inbox alerts me.

To: Rylee Thomas
From: Ace
Subject: Chivalry isn't dead

Ryl-E-E—
A gentleman never kisses and tells, Ryles. You should know that.
When you think about me, make sure to note that my demands will only result in your pleasure.
And you never answered my question. A bet's a bet. Time to pay up, sweetheart.
—Ace

I laugh out loud to his response. Maybe if I ignore his question, he'll just go away. Good luck with that! Despite detesting the game he's playing, I find myself smiling as I type my reply. I'm a challenge to him, plain and simple. If I'd acquiesced to his request for a date, or maybe even if I had continued kissing him in the hallway without backing away, he'd never have given me a second thought. He would have had his wicked way with me and walked away without a backwards glance.

To: Ace
From: Rylee Thomas
Subject: Fat ladies and yellow birds

Ace—
I read somewhere that a boy needs the adulation from many girls to be satisfied, whereas a gentleman needs the adoration

from just one woman to be fulfilled. By that definition alone, you are definitely not a gentleman. That means you should be singing like a canary, then.
Besides, a date is WAY ABOVE my pay grade.
—Rylee
P.S. Oh, and don't worry, I don't think of you. At all.

Take that! I think, proud of myself for my wit despite the blatant lie in the last comment. I stand and pack up my stuff, straightening my desk. As I reach to turn my computer off, my inbox alerts me again.

To: Rylee Thomas
From: Ace
Subject: You need a raise

_____

Rylee—
I may be a man, but I'm nowhere near gentle. In fact, I think you're a little curious just how I like it. Step over the edge with me, Ryles—I'll hold your hand and revel in making you lose that self-control you pride yourself on. I'll be anything and everything but gentle.
I promise. You'll never know your limits until you push yourself to them.
If you refuse to give me availability, I may have to take matters in my own hands. Maybe someone taking control is exactly what you want? What you need?
—Ace

"Egotistical asshole," I mutter as I switch off my computer, refusing to respond. Like he knows what I want or need. But despite my anger, his words reverberate through me more than they should.

My phone rings as I drive to The House. I'm in a foul mood for some reason, and I can only blame it on Donavan and his damn emails. Damn him for filling me with wants and needs and desires again. I glance at the screen on my phone and groan.

It's Haddie, my best friend and roommate. I've successfully avoided her and one of her notorious inquisitions since the event on Saturday night. Luckily, she'd had plans that kept her out of the house because one round of her questions and she would've known something had happened.

"Hey, Had!"

"Ry! Where've you been? You're avoiding me!" she reprimands.

Geesh, five words into the conversation and she's already starting in on me. "No, I'm not. We've just both been busy with—"

"Bullshit," she argues. "I talked to Dane and know the story! Why didn't you wake me up and tell me when you got home?"

I blanch, wondering what Dane told her, and then I realize that she is probably talking about the auction. "Because nothing happened but absolute humiliation. It was awful."

"Oh, it couldn't have been that bad!" she says sarcastically. "At least you got a hot date out of it. Who is he?"

I roll my eyes at her as I turn my car into the driveway of The House. "Some guy—"

"Well, obviously. I'm glad it wasn't *some* girl because that would put a whole different spin on this." She laughs, and I can't help but smile. "So spill it, sister!"

"Really, Haddie, there's nothing to tell." I can hear her guffaw. "Oh, will you look at that? I just pulled up to The House. I gotta go."

"Likely story, Ry. Don't worry, I'll get the scoop out of you when you get home tomorrow from work." I cringe at the Haddie Montgomery promise to dig deeper. She never forgets.

"Look, I don't know the guy," I relent, hoping if I give her some information she'll be satisfied and not pry any further. "Teddy introduced me to him before I was pulled into being a *contestant*. His name is Donavan something, and he's the son of one of the chairpersons. That's all I know." I cringe at my blatant omission.

I hear her hum of approval on the end of the line and know the exact expression that is on her flawless face. Her button nose is scrunched up in disbelief while her heart-shaped lips purse as she tries to figure out if I'm telling the truth. "I really am at work now, Had. I have to go. Love ya, bye," I sign off with our usual parting words.

"Love ya, bye."

There is chaos in The House as usual when I walk in the door. I step over six book bags that lay haphazardly in the entryway. I can hear Top 40 music coming from one bedroom and the beginning of an argument coming from another as I pass the hallway on my way to the core of the house.

I hear the pop of a baseball mitt coming through the open windows at the rear of the house, and I know that Kyle and Ricky are in the midst of their frequent bout of catch. Any minute, one of them will be complaining that the other one has horrible aim. They'll argue and then move to the next activity, playing with their Bakugan or competing at baseball on the Wii.

I walk into the great room to hear Scooter giggling as he sits next to my fellow counselor, Jackson, on the couch, arguing the merits of Spiderman versus Batman.

The great room is a common area of the house, combining the kitchen with a large open living area. Large windows open up to the backyard where I can see the boys playing catch. The room has couches on one end that form a U-shape around a small media center, while the other end houses a big wooden table, currently covered with what appears to be incomplete homework. The earth tone furniture is neither new nor shabby but gently worn and well used.

"Hey, guys," I say as I place my bag on the kitchen island, appraising the state of dinner in two large Crock-Pots on the counter.

I hear various versions of "Hi, Rylee" in response.

Jackson looks up from the couch, his brown eyes full of humor over his debate with eight-year-old Scooter, and smiles. "We were just taking a break from homework. They'll have it finished before dinner is ready."

I lift the lid off a Crock-Pot and stir what appears to be pot roast and vegetables. My stomach grumbles, reminding me that I'd worked through lunch today at the corporate office.

"Smells good," I say, smacking Shane's hand as he reaches to pinch a piece of the freshly baked loaves of bread that sit on cookie sheets on top of the stove. "Hands off. That's for dinner. Go get a piece of fruit if you're hungry."

He rolls his eyes at me as only a fifteen-year-old boy can. "Hey, can't blame a guy for trying," he counters, his prepubescent voice cracking as he skirts around me, brushing his shaggy blonde hair off his forehead.

"You need a haircut, bud." He shrugs at me, his lopsided grin stealing my heart as it does regularly. "Did you finish your paper yet so I can review it?"

He turns around to face me, walking backwards. "Yes, *Mom!*" he replies, the term of endearment not lost on me. For that, in fact, is what the staff here is to these boys; we are the parents they no longer have. And in most instances, the chance of adoption above a certain age diminishes drastically. The state has turned over their guardianship to my company.

I work mostly in the corporate office several miles away, but require that all of my trained staff work at least one twenty-four hour shift per week. This time allows them to connect with the boys, and to never forget whom exactly we are fighting on behalf of on a daily basis.

These boys and my staff are my second family. They fuel me emotionally and challenge me mentally. At times they try my patience and push my limits, but I love them with all my heart. I'd do anything for them.

Connor comes flying through the kitchen, running to the back door with something under his arm, while Aiden is chasing after him. "Hey, guys, calm down," I reprimand as I hear Aiden shout that he's going to get it back and make him pay.

"Cool it, boys," Jackson says in his deep baritone, rising from the couch to watch the interaction. Those two have a habit of antagonizing each other, sometimes to the point of becoming physical.

I feel small hands wrap around my thigh, and I look down into the angelic eyes of Scooter. "Hey, bud." I smile, taking slow and deliberate movements to reciprocate the hug. I can see him steel himself for my touch, but he does not flinch. It has taken me sixteen months to elicit this reaction from an eight-year-old whose only physical contact with his mother was through fists or objects. I squat down to his eye level and kiss him softly on the cheek. Trusting, chocolate-brown eyes look at me. "I agree with you. Spiderman is *way cooler* than Batman. He's got that spidey-sense that Batman only wishes he had." He smiles at me, nodding his head enthusiastically. "Why don't you go pick up your mess? It's almost time for dinner."

He nods, flashing me a shy smile, and I watch him walk back to the family room where his beloved comic books are sprawled haphazardly across the floor. I move my gaze from Scooter to the figure huddled on the other couch.

Zander is static. He is in the same mute state he's been in for the past three months he's been in my care. He is curled into himself, an impassive expression on his face, as he watches the muted television with large, haunted eyes. He has his beloved stuffed dog, ratty and coming apart at the seams, a lifeline held tightly against his chest. His wavy brown hair curls softly at the nape of his neck. He desperately needs a haircut, but I can still hear his terrified shrieks from a month ago when he caught sight of the scissors as I approached him for a trim.

"No change, Jax?" I murmur to Jackson who has walked up beside me, keeping my eyes on Zander.

"Nope." He sighs loudly, empathy rolling off him in waves. He continues in a muted tone, "His appointment with Dr. Delaney was the same. She said he just stared at her while she tried to get him to participate in the play therapy."

"Something is going to trigger him. Something will snap him out of his shock. Hopefully it will be sooner rather than later so we can limit damage to his subconscious..." I hold back my sorrow for the lost little boy "...and help the police figure out what happened."

Zander had come to us after the police found him covered in blood in his house. He had been trying to use a box of Band-Aids to stop the bleeding from the stab wounds that covered his mother. A neighbor walking her dog had overheard his mother's strangled cries for help and called the police. She died before they arrived. It is assumed that Zander's father committed the murder, but without Zander's statement, the events that led up to the actual act are a mystery. With his father missing, he's the only one who knows what happened that night.

Zander has not uttered a word in the three months since his mother's murder. It's my job to make sure we provide for him in every way possible so he can dig his way out of the catatonic, repressed state he's in. Then we can help him begin the lengthy process of healing.

I turn from the heartbreak that is Zander and work with Jackson to get dinner finished. We work in sync, side by side, like an old married couple; we've had this shift together for the past two years and can now anticipate each other's movements.

We both work in silence, listening to the flurry of activity in The House.

"So I heard the benefit was a success—with an unexpected entrant in the auction." He wiggles his eyebrows at me, and I roll my eyes in response before turning back to the sink. "And one hot and heavy make-out session backstage."

I drop the knife I'm washing. It clatters loudly against the stainless steel basin. I'm grateful that my back is to Jackson so he can't see the stunned look on my face. *What the hell?* Someone must have seen me with Donavan. I have to remind myself to breathe as I panic, trying to figure out how to respond. I don't need my staff gossiping about my backstage encounter.

"What—what do you mean?" I try to sound casual, but I hope I am the only one who can hear the distress in my voice. I turn the water off, waiting for the response.

Jackson laughs his deep, hearty laugh. "I would have loved to see you in action, Ry."

Shit, shit, shit! My heart races. How am I going to explain this one? I feel warmth on my cheeks as my flush spreads. I open my mouth to answer him when he continues.

36

"Parading around on stage at the event you so desperately fought against." I can hear the amusement in his voice. "My God, you must have been pissed!"

"You have no idea." My response is almost a whisper. I have nothing left to wash, but I keep my back to him, afraid the questions will start if he sees my face.

"And then Bailey told me she met this hot guy—her words, not mine—and lured him backstage in typical Bailey fashion and had a hot and heavy make-out session with him."

I release the breath I'm holding, grateful that it was our intern Bailey bragging about her exploits rather than gossiping about her boss's. And then I realize that sexy siren Bailey, whom all the guys at work want to date, was most likely Donavan's first conquest on Saturday night.

If that were the case, why would he want to go from the leggy, auburn-haired bombshell to me? Talk about reinforcing my feeling of being second choice.

I blow my hair up out of my face. "Well, you know Bailey," I counter, trying to phrase my next words carefully. "She definitely likes to have her fun."

Jax laughs, patting my back as he walks by. "That was a nice way of putting it," he says as he starts to make the boys' school lunches for the next day. "She's a great girl, works hard, the kids love her … just not a girl I'd want my son to date."

I murmur an agreement thinking about our beguilingly sweet intern, who is only five years my junior, and her *free* ways. A part of me has always been jealous of girls like her. Girls who throw caution to the wind and live their life without regrets, kiss random boys recklessly, take spur of the moment road trips, and are always the life of the party. I often worry that one day I'll look back on my life and feel like I haven't lived. That I haven't taken enough chances, sown my wild oats, or ventured outside my comfort zone.

My life is safe, predictable, controlled, and always in order. I like it that way most of the time. It's not that I'm not jealous of her because she kissed Donavan first—well maybe a little—but rather that she lives without regrets.

I shake myself out of my thoughts, ones that I have been having more frequently with *the anniversary* approaching. If anything, I should have learned that life is short and I need to *really* live it, not stay in my safe corner as it passes me by. I pull myself from my thoughts and refocus on the task at hand.

"Boys," I shout over the chaos, "it's time to come finish your homework." I hear groans coming from various rooms because I've said the dreaded "H" word. Six boys, varying from eight to fifteen years old, sullenly walk toward the table, grumbling as they go.

I look over toward the couch where Zander remains curled into himself, rocking back and forth for comfort.

I slowly walk toward him and kneel in front of him. "Zander, do you want to join us? I can read you a book if you'd like?" I speak softly to him, slowly reaching my hand out, holding it still for him to see my intention, and rest it on his hand that rests on his knee. He continues rocking, but his blue eyes flicker over to hold mine.

I see so many things in the depths of his eyes that shake me to the core. I smile softly at him and squeeze his hand. "We'd love for you to join us." He remains silent but his eyes are still fused on mine. A small sliver of hope springs within me since he normally looks at me and glances away after a few seconds. "Come on, Zander, take my hand, I won't let go if you don't want me to."

He continues to stare at me for some time as I remain stock still, a reassuring smile on my face. His tiny hand moves, and he closes his fingers around my palm. He stands slowly, and we move to join the rest of the boys at the table.

Chapter Five

I'M DRAGGING BIG TIME. I'VE hit the last hour of my shift at The House, and the long hours of the past couple of days have caught up with me. The boys were a handful today.

Kellen, my co-counselor, is playing tag with the boys outside. I can hear their laughter and squeals through the open windows.

I'm in the kitchen getting everything together for dinner for the next shift when the house phone rings.

"Hello?"

"Oh, good! You're still there." I hear relief tinged with excitement.

"Just barely." I laugh. "I have about fifteen minutes left. What can I do for you, Teddy?"

"I know you're probably exhausted, but is it possible for you to stop by the office on the way home?"

It's the last thing I want to do, as much as I love him. I just want to go home, crawl into bed, and sleep until tomorrow. "Um, okay. Sure. Is something wrong?"

"Just the opposite! I think we found the solution to find the rest of the funding for the new facilities." He says enthusiastically. "I'll tell you about it when you get here. We're just hammering out all of the details now."

"Wow! Are you serious?" My hopes start to rise. Even with the charity event and the numerous other donations we have already received, we are still shy of our goal by several million dollars. "I—I will be there as soon as I can, depending on traffic."

I hang up the phone, excitement bubbling inside me. All my hard work over the past two years to get the approvals, the board's backing, the plans, the funding—it all might finally come to fruition.

I finish preparing the dinner so all that the next shift has to do is put it in the oven. I grab my purse and overnight bag and start to gather my things. I glance at my cell phone and begrudgingly decide to check my email. Maybe I can tackle a few phone calls from them while I am in traffic.

I scan my inbox and notice an email I'd received earlier in the day from Donavan. I contemplate just deleting it, but curiosity gets the best of me and I open it up.

To: Rylee Thomas
From: Ace
Subject: Dexterous Fingers

_____

Rylee—
You've left me no choice. Your lack of response has left me to take matters into my own hands.
You remember how those felt, don't you?
—Ace

Arrogant ass. I delete the email. What's he going to do? I'm even more indifferent to him now that I know about his and Bailey's tryst in the dressing room. Or at least I am trying to be. Come to think about it, they probably fit each other perfectly. *Manwhore and ma-neater.*

I smile at the thought as I finish collecting my things and say goodbye to the troops.

Traffic is unusually light as I drive toward the office. I take this as a sign that good things are going to happen. It's a beautiful, sunny California day, unusually warm for the ending of January. What I would give to grab a towel, head to the beach and lie there, letting the sun's warmth rejuvenate me.

In no time at all, I pull into the parking lot of Corporate Cares. I walk quickly up to the building's lobby, checking my reflection in the mirrored windows. I have on my favorite blue jeans that sit low on my waist and a snug, red V-neck T-shirt. Luckily I had an extra one in my bag because I don't think Teddy would enjoy my original one that's now splattered with Ricky's vomit. I fuss with my hair a moment, pulling the clip from it and letting my curls fall down my back.

After a short elevator ride, where I'm able to touch up my lipgloss and pinch my cheeks for color, I arrive on the floor of the main office. I walk past my office, nod to several people, and exchange pleasantries on my way to Teddy's receptionist. I note that the shutters on the conference room windows are closed and wonder what's going on in there.

"Hi, Sandy."

"Hey, Rylee. I'll let him know you're here. He's expecting you."

I smile. "Thanks." I walk toward the wall of windows that extends throughout the office and watch a line of cars on the freeway heading home. *The ants go marching one by one.*

"That was quick!" I turn to face my boss, a broad grin on his face. "I can't wait to bring you up to speed."

"I can't wait to hear what's going on," I say as I follow him into his office.

I sit down across from him in the black leather chair, happy to be off my feet.

Teddy sits across from me, unable to contain his enthusiasm. "I got a call earlier today and have been in a meeting all afternoon hammering out a deal. Get this," he says as he leans toward me, placing his hands on his desk, "CD Enterprises has come forward wanting to put up half of the remaining cash for the facilities as well as raise the remainder of the money by getting other companies to match or sponsor them." His words come out in a rush of air, excitement in his eyes.

I process his words, trying to formulate a coherent thought. I can't believe this is really happening. "What? How? Wow!" I laugh, caught up in Teddy's whirlwind.

"I am still fine-tuning the finishing details of it. Colton's in the conference room right now." He motions with his hand toward the hallway. "I'll bring you in there in a second to reintroduce you."

"We've met?"

"Yes, I introduced you to him on Saturday at the benefit."

"You introduced me to a lot of people at the benefit," I tell him, laughing. "So many I couldn't keep their names and faces straight.

Let's hope I remember what conversation I had with him so I don't look like an ass."

He laughs at me, the reassuring sound booming off the walls of his office. "I'm sure you'll be fine! Anyway, this could be it, kid! All your hard work finally coming to fruition!"

"This is so great, Teddy!" Relief overtakes me. We'd been told earlier in the week that without the complete funding, the project might be delayed for another eight months to a year.

"Almost too good to be true, really." He shakes his head. "I have to tell you though, Ry, I'm gonna have to depend on you to help me with this. They want a dedicated person from our office to work side-by-side with theirs, and they requested you."

I nod despite being confused by why or how the company knows me. It doesn't matter. What matters is getting the funding. "Sure, I'll do anything. You know that." I put my hand up to my chest, covering my heart. "I can't believe it! Whatever you need, I'll do, to get this funding—to keep this ball rolling."

"That's my girl! I knew I could count on you!" He rises from his desk. "C'mon, I can't wait for you and Colton to reacquaint yourselves and go over the fine print on the agreement."

I follow him down the hallway, feeling a little insecure about my attire. I'm underdressed for a business meeting, but if Teddy doesn't care, neither should I.

"Here she is, Colton," Teddy announces as he enters the conference room ahead of me.

I turn the corner, walk through the doorway and come to a dead stop. Donavan is sitting in a chair at the other end of the conference table, a stack of papers in front of him. His arms are crossed casually over his chest, and his biceps pull noticeably at the sleeves of his polo shirt. His eyes meet mine and his mouth spreads into a slow, smug smile.

What the hell? I stop in the doorway looking at Teddy and back to Donavan. "I—I don't under—understand?" I stammer.

The appalled look on Teddy's face tells me that I've made a serious blunder in my reaction. "Rylee?" he questions as he looks at Donavan quickly, making sure I haven't offended him, and then back at me, a warning on his face. "Rylee, what are you talking about? This is Colton Donavan, among other things, the CEO of CD Enterprises—I introduced you to him the other night?"

All at once, my world turns and tilts on its axis. My head is reeling from the fact that the man across from me—the man who reduced me to a puddle of sensation the other night—is none other than Colton Donavan. *The* Colton Donavan—hot and upcoming racecar driver extraordinaire, son of a mega-Hollywood-movie director, and the serial philanderer who provides the tabloids constant fodder for their gossip columns.

The Colton Donavan who left me with salacious dreams and a carnal, unrequited craving since last Saturday. *Fuck me!*

I can't believe that I didn't put it together sooner. I knew he seemed familiar when I met him, but I realize I wasn't thinking rationally either. I'm having a hard time wrapping my head around this. All of the air has been punched out of my lungs.

My head swivels from Teddy to Dona-er-Colton and back to Teddy. From the way Teddy is staring at me, the look on my face must be quite unpleasant. I look down, take a deep breath, and try to compose myself and quiet the emotions rioting through my head. I can't screw up this donation regardless of my feelings—there is too much at stake.

"Um—I apologize," I say softly, "I just—I thought your name was Donavan." I walk further into the room, gaining confidence, telling myself I can do this. "I misunderstood when we met the other night …" The quick flash of Colton's grin stops me cold.

You can do this, I repeat to myself like a mantra. I refuse to let him know that he has this effect on me.

I hold my head up and walk with purpose to where he sits, holding out my hand and plastering a smile to my face. "Nice to see you again, Mr. Donavan."

I can hear the deep breath Teddy has been holding—afraid my reaction has possibly hampered this deal—release. The tension in his face ebbs.

"Colton, please," Donavan says as he unfolds himself gracefully from his chair and rises, taking my hand in his, holding it a beat longer than necessary. "Nice to see you again too." A spark flashes through his emerald eyes.

"Please, let's all sit," Teddy says enthusiastically. "Colton, I'll let you fill Rylee in on your company's proposal."

"I'd be glad to, Teddy." Colton says professionally, all business, as he shifts his chair to face me, placing a packet of paper in front of me. "CD Enterprises is invested in giving back to our community. On a yearly basis, my team and I choose an organization and devote time, connections, and funds to create awareness for their cause. After unexpectedly attending your function last weekend in my mother's place when she fell ill, I found your organization to be inspiring."

I observe him while he continues on with facts and figures of past organizations that CD Enterprises has supported. I'm having a hard time understanding how this professional, put-together man is the same person who reduced me to tremors and whimpers.

This is the type of man I usually fall for. Black and white, no grey area. Knowledgeable and passionate. This is what I find sexy. Not the arrogant, self-serving bastard from the other night who was reckless and uninhibited. Thank goodness I know the truth so I won't fall for his act.

At least this is what I'm telling myself when I hear my name pass from his lips.

"What?" I ask as I shake myself from my thoughts.

"Do you have any questions?" Colton asks, cocking his head to the side thoughfully. I can tell he knows exactly what I'm thinking about—*him.*

"First of all, let me say that I hope your mother is feeling better," I say, letting my manners override my contempt for him. When he nods, I continue, "What exactly does CD Enterprises do, Mr. Donavan?" I ask.

"My mother is doing better, thank you. As for CDE, the company's primary function is ownership and management of a race team. My race team," he says, exuding pride. "Among other things, our biggest venture is a cutting edge technology that will help increase the safety quotient for drivers. It is currently patent pending."

"Hmmmm," I contemplate, trying to figure out how this can all tie in. "And how exactly are you going to tie a race car or team, per se, into raising funds for orphaned kids and Corporate Cares?" I am back in business mode, my intellect unaffected by his charm. *For the most part*. But I have a feeling there's a catch here.

Once bitten, twice shy.

"Thank you for the segue," he says. "On Monday, I brought your organization to my team's attention. After some research, discussions, and brainstorming, we created the following proposal." He flips open the packet in front of me and looks at me, pleasure softening his hard features as he announces, "CD Enterprises proposes that up front, we donate one and a half million dollars to Corporate Cares."

Holy shit! I try to stifle the words from tumbling out of my mouth. Pride is evident in his eyes as he watches me pensively, quietly gauging my reaction before continuing.

"In addition to the immediate funds, we plan to devote a portion of my car's graphics in the upcoming season to promote your cause or mission, if you will." He sees the confusion on my face and puts his hand up so he can finish. "We plan on using this advertising spot to entice other companies and race teams to add to the sponsorship. My team will get them to commit to paying a set dollar amount per lap that my car completes or a blanket sponsorship."

I widen my eyes in disbelief; this could bring in a staggering amount of money for the company. I glance over to Teddy, who is so excited he is fidgeting, a huge grin on his face. I look back to Colton and my eyes meet his, emerald to amethyst, warring between gratitude and confusion. Why us? Why our company?

He smiles softly at me as if he knows what I'm thinking and acknowledges my dilemma. Accepting the donation means I have to accept his date. He continues, "We're still figuring out whether we offer the sponsorship per race or over the whole season. My team is working on that as we speak, seeing as we only have a little under three months until the first race to get as many corporate sponsors as possible."

"Isn't that unbelievable?" Teddy bellows from beside me.

I turn to him and smile sincerely before turning back to face Colton. "It's very generous of you and your company; I'm just a little baffled about why. Why Corporate Cares?"

The corners of his mouth turn up. "Let's just say that you can be very persuasive, Ms. Thomas." He holds my stare as I inhale a sharp breath. "I think I'll enjoy working with someone as passionate and..."

he looks away, finding the word before bringing his eyes back to mine "...*responsive* as I found you to be on Saturday night." He keeps his face impassive, although his eyes are anything but, as his tongue darts out to lick his lower lip.

Despite the blood draining from my head at his words, I can feel a flush spread over my cheeks and down my neck. The corners of his eyes crinkle. I squirm under his gaze, wishing to be anywhere but here.

Like in his bed, under him, with his fingers dancing across my skin and his lips possessing mine. What the fuck? It's bad enough he's in my face, now he's corrupting my thoughts. This is not good. *Definitely not good.*

I suppress my anger at the nerve of Colton. I can't believe he's just said this. Is referring to my indiscretion in front of my boss really that necessary? How dare he come in my office and provoke me, remind me of something I'm not proud of. Something I'm not going to forget anytime soon.

"Responsive," Teddy says, rolling the word over his tongue in thought. "That is a great way to describe my Rylee here!" He pats me on the back and pride fills his voice. He is completely oblivious. "Always going above and beyond."

Colton shifts his eyes to Teddy, who is unaware of our sexual tension. "It is, indeed. And a very hard quality to find in someone." He nods, agreeing with Teddy. "I watched her in *action* on Saturday night and was quite impressed."

I've had enough of this, yet I don't want to give him the satisfaction of knowing he's agitated me. I don't want to work with this man, but let's face it, Corporate Cares has no other option to make all my blood, sweat, and tears over the past two years come to fruition. He's stepping up to the plate, even if his motives aren't completely wholesome.

I have to think of this collaboration as *a means to an end.* My boys and the many others who can benefit from this new facility.

"So Mr. Donavan—"

"Colton, please," he reiterates.

"Colton, I understand the premise," I state primly, wanting to get this conversation back on track. "What exactly is my involvement in this collaboration?"

"Well, Ms. Thomas, I won't need much from you from a business standpoint. I have a team that is very experienced in this type of thing. Obviously though, I'll need you to be the point of contact for their questions and other miscellaneous things."

These "other miscellaneous things" have me worried. "So why —"

Colton holds up a hand again, and I am getting rather annoyed by this habit. "As I discussed with Teddy, the contract between our companies for the donation is contingent on several factors." He pauses, organizing the papers on the table before him. He looks up, his attention focused solely on me. "For the next several months and into the season, I will need a representative of Corporate Cares with me for numerous occasions."

He stops as I purse my lips, my eyes growing large as I hope my assumptions are incorrect. "Me?" I question, already knowing the answer.

"Yes. You." He mouths. I watch his eyes narrow as I lick my lips. All of a sudden, I feel hot. His lips part just a bit as he watches me, and I have to shake the inappropriate thoughts of them out of my head as he continues. "In conjunction with the announcement of our joining forces, there will be several events—some locally, some out of town— black tie affairs, press junkets, et cetera," he says, casually waving his fingers, "that I will need you to escort me to."

"What?" I stand up, pushing my chair back with force and look between Colton and Teddy in bewilderment. How dare he? I turn down a date, turn down going beyond second base backstage, and he schemes up a way to tie me to him with a contract? What an immature prick! His ego must really be bruised from my rejection.

I'm dumbfounded. *No way.* This is not happening. Words I'd love to say to him, to call him, run through my head as I seethe with anger.

"Is there something the matter, Rylee?" Teddy asks, breaking through my haze of frustration. "I think it's a brilliant idea." I turn my head to him, opening my mouth to respond but nothing comes out. "If Colton's willing to use his name, his *connections*, and popularity by standing beside you at a press filled event to get the word out about Corporate Cares, then—"

"Why not take advantage of it?" Colton finishes for him, a smug smile spreading across his face.

I'm starting to feel dizzy, my head spinning from the turn of events. I place my hand on the table to brace myself as I slowly sink into the chair, my eyes focusing on an imaginary spot on the papers in front of me.

"Ry? You okay?" Teddy asks, concerned.

"Huh?" I raise my head up to meet his empathetic eyes.

"You look a little flushed. Are you feeling okay?"

"Yeah. Yes," I answer, taking a deep breath. "I'm just—it was a long shift. That's all," I say, gathering myself. *It's a means to an end.* "Sorry," I apologize. "I'm just overwhelmed that the new project is going to be a reality." Colton sits silently, analyzing me. I shift uncomfortably under his scrutiny.

"Look, Rylee," Teddy says, "I know you have a lot on your plate right now and this is just adding to it, but it's so close now we can taste it. There is no one I'd rather have be the face of this organization. You're the one, kiddo."

His high praise warms me despite the panic I feel from being trapped. From being forced into a situation that I know will be beneficial for Corporate Cares but no doubt devastating for me.

Teddy glances at his watch and reaches over to pat my hand. "I have a conference call in five minutes." He rises from his seat as does Colton. "I trust that I can leave you two in here to fine-tune the remaining details."

He reaches his hand out to Colton, sealing the agreement with a handshake. "Thank you, for your unexpected generosity. You have no idea how many lives you are helping to change with this gift."

An unexplained darkness flickers across Colton's face. "I understand more than most people might think," he says before releasing Teddy's hand. "Thank you for your warm reception to the idea. My lawyer will be contacting you in the morning to draw up the paperwork."

With that, Teddy nods and exits the conference room. I stand watching the empty doorway, my back toward Colton as I contemplate my next move.

I'm overwhelmed by his generosity. At his attempt to make *my dreams* come true, so why can I not feel gratitude toward him? Why do I just want to turn around and throttle him? I hate being forced into anything. It's not that I have to be in control—well, maybe just a little bit. But at least I want to make my own decisions, not be treated like some compliant woman who submits without question.

Why does he irritate me so much? Is it because every time I look at his lips or watch his fingers rub over his jaw, my body tightens in anticipation of how they felt on me? Or is it because I can hear his rasp of a voice in my dreams telling me how much he wants me? *Shit!* My life was perfectly fine until last weekend. And then I meet him and now I'm a flustered mess.

I shouldn't care that he was making out and doing God knows what with Bailey, but I do. I'm embarrassed that he probably thinks I let any guy I meet put his hands on me. I'm irritated that I know the only reason for his pursuit is because I'm not falling for his smooth lines and eloquent bullshit. I'm confused why a man who is like a Pied Piper to women much prettier, sexier—everything—than me is even glancing twice in my direction.

My life is not some Hollywood romance movie where boring girl meets famous boy and they fall madly in love. I'm not naïve enough to believe that this is going to happen to me.

And then, my feelings for Max further confuse things. I feel guilty that, despite loving him, I never felt as alive with him as I did with Colton.

I sigh loudly, my body aware of his proximity.

He chuckles, fueling my irritation, as I turn to face him. He is leaning back in his chair, an ankle resting on the opposing knee, his arms casually resting on the armrests. We stare at each other, observing and scrutinizing each other for the first time without observers. His eyes lazily wander over my body, pausing at my cleavage. I watch his smile widen in what I can assume is an appreciation of the feminine form in general, not just mine, before they travel further down.

His beauty really is magnificent. Thick, dark lashes starkly contrast his green eyes. His strong nose has a slight curve, as if it had been broken. This imperfection in an otherwise perfect face adds to his overwhelming sex appeal. I take in his full lips, the top one slightly thinner than the lower, the darkened stubble that shadows his face, and the pulse that beats steadily under the curve of his jaw. I have the sudden urge to kiss him and nuzzle into him, to feel the pulse of this vibrant man beneath my lips. To be enveloped in his clean, earthy scent.

I shake my head, trying to break the trance. He quirks his eyebrows and waits for me to make the first move. We stare for several moments as we measure each other. I finally break the silence. "Is this what you call taking matters in to your own hands?"

"What's wrong? Can't handle the temptation, Ryles?" He flashes a wicked, arrogant grin at me, and as much as I want to roll my eyes, he's all I can think about.

"Hardly," I snort.

He shrugs indifferently. "A man's gotta do what a man's gotta do, Ry," he says. "You left me no choice."

"No choice? Really?" I scoff, throwing my hands up in disgust. "What are you, fifteen years old throwing a tantrum because you didn't get your way?"

"You owe me a date."

"All this for a frickin' date, Ace? Or is it because I denied your sexual ministrations after I came to my senses?" Ugh, he is so frustrating!

"*Oh, you would've come all right,*" he rebuts sardonically, raising an eyebrow, "and from what I recall, your senses? Those were strewn all over the backstage floor."

Smartass! How can he get me so fuming mad when it takes so much more to get me to this point with other people?

"So because I said no, you offer up tons of money and bind me to a contract? Forcing me to *have* to spend time with you? Money in exchange for a date? I'm not a *whore*, Colton," I rant, waltzing to the window trying to abate my anger. "Especially not *yours*!"

I can hear him shuffling behind me as he rises and walks toward the window. He looks at me through his reflection in the glass and holds my stare. My body vibrates.

"Let's get something straight," he growls. "First of all, I have my own reasons for donating the money that have absolutely nothing to do with you. Nothing! Second, I don't *ever* pay for dates, Rylee. *Ever.* I have more class than that." I can feel his fury roll off him in waves.

"You paid for a date with me," I retort.

"Charity. Auction. Does. Not. Equal. Escort. Service." He snarls, taking a step closer, but never breaking our stare. "Lastly," he seethes, grabbing hold of my arm to emphasize his point, "I don't ever want to hear you refer to yourself as a *whore* again."

We stand in silence as his words settle around us. Why the hell does he care what I call myself? He has no claim over me. I know better than to provoke when someone is angry, but I can't help myself. For some reason I want to push his buttons. If I'm going to be forced to do something, then I might as well say my peace.

"Then why the contract? The events that I'm required to be your *escort* for." I yank my arm out of his grip. "Sounds like your ego is bruised because I won't succumb to your dazzling charm, so you need to tie me to you to prove to yourself that you still have that magic *Colton touch.*"

"I didn't say anything about bondage," he cuts me off, smirking. "But if that's your thing, Rylee, I'd be more than happy to oblige. I can teach you *the ropes.*"

I shake my head in disbelief as the meaning of his words sink in. Blood rushes to my cheeks before I can meet his eyes in the glass again. "I'm ignoring your last comment," I say dryly, trying to recall what my point was since he has scattered my thoughts. *Um—where was I? Oh!* "Your ego's bruised because I won't fall helplessly at your feet and become your compliant sexual plaything, so you come to my job—take the one thing that I really want, the one thing that I've been working toward for over two years—and you serve it up to me on a platter."

"And the problem with that is …?"

"The problem is that you offer it to me with terms that are self-satisfying to you …" I falter because I realize I'm rambling now. And at some point I'm afraid that if I keep talking, private thoughts may tumble out—thoughts about him. And if I slip, then … he'll know I think about him more than I should.

Colton sidles up next to me, leaning his shoulder on the glass, staring at my profile. Our silence extends for several moments, my anxiety ratcheting from his quiet scrutiny.

When he speaks, his voice is demandingly soft, "Why won't you go out on the date with me?"

Whoa, change of subject! A sliver of a laugh escapes my mouth from nerves. I keep my face averted, watching the world outside. "For what reason? You and I come from different worlds, Colton, that have different rules. You want a date so you can add another to the many notches in your bedpost. You said you wanted to fuck me to get me out of your system and move on," I say, repeating his threat. In my periphery, I see him blanch at my words. "You may be used to women declaring their love for you and dropping their panties at *clever* lines such as that but not this one."

Colton starts to speak. I know he's going to drop a witty one-liner about how I'll have no problem dropping mine for him. Using his own tactic, I stop him before he can interrupt by holding up my hand. "Our encounter was a momentary indiscretion on my part. One that will never happen again." I turn my face to look Colton in the eyes. "I'm not that kind of girl, Ace."

He regards me, the muscle in his jaw pulsing. He leans in, the coarseness of his voice making his words resonate with truth. "You know that deep down, a tiny part of that proper, respectable woman that you are wants to visit that reckless, sexy, uninhibited place inside you that's begging to get out. A place I can undoubtedly help you find."

My eyes blaze while I try to reject the truth behind his words. He watches my internal struggle until I turn from him and walk back toward the conference table. I don't want him to see the despair on my eyes. "You play dirty, Colton."

"And your point?" he retorts, turning and leaning his backside against the glass, a lopsided smile flashing. "Sometimes you have to play dirty to get what you want."

"And what exactly is it that you want?" I ask, crossing my arms across my chest as an invisible means of protection against him. As if anything really could protect me.

Colton pushes off the wall and stalks toward me, like a lion about to pounce on his prey. He stops in front of me, closer than necessary, and reaches out, using a finger to lift my chin up so that my eyes meet his. "You," he states simply.

I feel as if all of the air has been vacuumed out of the room; I can't breathe. Incredulity and willingness flood me momentarily as I accept his answer. The warmth is fleeting as I realize that this is how he does it. This is how he gets so many notches on his bedpost. He makes you feel like you're the only one on his radar. He's good. He's really good. But I'm not going to fall for it.

I walk away from him, creating some distance so I can think clearly. "So why a contract? What are you trying to achieve?" I toss over my shoulder as I circle the conference room table. When I'm across it, I turn to face him. "Are you going to threaten my job if I don't *fuck* you?"

"No..." a wry smile turns up the corners of his mouth "...but there's always that option."

"Well, why don't we just save us both the time and effort and get it over with?" I rebuff, exhausted by this game we're playing. "Then we can move on to what really matters. Hell, we can even use the conference table if you're that desperate."

"We could," he says, laughing, a sincere smile on his face. He presses both hands on the table, testing its stability. "It's sturdy enough." He shrugs. "Although it's not exactly what I had in mind." His eyes express the lascivious thoughts he's left unspoken. "And believe me, sweetheart, I'm far from desperate."

His look sends shivers down my spine. I try to change tactics. Obviously the avenue I've taken is not working to deter him. "We both know you don't need an escort to these functions. Why not have one of your girlfriends escort you?" I continue moving, knowing that if I stand still, I risk the chance of coming into contact with him. And the pull he has over my body is too strong to resist his touch. And if he touches me, then I think my resolve will crumble. "I'm sure that you have a bevy of beauties waiting for you to snap your fingers."

"I don't do the girlfriend thing," he deadpans, stopping me in my tracks.

"Oh, I see. *The casual fucking thing is more your style then*?" I see anger flash in his eyes before he reins it in, covering it with a diminutive smirk. "I guess I was right to not expect too much from you."

"Why tie myself to just one woman when there are so many out there vying for my attention?" he goads, trying to push more of my buttons.

"Do you actually believe your own bullshit lines?" My God, the man is relentless and exasperating at the same time. He just flashes me a smarmy smile and folds his arms across his chest. I try to not focus on the play of muscles beneath his shirt. Try not to imagine what he looks like with his shirt off. "You sure are full of yourself, aren't you, Ace?"

He cocks his head and looks at me. "I can arrange for you to be full of me instead, if you'd like?"

Again, I stop at his words. Regardless of how forward and crass his comment is, all of the muscles south of my waist clench with desire. I can feel the flush of heat creep up my cheeks, staring at a non-existent spot on the wall for a moment, hoping he doesn't notice. He chuckles softly at my reaction, and my eyes flash up to meet his, my expression belying how dumbstruck I am from his words. It's only when I stare at him incredulously for a few moments, my mouth opening and closing trying to form words to berate him for his arrogance, that I see the crack in his game. A smile graces his lips, causing the lines around his eyes to crinkle.

"C'mon," he teases, taking a step closer to me. "You walked right into that one. I couldn't resist."

I know the feeling. I stare at him, shaking my head. "Okay," I concede. "I'm going to pretend that you didn't just say that. But seriously, why don't you do the girlfriend thing?"

He shrugs casually. "Not my thing. I don't like strings attaching me to anything. Relationships equal drama."

A guy with commitment issues, like that's something new.

"So I was right?" I mutter more to myself than to him, astounded by his brutal honesty.

"About what?" he asks, angling his head to the side as he approaches me slowly. My heart beats faster. The tone of his voice and his aura have changed. I can sense raw desire as he nears. The danger. My body clenches in anticipation, while my brain tells me to retreat quickly.

"What I told you on Saturday—you do like to just *fuck 'em and chuck 'em.*" My voice is quiet. The temerity behind my words fades with every step he takes in my direction.

"I told you once I don't take kindly to insults. You just did it again. For that alone you deserve to be taken over my knee." My thighs clench in expectant desire. I'm not into that type of thing. And yet that type of thing with Colton, his hands on me, possessing me, pushing me to ride that fine line bordering between pleasure and pain arouses me beyond coherence.

I part my lips as he comes within inches of mine. My body is attuned to him. His scent. The intake of his breath. My back arches as he lifts a hand to my cheek. "It sucks, doesn't it?" he asks as he trails a finger along my jaw line, stopping, then brushing against my bottom lip.

"What does?" I sigh softly as his finger leaves my skin.

"When you have to stick to your guns out of principal rather than giving into the temptation right in front of you," he whispers, turning the tables on me. "There is no shame, Rylee, in letting your body have what it craves."

We stand, inches from each other, letting the weight of his words settle in my psyche. I know he is right. My body's deepening ache tells me so. That I want exactly what he is offering.

"It's hard to deny it, sweetheart, when it's written all over your body."

I jerk back from him as if I've been bitten. His words fuel my ire and irritate me. "No! I—"

"Shhh," he murmurs, stepping back toward me, pressing a finger to my lips, his eyes ablaze with salacious intensity. "Just know, Rylee, the best sex you will ever have … will be with me," he says in a low, hypnotizing voice that seems to knock all of the air from my lungs and reason from my usually sensible head.

I jump back, needing space from his carnal words and unending arrogance. He's so forward, so cocksure it's almost unattractive. *Almost.* The man can definitely talk a good game. Too bad I'll never know if it's true or not, if for no other reason than to teach his oversized ego a lesson.

"I'll comply with the damn agreement, Colton," I huff. "For my boys. For the many kids to come." I stalk toward the table to collect my things. "Not for you. Or your stupid machinations behind it." I forcefully square up the papers on the table, paper hitting wood is the only sound in the room. I look up, my steely eyes pinning his. "I will not sleep with you, Ace."

"Yes, you will." He smiles smugly.

Despite the vicious bang his words spark between my legs, I manage a single chuckle. "Don't even think for a single minute—"

"Colton!" A sexy voice purrs at the door to the conference room, interrupting me.

I snap my head up to see the svelte Bailey smiling seductively, all wide eyes and batting eyelashes. My insecurities rise to the surface as I swallow loudly, looking to see Colton's reaction. My eyes meet his because, despite the interruption, his eyes have never left mine. I am unsure what to make of this. He purses his lips, the unresolved issues left hanging between us.

All of the sudden, I'm not feeling well and want desperately to escape from this room. From this man. From witnessing the familiarity between Bailey and Colton. From being jealous despite expressing that I don't want him.

Oblivious to the tension, Bailey sashays into the room, heading toward Colton, finger twirling her perfectly straight, perfectly bottle-dyed auburn hair.

Regret flashes across Colton's eyes as he glances toward her and smiles a warm hello, ever the consummate gentleman. I turn abruptly to leave, knocking into my chair so it scrapes loudly against the hardwood floor.

"I didn't realize you'd snapped your fingers," I mutter as I try again to get around my chair.

From behind me, Colton releases a hearty, sincere laugh at my comment that, despite my frustration, makes me smile. As I exit the room, I hear him call my name. I keep walking, wanting to distance myself from him.

"This is by no means over, Rylee," he yells out.

I continue without responding, right past my office and straight to the elevator doors. I ignore Stella's call, the blinking voicemail light on my phone, and luck out when the elevator door opens as I approach. I need fresh air to clear my head.

I am a confident woman and not afraid to speak up, so why do I feel like one of those blubbering girls I can't stand? Why is it that Colton reduces me to a mass of hormones—angry one minute and wanting his lips on mine the next?

I sag against the wall of the elevator in frustration. He gets me so worked up. So angry. I can't figure out what I want to do more, punch him or fuck him.

Chapter Six

THE CALIFORNIA SUN RELAXES ME as I drink in its warmth in my backyard. I recline in the chaise, tilting my head to catch the last rays before they sink and fade to dusk. The leaves of several palm trees that line our backyard fence rustle from the light breeze, calming me.

The day's events have taken their toll on me. And with Josie down with the flu, I'll be back at the house in less than twenty-four hours to cover her shift. Despite it being early evening, I really should be getting ready for bed and sleeping off some of my exhaustion. But I've let Haddie talk me into a glass of wine and some pizza that she's making in the house.

I close my eyes, leaning my head back, sighing as I allow myself to believe that the new facilities will become a reality. That our new approach for treating orphaned children can expand and hopefully become the pioneering protocol for change in our foster system. We can strengthen our case that creating small groups of kids under one roof—where they consistently have guardians, rules, school, counseling—will lead to well-adjusted adults. They will have a place where they belong.

A shiver of pride runs through me as I think of all of the possibilities and all of the hope that we can create with the completion of this project.

And then I suddenly feel sick from thinking about him. I still can't figure out what to make of his comment that he doesn't do the "girlfriend thing." Why do I still keep thinking about him if there's nothing there? *Because there is.* I can't deny that he's more than easy on the eyes. And I definitely can't act as if the sparks that shoot up my arm when he touches me are imaginary. But I don't want to get involved with him and his womanizing ways, especially now that I have to because of work.

I sigh heavily when I hear the sliding door open and Haddie walks out with a bottle of wine, two glasses, and a pizza box stacked with plates and napkins on top. I suddenly realize how hungry I am. She walks toward me, the sun framing her tall figure, setting her blonde hair alight like a halo around her head. Long, lean legs stretch from short khaki shorts, and her oversized bosom is covered in an orange camisole. As usual, she is accessorized perfectly and styled flawlessly. And despite her tireless perfection that makes me feel inadequate in so many ways, I love her like the sister I never had.

"I'm starving," I announce, sitting up from the chair to help Haddie place everything on the table.

"And I'm starving for information on what's going on with you. On why you're out here so deep in thought," she prods as she pours red wine into the glasses, and I serve the pizza.

"Just like in our dorm room," I say nodding at our meal, laughing at the memory .

She was my freshman year roommate. I could have never of guessed that first week of college orientation that the Barbie doll I roomed with would turn out to be my best friend. She waltzed into our dorm room looking like a model out of a Ralph Lauren ad campaign, so confident and sure of herself, her picture-perfect family following behind her. She slowly took in our meager surroundings, the painted brick walls and small closet space. My gawky self watched her, cringing at the thought of having to be reminded every morning of how inferior I was to this beautiful creature.

I sat picking at the hem of my dress as her parents left for good. She shut the door, turned to me, a huge grin on her heart-shaped lips, and said, "Thank God they're finally gone!" I watched her out of the corner of my eye as she sagged against the door in relief. She angled her head, studying me, sizing me up. "I think it's time to celebrate!" she said, hurrying over to her suitcase.

Within moments, she produced a bottle of tequila hidden deep in her belongings. She then flopped on my bed next to me. She unscrewed the cap and held the bottle up in the air between us. "To Freshman year!" she toasted, "To friendship, freedom, cute boys, and having each other's backs." She winced as she took a swig of the strong alcohol and then handed the bottle over to me. I looked nervously back and forth between her and the bottle, and then wanting desperately to be liked by her, took a swallow, the burn bringing tears to my eyes.

"My God, we were so naïve then. And young!" she reminisces. "We've been through so much since freshman orientation!"

"All we need is that cheap tequila to bring us back." I laugh and then fall silent as the impending night starts to eat the sun's rays. "Eight years is a long time, Had," I say, taking a long drink of the tart wine, letting it soothe the anxiety gnawing at the edges of my mind.

"Long enough," she says, taking a seat, looking at me, "that I know something is bugging you. What's going on, Ry?"

I smile, so grateful to have a friend like her and feeling cursed at the same time because I can't hide anything from her. I feel tears burn my eyes, the sudden onset of emotions surprising me.

Haddie leans forward, her perfectly tanned legs bending beneath her as she reaches out and places a hand on my leg. "What is it, Rylee? What has you so twisted up?"

I take a moment to find my voice, wanting to tell her everything, to get her opinion on whether I'm being obtuse about Colton. Maybe I know what she is going to tell me if I confess, and that's why I find myself holding back. Not wanting to hear that it's okay to let go and feel again. That being with someone else does nothing to tarnish Max, his memory, or what we had together.

"There are too many things. I don't even know where to start," I confess, trying to sift through my mental baggage. "I'm exhausted from work—worried about Zander's lack of progress, wrapping up all of the details from the benefit last Saturday night," I say, running my hands through my hair, "and the fact that I'm back to the house tomorrow to cover Josie's shift because she's sick …"

"Can't someone else cover it?" she asks, taking a bite of pizza. "You've worked way too many hours this week. I've barely seen you."

"No one can. Not this week. Everyone's hours are maxed out because of all the extra time I had them put in for the benefit … and since I'm on salary … it's left to me," I explain.

"I understand why you do it, Ry—why you love it—but don't let it kill you, sweetie."

"I know. I know. You sound like my mother!" I take a bite of my pizza and chew it slowly. "The good news though, is that I think we secured the rest of the funding for the facility."

"What?" she sputters, sitting up quickly. "Why didn't you tell me? This calls for a celebration," she says, clinking her glass with mine. "What happened? How? Details!"

"We're still ironing out the final details before making anything public," I say, trying to hide my contempt for how we secured the funding, "and then we'll make an announcement." I hope that my answer will be enough to keep her questions at bay.

"Okay," she says slowly, eyeing me, wondering why I'm not being more forthcoming. "So then what's up with your auction date thing that Dane was telling me about?"

I look down, twisting the ring that sits on my right ring finger. I worry it around and around out of habit. "Not sure yet," I say, looking up, noticing her watching me twist my ring.

She looks up, tears in her eyes. "It's because the anniversary is coming up soon isn't it? That's why you seem so overwhelmed?" She scoots out of her chair and sits next to me, wrapping her arms around me.

For a brief moment, I allow myself to give in to the memories and to the thoughts that surround the approaching date. I haven't really put the two together, my sudden sentimentality and my scattered emotional state over the possibility of acting on the nonexistent connection with Colton. I guess I'm subconsciously ignoring the traumatic date, wanting to close my eyes to the grief that will forever exist in the depths of my soul.

I wipe a tear from my cheek and withdraw from the warmth of Haddie's embrace. "Yeah." I shrug. "Just too much all at once." This is the truth, but I feel guilty about not telling Haddie the whole of it.

"Well, sister," she says, handing back my glass of wine, "let's drink a bunch more wine, wallow in pity, and laugh at our stupid selves." Her sincere smile lifts my mood.

I clink my glass to hers, thankful for her friendship. "Cheers, my dear!"

Chapter Seven

I GLANCE AT THE CLOCK as I finish helping Ricky with his spelling words and shoo him off to play with the others. I have thirty more minutes on shift and then I'm off for a whole glorious two days. I actually have the elusive, rare weekend off, and despite letting Haddie talk me into being her date for a launch party for the newest rum product her company is promoting, I'm excited to have time to myself.

It's been quite a day to say the least.

Earlier, the school called for me to pick up Aiden because he'd been in yet another fight. I received a lecture from the principal that if this keeps up, other measures might need to be taken for his education. I questioned him about whether the other boys, the ones who keep bullying Aiden, were receiving the same threat. He responded with a non-committal grunt.

I was happy to be able to work one-on-one with Zander while the rest of the boys were in school. Our counseling staff thought it was best to home school him until he started communicating verbally. Trying to teach someone who, for the most part, is unresponsive is a frustrating endeavor to say the least. All I want is for some kind of break through. Something tells me he knows how much I care for him. That I wish he still had his mother to soothe him. To hug him. To tell him she loves him.

The boys are keeping themselves busy while I'm at the table reviewing Shane's paper for school. Jackson's shift ended an hour ago and his replacement, Mike, is at a counseling appointment with Connor.

I'm thoroughly impressed with how well Shane is improving in school, a result of our many one-on-one sessions with him. I glance over to the family room area where Kyle and Ricky have brought their box of baseball cards. They sit down on the floor next to the coffee table and turn their attention to the basketball game on the television. Zander is in his usual place, stuffed animal held to his chest and his eyes staring into space. Scooter is lying on the carpet, coloring in one of his Spiderman coloring books. I listen for the telltale sign of music in the back bedrooms to indicate that Shane is in his room. I finish making comments on Shane's paper and shift my attention toward reviewing the meal and afterschool activity schedules for the next week.

I hear a knock at the front door and before I can even put my pen down, I hear Shane yell, "I got it!" from his bedroom. I smirk because I know he's hoping it's his "girl that is a friend." She came over last week, and Shane is still on cloud nine.

"Look before you open," I tell him as I rise from the table and walk toward the hall. As I reach the corner that leads to the foyer, Shane breezes past me, disappointment on his face. "It's for you," he says, plopping on the couch.

I turn the corner, figuring that there's a delivery. The House is always receiving legal documents via courier, regarding our kids' situations. I reach the doorway and when I step out, I come face to face with Colton. Despite his sunglasses, I know he's looking me up and down. A lazy, lopsided grin on his face that causes his dimple to deepen, spreads across his face.

Damn my breath for catching at the sight of him. As much as I don't want him here, don't want the complication of what he has to offer in my life—a quick fuck that's easily discarded—I am giddy at the sight of him. And this turn of events is not looking good for me.

I stop in the doorway, a smile spreading on my face despite knowing that he's bad news for me. We stand, looking at each other, taking each other in for several moments. He's in a well-worn pair of jeans, and a black T-shirt clings to his muscular torso. The simplicity of his clothing only adds to his devastating looks. His dark hair is windblown, wild, and sexy as hell.

Everything about him screams here comes trouble. And I'm standing right in his path like a deer in the headlights, unable to move.

Willpower is only going to last me so long. *I'm seriously screwed.*

"Hello, Rylee." The simple rasp of his voice saying my name has me flashing back to his mouth on mine. His hands on me. His vibrations propelling shockwaves through my body.

I cock my head to the side regarding him. "Hi, Ace," I say guardedly. "Since when did you add stalker to your repertoire of talents?"

I slip my hands into the rear pockets of my jeans as I lean against the doorjamb. He removes his sunglasses, his emerald eyes blazing into mine, and then folds them to hang in the neck of his shirt. Their weight pulls the neckline down so several dark hairs curl out. I drag my eyes from the sight back up to his eyes.

He flashes me a lightning fast grin. "I'd be more than happy to show you my talents, sweetheart."

I roll my eyes. "Womanizing is not a talent."

"True." He draws the word out and slowly nods his head, "but you've yet to see the true depths of my many others." He arches an eyebrow, a roguish smile turning up the corners of his mouth. "And since you keep running, I can't show you and we can't solve our little problem about that date you owe me." He takes a step closer, a playful look in his eyes. I retreat a step back into the foyer, leery of this dance we are engaging in. "Aren't you going to invite me in, Ryles?"

"I don't think that's a good idea, Donavan. I've been warned about guys like you."

He smirks. "You have no idea," he murmurs, eyes locked on mine. His patronizing smile irks me. He takes another step closer, causing my pulse to quicken.

"What do you want? Why are you here?" I huff.

"Because I want my date with you," he says, slowly enunciating every word. "And I always get what I want." He places both hands on the doorjamb, leaning into it, his silhouette blocking the afternoon sun, his dark features haloed by the bright light.

I shake my head at his nerve and boundless conceit. "Not this time," I disagree. I push the front door to shut and turn back on my heel down the hallway.

In less than a heartbeat, Colton grabs my upper arm, whirls me around, and has me pressed up against the doorjamb. "Keep fightin' me, sweetheart. The feistier you are, the harder you make me." There is a dangerous amusement in his tone that scrapes over me and prickles my senses.

Shit! How can he make those words sound like a seductive promise?

He presses his hips against mine, holding me against the hard, unforgiving wood. We're both breathing heavily, and I'm unsure if it is from the physical exertion or from our proximity to each other.

Colton releases my upper arm and brings both of his hands to cradle my face, his thumbs brushing at my jaw line. His translucent eyes burn into mine, and I can sense an internal struggle in him, his jaw tensing in deliberation.

"As much as I'd like to warn you away from me, Rylee—for your own sake," he murmurs, inches from my mouth, "all I crave is the taste of you." His finger trails a line down the side of my neck, lighting my skin on fire. "It's been too long since I've savored you. You. Are. Intoxicating." His words are a staccato that match the quickening of my heart.

Oh fucking my! If that comment didn't make desire flood every inch of my skin, nothing will. The man can seduce me with words alone. He's pulling at me, testing my willpower, and making me want way more than I should. We breathe each other in for a moment as I try to form words in my head. Gain some semblance of coherence. His mere presence makes my synapses misfire.

"Why are you warning me," I breathe, completely immobilized by the intensity of his stare, "when you're going to take what you want anyway?"

He quickly flashes a grin before his lips are on mine, his hands on me, proving my point and then some. This kiss is not gentle by any means. I can sense his hunger, his fiery need as our teeth clash. His lips and tongue move at a frenzied pace against mine while his hand grabs hold of my ponytail and tugs down, holding me in place.

I relish this kiss as much as he does, for all of my pent-up frustration over him explodes within me. I am caught up in the hurricane that is Colton. I take as he is taking. I curl my arms around his torso, running my hands up his back, enjoying the firm delineation of his muscles as he moves with me. I nip at his bottom lip, aroused by the low moan that comes from the back of his throat. We press into each other, unable to get enough of each other's touch—the only thought running through my head is that I want *more*.

I'm suddenly shocked back to reality like an angel losing her wings when I hear the boys cheering loudly in the family room at something to do with the basketball game. I push Colton back with two hands against his chest.

I try to catch my breath and my bearings by placing my hand against the wall and trying to steady myself. What the hell am I thinking? I'm making out in the doorway at work. *For the second time.* What the hell is this guy doing to me? When I'm around him it's as if I've lost all sense of reality. I can't do this. I just can't. I'm shaken. Really shaken. No one has ever elicited such a blatant carnal reaction from me, and it scares me.

Colton stands across from me, calm as can be, keenly watching. Why do I feel as if I have just run a marathon and he looks like an uninterested bystander?

I finally find my voice. "You're right," I say ruefully. "I most definitely should stay away from you." I look back toward the hallway as I catch a slight grimace on his face. "I need to check on the boys. You can see yourself out," I tell him as I turn abruptly and walk back toward my responsibilities. My reality.

I enter the great room trying to plaster a natural smile on my face, but failing miserably. All the boys are where I left them and for that I am thankful—glad that no one ventured into the hallway to see their guardian acting like a teenager filled with raging hormones.

Something in my periphery catches my eye. I turn to see Colton standing at the edge of the hallway, thumbs hanging in the pockets of his jeans, shoulder casually leaning against the wall. His face is expressionless, but those iridescent eyes say so much.

What now? Can't he just leave me alone?

I glare at him, hoping my angst is reflected in my eyes. I see that Shane has taken notice of the stranger standing in his home. He turns his attention to Colton, sizing him up. His face scrunches as he contemplates the stranger, trying to place him.

"What do you want?" I scowl despite trying to keep the contempt out of my voice. The last thing the boys need to witness right now is a confrontation. I notice Kyle and Ricky's heads pop up to look over the table like a pair of meerkats.

Colton glances at the boys and smiles politely, although I can see the tension in his eyes. "I told you, Rylee, I'm here to collect my winnings," he drawls. "To collect what's mine." He smiles insolently at me, waiting for my reaction.

"I beg your pardon?"

"You owe me a date, Ryles."

The boys have all turned their attention to us now. The basketball game has been forgotten. Shane is smirking since he's old enough to sense sexual tension, even if he doesn't quite understand it.

Colton walks toward me, purposely placing his back to our audience, blocking me from their vision so they can't watch our interaction. I am grateful when he stops and stands at a respectful distance.

"Sorry, Ace," I say sweetly so only he can hear me. "Hell hasn't frozen over yet. I'll let you know when it does."

He takes a step closer, his voice just above a whisper. "It seems you know all about being cold, Rylee. Why stay frigid when you know I can heat you up?"

His words take a direct hit at my self-esteem. I see the anger at his arrogance but know I must calm myself down before I cause a scene in front of my kids.

I break my glare from Colton when something over his shoulder catches my attention. I step to the side so I can get a better look at what it is. I stifle a gasp as I watch Zander, holding his stuffed animal tightly, move slowly around the couch toward us. He has a curious look on his usually stoic face as he approaches.

Colton turns around to see what I'm reacting to. He starts to ask me a question, and I raise my hand up forcefully, telling him to be quiet. Fortunately, he complies. The other boys in the room have all turned to watch, expectant expressions on their faces, for this is the first time that Zander has ever purposely taken the initiative to interact with someone.

Zander walks up to us, staring at Colton, his mouth opening slightly and closing several times. His eyes are saucers. I kneel down to eye level with him. I sense Colton next to me trying to understand my reaction.

"Hi there," I hear Colton say gently.

Zander stops and just stares. I fear that something about Colton's looks or something he is wearing has triggered a reaction in Zander. Some negative memory that is forcing him to come see for himself if it's real. I'm waiting for the fallout to start—the screaming, the fighting, and the terror to fill his eyes.

"Zander. It's okay, baby," I croon, wanting to break through his trance, letting him know that a familiar, comforting voice is nearby. I turn my head slightly toward Colton, locking my eyes with his. "You need to leave now!" I order him, afraid of what Zander sees in him.

Against my wish, Colton steps forward and slowly crouches down beside me. I hear his boots squeak on the tile, the house is so quiet. One of the boys must have muted the television.

"Hey, buddy," he soothes, "How ya doin'? You okay?"

Zander takes a step closer to Colton and a smile ghosts his mouth. My eyes widen. He is not scared. He likes Colton. I quickly glance to Colton, afraid to miss anything Zander does, and he holds my gaze, nodding his head. He understands that something is happening. Something important. Something that he needs to be cautious about.

"Zander is it?" Haunted eyes meet Colton's, and then he moves his head in a small, discernible nod. I suck in my breath, tears threatening as I watch a small breakthrough happening. "So Zander, do you like racing?"

I can hear the boys in the family begin murmuring excitedly as they realize who Colton is. The boys get louder until they see me staring intensely at them, and then they become silent.

Colton holds his hand out to Zander. "Nice to meet you, Zander. My name is Colton."

For the second time in three days, I am rendered speechless. My head is reeling from the sight of little Zander slowly reaching out to shake the hand of the man next to me.

I watch the first steps of a little boy breaking free from the devastating grasp of a violent trauma. This is his first time initiating physical contact with someone in over three months.

Colton holds Zander's small hand in his, shaking it gently. When they finish their greeting, Zander keeps his hand there, with no indication that he wants to move it. Colton obliges and holds the tiny hand, a soft smile on his face.

Tears burn my eyes as I struggle to hold them back. I want to jump up and shout in excitement at this breakthrough. I want to grab Zander and hug him and tell him how proud I am of him. I do none of these. The power of this moment is so much greater than any of these things put together.

"I'll tell you what, Zander, if Rylee here agrees to the date with me that she's trying to get out of," Colton says, never breaking eye contact with him, "then I'll take you as my personal guest to the track the next time we test. How's that?"

A ghost of a smile returns to Zander's lips, his eyes lighting up for the first time as he nods his head yes.

I hold my hand over my heart as joy races through me. Finally! And all because Colton followed me in the house. All because he didn't listen to me. All because he's using one of my kids to blackmail me into going out with him. I could kiss him right now! Well, I guess I've already done that, but I could do it again. At this point, I'll do anything Colton asks me to do just to see the smile on Zander's face again.

Colton squeezes Zander's hand again and shakes it. "It's a deal then, buddy." He releases his hand and leans in closer. "I promise," he whispers.

Zander's lips curve into a smile. Small dimples form in his cheeks. Dimples I didn't even know he had. He slowly withdraws his hand from Colton's but continues to look at him expectantly, as if to ask when this will take place. Colton glances over at me for help, and I step up.

"Zander, sweetie?" He moves his eyes from Colton's and looks over to me. "Colton and I are going to go over and sit in the kitchen and plan a time, would you like to join us or would you like to go finish watching the basketball game with the boys?" I ask softly.

Zander's eyes glance rapidly back and forth over the both of us before Colton interrupts. "Hey, buddy, I'm gonna stay right here in the kitchen for a couple of minutes with Rylee. Can you go watch the game for me to let me know what I've missed when we're done?"

Zander nods slightly, locking eyes with Colton, once again gauging if he's being sincere. He must believe him because he clenches his stuffed doggy tighter and heads back to the couch. Shane's eyes catch mine, his face blanketed with disbelief before he picks up the remote and turns the sound back up.

I rise from the floor, noticing that all of the boys except Zander have their attention still focused on Colton. It's not every day that a celebrity is in our house. Colton notices the pairs of eyes on him and gives them a heartfelt smile.

"Don't worry," he says to them, "you can all come too when I take Zander to the track."

A large cacophony of whoops ring out as excitement electrifies the boys. "Okay, okay," I placate. "You guys got what you wanted. Please turn around and pay attention to the game so Colton and I can discuss some things."

They obey, for the most part, as we move to the barstools in the kitchen. I offer Colton a seat, and I walk around the island so I can face him. I notice Shane still observing us though, a protective look on his face, wondering why Colton has upset me.

For the myriad of emotions that Colton has made me feel in the week's time I've known him, the gratitude I have for him at this moment trumps them all.

I look up at him and meet his eyes, trying unsuccessfully to keep the tears from filling mine.

"Thank you," I whisper. It's only two words, but the look on his face tells me that he understands how much is behind them.

He nods. "It's the least I can do." His voice is gruff. "We all have our stories," he says, more to himself than to me.

"You got that right," I say, still overwhelmed by the situation. I look over to Zander and smile. He did it. He really did it today. He took a step out from under the fog. And suddenly I feel filled with hope. I feel impulsive from the possibilities.

"Colton!" I jolt him out of his thoughts. He whips his head up, startled by my urgency. I know I will regret this later, but I decide to go with my instinct. I decide to be impulsive and act in the moment. "I'm off in ten minutes," I say, and he looks at me as if he is not following my train of thought, so I continue. "I owe you a date, so let's go on a date."

He shakes his head as if trying to make sure I said the words he heard. "Oh— okay," he stumbles, and I love the fact that I've taken him by surprise. He starts to rise, the corners of his lips curving. "I don't have any reservations or—"

"Who cares?" I motion with my hands. "I'm not high mainte-nance. Simplicity is rewarding. I'm good with a burger or anything really." I watch his eyes widen in disbelief. "Besides, you paid enough for the date, who needs to drop a bunch of money on food that we eat anyway?"

He stares at me for a beat, and I sense that he is trying to figure out if I'm being serious or not. When I just look at him like he's being dense, he continues. "You are incredible. You know that right?" His simple words go straight to my heart, I can tell that he is being sincere.

I flash a grin over my shoulder as I head to my quarters to grab my things and freshen up. "I'll be right back."

I return in moments to find Mike staring awestruck, shaking Colton's hand in the kitchen. Colton turns to me when he hears me come in. "You ready?" he asks.

I hold up my finger indicating one second. "I'm outta here," I announce to the boys as they rise to give me hugs goodbye. I think the presence of Colton and my acquaintance with him has suddenly elevated me to rock star status, judging by the way they're hugging me so tightly.

As I'm receiving my hugs, I notice Colton walk over to the couch and squat down in front of Zander. He says something to him, but I can't hear what.

Chapter Eight

Aᴄ Colton and I stroll out of the house, an odd feeling of calm settles over me. I think this may be the best approach for a date with Colton. I've caught him off guard so he can't do any extensive planning. Extensive planning might equal overstated indulgences and premeditated seduction. Two things that I definitely do not need. It's hard enough to resist him as it is.

"We'll take my car," he says, placing a hand on my back, the warmth comforting me as he steers me toward a sleek, carbon-black convertible parked at the curb. The Aston Martin is beautiful and looks as if it is meticulously taken care of. It looks like it can really fly, and for just an instant, I imagine getting behind the wheel, flooring the pedal, and leaving all my ghosts behind.

"Nice ride," I grant him, although I try not to show any interest. I'm sure he's used to women fawning all over him and his car. Not me. *Let the games begin*, I think.

"Thanks." He opens the passenger door for me, and I slide onto the black leather, admiring the crafted interior and utter opulence. "I thought it was a beautiful day to drive with the top down," he says, rounding the back of the car and sliding in next to me. "I just didn't realize I was also going to be taking you out in it, too. An added bonus!" He says, giving me a megawatt grin as he puts on his sunglasses.

I can't help but flash him a smile back. "Whatever happened to good ol' fashioned pickup trucks?" I ask as he leans forward, opening the glove box, brushing his arm across my thigh and laughing loudly.

His touch is electrifying, even when it is accidental. He pulls out a worn, molded baseball hat with "Firestone" emblazoned across the bridge and puts it on his head, his dark hair curls out from under it at the nape of his neck. He pulls the brim down low enough to touch his sunglasses.

I guess this is his "incognito" look, but all I can think is he looks sexy as hell. All smoldering, edgy bad boy wrapped up in a drool-worthy body. I'm seriously fucked here if I actually think that my willpower will prevent me from giving in to any request from him. He reaches over and gives my thigh a quick squeeze before pressing a button on the dash in the center console.

"Don't worry, I have a truck too." He chuckles before the car roars to life, the vibration of the engine reverberating through my body and sending a thrill through me. "Hold on!" he says as he zooms out of the neighborhood, the excited look of a little boy on his face.

Boys and their toys, I think as I watch him from behind my aviators. I shouldn't be surprised by his skill maneuvering the car—this is how he makes his living—but I am. I shouldn't be turned on by his complete competence as he weaves smoothly in and out of traffic, the car accelerating quickly, but I find myself wanting to reach out and touch him. To connect with him, despite knowing that's a dangerous line for me to cross.

The roar of the engine and the whipping wind are loud enough that talking is not an option. I sit back, enjoying the feeling of freedom as the wind dances through my hair and the sun warms my skin. I lean my head back and give in to the urge to raise my hands over my head as we zip onto Interstate 10 heading west.

I glance over to see him watching me, a curious look on his face. He subtly shakes his head, a diminutive smile on his lips before he looks back toward the road. After a beat, he pushes a button and music pours through the speakers.

The song ends and another begins. I throw my head back, laughing at the song. It's a catchy little pop tune that I have heard on Shane's radio enough times. In my periphery, I notice Colton give me a quizzical look, so despite my average voice, I belt out the chorus, hoping he hears the words.

"You make me feel so right, even if it's so wrong, I wanna scream out loud, boy, I just bite my tongue." I raise my arms over my head again, letting myself go, reveling in the thought that I am telling

Colton how I feel without telling him. This is so unlike me—singing out loud, letting loose—but something about being with him, sitting next to him in this flashy sports car, has rid me of my inhibitions. As we exit the freeway, I finish the chorus with gusto. "It feels so good, but you're so bad for me!" Colton hears the words and laughs good-naturedly at them.

I continue singing the song, with less gusto since the car's purring engine is quieter now that we are on Fourth Street. He suddenly swerves abruptly and parks the car with adept precision along the curb.

I glance around trying to figure out where we are as he pushes a button in the sleek dashboard and the sexy purr of the engine ceases. "You okay to sit tight for a sec?" he asks, flashing me an earnest grin that affects me more than I care to admit.

"Sure," I answer, and I know at this moment that I am saying yes to so much more than just sitting patiently in the car. I push the fear out of my mind and vow to embrace the idea of feeling again. Of wanting to feel again. I flick my eyes from his, down to his mouth and back up, salacious thoughts running rampant through my mind. His smile widens.

"I'll be right back!" he announces before unfolding himself gracefully out of the car and standing to give me an incredible view of his ass. I bite my lip to suppress the urges whipping through my body. He glances over his shoulder and laughs, knowing full well the impact of his actions. "Hey, Ryles?"

"Yeah, Ace?"

"I told you you wouldn't be able to resist me." He flashes me a disarming smile before hopping up on the curb and walking briskly down the block, long legs eating up the sidewalk without a look back.

I can't help but grin as I watch him walk away. The man is captivating in every way and the epitome of sexy. From that boyish grin that disarms me in seconds to his sexy swagger that says he knows exactly where he's going and what his intentions are. He exudes virility, evokes desire, and commands attention all with a single look from his stunning eyes. He's edgy and reckless and you want to go along for the ride hoping to get a glimpse of his tender side that breaks through every now and again. The bad boy with a touch of vulnerability who leaves you breathless and steals your heart.

I shake myself from my thoughts to admire the view of Colton's broad shoulders and sexy swagger as he strides down the sidewalk. He tugs down on his baseball cap before he walks past two women. They both turn their heads as he passes by and admire him before turning back to each other and giggling, one mouthing the word, "Wow!"

I know how they feel, multiplied by a hundred. I watch as Colton stops and disappears into a doorway. I can't see the sign above the entrance on the worn down façade.

I pass the time admiring the sleek interior of the vehicle and watching people walk by the car and stare at it. The ring of Colton's cell phone sitting in the console startles me. I glance down to see the name *Tawny* flashing across the screen. A pang of irritation flickers in me before I rein in my jealousy. *Of course he has women calling him,* I tell myself.

Probably *all* the time.

"We're all set," Colton says, startling me as he places a paper grocery bag behind me. He walks around the car and slides into his seat. As he buckles his seatbelt, he notices his phone's missed-call message on the screen and thumbs to it. An enigmatic look crosses his face as he sees the caller's name, and I chastise myself for hoping he would scowl when he saw it.

A girl can dream.

Within moments we are back on the road and headed up the Pacific Coast Highway. I'm admiring the sight of the surf crashing on the beach with the sun in the background slowly ebbing toward the horizon before I realize that we're pulling into a nearly empty parking lot. I'm surprised there are so few people here considering the weather is unusually warm for this time of year.

"We're here," he says, pushing a button that has the top of the car lifting and closing in over us before he turns off the car. I look at him, surprised; I was hoping for a non-romantic "date," and yet he has brought me to my favorite place on earth—a near-empty beach just before sunset. He simply is not playing fair, but then again, he doesn't know me well enough to know my preferences, so I just chock it up to luck on his part.

He grabs the bag behind my seat and exits the car. He then collects a blanket from the trunk before coming around to my side. He opens the door with a playful flair as he reaches for my hand to help me out of the car.

"Come," he demands as he tugs on my hand, a thousand sensations overtake me as he pulls me toward the sand and surf. I am giddy with the fact that he continues to hold my hand in his even though I've followed him. The rough calluses on his palm against my smooth skin are a welcome feeling, almost like being pinched to make sure I'm not dreaming.

We walk out onto the beach past a pile of towels and clothes that I assume belong to the two surfers in the water. We walk in silence, both taking in our surroundings as I try to figure out what to say. Why am I all of the sudden nervous over Colton's intensity? Over his proximity?

When we get about ten feet from the wet sand, Colton finally speaks. "How about right here?"

"Sure, although I would've brought my swim suit if I'd known we were coming to the beach," I say, my nerves giving way to stupid humor as it usually does. If I could roll my eyes at myself right now, I would.

"Who said anything about suits? I'm all for skinny dipping."

I freeze at the comment, eyes wide, and swallow loudly. Odd that the idea of stripping down naked with this ruggedly handsome man unnerves me, despite the fact he's had his hands on me.

His perfection next to my ordinary.

Colton reaches out with his free hand and puts a finger under my chin, raising my head so that I can meet his gentle eyes. "Relax, Rylee. I'm not going to eat you alive. You said you wanted casual, so I'm giving you casual. I thought we could take advantage of the unusually warm weather," he says, releasing my chin and handing me the brown bag so that he can lay a large Pendleton blanket on the sand. "Besides, when I get you naked, it's going to be somewhere a lot more private so I can enjoy every slow and maddening second of it. So I can take my time and show you exactly what that sexy body of yours was made for." He glances up, eyes flashing desire and mouth turning up in a wicked grin.

I sigh and shake my head, unsure of myself, of my reaction to him, and how I should proceed. The man can seduce me with words alone. That's definitely not a good sign. If he keeps it up I'll be handing over my panties to him in no time at all.

I fidget under the intensity of his stare and from the direction my thoughts have taken. "Take a seat, Rylee. I promise, I don't bite." He smirks.

"We'll see about that." I snort, but I oblige him and sit down on the blanket, distracting myself from my nerves by unzipping my ankle boots. I pull off my socks, free my feet, and wiggle my toes, which are painted fire-engine red. I pull my knees up, and wrap my arms around them, hugging them to my chest. "It's beautiful out here. I'm so glad the cloud cover stayed away today."

"Mmm-hmm," he murmurs as he reaches into the brown bag from Fourth Street. "Are you hungry?" he asks, producing two packages wrapped in white deli paper, followed by a loaf of French bread, a bottle of wine, and two paper cups. "Voila," he announces. "A very sophisticated dinner of salami, provolone cheese, French bread, and some wine." The corners of his mouth turn up slightly as if he is testing me. As if he is checking to see if I really am okay with a casual, no-frills dinner in this land of Hollywood glitz, glamour, and pretension.

I eye him warily, not liking games or being tested, but I guess someone in his shoes is probably wary of others. Then again, he's the one begging me for a date, although I'm still not sure why.

"Well, it's not the Ritz," I say dryly, rolling my eyes, "but it'll have to do."

He laughs loudly as he pulls the cork out of the wine, pours it in the paper cups, and hands one to me. "To simplicity!" he toasts good-humoredly.

"To simplicity," I agree, tapping his cup and taking a sip of the sweet, flavorful wine. "Wow, a girl could get used to this." When he eyes me with doubt, I continue, "What more could I ask for? Sun, sand, food—"

"A handsome date?" he jokes as he breaks off a piece of bread, layers it with provolone and thin-sliced salami, and hands it to me on a paper napkin. I accept it graciously, my stomach growling. I've forgotten how hungry I am.

"Thank you," I say. "For the food, for the donation, for Zander ..."

"What's the story there?"

I relay the gist of it to him, his face remaining impassive. "And today, with you, is the first time he's purposely interacted with anybody, so thank you. I'm more grateful than you will ever know," I conclude, looking down sheepishly, a blush spreading across my cheeks as I'm suddenly uncomfortable again. I take a bite of the makeshift sandwich and moan appreciatively at the mixture of fresh bread and deli fare. "This is really good!"

He nods in agreement. "I've been going to that deli forever. It's definitely better and more my speed than caviar." He shrugs unapologetically. "So why Corporate Cares?" he asks, his mouth parting slightly as he watches me savor my food.

"So many reasons," I say, finishing my bite. "The ability to make a difference, the chance to be part of a breakthrough such as Zander's today, or the feeling I get when a child left behind is made to feel like he matters again ..." I sigh, not having enough words to express the feelings I have. "There are so many things that I can't even begin to explain."

"You are very passionate about it. I admire you for that." His tone is earnest and sincere.

"Thank you," I reply, taking another sip of wine, meeting his eyes. "You were quite impressive yourself today. Almost as if you knew what to do despite me telling you to leave," I admit sheepishly. "You were good with Zander."

"Nah," he denies, grabbing another piece of cheese and folding it in the bread. "I'm not good with kids at all. That's why I'm never having them." His statement is determined, his expression blank.

I'm taken aback. "That's a bold statement for someone so young. I'm sure at some point you'll change your mind," I reply, my eyes narrowing as I watch him, wishing I still had the option to make a choice like his.

"Absolutely not," he states emphatically before averting his eyes from my gaze for the first time since meeting him. I can sense his discomfort with this topic—an oddity for a man so confident and sure of himself in all other areas of life. He looks out toward the tumultuous ocean and is quiet for a few moments, an unreadable look on his rugged features.

I think that my questioning statement will go unanswered, until he breaks the silence. "Not really," he says with what I sense is a resigned sadness in his voice. "I'm sure you experience it first hand every day, Rylee. People use kids as pawns in this world. Too many women try to trap men with them and then hate the kid when the man leaves. People foster kids just to get the monthly government stipend. It goes on and on." He shrugs nonchalantly, belying how affected he is by the hidden truth behind his words. "It happens daily. Kids fucked up and abandoned because of their mothers' selfish choices. I'd never put a child in that kind of position." He shakes his head emphatically, still refusing to meet my eyes, his gaze following the surfer riding a wave in the distance. "Regardless, I'd probably fuck them up as much as I was as a kid." He breathes deeply with his last statement and removes his cap with one hand while running his other hand through his hair.

"What do you mean? I don't understand," I falter as I start to ask without thinking. This conversation has unexpectedly gotten heavy quickly.

Annoyance flashes across his face before I watch him rein it in. "My past is public knowledge," he states, my furrowed brow showing my confusion. "Fame makes people dig out ugly truths."

"Sorry," I say, raising my eyebrows, "I don't make it a habit of researching my dates." I hide the unease I feel with this conversation in the sarcasm of my tone.

His green eyes lock onto mine, his clenched jaw pulsing. "You really should, Rylee," his steely voice warns. "You just never know who's dangerous. Who's going to hurt you when you least expect it."

I'm taken aback. Is he warning me about him? Warning me away from him? I'm confused. Pursue me and then push me away? This is the second time today he's issued a statement like this. What should I make of it?

And what the hell is with his comments about being messed up as a kid? His parents are practically Hollywood royalty. Is he saying that they did something to him? The fixer in me wants to probe, but I can tell how unwelcome that would be.

I cautiously glance over at him to see his attention turned back toward the surf. It is in this moment I can see the pictures painted by the media of him. Dark and brooding, a little rugged with the dark

79

shadow of hair on his jaw, and an intensity to his eyes that makes you feel as if he's unapproachable. Unpredictable. The broad shoulders and sexy swagger. The bad boy who is too handsome for his own good mixed with a whole lot of reckless. The rebel who women swoon over and swear they could tame—if they had the chance.

And he's sitting here. *With me.* It's mind-boggling.

I clear my throat, trying to dispel the awkwardness that has descended on our picnic. "So, how 'bout them Lakers?" I deadpan.

He throws his head back and laughs loudly before turning back to me. All traces of Brooding Colton have been replaced by Relaxed Colton, with eyes full of humor and a megawatt smile. "A little heavy?"

I nod, pursing my lips, as I grab for another piece of cheese. Time for a change in topic. "I know it's an unoriginal question, but what made you get into racing? I mean why hurl yourself around a track at close to two hundred miles an hour for fun?"

He sips from his Dixie cup. "My parents needed a way to channel my teenage rebellion." He shrugs. "They figured why not give me all the safety equipment to go along with it instead of racing down the street and killing myself or someone else. Lucky for me, they had the means to follow through with it."

"So you started as a teenager?"

"At eighteen." He laughs, remembering.

"What's so funny?"

"I got a ticket for reckless driving. I was speeding ... out of control really ... racing some preppy punk." He glances over at me to see if I have any reaction. I just look at him and raise my eyebrows, prompting him to continue. "I was spared being hauled off to juvie because of my dad's name. *Man, was he pissed.* The next day he thought he'd teach me a lesson. Dropped me off at the track with one of the stunt drivers he knew. Thought he'd have the guy drive me around the track at mach ten and scare the shit out of me."

"Obviously it didn't work," I say dryly.

"No. He scared me some, but afterward I asked him if he could show me some of the stunt moves." He shrugs, a half smirk on his lips, as he looks out toward the water. "He finally agreed, let me drive his car around the track a couple of times. For some reason one of his friends had come with him to the track that day. The guy's name was

Beckett. He worked for a local race crew who'd just lost their driver. He asked if I'd ever thought about racing. I laughed at him. First of all, he was my age so how could he be part of a race team, and secondly, how could he watch me take a couple of laps and know that I could drive? When I asked, he said he thought I could handle a car pretty well, and would I like to come back the next day and talk to him some more?"

"Talk about being at the right place at the right moment," I murmur, happy to learn something about him that I couldn't read about by looking on the Internet.

"You're telling me!" He shakes his head. "So I met up with him. Tried out the car on the track, did pretty well and got along with the guys. They asked me to drive the next race. I was decent at it so I kept doing it. Got noticed. Stayed out of trouble." He grins a mischievous grin, raising his eyebrows. "For the most part."

"And after all this time, you still enjoy it?"

"I'm good at it," he says.

"That's not what I asked."

He chews his food, carefully mulling over my question. "Yes, I suppose so. There's no other feeling like it. I'm part of a team, and yet it's just me out there. I have no one to depend on, to blame, but myself if something goes wrong." I can sense the passion in his voice. The reverence he still has for his sport. "On the track, I can escape the paparazzi, the groupies … my demons. The only fear I have is that which I've created for myself, that I can control with a swerve of the wheel or a press of the pedal … not any inflicted on me by someone else."

The startled look on his face tells me that he has revealed more than he expected in an answer. That he's surprised by his unanticipated honesty with me. I brush aside his unease at feeling vulnerable, by propping my arms out behind me and raising my face to the sky.

"It's so beautiful here," I say, breathing in the fresh air and digging my toes in the cool sand.

"More wine?" he asks as he shifts to sit closer to me. The brush of his bare arm against mine leaves my senses humming.

I murmur in assent as warning bells go off in my head. I know that I need to create some distance between us, but he's just too damn attractive. Irresistible. *Nothing like I expected and yet everything I an-*

ticipated. I know that I need to clear my head because he is clouding my judgement.

"So is this what you imagined, Ace, when you spent all that money for a date with me?" I turn my head and come face to face with him— hair mussed, lips full, eyes blazing. I hold my breath, frozen in the moment, for all it would take is for me to lean in to feel his lips on mine again. To taste his carnal hunger as I did earlier on the porch.

He flashes a grin at me. "Not exactly," he admits, but I can sense our proximity is affecting him too. I can see the pulse in his throat accelerate. His Adam's apple bobs with a swallow. I bring my eyes back up to his, unspoken words flowing between us. "You really have the most unusually magnificent eyes," he whispers.

It's not as if I haven't heard this before about my unique, violet-colored eyes, but for some reason, hearing it from him has desire spiraling through me. Warning bells clang inside my head.

"Rylee?"

I raise my eyes to meet his, trepidation in my heart. "I'm only going to ask this one time. Do you have a boyfriend?" The gravity in his tone as well as the question itself take me off guard. I didn't expect this. I thought he'd already know the answer after the backstage ministrations from the other night. More surprising than the question itself, is the way he asks it. His demanding tone.

I shake my head "no," swallowing loudly.

"No one you are seeing casually?"

"You just asked twice," I joke, trying to shake the nerves skittering up my spine. When he doesn't smile but rather holds my stare in question, I shake my head again. "No, why?" I respond breathlessly.

"Because I want to know who's standing in my way." He tilts his head and stares at me as my lips part in response. My mouth is suddenly very dry. "Whose ass I have to kick before I can make it official."

"Make what official?" My mind flickers trying to figure out what I'm missing.

"*That you're mine.*" Colton's breath flutters over my face as the look in his eyes swallows me whole. "Once I fuck you, Rylee—it's official, you're mine and only mine."

Oh. Fucking. My. How can those words, so possessive, so dominantly male, make me want him that much more? I'm an independent, self-assured woman, and yet hearing that this man—yes, Colton Donavan—inform me that he is going to have me without asking, without giving me a choice, makes me weak in the knees.

"It might not be tonight, Rylee. It might not be tomorrow night," he promises, the rumbling timbre of his voice vibrating through my body, "but it will happen." My breath hitches as he pauses to allow me to absorb his words before he continues. "Don't you feel it, Rylee? This…" he gestures a hand between him and me "…this charge we have here? The electricity we have when we're together is way too strong to ignore." I lower my eyes, uncomfortable with his overconfidence yet turned on by his words. He takes a hand and reaches out, the spark he's referring to igniting when his index finger trails up the underside of my neck to my chin. He pushes up to lift my chin so I'm forced to stare into the depths of his eyes. "Aren't you the least bit curious how good it will be? If it's this electrifying with just the brush of our skin against each other, can you imagine what it will be like when I'm buried inside of you?"

The confidence in his words and the intensity of his stare nonpluses me, and I avert my eyes down again to focus on the ring I'm worrying around my right ring finger. The rational part of me knows that once Colton has his way with me, he'll move on. And even though I'd know this going into it, I'd still be devastated in the end.

I just don't want to go through it again. I'm afraid to feel again. Afraid to take a chance, afraid that the consequences will be life-altering for me again. I use my fear to fuel my obstinance; no matter how wild the ride, the inevitable fallout isn't worth it.

"You're so sure of yourself, do I even need to show up for the event?" I ask haughtily, hoping my words cover the deep ache he's responsible for creating in my body. His only response to my question is a heart-stopping smirk. I shake my head at him. "Thanks for the warning, Ace, but no thanks."

"Oh, Rylee," he says with a laugh. "There's that smart mouth that I find so intriguing and sexy. It disappeared for a little while with your nerves. I was getting worried." He reaches over and squeezes my hand. "Oh, and Ryles, just so you know, that wasn't a warning, sweetheart. That was a promise."

And with that he leans back on his elbows, a cocky grin on his face and challenge in his eyes as he stares at me. I travel the length of his lean body with my eyes. My thoughts running through how I should resist this over-the-top, reckless, troubled, and unpredictable man whose continual verbal sparring makes me uncomfortable. Makes me desire. Churns up feelings and thoughts that died that day two years ago. And yet, rather then head the other way as I should, all I want to do is straddle him right here on that blanket, run my hands up the firm muscles of his chest, fist my hands in his hair, and take until I surrender all my rational thoughts.

I brave meeting his eyes again for I know he is watching me appraise his body. I make sure that my eyes reflect none of the desire I'm feeling. "So, what about you, Colton?" I question, turning the tables on him. "You said you don't do the girlfriend thing, and yet you always seem to have a lady on your arm?"

He arches his eyebrows at me. "And how would you know what I always have on my arm?"

How do I know that? Do I admit to him that I occasionally glance through Haddie's subscription of *People* and roll my eyes at the ridiculous commentary? Do I confess that I peruse Perezhilton.com as a distraction when I'm in the office sometimes and that I usually skip over the gossip about self-absorbed Hollywood brat-packers like him, who think they're better than everyone else? "Well, I do stand at the checkout lines in the grocery store," I admit. "And you know how true all of those tabloids are."

"According to them I'm dating an alien with three heads and my photoshopped picture is right next to the caption stating a chupacabra was found in a movie theater in Norman, Oklahoma," he says, animating his expression, eyes wide in a mock stare of horror.

I laugh out loud. Really laugh. So glad that he takes the media in stride. Happy that he's added some levity to the heavy topics of conversation. "Nice change of topic, but it's not going to work. Answer the question, Ace."

"Oh, Rylee—all business," he chides. "What is there to say? I hate the drama, the points system of who is contributing how much, the expectation of the next step to take, trying to figure out if there is an ulterior motive for them being with me ..." He shrugs. "Rather than deal with that bullshit, I come to a mutual agreement with someone, stated rules and requirements are laid out, specifics are negotiated, and expectations are managed way before they even have a chance to begin or get out of hand. It simplifies things."

What? Negotiations? So many things run through my head that I know I'm going to have to think about later, but with his eyes boring into mine, awaiting my reaction, I decide that humor is the best way to mask my surprise at his response.

"So a guy with a commitment issue…" I roll my eyes "…like that's something new!" He remains quiet, still regarding me as I think about him, about *this*, about *everything*. "So what were you hoping for?" I continue sardonically, "that I'd just look into your gorgeous green eyes, drop my panties, and spread my legs when you admit that you like women in your bed but you won't let them in your heart?" Despite my sarcasm, I'm being brutally honest. Does he think that just because he is who he is, it'll negate all my morals? *"And they say romance is dead."*

"You do have such a way with words, sweetheart," he drawls, shifting onto his side, propping his head on his elbow. A slow, measured smile spreads across his face. "I assure you, romance is not something I actively subscribe to. There's no such thing as happily ever after."

The hopeless romantic in me sighs heavily, allowing me to ignore his comment and the smirk on his face—the one that makes me forget all the thoughts in my head because he is in fact that damn attractive and his eyes are that mesmerizing. "You can't be serious? Why the emotional detachment?" I shake my head. "You seem to be such a passionate person otherwise."

He shifts on the blanket, lying on his back and placing his hands behind his head, exhaling loudly. "Why is anyone the way they are?" he answers vaguely, the silence hanging between us. "Maybe that's how I was born or what I learned in my formative years … how's one to know? There's a lot about me you don't want to know, Rylee. I promise you."

I look at him, trying to decipher his verbal maze of explanations as he lies quietly for a few minutes before reaching a hand out from behind his head and placing it on mine. I revel in this rare sign of affection. Most of the time when we touch it's explosive, carnal even. Rarely is it simple. Undemanding. Maybe that's why I enjoy the warmth of his hand seeping through the top of mine.

I'm still pondering what he's said despite the distraction of his touch. "I disagree. How can you—"

I'm stopped mid-sentence as he tugs on my arm, and within seconds has me lying on the blanket, looking up at his face hovering over mine. I'm not sure how it's possible, but my breath speeds up and stops at the same time. He very slowly, very deliberately uses one hand to brush an errant hair off of my face while the other rests on the base of my neck just under the crease of my chin.

"Are you trying to change the subject, Mr. Donavan?" I ask coyly, my heart thumping and desire blooming in my belly. His touch leaves electric charges on my skin.

"Is it working?" he breathes, angling his head to study me.

I purse my lips and narrow my eyes in thought. "Hmmm … no, I still have my questions." A smile plays on my lips as I watch him watch me.

"Then I just might have to do something about that," he murmurs with painstaking slowness as he lowers his head until his lips are a whisper from mine. I fight the urge to arch my back so that my body can press against his. "How about now?"

How is it we are outdoors but I feel as if all of the oxygen has been vacuumed away? Why does he have this effect on me? I try to slowly breathe in and all I smell is him—woodsy, clean, and male— a heady, intoxicating mixture that is pure Colton.

I can't find my voice to answer his question, so I just give him a noncommittal "Hmm-hmmm." I'm oblivious to everything around us: the seagulls squawking, the surf crashing, the sun heading slowly toward the ocean on the horizon.

Due to our proximity, I can't see his lips but I know that he smiles because I see the lines crinkle at the corners of his eyes. "Should I *take* that as a yes or should I *take* that as a no?" he asks. His eyes hold mine, daring me. When all I do is breathe in a shaky breath, he says, "Then I guess I'll just *take*."

And with those words, his mouth is on mine.

He sets a slow, mesmerizing pace, feathering light kisses over my lips. Each time I think he is going to give me what I want—deep, passionate kisses—he pulls back. He leans on one elbow, and then cups the back of my neck. His other hand slowly travels down the side of my body, and stops on the side of my hip. He grabs hold there, gripping my flesh through my jeans and presses my body closer to him.

"Your. Curves. Are. So. Damn. Sexy," he murmurs between kisses. The riot of sensation he is causing within me is both exhilarating and tormenting. I run my hands under his shirt, up the plains up of his torso and then his back, as he continues his languorous assault on my lips.

If I were the intelligent woman that I claim to be, I would step back a moment and rationally assess the situation. I'd realize that Colton is a guy used to getting what he wants without preamble or precaution. And at this time, he wants me. He has tried the direct, get-to-the-point approach and basically had me up against a wall within ten minutes. He's tried coercion, a contract, annoyance, and even admitted he doesn't do girlfriends, commitment, or relationships. The rational part of me would acknowledge these facts and realize he's failed the challenge thus far, so now he is moving onto seduction. I'd argue that he's changing his approach, taking his time by making me feel and making me want him. Letting me think this situation is on my terms now. I'd realize that this has nothing to do with emotions and wanting 'an after' with me, but rather he is trying to get me in his bed any way he can now.

But I'm not listening to my rational self and the snarky doubts she's trying to cast. I vaguely push away the niggling feeling that she's trying to force into my subconscious. My common sense has long been forgotten. It has been overrun, inundated, and is being thoroughly obliterated by my new addiction, otherwise known as Colton's mouth. His mouth worships mine with slow, leisurely licks of tongue, grazes of teeth, and caresses of lips.

"Uh-uh-uh," he teases against my lips as I thread my fingers through his hair at the back of his neck and try to pull him closer so I can give into the blistering need he's built inside of me and take more.

"You're frustrating." I sigh because now his lips have moved steadily up my neck, lacing open mouth kisses to nip at my earlobe, causing little sparks of frisson in their path.

I can feel his smile spread against the hollow spot beneath my ear in response to my words. "Now you know how it feels," he murmurs, "to want something …" He withdraws from my neck so his face hovers an inch from mine. There is no doubt about the desire that clouds his eyes when they fuse to mine. He repeats himself. "To want something that someone won't give you."

I don't even have a moment to register his words before his mouth crushes down on mine. This time he doesn't hold back. His lips possess mine from the very moment we touch. He commands the kiss with a fiery passion that has my head spinning, my sanity ebbing, and my body craving. He kisses me with such an unrequited hunger, it's as if he'd go crazy if he didn't taste me. I have no choice but to ride the wave that he is controlling because I'm just as caught up as he is.

His tongue darts in my mouth, tasting of wine, before he eases and pulls gently at my bottom lip. I arch my neck, offering him more, wanting him to take more because I can't get enough of his intoxicating taste. He acquiesces, laying a row of feather-light kisses along my jawline before coming back to my mouth. He licks his tongue back in against mine—caressing, possessing, igniting.

I revel in the feeling of him. His hand spanning my hip in ownership. The weight of his leg, which is bent and resting on mine, pressing his evident arousal into my hip. His mouth controlling, taking, and giving all at the same time. The low growls of desire that emanate from deep in his throat in pure appreciation, telling me that I excite him. That he wants me.

I could stay in this state of desire all day with Colton, but the sound of approaching laughter brings me to my senses. Brings me to the realization that we're in public view. Colton brushes my lips gently one more time as we hear the surfers walking several feet away, back to their towels. His hands remain cupped on my face though, and he rests his forehead against mine, both trying to calm our ragged breathing.

He closes his eyes momentarily, and I sense him struggle with his control. He rubs his thumbs back and forth on my cheeks, a gentle caress that calms me.

"Oh, Rylee, what do you do to me?" He sighs, kissing the tip of my nose. "What am I going to do with you? You're such a breath of fresh air."

My heart stops. My body tenses. I flash back to three years prior,

Max on one knee, ring in his hand, staring up at me expectantly. His words, chock-full of emotion, ring in my ears like it was yesterday. "Rylee, you are my best friend, my ride off into the sunset, *my breath of fresh air*. Will you marry me?"

I am thinking of Max—bright, open, and carefree—but I am looking at Colton: reserved, unattainable, and inescapable. A sob escapes my throat as the memory takes hold of me, of that day, of the aftermath, and guilt washes over me.

Colton is startled at my reaction. He jolts back away from me, but his hands still cup my face, concern filling his eyes. "Rylee, what is it? Are you okay?"

I put my hands on his chest and push him away as I rise up to sit, pulling my legs to my chest and hugging them. I shake my head for him to give me a minute and take in a deep breath, aware that Colton is watching me very closely, curious about what caused my reaction.

I try to push the words out of my head. His mom yelling at me that I killed him, his dad telling me he wished it had been me instead, and his brother telling me it was my fault. That I don't deserve to ever know that kind of love again.

I shudder at the thoughts, collecting myself, preparing myself for the questions I'm waiting for Colton to ask. But they never come. I look over at him, his face somber as he studies me, and I look back out to the sea. He rubs his hand over my lower back, the only form of solace he gives me.

I shake myself out of my thoughts, upset at what they interrupted. Why can't I just let it all go and enjoy this man—this virile man within my grasp—who for some ridiculous reason wants me? Why can't I just give in to his sordid excuse of a one-night-stand-type relationship just to get me out of this revolving nightmare? Use him, as he wants to use me.

Because that's not you, I whisper to myself. *You are a breath of fresh air.*

I'm thankful to Colton for his silence. I'm not sure if it is a silent understanding, or a detachment from someone else's drama, but regardless, at this point I'm glad that I'm not being asked to explain myself.

I reach back to grab for my plastic cup of wine. Colton hands it to me as he takes his and sips. "Well, I guess it's a good thing we're outside," I say, trying to diffuse the awkwardness with humor.

"Why's that?"

I take a long swallow of my drink before I continue. "To keep us from getting out of hand *in public*," I respond, turning my head so that I can smile at him.

"What makes you think that being outside would stop me?" He flashes a devilish grin before laughing out loud, throwing his head back when he sees the shocked look on my face. "The danger of being caught only heightens sensation, Rylee. Increases the intensity of your arousal. Your climax." His voice wraps seductively around me, spinning me in his web.

I stare at him, trying to unwrap my thoughts from his snare. Trying to find my wits about me so I can respond and appear to be unaffected by his hypnotic words. "I thought you said you wanted somewhere private the first time?" I smirk, arching an eyebrow at him.

He leans in close to me, his breath feathering over my face and amusement dancing in his eyes. "Well at least I just got you to admit that there's going to be a first time."

My eyes widen as I realize what I'd just willingly walked into. I can't help the smile that breaks across my lips as I take in the mischievously wicked one on his. He shakes his head and as his eyes break from mine he says, "Look at that." He points to the horizon where the bottom of the sun hits the edge of the water, a bright ball sinking and spilling pastels across the sky.

Grateful for the change in topic, I turn my head to look. "Why is it that the sun seems to take forever to reach the horizon and the minute it gets there it sinks so fast?"

"It reflects life, don't you think?" he asks.

"How so?"

"Sometimes our journeys in life seem to take forever to get to the culmination of our efforts—to achieving the goal. And once we do, it goes so fast and then it's over." He shrugs, surprising me with his introspection. "We forget that the journey is the best part. The reason for taking the ride. What we learn the most from."

"Are you trying to tell me something in a round about way, Colton?" I ask.

"Nope," he says, a smile lighting up his features. "Just making an observation. That's all."

I eye him cautiously, still unsure what he's trying to tell me despite his denial. I dig my toes into the sand still warm from the sun's rays. I scrunch my toes back and forth, loving how it feels.

I hear Colton move next to me before I hear the paper bag from the deli rustling. I turn to see him stretched out across the blanket, pulling two Saran-wrapped squares from the bag. He sits back up next to me, crossing his legs like a kid in grade school. He holds a square up between us. "The cure for all woes," he says, handing it to me.

Our fingers brush as I take the brownie from him, his touch welcome. "You thought of everything on this twenty-five thousand dollar date, didn't you?" I tease him, making quick work of the package. He watches me as I take my first bite, the scrumptious chocolate is delectable and has me rolling my eyes in appreciation, and moaning with ecstasy. *This* is the way to get to my heart.

I look from the brownie back up to Colton, a captivated look on his face. "Do you have any idea how fucking sexy you are right now?" His voice is gruff, pained even.

I stop chewing, mid-bite, at his comment. How is it he can make such simple words so spellbinding at the oddest times? The candor on his face throws me off. We just sit there, a few feet apart on a blanket on a beach, and stare at each other. No pretenses. No audience. No expectations. The unspoken words that flow between us are so powerful I'm afraid to blink, afraid to move, afraid to speak for fear of ruining this moment. I'm seeing the true Colton Donavan—the unmasked version with a vulnerability that makes me want to reach over and take away the hurt that often flickers through those green eyes and make it better. To show him that love and commitment are possible without complications. That it is real and pure and much more powerful than ever imagined when it is built and shared between two people.

I feel a phantom ache in my heart as a tiny piece tears off, lost forever to Colton in this moment.

I finally break eye contact, lowering my eyes back to watch my fingers pick at my brownie. I know that I'll never get to express this to him. I'll never get the chance. At some point in the near future I will give my body to him willingly, despite my head telling me it's a mistake. I will revel in that moment with him which will be filled with reverent sighs and entangled bodies, and I'll be devastated when he walks away after having his fill of me. I blink away the tears that burn in my eyes.

It has to be the approaching anniversary, I tell myself. I'm never this emotional—this unstable.

I pick a chunk off the corner of my brownie and push it in my mouth. I look back up at him, a shy smile creeping onto his face, telling me that he felt the moment between us as well. I shiver .

"You cold?" he asks, reaching out with his thumb to wipe a piece of chocolate from the corner of my mouth. He brings his thumb and holds it out to my mouth. I open my lips and suck the chocolate off. A groan rumbles in the back of his throat, and his lips part slightly as he watches me. If I knew it'd be this erotic to watch his reaction, I'd leave a Hansel and Gretel trail of brownie crumbs all over my body and enjoy watching him find them.

I shiver again in response to his question, despite the heat burning within me.

"Since this was so impromptu, I didn't bring a jacket or an extra blanket for you," he says with disappointment in his voice. "We can go somewhere else if you'd like?"

I look up at him, a sincere look on my face. "Thank you, Colton. I really had a good time …"

"Despite the heavy conversation," he adds when I pause.

I laugh at him. "Yes, despite the heavy topics, but I've had a really long week and I'm exhausted," I apologize, "so I think it's best if we head back." I really don't want to, but I am desperately trying to keep a level head here.

"Ooooh, the blow off!" he teases, pressing a hand to his wounded heart. "That's harsh, but I understand." He laughs.

I help him start to wrap up the left-over food and place it back in the bag. I start putting my socks and shoes back on when he says, "So Teddy signed the deal today with CDE."

"That's great!" I say sincerely. Excited for the opportunity and uncertain about the effect it will have on my personal life—being forced to be with him. "I can't express how thankful I am—"

"Rylee," he says with enough force to stop me short. "That, the donation, has nothing to do with *this*," he says, gesturing between the two of us.

Like hell it doesn't. I wouldn't be here with him if it weren't for that arrangement.

"Sure," I mumble in agreement, and I know that I haven't convinced him.

"That's mine," I point toward my red and white Mini Cooper parked on the street outside of The House. He pulls up behind it, pushing the button to quiet the sexy purr of the engine. The streetlights are on and the one nearest The House keeps flickering on and off. I can hear a dog barking several houses down, and the smell of meat cooking on charcoal hangs in the air. It feels like home, normalcy, just what the seven boys tucked inside the house in front of me deserve.

Colton comes around the side of the car and opens the door, holding a hand out to help me from my seat. I clutch my purse to my chest, suddenly feeling awkward as I make my way to my car with Colton's hand on the small of my back.

I turn to face him, leaning my back against my car. I have my bottom lip between my teeth and worry it back and forth as my nerves seem to be getting the better of me. "Well … thank you for a nice evening, Colton," I say as I look around the street unable to meet his eyes. Am I afraid that this might be it? Of course not, because I know I'll have to see him for work. Then why do I suddenly feel a mixture of unease and sadness over parting with him? Why am I mentally kicking myself for not taking him up on the offer to go somewhere else?

Colton reaches out and places a finger under my chin, turning my face so I'm forced to meet his eyes. "What is it, Rylee? What has you so afraid to feel? Every time you start to get caught up in the moment and hand yourself over to the sensation, something flashes across your face and has you withdrawing. Pulling back and becoming unavailable. Has you bottling back up all of that potential passion of yours in a matter of seconds." He searches my eyes in question, his fingers firm on my chin so I can't avert my eyes. "Who did this to you, sweetheart? Who hurt you this badly?"

His eyes probe mine looking for answers I'm not willing to give him. The muscle in his jaw tics in frustration at my silence. His features, darkened by the night sky, are tense, awaiting my response. The flickering streetlight creates a stark contrast with his warring emotions.

I can feel my protective wall bristle at his unwanted attention. The only way I know how to deal, how to keep him at arm's length, is to turn the question back on him. "I could ask you the same question, Colton. Who hurt you? What haunts those eyes of yours every so often?"

He quirks his eyebrows at my tactic, his concentrated stare never wavering. "I'm not a very patient man, Rylee," he warns. "I'll only wait so long before—"

"Some things are better left alone," I cut him off, my words coming out barely above a whisper and my breath hitches.

He moves his thumb from my chin and drags it over my bottom lip. "Now that," he whispers back to me, "I can understand." His response surprises me, reaffirming my assumption that he is in fact hiding from something himself. Or running.

He leans in slowly, brushing a reverent, lingering kiss on my lips, and all thoughts in my head vaporize. His tenderness is unexpected, and I want to capture this moment in my mind. Revel in it. I sigh helplessly against his lips, our foreheads touching briefly.

"Goodnight, Colton."

"Goodnight, Rylee." He leans back, grabbing the handle of my door, opening it for me and ushering me in. "Until next time," he murmurs before shutting the door.

I start the engine and pull away from the curb. Instinctively, I reach out and push the stereo on, shuffling for the sixth disc in the changer. I glance in my rearview mirror as I make my way down this street, music flooding the car. I can see his figure as he rocks back on his heels with his hands in his pockets, standing beneath the flickering streetlight. *An angel fighting through the darkness or a devil breaking into the light?* Which, I'm not sure. Regardless, he stands there, my personal heaven and hell, watching me until I turn the corner and am out of his sight.

Chapter Nine

I PULL INTO MY DRIVEWAY and sit in the car for several moments humming to the music pouring out of the speakers, running through my time with Colton. I sing the song out of habit. The words and the rhythm are comforting to me. I place my hands on the top of the steering wheel and rest my head on top of them. It's not like I have been out with many guys in my life, but that was one of the most intense, passionate, and strangely comforting dates of my life. I shake my head as I replay it again.

Holy shit! That's all I can really think about my evening. About Colton's unexpected pursuit. The devil on my shoulder reiterates to me that this is all my fault. That if I'd acted like the *normal* me, I would've never been a willing victim to his deft hands in a backstage alcove. I would've never been in the position to tell him "thanks but no thanks," spurring on this whole chase—this whole challenge—a welcome change in his world of overly eager, willing women.

I scream out, startled by the knock on my car window. I am so deep in thought, I never saw Haddie approach my car. My heartbeat returns to normal as I open the door to her.

"Hi, Had. Just a sec," I say as I reach across my seat to grab my belongings.

I sense Haddie's presence shift into the doorway as her body blocks the garage light, throwing a shadow over the front seat. "Is that Matchbox Twenty?" she questions as she strains to hear the music playing quietly on the stereo system.

Uh-oh, I tell myself, *she knows something is up.* She knows I listen to Matchbox Twenty whenever I'm upset. Haddie knows this all too well from the dark period of my life.

I look over at her, hands on her hips, irritation emanating off of her in waves, and I'm not sure just how much she knows. And depending on what she knows is how hurt she'll be that I've kept it from her.

There is no rationalizing with Haddie when she's angry. When she feels wronged. I silently groan and know my interesting day is about to get longer. She never backs down until she gets the answers she wants. She can fool everyone because behind her innocent beauty is her razor sharp wit—but not me.

I know better.

I turn off the car quickly before she can hear which song I have on repeat, *Bent*. At least it's not *Unwell*. I have my bag in my hand but can't exit the car because she is standing in the way.

"I think we need to have a little chat," she says haughtily. "Don't you?" She moves out of the way, her hands on her hips. All she needs is to tap her foot and I'll be transported back to being in the principal's office in grade school.

I force a cheerful smile on my face. "Sure, Had. What's up? You seem pissed at something?"

"You."

"Me?" I respond, walking to the front door, rolling my eyes.

"Don't roll your eyes at me either, Ry," she demands as we walk through the front door.

I drop my stuff by the tall table that stands against the entry wall. I skulk over to the couch in our front room and sink into it, wishing I could just close my eyes and fall asleep. But I can't because Haddie sits down on the other end of the couch and curls her lithe legs beneath her.

"When were you going to tell me?" Her voice is chillingly quiet. This is not a good sign. The quieter she is, the more pissed she is.

"About?" I prompt, figuring if she gives me what she knows, I can at least get credit for telling her the rest.

"Colton freakin' Donavan?" she sputters, eyes wide, trying to suppress a grin that threatens to break through her implacable façade. "Are you fucking kidding me? And you didn't tell me?" The pitch of her voice escalates with each word. She grabs her glass of wine on the end table next and sips it, never breaking eye contact. "Why?" she says quietly but clearly hurt.

"Oh, Haddie." I blow out, scrubbing my hands over my face, trying to bite back the tears that threaten to break free. I lose the battle and a single tear slips down my cheek. "I'm so confused." I sigh, closing my eyes momentarily to gain control of my slipping emotions.

Haddie's face softens at my confession. "I'm so sorry, Ry—I just— I'm hurt you didn't tell me—I didn't mean to—"

"It's okay," I tell her, slipping my shoes off, the grains of sand stuck to my feet, reminding me that I really was with Colton tonight. As if I need a reminder. The scent of his cologne mixed with the smell of *him* still fresh in my mind. "I didn't mean to hurt you. How did you—"

"You didn't answer your phone ... like at all. I was excited to tell you about someone we confirmed for the big launch party tomorrow. I texted and called several times and didn't get a response," she says. "I was concerned. It's not like you to not give me at least a one-word answer if you're busy. I was worried so I called Dane." My eyebrow rises. "I guess he just put two and two together." She shrugs. "So what's going on, Rylee? What are you hiding from me?"

"It's just—I am just so overwhelmed with everything." I continue to tell her the story, every sordid detail despite my embarrassment at our first ten minutes of interaction. Her face remains impassive during my replay of events as she digests everything.

When I'm finished, she is quiet for a few moments, staring at me with unconditional affection on her face. "Well," she says, rising to get more wine and returning with a glass for me, "there are many things to say, to discuss, but first and foremost," she grabs my knee, excitement vibrating off of her, "Holy shit, Rylee! Colton Donavan? Backstage at the theater! Woohoo!" She raises her arms above her head, and I mentally cringe, hoping she won't spill her wine. "I'm so proud you finally got a little crazy. What's gotten into you?"

I feel the deep crimson flush over my face as I bow my head and start twisting the ring around and around my finger. "I know," I mumble. "I don't get it either."

"What?" she shouts at me. "What the hell are you talking about?" She shoves my knee vigorously. "I meant wow in admiration, not wow in why would he pick you. Snap out of it, Ry." She snaps her fingers in front of my face, forcing me to look at her. "He is fucking gorgeous! All rebellious and smoldering bad boy …"

As if I need to be reminded.

Haddie looks back at me. I can see her giddiness rising to the surface. "Is he as good looking in person as he is on TV?"

I try to find the perfect word, but I say the first one that comes to my mind. "He's breathtaking," I say reverently, "and sexy and domineering and frustrating and his eyes are just … and his lips … ugh!" I am caught up in the memory of him, my mind drifting over bits and pieces. When I come back to the here and now, I find Haddie staring at me, a ghost of a smile on her mouth.

"You really like him, don't you?" she asks quietly, sensing what I feel but refuse to say.

Tears pool in my eyes at the thought despite the smile plastered on my face. "It doesn't matter if I do or don't, he made it clear he only wants me for one thing." I shrug, taking a long swallow of my wine. "Besides, I can't do that to M—"

"Whoa, whoa, whoa!" she yells, waving her arms in the air to stop me. "I'm going to take this discussion and break it up into two different parts—compartmentalize it for you and your anal ways, if you will—because both really need to be addressed." She scoots closer to me. "Rylee, honey…" gravity in her voice "…who cares what the future holds when it comes to Colton. If he only wants you for your body and some earth-shattering sex, then so be it. Go for it. Just because it's not what you're expecting doesn't mean it's not everything you might need. And who better to do it with than a fucking Adonis like him?" She swigs another drink, amused. "Shit, I'd take that for a ride in a heartbeat," she murmurs, her lips pursing in thought at what it would be like.

I laugh out loud. "You would," I tease, slowly feeling my body unwind from the tension. "That kind of thing is easy for you."

She shoves at my leg. "Gee, thanks! I'm not a slut!" she contemplates. "Well, unless I want to be." She laughs.

"No," I huff, "I mean you are so carefree and sure of yourself. Everything you do you're sure about. No regrets." I cock my head to the side. "*And you sure are attracted to the bad boys.*" I smirk at her.

"Hmm-hmm, I do love them naughty." She laughs, momentarily

lost in her thoughts. "But back to you. No need getting me all twisted up over a man that's into you."

I roll my eyes at her comment.

"Rylee, the guy can have any woman he wants, and he is busy chasing you around, paying thousands for dates, spending millions to make your dream come true, and taking you on impromptu romantic dates to the beach. At sunset."

"According to him, he doesn't do romance."

She snorts loudly. "Well maybe he needs to redefine what romance is," she rebukes, "because all of those things spell out a man in pursuit."

I shake my head and her Haddie frankness. "He just wants me because I told him no. I'm a challenge to him in an otherwise willing world of women."

"You were quite the challenge when he had you up against the wall backstage, huh?" She quirks her mouth, goading me.

"You know that is so not like me, Haddie! I haven't been touched since ..." The silence settles and I shake my head to clear it of the memories holding me hostage. "Besides, I came to my senses. It was just the adrenaline from being trapped—"

"You just keep telling yourself that, sweetie, because I'm not sure if you're trying to convince me or yourself that it's just a simple lapse in morality." She shrugs, not breaking eye contact with me. "It's nothing to be ashamed of. It's okay to feel again, Rylee. To live again."

Tears threaten again, and I dash them away with the back of my hands before they can fall. "And even though we aren't done with item number one on our agenda, let's visit item number two." I level my eyes with hers, apprehension filling me. All of a sudden, her expression changes into understanding as the realization hits her. "You didn't want to tell me because you didn't want me to tell you that it's okay to live again. That it's okay to move on." Her questioning voice is soft, soothing.

I nod slowly as I swallow the huge lump in my throat. She scoots close to me, wrapping her arms around me, rocking me slowly and making hushing noises. A huge sob escapes and I succumb to the tears that have threatened me for several days. It feels so good to let them out, cathartic really.

After a few moments I find a semblance of control and am finally able to speak. "I just—I feel like I'm betraying Max. I feel like I don't deserve..." my breath hitches from my sobbing "...I feel guilty—"

"Rylee, honey..." she tucks an errant curl of hair behind my ear "...it's normal to feel that way, but at some point you have to start living again. It is a tragic, horrific thing that happened to you guys. To him. To you. But it's been over two years, Ry..." she grabs my hand "... and I know you don't want to hear it, but at some point you have to move on. You don't have to forget, but you—the wonderful, beautiful woman that you are—needs to live again. You too were once carefree. It's not too late to find that again."

I stare at her, tears blurring my vision, afraid that my next admission will make me a horrible person. I avert my eyes, afraid to look at her when I speak. "Part of the reason I feel guilty ... I ... the intensity, the desperation, the everything that Colton makes me feel is so much more, so much stronger, than I ever felt with Max." I take a chance and look back at her face, finding the exact opposite expression than what I had expected. I find compassion rather than disappointed disgust. "And I was going to marry Max," I choke out, relieved to have gotten this huge burden off of my chest and off my conscious. "I know it's stupid, but I can't help feeling it. I can't help that it pops into my head in that moment when all I feel, breathe, and want is more of Colton."

"Oh, Ry ... why have you been holding all of this in by yourself?" She wipes one of her own tears before pulling me to her and squeezing me again. She rests her cheek on the top of my head. "Rylee, you were a different person then. Your life is different now. Back then, anyone that saw you and Max together—we just knew that you were perfect for each other—just as you knew." I can hear the smile in her voice as she reminisces. "And now," she sighs, "you've been to hell and back in a little over two years. You are not the same person you were. It's natural to feel differently—to love deeper, feel stronger—no one is going to fault you for that. No one has touched you in two years, Rylee. Your reaction is going to be more intense."

We sit there in silence as I absorb the truth in her words. I know she's right, I just hope that I can believe it when the time comes. My contemplative silence is broken when Haddie suddenly starts laughing. She releases me from her hug, and I lean back to look at her perplexed. What in the hell is so funny? "*What?*"

She looks at me and I can see debauchery in her eyes. "He's probably great in bed." She smirks wickedly. "I bet he fucks like he drives—a little reckless, pushing all the limits, and in it until the very last lap." She raises her eyebrows at me, her grin sassy.

Her words make me bite my bottom lip at the thought of him hovering over me, sinking into me, filling me. I relive the feel of his lips on mine, the firm muscles beneath his clothes flexing with me, and his raspy voice telling me he wants me. I break from my thoughts, my core dampening at the thought of him. I look back to Haddie, watching her watch me, her eyebrows still raised, as if she is asking me if I think her assessment is accurate.

Oh boy, do I. *And then some.*

"Since when do you watch racing? Know how he drives?" I shift the focus of the conversation.

"Brody watches it. I pay attention when they say Colton's name," she says of her brother and then smirks devilishly. "It's definitely worth watching when they flash his face on camera."

"The man can kiss," I confess, grinning like a loon. "He can definitely kiss." I nod my head in agreement.

"Don't think about it, Rylee … just do it! Be reckless. Let your hair down," she urges. "Do you want to wake up twenty years from now with a perfectly ordered life with everything in its proper place but never having really lived? Never really putting yourself out there?"

"Well, I like the everything in order part," I kid as she rolls her eyes at me.

"Of course, that's what you would focus on! Just think of the stories you can tell your grandkids someday—about the sordid affair you had with the hot playboy race car driver."

I take a sip of my wine, contemplating her comments. "I know what you're saying, Haddie, I really do, but the sex without commitment thing. Without the relationship thing … how do you do that?"

"Well you stick flap A in slot B," she answers wryly.

"It was a rhetorical question, you bitch!" I laugh, throwing a pillow at her.

"Thank God! I was worried it had been so long that I was going to have to give you a sex-ed lesson." She reaches over to the table and uncorks another bottle of wine, topping off both of our glasses. She settles back in the couch, and I can see her mentally choosing her words before she speaks. "Maybe it's best that way?" When all I do is raise my eyebrows in question, she explains. "Maybe for your first guy since Max, maybe it's best that he isn't relationship material. You're bound to have some hiccups—after everything you've been through—so maybe it's best to throw caution to the wind and embrace your inner slut for a little bit. Have some fun and a lot of mind blowing sex!" She wiggles her eyebrows and I giggle at her, my over-consumption of wine slowly taking effect, smoothing over my frayed nerves.

"My inner slut," I reiterate, nodding my head, "I like that, but I think she's lost."

"Oh, we can find her, sister!" she snickers. "She's probably hiding behind the layers of cobwebs covering your crotch."

We both laugh before we start giggling uncontrollably. My over-wrought emotions from the week welcome this release. I giggle until tears seep from the corners of my eyes. Just when I think my laughter is going to subside, Haddie shakes her head. "You have to admit, Ry, the man is fucking hot!"

I start giggling again. "Scorching hot!" I confirm. "Man, I can't wait to see him naked!" The words are out before my fuzzy brain has had a chance to filter them.

Haddie stops mid-laugh, a knowing smile playing over her lips. "I knew it!" she yells at me, pointing at my face. "I knew you wanted to fuck him!"

"Well, duh?" I respond before we collapse again in another fit of giggles.

"Let's get you drunk tomorrow night at the event, and then we'll drunk dial his ass for a booty call."

"Oh God, no!" I blanch. *What have I gotten myself into?*

Chapter Ten

THE LIGHT FILLING THE ROOM is way too bright. The pounding in my head makes me groan out loud and grab my pillow from under my head, pulling it down over my eyes. I curse the numerous glasses of wine that Haddie and I drank last night but smile remembering our tears, and our laughs.

And Colton. Hot, delectable Colton.

Hmmm, I sigh at the memory of yesterday and him. He's going to have to do something to take care of this ache he's churned inside of me. I press my thighs together to abate it without success.

Since I can't get him out of my head, my hopes of falling back asleep are now gone. I reach my hand out blindly and fish around for the cell phone on my nightstand, knocking over an empty bottle of water. It clatters loudly on the hardwood floor, the sound making me cringe. I lift the pillow slightly to glance at the screen of my phone, wanting to know what time it is.

I lift the pillow further when I see my screen. I have numerous missed calls and texts from last night. I scroll through them quickly noting Haddie's texts getting more frantic as time passed. There are several from Dane and as I scroll to the next screen, the very last alert shows me there is a text from an unknown number. It was sent after I'd gotten home last night, during my discussion with Haddie. I open the text, and a smile spreads across my face. The text is from Colton:

Ryles—Thanks for the unexpected picnic. Since you seem most comfortable telling me what you think through music, I'll do the same. Luke Bryan, "I Don't Want This Night to End"—take

it for what it is. ⃰Ace

I smile at his words when I realize he heard the words I sang to him yesterday in the car. I'm unaware of the song he's mentioned, so I scramble quickly, ignoring my hangover to grab my MacBook Pro. I pull it off my dresser and plop back on my bed, anxiously waiting for it to power up. I immediately Google the song and am surprised to find that it is country; Colton does not seem like a country music kind of guy to me, more hard rock or something with a thumping bass. I click on the link and within seconds the song is playing.

I lie back on my bed, close my eyes, and listen to the words of the song. A soft smile plays on my lips as the song washes over me. My first peek inside of Colton's head—sure, he verbally tells me he wants me, but the gist of the words is that he enjoyed his time with me last night. That he didn't want the night to end. I enjoy the little boost to my ego and the flutter in my stomach from the thought that Colton wants to *get drunk on my kiss*.

Don't jump to conclusions. I warn myself. This is the same man who warned me off of him. Who tells me I need to research my dates to know who's dangerous and will hurt me when I least expect it.

I sit back up and grab my computer. I immediately replay the song and open up another window to Google "Colton Donavan." The search is immediately populated with page upon page of links referencing him: racing sites, the Speed Channel, fan-created sites, and so many more.

I decide to narrow the search and type in "Colton Donavan Enterprises." I click on the company's website. The opening page is a picture of what I assume is Colton's racecar next to a picture of the office facility. I click through the menu and am led through a corporate mission statement, history, products, media, and race team information. It's all very impressive, but I stop when I click on the tab "drivers" and Colton's face fills the screen. It is a close-up, candid shot of him in his fire suit. He is looking intensely at something off-camera, and his green eyes are clear and intrigued. He has a half-smile on his face as if he is remembering a fond moment, the dimple in his right cheek winking. His hair is in need of a cut and curls over the neck of his suit.

I suck in my breath. My God, the man is sex on a stick.

I bookmark the picture for good measure before I force myself to change the page and search Google Images. I reluctantly type in his name, afraid of what I'll see. The page refreshes and dozens of images of him pop up on the screen, most of them with a gorgeous woman draped on his arm or looking up in obvious adoration of him. I know I have no reason to be jealous—these pictures are dated—but I find myself rolling my shoulders to ease my agitation. Knowing I should close the page, I do just the opposite and find myself clicking on each picture. Staring. Comparing. None of the captions refer to the women as girlfriends, just dates or companions.

I realize that most of his *escorts* are long, leggy blondes, stick thin, with some type of plastic enhancement. And all are drop-dead gorgeous. Much to my chagrin, I realize they look very similar to Haddie, *except hers are real.* Ironically, the pale hair next to his dark features makes him seem more aloof and edgier somehow.

I note that each girl only seemed to exist in his life for a short period of time, except for one. I wonder why that is. Is she an escort? The one he takes when his other *cookie-cutter blondes* have fallen through and he needs a date? Or is she the one he keeps going back to because there is really something there? After clicking on several of their pictures together, I finally get a caption that offers her name. *Tawny Taylor.* The caller on his phone yesterday. What is she to Colton? I know I could dwell on this for hours so I force myself to push it to the back of my head and resolve to think about it at another time, even though I'm afraid to know the answer.

I look like none of them. I may be tall, but I'm definitely not petite like them. I'm thin but I have curves in all the right places, unlike their ruler-straight physiques. I have an athletic body that I'm proud of—that I work hard to maintain—whereas they look like they have no need to even think about exercise. I have rich chocolate brown curly hair that stops midway down my back; it is unruly and a pain, but it suits me. I continue the comparisons until I tell myself that I need to just get off the page before I become depressed. That my hatred toward them has nothing to do with them in particular.

I go back to Google and type in "Colton Donavan childhood." The first few pages reference children's organizations that he is involved with. I quickly scan through the links, looking for one mentioning his childhood.

I finally find an old article written five years ago. Colton was interviewed in connection with a charity he was supporting that benefited new changes speeding up the adoption process.

Q: *It is public knowledge that you were adopted, Colton. At what age?*

CD: *I was eight.*

Q: *How was the adoption process for you? How would you have benefited from these new initiatives that this foundation supports?*

CD: *I was lucky. My dad literally found me on his doorstep, took me in, for lack of a better term, and I was adopted shortly after that. I didn't have to go through the lengthy process that occurs today. A process that makes kids who desperately crave a home, a sense of belonging, wait months to see if an application will be approved. The system needs to stop looking at these kids as cases, as paperwork to be stamped with approval after months of red tape, and start looking at them as delicate children who need to be an integral part of something. A part of a family.*

Q: *So what was your situation, prior to being adopted?*

CD: *Let's focus less on me and more on the passing of these new measures.*

Does he not want to talk about it because it draws attention away from the charity, or was it so bad he just doesn't talk about it? I scan the rest of the article but there is nothing else about his childhood. So he was eight. That leaves a lot of time to be damaged, conditioned as he's said, by whatever situation he was in.

I stare at the screen for a couple of minutes imagining all kinds of things, mostly variations of the kids who have come through my care, and I shudder.

I decide to look up his parents, Andy and Dorothea Westin. The pages are filled with Andy's movie credits, Oscar nominations and wins, and top-grossing movies amongst other things. His family life is referenced here and there. He met Dorothea when she had a bit part in one of his movies. At the time she was Dorothea Donavan. Another piece clicks into place. I wonder why he uses his Mom's surname and not his Dad's. I continue scanning and see the basic Hollywood mogul background, less the tabloid drama or stints in rehab. There are a few mentions of his children, a son and a daughter, but nothing giving me the answers I'm looking for.

I return to search again and scan through the different links that mention Colton's name. I see snippets about a fight in a club, possible altercations with current-generation brat-pack actors, generous donations, and gushing comments from other racers about his skill and the charisma he brings to his sport that had been tinged after the CART and IRL league split years ago.

I sigh loudly, my head filled with too much useless information. After over an hour of research, I still don't know Colton much better than I did before. I don't see anything to validate the warnings he keeps giving me. I can't help myself. I open up the page again for CDE and click on the picture of him. I stare at it for sometime, studying every angle and every nuance of his face. I glance up and sadness fills my heart as the picture on my dresser of Max catches my eye. His earnest smile and blue eyes light up the frame.

"Oh, Max," I sigh, pressing the heel of my palm to my heart where I swear I can still feel the agony. "I will always miss you. Will always love you," I whisper to him, "but it's time I try to find me again." I stare at his picture, remembering when it was taken, the love I felt then. Seconds tick by before I look back at my computer screen.

I close my eyes and breathe deeply, strengthening my resolve as the song on my computer, Colton's song, repeats itself for the umpteenth time. *It's time.* And maybe Haddie is right. Colton may be the perfect person to help me find myself again. For however long he lets me, anyway.

I look back at my phone, suppressing the overwhelming urge to text him back. To connect with him. If I'm going to do this, I at least need to make sure a couple things are on my terms.

And chasing after him is definitely not going to allow me to achieve that.

Chapter Eleven

I BARELY RECOGNIZE THE GIRL in the mirror who stares back at me. Once again, Haddie has gone all out with her preparations for the launch party tonight thrown by the public relations company she works for. She spent almost an hour blowing my ringlets out so that my hair hangs in a straight, thick curtain down my back. I keep staring at myself in the mirror, trying to adjust to this different person. My eyes are subtly smoked so the dark smudges have an opalescent quality, reflecting the violet in my irises. My lips are lined with nude liner and lip-gloss, making the slight touches of bronzed blush on my cheeks stand out.

She has talked me into wearing a little black number that shows off more skin than I'm comfortable with. The bust of the dress runs into a deep V, hinting suggestively at my abundant bra-proffered cleavage without being trashy. The straps go over the shoulders and connect the non-existent back with thin gold chains that drape loosely and attach at the swell of my butt. I tug down on the hemline that falls mid-thigh, something I'm not altogether used to.

I look again in the mirror and smile. This is not me, the girl I know. I sigh shakily as I add chandelier earrings to complete the look. This may not be me, I think, but this is the confident girl I want to be again. The new me who's going to go out tonight, let loose, and have fun. The girl who has resolved to have a night of fun and gain some self-assurance before I undertake all that is Colton and his warning-laced pursuits.

"Holy shit!" Haddie walks into my bathroom, a whistle blowing from her lips. "You look hot! I mean—" She stumbles over her words.

"I'm at a loss here. I don't think I have ever seen you this smokin' sexy, Ry." I smile widely at her praise. "You're going to have them lining up tonight, baby. Hot damn, this is going to be fun to watch!"

I laugh at her response, my self-esteem bolstered. "Thanks. You're not so bad yourself," I compliment her harlot-red dress that shows off all of her best assets. I slip my heels on, wincing and smirking at the memory of the last time I wore them. "Give me a sec and I'll be ready."

I grab my clutch and stuff my driver's license, money, and keys into it. When I grab my phone to place in the small purse, I realize I never asked Haddie about the voicemails from her that I'd listened to earlier.

"Had? I never asked you what was so exciting about the event tonight. What hot celebrity did you guys secure as a carpet walker?"

She gives me an enigmatic smile. "Oh, it fell through," she dismisses casually. I shake off the feeling that for some reason she is laughing at me. I quirk my head at her and she turns around, "Let's go!"

The entrance to the trendy club downtown is quite the spectacle with criss-crossing searchlights, velvet ropes, and a celebrity ready red carpet complete with a backdrop displaying Merit Rum, the new product being launched. We park in reserved spots for Haddie and her fellow PRX employees at the trendy, upscale hotel that owns and is connected to the club. Haddie flashes her credentials, which allows us to whisk past the hoopla, and within moments we are inside the crowded club, the dull throb of the music pulsing through my body.

It has been years since I've been in a club like this and it takes me a while to acclimate to the dim lighting and loud music and not feel intimidated. I think Haddie realizes my nerves are kicking in and that my confidence is waning despite my sexed-up appearance. Within moments she has pushed us through the throng of people to the bar. With disregard to the numerous bottles of Merit lining the slick countertop, Haddie orders us each two shots of tequila.

"One for luck." She grins at me.

"And one for courage," I finish our old college toast. We clink glasses and toss back the liquid. It burns my throat. It's been so long since I've done a shot of tequila, I wince at the burn and put the back of my hand to my mouth to try and somehow stifle it.

"C'mon, Ryles," Haddie shouts, unfazed by the liquor. "We've got one more to go!"

I raise my glass, an intrepid smile on my face, tap it to hers, and we both toss them back. The sting of the second one isn't as bad, and my body warms from the liquid, but it still tastes like shit.

Haddie gives me a knowing glance and starts to giggle. "Tonight's going to be fun!" She hugs her arm around me and squeezes. "It's been so long since I've had my partner in crime back."

I flash a smile at her as I take in the club's atmosphere. It's a large room with purple, velvet-lined booths around the bottom floor. A glossy bar with a mirror placed behind it fills one whole wall, creating the illusion that the massive space is even larger. In the middle of the main floor is a large dance floor, complete with trussing lined moving head lights that are creating a dizzying array of colors. Stairs rise up from the floor to a raised VIP area where teal booths are sectioned off by velvet stanchions. In one section of the VIP area, a plexiglass partition allows all below to see the DJ spinning the music pumping through the club. Model-worthy waitresses flit around in hot pants and fitted tank tops, purple flowers adorning their hair. The club is swanky class with a touch of sophistication, despite the advertising for Merit Rum around the room.

It's nearing eleven o'clock, and I can see the crowd thickening, feel the pulsating energy. In the VIP area, there is a crowd of people gathered in one corner, and I wonder what trendy celebrity Haddie's team has secured to promote their newest product. I've been to enough of these functions with her to know the drill. Hot celebrities shown taking photos with new product equals big-time press for not only the item but Haddie's company as well.

I take the glass Haddie hands me, my usual Tom Collins, and I sip from the straw as I point to the upper section. I raise my eyes in question rather than shout over the music that is starting to increase in volume as the club becomes more crowded. I figure we have about thirty minutes left until the decibels are so loud that the only way to communicate will be to yell.

She leans over to talk in my ear. "Not sure. We have several people confirmed for tonight." She shrugs a noncommittal answer. "Some surprises are in store as well."

I narrow my eyes at her, wondering why she is being vague. She just smiles broadly and tugs my hand to follow her. We navigate through the mob of people, moving together as one unit. I can feel the alcohol slowly starting to buzz through my body, warming me, easing my tension, and relaxing my nerves. For the first time in longer than I can remember, I feel sexy. I feel beautiful and sensual and at ease with those feelings.

I squeeze Haddie's hand as she pushes through to a purple booth, which is reserved for PRX staff. She looks back and smiles genuinely at me, realizing that I'm starting to relax. We break through the crowd to the booth to find two of Haddie's colleagues there. I smile at them and say a quick hello, having met them before at previous events I've attended. I thank one of them for his compliments on my vamped-up style for the evening. As we sit down there is a large cheer from the other side of the room on the upper level where the crowd had been. I glance up to see what's going on and notice nothing but a number of women showing way too much skin hoping for whatever hot item PRX has invited up there to take notice of them.

I roll my eyes in disgust. "Fame whores," I mouth to Haddie and she bursts out laughing.

I finish my drink as the catchy beat of a Black Eyed Peas song fills the club. I start moving my hips to the tempo, and before I know it, I grab Haddie's hand and drag her through the people out onto the dance floor. The surprised look on her face has me laughing as I close my eyes and let the music take me. We sing the words together, "I gotta feeling, that tonight's gonna be a good night," as we let loose on the dance floor.

I haven't felt this liberated in so long that I just want to suspend this moment in time. I want to capture it in my memory so the next time I start to fall into that dark place, this feeling can help me hold on to the light.

Haddie and I move to the music, working our way through several songs, each one strengthening my confidence and increasing my fluidity on the floor. Several of her co-workers, Grant, Tamara, and Jacob, join us as the song switches to *Too Close*, an old song but one of my favorites. I flirtatiously dance with Grant, acting out the song with him. We laugh, our bodies rubbing innocently up against each other.

I raise my arms over my head, crossing them at the wrists and swivel my hips to the rhythm, the alcohol buzzing through my system. I close my eyes, absorbing the atmosphere around me. A tingling sensation up my spine has me flashing my eyes back open.

I look up, and despite the synchronized unison of the mass on the dance floor, I stop, frozen in place. I see Colton. He is standing on one of the stairways that angles down from the VIP section. He has a drink in one hand and his other arm drapes casually around the shoulder of a statuesque blonde. She is turned into him, her hand rubbing gently through the top unbuttoned portion of his dress shirt. Her face tilts up to him and even from a distance I can see her reverence and adoration, although he has his head turned away from her, laughing with a rakish man on his left. A large daunting man stands behind him, eyes scanning the crowd. His security, maybe? Colton flashes a smile at his male cohort, and it's natural and unguarded, allowing me to momentarily appreciate his absolutely devastating looks. The blonde says something and Colton turns his attention back to her. She lifts her hand from his chest to rest on his cheek and lifts her face up, placing a slow, seductive kiss on his lips in ownership.

My insides churn at the sight, clouding my vision so much that I don't pay enough attention to see if Colton is encouraging and returning the kiss or merely just tolerating it. My mouth is suddenly dry. I am paralyzed as I watch him with her. Numb really. We're not together—my constant refusal of him has not demonstrated that I want otherwise. And despite my intense and unfounded hurt right now, all I want is that to be me he is holding. *Me* he is kissing. In the seconds that all of this swirls within me, my hurt begins to shift to anger. How stupid was I to think a guy like him could actually want a girl like me when he could have a girl like her?

I notice Haddie fall motionless in my periphery, taking notice of what I see. I'm about to turn to say something to her when Colton lifts his chin away from his arm candy, and looks up, his eyes locking onto mine. My heart skips over a beat and lodges itself in my throat. Despite the distance between us, I see shock flash in his eyes.

Even though a fellow dancer jostles me, my eyes hold steadfast to his. I know I need to leave the floor before my emotions get the best of me and my threatening tears begin to fall, but I am riveted in place, unable to break the inescapable, magnetic pull he has over me. He releases his hold on the blonde immediately, discarding her easily. He hands his drink off to his male companion without looking and strides unfaltering down the stairs. His emerald eyes burn into mine, never losing our connection.

As he reaches the dance floor, the music changes to a deep, pulsating throb enveloping Trent Reznor's hypnotic voice. Without a word or a look, the horde of dancers seems to move apart as he stalks onto the floor toward me. His expression is indiscernible, the muscle pulsing at his jaw, the shadows from the lights playing over the angles of his face. His long legs eat up the distance quickly. Numerous people turn their heads in recognition, but the hungry look in his eyes stops them from approaching. Despite the music's volume, I hear Haddie suck in a breath as he reaches me.

All of the things I want to yell at him, all of the hurt I want to spew at him, disappears as he walks up to me, and without preamble grabs my hips in his hands, forcefully yanking me up against him. He holds me there, pressed against him, as his body starts to move, hips begin to grind into mine in sync to the punishing tempo of the song. I have no other option than to move with him, respond to the animalistic rhythm of his body. I slide my hands over his hands on my hips and lace my fingers through his, holding him.

Holding on to the ride that is undeniably coming.

Our eyes remain locked. My head tilts back to look up at him. His lips part slightly, and I can hear him hiss out as my hips respond to him. His eyes darken, glazing with desire, filling with heat—with a predatory need. His scorching look has my nipples tightening and my body becoming a melting mess of need in anticipation of his touch. *Of his undoubted possession of me.*

I bite my bottom lip as he moves our combined hands from my hips to behind my back, kneading my backside through my dress, handcuffing me there. We continue to move as one with the music, the feeling of his firm, defined thighs pressing against mine. His arousal rubs against the lower part of my belly. He leans his face down so we are within inches of each other. I can smell the alcohol on his breath as he sighs.

It is by far one of the most erotically sensual moments of my life. The rest of the world has fallen away. The intoxicating effect he has on my body blocks out the crowd around us, all looking our way, noticing me because of the man I am with. It's just he and I— Moving. Responding. Arousing. Anticipating.

The song comes to an end, but we remain entranced in each other's spell. I breathe for what I feel like is the first time since we've touched, a long shaky breath. I don't realize that the music has stopped, and that the event's emcee is speaking over the microphone about the product of the evening. That except for the small crowd around us, the attention of the club has turned and is focused on the stage.

Colton and I stand there, not moving, feeling like we are barely breathing despite our heaving chests, absorbing each other and the sparks of sexual tension that are igniting between us.

"Colton! Hey, Colton," a voice breaks through our connection, snapping me out of my spellbound state. Colton swivels his head to find one of the PRX staff calling his name. "It's time. We need you on the stage. Now."

He nods curtly before looking back at me, eyes smoldering with an urgency that makes my insides shiver. He unlaces his fingers from mine, releasing his hold on my hands and pulls away slightly. The warmth of his body is gone immediately, but my body is still humming from the connection, aching with need. He gives me a slow, suggestive smile and shakes his head softly. At me? At his own thoughts? At which one I'm not sure.

He reaches up a hand and tugs on my hair, his eyebrows quirk up as if to ask me why the change in my hair. I shrug shyly at him, words escaping me. His name is called again. He turns to go, but not before I watch the transition on his face from the Colton Donavan I know to the public persona. Aloof and untouchable. Sexy and untamable.

We haven't uttered a single word, and yet I feel like we've said so much.

I watch his broad shoulders as he walks through the crowd toward the stage, his bodyguard falling in step beside him, pushing back the swarming people. I watch the spectacle and a little part of me smiles about the fact that I've seen the real Colton. At least, I hope I have.

Before I can finish watching his ascent to the makeshift stage, Haddie has me firmly by the arm and is pulling me from the dance floor. My resistance is futile as she drags me down a corridor, past the line for the bathrooms, and toward a small alcove near the exit. She spins me to face her, an incredulous look on her face.

"Ow, you're hurting me!" I snap at her, yanking my arm away, not exactly thrilled at being taken away from watching Colton.

"What. The. Fuck. Was. That?" she asks, each word a staccato. I don't even know how to answer her. I think I'm still under his spell. "Holy shit, Rylee! You two were basically fucking each other with your eyes. I mean, I felt uncomfortable watching you, like I was peeping into your bedroom," she rambles on as she does when excited, "and you know I never get uncomfortable." She leans back against the wall and tilts her head up to the ceiling, an unbelieving look on her face.

I stand there and stare at her. I don't know how to answer her, so she continues. "I knew you said you guys had made out," she continues, ignoring the childlike snort of laughter that comes from me, "but you never told me that there was … that spark … that chemistry … such intensity … My God! I mean, I was hoping when you saw him that—"

"What?" Her last sentence triggers my brain to function. "What do you mean *you were hoping?*"

She smiles sheepishly at me. "Well …"

What the fuck is going on here? "Quit stalling, Montgomery!"

"Well, I was calling you last night to tell you we had landed him as a guest—Merit's one of his new sponsors. Anyway, I called just because I was excited. I thought we could sit back and lust after him tonight—I didn't know anything about what had happened. I talked to Dane and that was when I found out you were out with him." Her words are tumbling out now. I nod at her to continue, my eyes narrowed, lips pursed. "Then you came home and everything unfolded …"

"And what? You decided not to tell me because …"

116

"Well," she contemplates, "After you told me everything, I had no idea that you two—your connection—is that magnetic. That captivating. I thought maybe if you saw him here, I could help you—I could push the issue. Help you have some fun."

I blow out a loud breath, silently staring at her. I know she means well, but at the same time, I don't need my hand held like a child. I'm mad at her. Mad at Colton for being here with that bimbo. Mad at him for waltzing up to me and taking hold of me as if I belonged to him. Mad at him for making me want him so badly my insides are burning. Silence settles over us.

"Don't be mad, Ry. I'm sorry. I was doing it from a good place." She bites her bottom lip, pouting at me, knowing I can never stay mad at her. I smile softly, forgiving her.

I sag back against the wall and close my eyes, listening to the cheering of the crowd at something the emcee said. The question rattling around my brain comes to the surface. "Who's his plus one?" I ask, referring to the blonde. Is she one of his *permanent go-to girls that know there is no hope of commitment*? Someone he picked up in the club? Why is he kissing her if he is telling me he wants me? Did he not ask me because I'm not *enough*—pretty enough, sexy enough, glamorous enough—to be on his arm in public?

"Does it matter?" she sputters, "I mean, Jesus, Rylee, you two are—"

"Who?"

"Not sure." She shakes her head. "His people just asked for clearance for ten. No names were given."

I let out a slew of curses that make no sense, it's just something I do when upset. Haddie eyes me cautiously. "Talk to me, Ryles," she urges. "What's going on in that head of yours?"

"I'm not lying to myself, am I?" Haddie looks at me, confusion etched on her face. "I mean, I'm not making it up? The chemistry? Colton?"

"Are you crazy?" she stammers, grabbing me by the shoulder and giving me a little shake. "I thought you two were going to spontaneously combust out there! How can you question it?"

The crowd erupts again, the sound echoing down the hallway. I can hear Colton's voice on the microphone. The rasp of his voice pulls at me. The crowd cheers again at something he says, and I wait for the noise to subside some before I can continue. "If he's that into me. If there is that much chemistry … then why is he here with that blonde? Kissing her? Why not ask me? Or am I just the girl he wants to fuck on the side?" The confusion and hurt are evident in my voice.

Haddie twists her lips up as she thinks about my comments. "I don't know, Rylee. There are so many scenarios here." I raise my eyebrows as if I don't believe her. "He could have already had her as a date before he met you. Or he could really want you and she could be the piece on the side until you say yes."

I snort again. "Really? Did you see her?"

"Have you seen *you*?" she rebukes. "Have you looked in the mirror, Ry? You're gorgeous on a normal day and you look unbelievable tonight! I'm kind of getting sick of telling you that. When are you going to start believing it?" I roll my eyes at her like a child. She ignores me. "She could be one of his *arrangements*? Or maybe she is a fame whore who met him here? Or maybe she's a friend."

"When's the last time you kissed a friend like that?" I snip. She just stares at me, arms folded across her chest. "What am I supposed to do?"

"I'd say keep doing what you're doing. He obviously likes you, including your stubborn streak and smart mouth."

"But, how do I—what do I?"

"Rylee, if you're mad at him, be mad at him. It hasn't stopped you from saying something to him before, and he still wants you. Just because you've decided to sleep with him doesn't—"

"How do you know I've decided that?"

"Oh, honey, it's written all over your face—and your body for that matter. Besides, anyone watching that display out there already thinks that you have." She laughs sympathetically at me as my eyes widen. "Look, Ry, every girl in this club would fall into line if he snapped his fingers. Everyone, that is, but you. He's the one pursuing you. How many times in his life do you think a woman has said no to him? Has walked away from him? Maybe he likes that. And if he does, don't change it just because you've decided you want to do the deed with him." She wiggles her eyebrows.

"But that's just it," I confess. "Am I a challenge or does he really

118

want me? And if it does happen, then will the challenge be over and then he'll be done with me?"

"Honestly, who the fuck cares?" she castigates me. "You always overthink, overanalyze *everything*, Ry. Just forget your head for once, ignore its sensible warnings, and follow what your body wants. Follow Colton's lead, for God's sake." I let out a shaky sigh, heeding her words. "Be yourself, Rylee. That's what he's liked all along."

I nod my head several times, looking at her. A timid smile forms on my face. "Maybe you're right."

"Well, hallelujah!" she yells, flailing her hands over her head. "You finally listened." She grabs my hand and starts tugging me down the hallway. "Let's get you freshened up, get you some more liquid courage, and see where the evening and Mr. Sexy Colton lead you."

It's been about an hour since Haddie's pep talk, and my confidence, bolstered by my steady intake of alcohol, is back in full force. We have danced and socialized with some of her co-workers and are now sitting at the purple booth, taking a breather before hitting the floor again. I have tried desperately to not search out Colton. Tried to ignore the fact that he is probably kissing *her* somewhere in the vicinity. But I do catch my eyes flitting here and there whenever I see a big mob of people. I also note Haddie watching me as I look for him, so I try to sneak glances and be subtle about it. She assures me that he is probably busy with Merit Rum executives. I appreciate the explanation, her trying to make me feel better, so I just push him out of my head. Or try to, with the aid of Tom Collins.

Haddie's drinks have disappeared at a much slower pace than mine since she is technically "at work" and wants to make sure she has her wits about her. I have a steady buzz, but I'm not drunk. I hate the lack of control that comes with drinking too much alcohol. She is laughing at me as I ask her for the third time to explain a situation with a pretentious A-lister she had to deal with earlier in the week.

"Rylee, my dear, you are—"

"Excuse us ladies, would you mind if we joined you?" I turn to see two attractive gentlemen behind me.

Haddie raises her eyebrows at me in question and looks back at the taller one who'd spoken. "By all means, gentlemen," she answers, a slow, sexy smile growing on her lips. "I'm Haddie and my friend here is Rylee." She nods at me as they slide into the booth with us. The tall, dark haired one sits next to Haddie and the other, a blond haired surfer type, sits next to me in the open-ended booth. He has a kind, nervous smile and takes a long sip of his drink.

"Hi, Rylee, my name's Sam." He holds out his hand to mine, and I shake it, giving him a shy smile. I glance over to see Haddie engaged in conversation with his pal, her giggly, flirty face on. "So uh, I would offer to buy you a drink, but I can see your glass is already full."

"Thanks." I lower my gaze from his and bring my glass to my mouth to take a timid sip through my straw.

"Crazy crowded here tonight."

"Yeah, I know," I shout over the noise.

He says something else to me, but I'm not sure what because a loud cheer erupts from the booth next to us. I hold my hand to my ear, indicating that I can't hear him. He scoots closer, placing his arm behind me on the booth and leans in. "I said that you seem to be having a good time and that I noticed you earlier and am glad I—"

"*The lady's with me.*" I suck in my breath at the sound of Colton's steely voice, the threat in his words clear. My eyes snap up to meet Haddie's, and I see delight flash in them before she gives me a careful, reassuring look. My heart is beating at a frantic pace, my skin laced with goose bumps, and all because I am so damn attuned to him and his body's proximity.

I slowly turn to face him, effectively turning my back to press into Sam's chest, his arm across the back of the booth brushing over my shoulder. I raise my eyes to meet Colton's and try to ignore the pang of lust that shoots straight toward the juncture of my thighs. His hair is a tad mussed, his shirtsleeves are rolled up to the elbow, that muscle I find so damn sexy is pulsing in his jaw, and his eyes smolder with annoyance. I've had just enough alcohol to feel defiant, to test just how irritated Colton really is.

"*I'm with you?*" I ask, my voice laced with sarcasm. I can feel

Sam's body tense behind me and shift nervously, unaware of the chess game he is currently a pawn in, as Colton's eyes narrow at me. "Really? Because I thought you were with her." I shift to the side to look behind him, looking for her. I raise my eyebrows and continue, "You know, the blonde from earlier?"

"Cute, Rylee," he spits out impatiently. I see his eyes shift, lock with Sam's behind me, and deliver the hands-off warning.

I'm irritated that he's been all over the club for the past hour and a half, doing God knows what with the blonde, and yet he thinks he can waltz up and lay claim to me? I don't think so. I reach back and place my hand on Sam's knee and squeeze it gently. "Don't worry, Sam, I'm not with him." I make my voice loud enough that Colton can hear me. I see Haddie's eyes widen as I hear a low growl from Colton. I can feel Sam flinch against me. I turn back to Colton, defiance in my smirk and challenge in my eyes.

"Don't push me, Rylee. I don't like sharing." I can see him clench and unclench his fists. "You. Belong. With. Me."

I quirk my eyebrows up, my insolence mounting. "How so, Ace?" I watch his eyes focus on the hand I've kept on Sam's knee. "Last night you were with me, and tonight you're with her." I shrug calmly at him, although inside I'm anything but—my heart is racing and my breath has quickened. "Seems to me like—She. Belongs. With. You," I mimic childishly.

Colton drags a hand through his hair and gives an exasperated sigh as his eyes flicker over everyone in the booth. I can see him try to rein in his frustration and at having to have this conversation in front our little audience. "Rylee." He blows air out in a sigh. "You—You…" he looks around, out into the crowd and then his eyes finally come back to mine "…you test me on every level. Push me away," he grunts, realizing he is saying this out loud. "What am I supposed to think?"

I look him up and down, my mouth twisting in thought. I'm kind of enjoying toying with him, making the man who is so sure of himself, who always gets what he wants, have to work at something. "*I'm not sure if I want you yet*," I bait him. I hear Haddie suck in her breath at my flippant comment and the ice clink in Sam's glass as he anxiously drinks what's left. "A girl's allowed to change her mind," I taunt, tilting my head as I regard him. "We're notorious for it."

"Among other things," he says dryly, taking a drink, watching me from over the rim of his glass. "Two can play this game, Ryles," he cautions, "and I think I have a lot more experience at it than you do."

My bravado falters slightly from the warning look in his eyes. I withdraw my hand from Sam's knee and scoot toward the edge of my seat, my eyes never wavering from his. We stay like this for several moments. "You're playing hard to get, Rylee," he admonishes.

I glance over at Haddie who's face is impassive, but her eyes tell me she can't believe what is unfolding. I stand up to face him, squaring my shoulders, defiantly raising my chin. "And your point is?"

He tsks at me, shaking his head, and takes a step closer. "I hope you're enjoying yourself because it's quite a show you're putting on here." He puts a finger under my chin, lifting it so my eyes meet his. "I don't play games, Rylee," he warns, his voice just loud enough for me to hear, "and I won't tolerate them played on me." Sexual tension radiates between us. The air is thick with it.

I breathe in a slow, calculated breath, trying to form an intelligent answer as his proximity clouds my thoughts and heightens my senses. "Well, thanks for the update." I slap a hand on his chest and lean in a little closer, my lips near his ear. "I'll let you in on a little something as well, Ace. I don't like being made to feel like I'm sloppy seconds to your *blonde bevy of babes*." I step back, forcing a confident smirk on my face. "You're developing a pattern of wanting me right after I know you've been with another. That's a habit you're going to need to break or nothing else is going to happen here," I finish, gesturing between the two of us as I raise my eyebrows. "That is, if I want it to at all." His lips curl.

God, he is gorgeous! Even when he is smoldering with anger, he emits a raw sensuality that my body has a hard time ignoring. I turn to glance at Haddie for encouragement as I hear his name being called by a seductive voice. "Colt, baby?"

The words make me want to vomit.

I turn back to him to see a well-manicured hand slide in between his arm and his torso, splaying over his chest. I see him tense at the touch, his eyes guarded in reaction, and he throws back the rest of his drink, hissing at the sting of it between clenched teeth. I proceed to watch as the blonde from earlier slithers up next to him, eyeing me up and down pityingly, trying to stake her claim. I see the spark in her eye when she recognizes that I'm the one he left her for on the stairs. If looks could kill, I'd be dead. But despite it all, Colton's eyes remain steadfast on mine.

I am nauseated by the sight of her hands on him and the thought of him giving any attention to her. I shake my head in condemnation as I cluck my tongue. "Case in point," I say. I glance back at Haddie and the two men sitting with us. "I apologize, but please excuse me." Haddie starts to gather her purse, concern on her face, and I subtly shake my head for her to stay.

I turn back and look at Colton one last time, hoping my eyes portray the message I'm sending. Here's your choice. *Me or her.* You pick. Right now. Last chance.

I avert my eyes, breaking our connection. He stands static with the blonde draped over him like a cheap jacket. I guess he's made his decision. I try to calmly exit the booth. Try to flee from the dangerous path that I undoubtedly know he will lead me down.

Once I feel like I'm clear from view, I blindly push my way through the mass of people, hurt bubbling up inside me. My heart aches from the knowledge that I'll never be able to compete with someone like her. Never. I try to contain it as I push my way to the bar, wanting to numb the feelings I let myself believe were valid. Were reciprocated. Were possible again.

Shit! I swallow back the threatening tears as I squeeze into an open space at the crowded bar and by some miracle the bartender is right in front of me. "What'll you have?" he asks above the noise.

I stare at him a moment, contemplating my options. I opt for quick and numbing. "Shot of tequila please," I request, garnering the attention of the man standing next to me. I can feel him looking me up and down, and I roll my shoulders, bristling at the unwanted attention.

The bartender slides a shot of tequila across the bar to me and I grab it, looking at it for a moment, silently saying our toast. Right now I definitely need the courage portion. *Even if it's false courage.* I toss it back without hesitation and scrunch my face up at the burn. I close my eyes as its warmth slides down my throat and settles in my belly. I sigh deeply before opening my eyes, ignoring the offer of another drink from the man beside me.

I grab my phone out of my purse and text Haddie that I'm fine, to enjoy herself, and I'll see her at home. I know that if she weren't here for work, she'd be at my side taking me home.

I glance up from my phone to look for the bartender. I need another shot. Something to numb the rejection. My eyes flicker down the length of the bar when I see Colton striding purposefully toward me.

Despite the hope surging inside of me, I mutter, "Fuck!" and throw some cash on the bar before turning on my heel and veering toward the closest exit. I find one quickly, and shove open the doors. I find myself in an empty, darkened corridor, relieved when the door shuts behind me, muffling the pulsating music. My moment of solitude is fleeting as the door is thrown open moments later, Colton pushing through. We lock eyes—I can see the anger in his and I hope he can see the hurt in mine—before I turn my back to him and rush down the hallway.

I let out a strangled cry in frustration as Colton catches up to me and grabs my arm, spinning me around to face him. Our ragged breathing is the only sound in the hallway as we glare at each other, tempers flaring.

"What the fuck do you think you're doing?" he growls at me, his grip on my arm holding firm.

"Excuse me?" I sputter.

"You have an annoying little habit of running away from me, Rylee."

"What's it to you, Mr. I-Send-Mixed-Signals?" I throw back at him, wrenching my arm from his grip.

"You're one to talk, sweetheart. Is that guy—is he what you really want, *Rylee*?" He says my name like a curse. "A quick romp with Surfer Joe? You want to fuck him instead of *me*?" I can hear the edge in his voice. The threat. In this dark corridor, his features hidden by shadows, his eyes glistening, he is every bit the intimidating bad boy that the tabloids hint at.

"Isn't that what you want from me, Colton? A quick fuck to boost that fragile ego of yours? It seems you spend an awful lot of time trying to placate that weakness of yours." I hold his glare. "Besides, why do you care what I do? If I recall correctly, you were pretty occupied with the blonde on your arm."

He clenches and unclenches his jaw regarding me, rolling his head back and forth on his shoulder before answering me. "*Raquel? She's inconsequential,*" he states as a simple matter of fact.

I can take that answer so many ways, and all of them paint his opinion of women in a less than stellar light.

"*Inconsequential?*" I question, "Is that what I'd be to you after you fuck me?" I stand my ground, shoulders squared. "*Inconsequential?*"

He stands there seething. At me? At my response? He takes a step toward me and I retreat, my back pressing into the wall behind me. I have nowhere left to run. He reaches out a hand and pulls it back in indecision, the muscles in his jaw clenching, the pulse in his throat pounding. He angles his head to the side, closing his eyes, swearing silently to himself. He looks back at me—frustration, anger, desire, and so much more burning in the depths of his eyes. Their intensity as they look into mine is unnerving, as if he is asking for my consent. I nod my head subtly, giving him the permission to take. The next time he reaches out, there is no hesitation.

Within a beat, his lips are on mine. All of the pent up frustration, irritation, and antagonism of the evening explodes as our lips clash, hands fist, and souls ignite. There is nothing gentle about our union. Rapacious need burns through me as one of his hands snakes around my back, grasps my neck and yanks me against him so his mouth can plunder mine. His other hand slides between the wall and my arching back, splaying against me in ownership. Gone are the gentle sips and the soft caresses from yesterday.

His lips slant over mine and his tongue darts in my mouth, tangling, teasing, and tormenting mine. His hands slide over mine where they're fisted in his shirt. He grabs my wrists and pulls them over my head, presses them to the wall, and handcuffs them with one of his hands. He brings his free hand down and cups my jaw as he breaks from our kiss. He draws his face back and his eyes, darkened and vibrant with arousal, hold mine.

"*Not inconsequential,* Rylee. You could never be inconsequential." He shakes his head subtly, the vibration of his voice resonating in me. He rests his forehead to mine, our noses brushing each other's.

"No—you and me—together," he grinds the words out, "that would make you *mine*." His words feather over my face, enter my soul, and take hold. "*Mine*," he repeats, making sure that I understand his intentions.

I close my eyes to savor the words. To relish the thought of Colton wanting me to be his *mine*. Our foreheads remain touching as I surrender to the moment, to the feeling, and to the easing of doubts. He steps back from me and gently releases my hands from above my head. Our eyes stay connected and I see what I think is a momentary flash of fear blaze through his.

I reach out tentatively to him and touch his hips, working my hands under his untucked shirt so that I can place my hands on his skin. So that I can feel this vibrant, virile man beneath my fingertips. It's always been his hands on my skin. Him in control. I haven't had the chance to appreciate the feel of him beneath my palms yet.

I find my purchase, my fingers caressing the firm warmth of his defined muscles as they tense at my touch. I slowly run them up the front of his torso, feeling each delineation, each breath he takes in reaction to my touch. It's a heady feeling to hear his response, see his pupils dilate in desire, as I glide my hands from his pecs, smoothing them over ribs and under his arms to scrape my nails up the plains of his back.

He closes his eyes momentarily in rapture, clearly enjoying my slow, teasing assault on his senses. I lean up on my toes and hesitantly lean into him and brush my lips against his. I press my hands into his shoulders, pulling his body into mine. I slant my mouth over his and run the tip of my tongue over his bottom lip.

His fingers slowly brush against my cheeks, his palms resting on the line of my jaw to frame my face as he tenderly deepens the kiss. His lips sipping, his tongue slowly, sweetly parting my lips and melding with mine. His quiet affection touches me in my core, slowly unraveling me and winding me into a ball of need. He takes my breath away with each caress. I sigh into the kiss, my fingers digging into his shoulders, the only sign of my impending impatience at wanting more. At *needing* more.

I can feel Colton's struggle to control his need, his body taut beneath my hands, his impressive erection pressing into my belly. He continues his tender and unrelenting assault on my senses by concentrating solely on my mouth. Seducing my lips. His breath is mine. His action is my reaction.

He stops abruptly, placing his two hands on the wall beside my shoulders and braces himself, letting his forehead drop to my shoulder so that his nose and mouth are buried in the nape of my neck. I feel his chest heaving for air like mine, and I'm relieved that he appears to be as affected by this encounter as I am. I'm a little confused by his actions, but I take the moment to allow him to collect himself while I settle my racing heart. I subconsciously squeeze my knees together to try and quiet the relentless pressure at the delta between by thighs.

I can feel the warmth of his breath as he pants against my neck, struggling for control. "Sweet Jesus, Rylee," he murmurs as he shakes his head, rolling it on my shoulder before scattering innocent kisses along my collarbone. "We need to get out of here before you unman me in the hallway."

He raises his head to look at me as I still from his words. There is no doubt that this is what I want. That he is who I want. But I can't deny the fact that I'm nervous—anxious—afraid I'll disappoint him with my lack of experience in this department.

"Come." He doesn't give me time to speak before he grabs my hand, wraps his arm around my shoulder, pulling me into him, and walks us deeper into the corridor. "I have a room here for the night." His strong arm helps support me, leading me toward my apple in the Garden of Eden.

I follow obediently, trying to quiet the doubt and noise in my mind, for it is actively chattering away now that his mouth is not on mine, blunting my ability to reason. We quickly make it to an elevator at the end of the hallway and within seconds we are stepping in. Colton pulls a key card out of his pocket and inserts it into the panel, effectively unlocking the top floor. The penthouse.

He steps back toward me as the elevator lifts and places a hand on the small of my back. The silence between us is audible and only intensifies the butterflies that are churning in my stomach. "Why the change?" Colton asks as he tugs on my straightened hair, trying to ease my mounting anxiety.

"Just trying to fit the mold," I quip reflexively, referring to the numerous pictures on the Internet of him with straight haired women. His brow furrows, trying to figure out what I mean, when I offer up, "Sometimes change is good."

He uses his hand on my back to turn me toward him. He angles his head down so that we are eye to eye. "I like your curls," he says softly, my ego preening from the compliment. "They suit you." Now that he has me positioned, he raises a hand up to wipe an errant strand off my face. He then places his fingers on the side of my jaw and holds me there, his eyes searching mine. "You have one chance to walk away," he warns me as the elevator alerts us we're at his floor. The husky tone of his voice wreaking havoc on my willpower.

My heart beats erratically. I shake my head in unconvincing acceptance when I can't find the words to speak to him.

He ignores the opening elevator door behind him and continues to look intently into my eyes. "I won't be able to walk away, Rylee," he says as he scrunches up his eyes as if the admission is painful. He blows out a loud breath, releasing me and running his fingers through his hair. He turns his back to me, reaches out, and stabs the door open button, bracing his hands against the elevator wall. His broad shoulders fill the small space. His head hangs down as he mulls over his next words. "I want to take my time with you, Rylee. I want to build you up nice and slow and sweet like you need. Push you to crash over that edge. And then I want to fuck you the way I need to. Fast and hard until you're screaming my name. The way I've wanted to since you fell out of that storage closet and into my life."

I have to bite my lower lip to stifle a groan. I fight the need to sag against the wall for some kind of relief.

"Once we leave this elevator, I don't think I'll have enough control to stop … to pull away from you, Rylee. I. Can't. Resist. You." His voice is pained, quiet, and chock-full of conviction. He turns back to me, his face filled with emotion. His eyes reflecting a man tinkering on the edge of losing control. "Decide, Rylee. *Yes. Or. No.*"

Chapter Twelve

I LOOK UP AT HIM through my lashes, my bottom lip between my teeth, and nod in consent. When he continues to look at me, I find my voice and try to push the nerves out of it. "Yes, Colton."

His mouth crushes down on mine instantly, his hunger palpable as he pulls me out of the elevator toward the penthouse. I giggle freely as he tries to insert the key in the door while trying to keep his lips on mine. He finally gets the key in and the door opens as we continue our ungraceful entrance, mouths never leaving each other's. He kicks the door shut and presses me up against it, his hands sandwiched between the door and my butt. His fingers grip my flesh fervently, pressing me into his muscular frame.

I lose myself in him. In his touch, his heat, his quiet words of praise as he rains kisses over my lips and neck and the bare skin in the deep V of my dress. I turn myself over to the moment and experience what it is to feel again. To want again.

I clumsily try to unbutton his shirt, needing to feel his skin against mine but am hindered by his constantly moving arms that are running fervently over every inch of bare skin that his fingers can touch. His lips find my spot just under my jaw line, and I forget the buttons and fist my hands in his shirt as sensation overwhelms me. Consumes me. A strangled cry escapes my mouth, little explosions detonating from my neck down into the pit of my belly.

Colton presses his hands to my backside again, and I wrap my legs around his hips at the same time he lifts me up. One hand supports my back while the other dips beneath the fabric of my dress to palm my breast. I bow into him as his thumb and forefinger rub my pebbled nipple. The electric shock of his touch spreads heat to my sex and wildfire to my senses.

Colton starts to move while holding me, his lips feasting on the ever-sensitive line of my shoulder, his erection pressing between my thighs. With every step he takes, he rubs against me, creating a glorious friction against my clit. I press into him, a ball of tension building, surmounting, and edging toward my need for release.

We enter the bedroom of the suite, and despite the overabundance of sensations surging through me, I'm still nervous. He stops at the edge of the bed, and I lower my legs, dropping my feet to the floor. I resume my attempt to free him of his shirt, and this time I'm successful. He lets go of me, momentarily stepping back as he slips his arms out and lets the shirt fall to the floor.

I get my first glimpse of Colton's naked torso, and he is *utterly magnificent*. His golden skin covers the well-defined muscles of his abdomen. His strong shoulders taper down to a narrowed waist, which give way to that sexy V that sinks below where his slacks hang. On his left flank is a tattoo of some sort, but I am unable to make out what it is. He has a slight sprinkling of hair on his chest and then below his belly button, amidst tightened abs, he has a sexy little trail of hair that disappears beneath his waistband. If my hormones weren't raging already, the sight of him alone would have sent my system into overdrive.

I drag my gaze back up his torso and meet his eyes. He looks back at me, eyes drugged with desire, enflamed with lust. A sexy grin spreads across his mouth as he pushes off his shoes and removes his socks before approaching me again. He raises his hands to my face and frames it, his mouth on mine in a slow, tormenting kiss that has me pressing into him. His hands slide from my face, down my shoulders, and make the slow descent down my torso until fabric gives way to the bare skin of my thighs.

"God, Rylee, I want to feel your skin on mine." His fingers play with the hem of my dress momentarily before grabbing it and slowly lifting. "Feel your body beneath me." His words are hypnotic. Inviting. "My cock buried in you," he murmurs against my lips before he leans back a fraction, his eyes never leaving mine, to pull the dress over my head.

I start to take my high heels off, but Colton reaches down to grab my hand before I can reach my shoe. "Uh-uh," he tells me, smiling lasciviously. "Leave them on."

I suck in my breath, insecurities rearing their ugly head as I stand before him in a bra, a scrap of lace as an excuse for panties, and my stilettos. "I think—"

"Sh-sh-sh," he whispers against my lips. "Don't think, Rylee. The time for thinking is over." He steps us backwards, the back of my knees hitting the bed, and he slowly lays me down, his mouth still lacing me with kisses. "Just feel," his husky voice demands of me. One of his hands cups the back of my neck while the other roams slowly down to the black lace of my bra and over my rib cage before starting the path back up again. A moan escapes my lips. I need his touch like I need my next breath.

"Let me look at you," he whispers, leaning back on his elbow. "God, you are beautiful."

I freeze at the words, wanting to hide the scars that mar my abdomen, wanting to twist away so that I'm not asked, not reminded. I do none of that though. Instead, I remind myself to breathe as his eyes wander down my body. I know the moment he sees them; shock flickers across his face before his eyes flash back to mine, concern etched in his brow.

"Rylee? What—"

"Not now," I tell him before I reach out and grab his neck, yanking him to me in a demanding kiss that obliterates all sense of control. Quiets all questions before they can be asked. A carnal passion ignites within me as I take hold of him—kissing, caressing, digging fingernails into his steeled skin. A feral growl comes from deep within him as his tongue skims a trail down my neck. He palms my breast, slipping the finger beneath the lace and pushing the cup below it. His mouth teases on its descent down before closing over the tight bud of my nipple.

I cry out in ecstasy as he laves my breast, sucking it into his hot, greedy mouth. His hand assaults my other breast, rolling my nipple between his thumb and forefinger—blurring the fine line between pleasure and pain. His acute attention to my sensitive buds mainlines a fire to my sex. It clenches, throbs, and moistens, silently begging him for more to push me over the edge. I shift beneath him to try and ease the intense ache that is building, but the coils of craving are so strong my breath pants out erratically.

I tangle my fingers in his hair as he moves from my chest, sucking, kissing, and nipping his way down my abdomen. I fist my hands in it and grate in a sharp breath as he deliberately lays a row of kisses along my worst scar. "So beautiful," he repeats to me again as he continues his tormenting descent. He stills at the top of my panties, and I can feel the smile form on his lips from his mouth pressed against my skin.

He looks up at me, a mischievous grin lighting his face. "I hope you're not overly fond of these." I don't even have a chance to respond before he rips the panties off of me. A low satisfied purr comes from the back of his throat as he trails a finger down the small strip of curls beneath the material. "I like this," he growls at me, his finger tracing below the strip where I'm void of hair, "and I like this even more."

My breath catches as he slips a finger between my folds, sliding it slowly back and forth. "Oh God," I groan as I grip my hands into the sheets of the bed, ecstasy detonating in sparks of white hot flashes behind my closed eyelids.

Colton sucks in an audible breath as he slips a finger tantalizingly slowly into my passage. "Rylee," he groans, the break in his voice as he says my name betrays his front of control. "Look how wet you are for me, baby. Feel how tight you grip me." I arch my back, shoulders pressing into the mattress as his finger leisurely circles inside of me, grazing over that sweet spot deep along my front wall before deliberately withdrawing, only to start the whole exquisite process again.

"The things I want to do to this tight little pussy of yours," he murmurs as I feel his other hand part me again. His blunt words turn me on. Incite feelings I didn't expect. I writhe beneath him as the cool air of the room hits my swollen folds. "Look at me, Rylee. Open your eyes so I can see you when my mouth takes you."

It takes everything I can to snap out of my pleasure induced coma and open my eyes. He looks up at me through hooded lids from between my thighs. "That's it, baby," he croons as his head drifts down until I feel the warm heat of his mouth as it captures my nerve laden nub at the same time he slips two fingers in me.

I cry out, throwing my head back as a raging inferno blasts through my center—taking, possessing, building. "Look at me!" he growls again. I open my eyes, the eroticism of watching him watch me as he pleasures me is more than I've ever known.

His tongue laves lazily back and forth, over and around as his fingers continue their delicious internal massage. He withdraws and then pushes back in, his fingers leisurely rubbing my walls within. I buck my hips up against him, begging for more pressure as I tinker on the edge of losing my sanity.

"Oh, Rylee, you are so responsive," he praises. "So fucking sexy." As he replaces the warmth of his mouth with the pad of his thumb, the tempo and friction of skin on skin is exactly what I need. He slides up my body as his fingers continue their mind-blowing torture on my sex, his lips kissing, nipping, and licking until he reaches my face. Making me want like I've never wanted before.

"Let go, Rylee," he demands with his erection pressing deliciously into my side. "Feel again, sweetheart," he murmurs as my hands wrap around his shoulders, fingernails scoring his sweat-ridden skin. The ball of tension mounts, begging for release. I buck my hips wildly against him, his fingers increasing their tempo, rubbing, penetrating, driving me into a rapturous oblivion.

"Come for me, Rylee," he growls as I reach the edge and scream out in release as my orgasm explodes within me, crashes around me, and ripples through every nerve and sinew in my body. My muscles flex reactively, clamping down on his fingers, causing him to groan at the sensation. "That's it baby, that's it," he croons as he helps me ride out the rippling waves of my climax.

I feel the bed dip as he leaves it, causing my eyes to fly open. He looks down at me, satisfaction on his face and desire in his eyes, as he slowly unbuckles his pants. "You are breathtaking," he praises as I watch him, struggling to catch my panting breath. "I can't figure out which is hotter, Rylee, watching you come or making you come." His eyes sparkle with his libidinous thoughts. "I guess I'll have to do it again to figure it out." He flashes a wicked grin at me, full of challenge. My muscles coil tightly at his words, and I'm startled that he has me so worked up that my body's churning to come again. I bite my lip as he pulls his pants down with his boxer briefs, his impressive erection springing free.

Holy shit!

He smirks at me as if he can read my thoughts and crawls on the bed with his lean, firm thighs. He grabs one of my splayed feet by the heel of my shoe and laces a row of kisses up my calf, stopping at my knee to caress his fingers at the sensitive underside before continuing the dizzying ascent of his mouth up my thigh. He stops at my apex and kisses me lightly there, swirling his finger gently over my sex, tickling, taunting, testing.

I grip my hand in his hair. "Colton," I pant out, his slight touch on my sensitized flesh almost more that I can bear.

He looks up at me as he plants another kiss on my strip of hair. "I just want to make sure that you're ready, baby," he replies, pulling a wet finger from my core. "I don't want to hurt you."

A dozen things flit through my mind as I watch him slip his finger into his mouth before flashing a devilish grin and humming in approval. He predatorily crawls the rest of the way up my body, his eyes never leaving mine, and covers my mouth with his, his hand palming my trussed up breasts, his cock pressing into the V of my thighs.

Emotions swirl within me as the dizzying pleasure surges again. He parts my legs with his knees and pushes himself up off of me to sit back between my thighs. He leans over toward the edge of the bed and produces a foil packet. My mind buzzes. I've been so overcome with everything in the past week that I haven't even thought about protection. And despite him not knowing about my inability to get pregnant, I am glad he has enough common sense to think of this.

I prop myself up on my elbows as he tears the packet open and watch as he rolls the condom down his iron length. His eyes flash up to mine, desire, lust, and so much more swarming within them. "Tell me what you want, Rylee."

I stare at him until my eyes are drawn down to watch as he runs his fingers over my delta and gradually parts me. I suck in a breath in anticipation. "Tell me, Rylee," he growls, "Tell me you want me to fuck you. I want to hear the words."

I bite my bottom lip, watching as he lays his length against my cleft. He stills, and I look up to meet his eyes. I can see him trying to rein in his control, the vein in his neck prominent as he stares at me, waiting for my words.

"Fuck me, Colton," I whisper as he slowly presses the blunt tip of his cock into my entrance. I tense at the thought of accepting him, at the sensation of him stretching my channel to its limits, at the slight pain from it telling me that I'm alive, that I'm here in this moment with this sublime man.

"Oh God, Rylee," he moans as he pulses slowly in and out. "You feel so good. So damn tight," he hisses, rubbing his fingertips softly up and down my inner thighs. "I need you to relax for me, baby. Let me in, sweetheart."

I close my eyes momentarily as the stretching burn fades to a full feeling. He pushes further, slowly, deliberately, until his cock is sheathed completely root to tip by my velvet walls. He stays motionless, allowing my body to adjust to him as he watches me. I can see his jaw clench as he tries hard to hold onto his control, and it's an invigorating feeling to know that I can push him over the edge.

I clench my muscles around him, gripping him reflexively as I push my torso up to allow me to see where our bodies are now joined as one.

"Sweet Jesus, Rylee," he warns, "you do that again, I'm gonna come right now."

I smile wantonly at him as he slowly starts to move. He pulls out all the way to the tip and then slowly slides his luscious length back in me. The feeling is exquisite and I fall back on the bed, allowing the sensation of my slick walls being penetrated to take over. I wrap my thighs around his hips as he starts to pick up the pace. His muscles ripple beneath his tanned skin as he moves with me. His eyes flick back and forth between mine and watching our union.

I can feel the warmth starting to spread through me again as my body arches into the friction of his length rubbing my patch of nerves inside. My walls bear down on him, tightening and milking his cock as his rhythm quickens.

He leans over me, balancing his weight on his forearms beside my head, and takes my mouth with his in a carnal, no-holds-barred kiss. Teeth nip, lips suck, tongues meld. I hook my arms under his shoulders and tighten my legs around his hips, locking my feet at the ankles. I need to get as close as I can to him. Need him to be as deep as he can be in me. Need to feel his sweat-slicked skin rubbing on mine.

The pressure in me mounts to the point where I can't kiss him anymore because all of my focus is on the insurmountable wave that's about to crash down all around me. He senses my tension, my nearing oblivion, and continues his punishing pace. He reaches a hand down and slides it under my ass, pressing my pelvis further into his, grinding his against mine, causing that slight friction I need on my clit. Before I know it, my world ignites.

I arch off the bed, bucking my hips uncontrollably as the strongest orgasm I've ever had spears through my center. I'm thrown off the cliff and hurled into a never-ending freefall. The pleasure is so strong, bordering on painful, that I sink my teeth into his shoulder trying to stifle it somehow. The wave crashes around me as Colton bucks into me a few more times before I hear him cry my name out. He tenses, his cock pulsing jaggedly within me as he finds his own release. His muscles jerk in torment as he lets his climax tear through him before slowly relaxing. He then buries his head in the curve of my neck, his breathing harsh like mine, his heart pounding against my own.

My orgasm continues to tremble through me, my muscles pulsing around his semi-hard cock still within me. With each tremor, I can feel his body tense from his sensitivity and hear the soft guttural moan from deep within his throat. His weight on me is comforting, reassuring, and I forget what a soothing feeling it can be.

Sex has never been like this for me. This earth shattering. This hedonistic. This unbelievable.

We lie like this for a moment, both silently coming down from our high. He nuzzles my neck, laying a kiss over and over in the same spot, his sated body unable to move. I close my eyes, unable to believe that I'm here. That this gorgeous man is here with me.

I run my fingernails lazily up and down his back, breathing in his earthy male scent. I wince as he grunts and slowly withdraws from me, the empty feeling unwelcome. He ties the condom in a knot and tosses it onto the floor beside the bed before shifting back next to me. He lies on his side and props his head on his hand to watch me while leisurely running a single finger up and down my chest, causing a slow, measured breath to exhale from my lips.

I glance over at him, our eyes holding for a second as we silently reflect on each other and the experience we just shared. I can't decipher the look in his eyes. He's too guarded. I shift my gaze to the ceiling as panic starts to take hold. What now? Colton's had his way with me and now the challenge is over. Crap. I've only ever had sex with Max. We were in a relationship. We made love. It wasn't a casual thing. And although what just happened might have meant a whole lot more to me than it did to Colton, what am I supposed to do now? With Max I didn't have to think about having to leave after. Or the etiquette of if I stay? Does Colton want me to stay? What the hell am I supposed to do? Is this what a one-night stand feels like? *Shit*.

"Stop thinking, Ryles," Colton murmurs. I can sense his eyes trained on me. I still quickly, surprised that he can be so in tune with me despite only knowing me for a short time. How does he know?

"Your whole body tenses up when you're overthinking," he explains, answering my silent question. "Turn that mind of yours off," he warns, reaching out to my hip, pulling me toward and up against him, "or I'll be forced to make you."

I can hear the smile in his voice and I laugh. "Oh, really?"

"I can be very persuasive," he taunts, running his free hand down my rib cage, stopping to idly palm my breast and run his thumb over my peaked nipple. "Don't you think?"

"Didn't you just tell me I'm *not allowed to think*?" I sigh a soft moan, raising my chin as he leans into me to plant kisses in various places.

"I love a woman who obeys," he murmurs softly. I can feel him start to harden against me, and before I can process his ability to recover swiftly, Colton has rolled us over, switching our positions, with me sitting atop his hips.

I sit astride him and stare down at him and his cocky grin. He returns my gaze, trailing his eyes up and down my torso. I can feel his length continuing to thicken against the cleft in my rear end. "My God, Rylee, you are enough to make a man go crazy," he tells me, leaning up and reaching around me to unclasp my bra. My breasts come free, heavy and weighted from desire. Colton groans in appreciation before he lifts himself up to suckle one, my thighs clenching viciously around him in response.

I lift my head up and arch my back so that he has full advantage of my chest. The thoughts I'd had moments before are now pushed away as he continues his barrage of incendiary kisses. I feel his arms wrap around me and fumble near my bottom before I hear the telltale rip of foil. He finishes jacketing himself as he trails kisses with his skillful mouth back up to my lips. He slants his mouth, taking tiny, delirious sips from mine as he brings one hand to my hair and fists it. He whispers gentle praise in between each kiss, each one stoking my craving for him.

"Lift up for me," he whispers as he brings one hand to my hip, helping raise me, while the other positions his turgid cock beneath me.

I bite my lip in anticipation as his eyes hold onto mine, watching as I gently sink down onto the tip of him. I stay suspended momentarily as I let my fluids coat him so it's easier for him to gain entry. It is empowering to watch the desire cloud Colton's eyes while I slowly lower myself inch by delirious inch onto him until he's sheathed entirely. I moan softly as he stretches me to the most incredible feeling of fullness. I'm forced to sit still for several moments so that I can adjust to the entirety of him. Colton closes his eyes, lifting his head back, lips slightly parted as a low rumble comes from deep in his throat.

He brings his hands to my hips, and I start to rock myself on him. I raise myself up to his very tip and then slide back down, leaning back so he rubs the patch of nerves within my walls.

"*Fuck*," he hisses. "You are going to make me lose my mind, Rylee," he moans loudly as he kisses me possessively before lying back on the bed. He starts to piston his hips up in unison with my movements and soon we are moving at a frantic pace. Each needing more from each other. Each driving, pushing, tantalizing each other to the precipice.

I look down at Colton, the tendons in his neck strained, the tip of his tongue peeking through his teeth, eyes darkened by lust—he is sexy as hell. His hands grip my hips, muscles tensing as he holds me, lifts me, and drives into me. I am climbing, spinning dizzily as pleasure washes over me. I grip one of Colton's hands on my hip, our fingers entwining, holding on. He moves his other hand to where we are joined, his thumb stroking my clit, manipulating it expertly.

My body quickens, my muscles clench around Colton, and once again I'm thrown into a staggering oblivion. I cry out his name as a rapturous warmth overtakes me, envelopes me, and pulls me under its all-consuming haze.

"Christ, Rylee," Colton swears, sitting himself up without stopping his voracious tempo, taking control to allow me to lose myself in my orgasm. He wraps his arms around me, strong biceps holding me tight, and brings his lips to mine in a devouring, soul-emptying kiss. The onslaught of sensations pulling at me from every nerve in my body are so overwhelming that all I can comprehend is that I'm drowning in Colton Donavan.

I can feel his body tense, his hips thrust harder, and his arms squeeze tighter with hands splayed wide on my back. Colton buries his face in my neck before yelling out my name, a benediction on his lips, as he crashes over the edge. I feel him convulse wildly as he finds his release.

We stay like this, me sitting astride him, arms wrapped around each other, heads buried into one another for some time, neither of us speaking. I am overcome with emotion as we hold each other.

Oh, shit! How stupid was I to think that I could actually do casual sex? Feelings bubble up inside me. Feelings that I know Colton will never reciprocate, and I find myself struggling to maintain composure. I tell myself to hold it together, that I can wallow and break down once I'm alone.

Colton shifts his legs and leans back. He takes my head in his hands and transfixes me with his intoxicating stare. "You okay?" he whispers to me.

I nod my head, trying to clear the worry from my eyes.

He leans in and kisses me. A kiss so gentle and affectionate that I have to fight back tears because his tenderness disarms me and strips me to the core. When he opens his eyes, he stares at me for some time. I see something flash through them quickly, but can't decipher.

He shakes his head quickly and lifts me off of him before scooting off the bed without a word. He stands hastily, averting my questioning look and runs his hand through his hair, muttering "fuck." I watch his toned, broad shoulders and very appealing ass as he walks to the bathroom. I hear the water run and another muffled swear.

I pull the sheet around me, suddenly feeling alone and uncomfortable. After a few moments, Colton reappears from the bathroom with a pair of black boxer briefs on. He stands in the doorway and looks at me. Gone is all of the warmth and emotion that was in his eyes minutes before. It's been replaced by a cold, aloof appraisal as he looks at me in his bed. He is no longer relaxed. The tension around his eyes and the strain of his jaw is obvious.

"Can I get you anything?" he asks, his voice a curt rasp. "I need a drink."

I shake my head no, afraid that if I speak, the hurt I feel from his sudden detachment will only make matters worse. He turns and walks out to the main room of the suite. I guess I have my answer. I was just a challenge to him.

Challenge conquered, now I'm disposable.

I hold the heel of my hand to my breastbone, trying to stifle the pain inside. Trying to lessen the feeling of being used. I think of Max and the way he used to treat me after we made love as if I was so fragile I'd break. He would caress me and hold me and make me laugh. Make me feel cherished. *My beautiful, idealized Max.* What have I done to him and to our memory by sleeping with someone when I'm technically engaged?

His mother's yells echo in my ears as she tells me it's all my fault his life is over—that I killed him and every hope and dream that went with him. Guilt and shame and humiliation wash over me. I have to get out of here. These thoughts fill my head as I throw the covers off of me and gather all of my discarded clothes before scurrying to the bathroom.

The pressure in my chest is unbearable from trying to hold back my tears as I fumble clumsily to get my bra clasped. I throw my dress over my head, struggling to get my arms in the straps. I don't have any underwear. They're ripped apart somewhere on the floor and aren't worth the hassle of finding. I'm missing an earring, and I don't care. I quickly tug its matching counterpart out as I glance in the mirror, noticing misery mingled with regret heavy in my eyes. I take a tissue and wipe away the smudged eyeliner as I steel myself for my departure. After a few moments of masking my emotions and gathering my thoughts, I'm ready.

I open the door to the bathroom and peek out, relieved and saddened that Colton is not sitting there waiting for me. Then again, what did I expect after how he just acted? For him to be sitting on the bed waiting to profess his undying love for me? "Fuck 'em and chuck 'em," I mutter under my breath as I walk out of the bedroom door to the main room of the suite.

Colton is standing in the suite's kitchenette, his hands pressed against the counter, his head hanging down. I stand for a moment and watch him, admire the lines of his body, and wish for so much more than he can give. Colton shifts and takes a long draw on the amber liquid in his glass. He sets it down harshly, the ice clinking loudly before he turns. His step falters as he sees me standing dressed and ready to go.

"What are—"

"Look, Colton," I begin, trying to control the situation before I can be humiliated further. "I'm a smart girl. I get it now." I shrug, trying to prevent my voice from breaking. He looks at me and I can see the cogs in his head turning as he tries to figure out why I appear to be leaving. "Let's face it, you're not a spend the night kind of guy, and I'm not a one-night stand kind of girl."

"Rylee," he objects, but says nothing more as he takes one step toward me until I hold my hand up to halt him. He stares at me, subtly shaking his head, trying to wrap his mind around my words.

"C'mon, that's probably what this is to you—what you're used to." I take a couple steps toward him, proud of myself for my false bravado, "So I'll just save myself the embarrassment of you asking me to leave and do the walk of shame now instead of in the morning."

Colton stares at me, struggling with some unseen emotion, his jaw clenching tightly. He closes his eyes for a beat before looking back at me. "Rylee, please just listen to me. Don't go," he utters. "It's just that …" He pulls a hand up to grip the back of his neck, confusion and uncertainty etching his remarkable face as he is either unable to find his words or finish his lie.

My heart wants to believe him when he tells me not to go, but my head knows differently. My dignity is all I have left, seeing as my wits have been thoroughly destroyed, scattered, and left on the bed. "Look, Colton." I exhale. "We both know you don't mean that. You don't want me to stay. You got a room here tonight hoping you'd get laid. You just probably thought it would be with Raquel. A nice little suite where there would be no drama and no complications—a place you could leave in the morning without a backward glance at who's still asleep in the bed. Well, I walked into it willingly," I admit, stepping up to him, his eyes never leaving mine as I place a hand on his bare chest. "It was great, Ace, but this girl," I say, motioning toward me and then the bedroom, "this isn't me."

He stares at me, his eyes piercing mine with such intensity that I avert my gaze momentarily. "You're right, this isn't you," he grates out, guarded, as I flick my eyes back to his. He lifts his glass and empties the rest of the glass' contents, pools of emerald continuing to watch my eyes from over the rim of the glass. When he finishes, he runs his tongue over his lips, angling his head as he thinks something through in his head. "Let me get my keys and drive you home."

"Don't bother," I shake my head, shifting my weight as I figure out how to save face as humiliation seeps through me. "I'll take a cab—it'll make this mistake easier on both of us." It takes everything I have to lean up on my toes and brush a casual, chaste kiss on his cheek. I meet his eyes again and try to feign indifference. "Don't worry, Colton, you crossed the finish line and took the checkered flag," I say over my shoulder as I start to walk toward the door, chin held high despite the trembling of my bottom lip. "I'm just throwing the caution out there before I can be black flagged."

I step through the door and into the elevator. When I turn to push the first floor, I notice Colton standing in the doorway of the penthouse. His mouth twists as he watches me with aloof eyes and a hardened expression.

I continue to stare at him as the doors start to close, a single tear falling down my cheek—the only betrayal my body displays of my sadness and humiliation. I am finally alone. I sag against the wall, allowing the emotions to overcome me, yet fighting the tears swimming in my eyes. I still have to find a way home.

The cab ride is quick but painful. My quiet sobs in the backseat do nothing to alleviate the brutal reality of what just happened. When we pull up to the house a little after three in the morning, I'm glad to see that Haddie is home but asleep because I can't handle her questions right now.

I slip into my room and flip on my IPOD speakers to a barely audible volume, scroll for *Unwell,* and push repeat. As I hear Rob Thomas' familiar words, I shed my clothes and step into the shower. I smell of Colton and of sex, and I scrub obsessively to get his scent off of me. It doesn't matter though. No matter what I do, I can still smell him. I can still taste him. I can still feel him. I allow the water to wash away my torrent of tears, hiding my sobs in its rush.

When I'm waterlogged and the tears have subsided, I pick myself up off the shower floor and make my way into my bedroom. I throw on a camisole and a pair of panties before collapsing into the comforting warmth of my bed and succumb to sleep.

Chapter Thirteen

I CAN SMELL FUEL AND dirt and something pungently metallic. It fills my nostrils, seeps into my head before I feel the pain. In that quiet moment before my other senses are assaulted with the destruction around me, I feel at peace. I feel still and whole. For some reason my consciousness knows I'll look back on this and wish I had this moment back. Wish I could remember what it was like *before*.

The pain comes first. Even before my head can clear the fog away enough so that I can open my eyes, the pain comes. There are no words to describe the agony of feeling like you have a million knives entering you and ripping you apart, just to withdraw and start all over again. And again. Endlessly.

In that second between unconscious and conscious, I feel a jagged pain. My eyes fly open, frantic breaths gulp for air. Each breath hurting, burning, laboring. My eyes see the devastation around me, but my brain doesn't register the shattered glass, smoking engine, and crushed metal. My mind doesn't understand why my arm, bent at so many odd angles, won't move to undo my seatbelt. Why it can't release me.

I feel as if everything is in slow motion. I can see dust particles drift silently through the air. I can feel the trickle of blood run ever so slowly down my neck. I can feel the incremental inching of numbness taking over my legs. I can feel the hopelessness seep into my psyche, take hold of my soul, and dig its malicious fingers into my every fiber.

I can hear him. Can hear Max's gurgled breathing, and even in my shock-induced haze I'm mad at myself for not looking for him more quickly. I turn my head to my left and there he sits. His beautiful wavy blonde hair is tinged red, the gaping gash in his head looks odd. I want to ask him what happened but my mouth isn't working. It can't form the words. Panic and fear fills his eyes, and pain creases his tanned, flawless face. A small trickle of blood is coming from his ear and I think this is a bad thing but I'm not sure why. He coughs. It sounds funny, and little specks of red appear on the shattered window in front of us. I see his hand travel across the car, fumbling over every item between him and me as if he needs touch to guide him, until he finds my hand. I can't feel his fingers grip mine.

"Ry," he gasps. "Ry, look at me." I have to concentrate really hard to raise my head and eyes to meet Max's. I feel the warmth of a tear fall on my cheek, the salt of it on my lips, but I don't remember crying. "Ry, I'm not doing too good here." I watch as he unsuccessfully attempts to take a deep breath, but my attention is drawn elsewhere when I think I hear a baby crying. I swivel my head to look—nothing but pine trees. The sudden movement makes me dizzy.

"Rylee! I need you to concentrate. To look at me," he pants in short bursts of breaths. I swing my head back at him. It's Colton. What's he doing here? Why is he covered in blood? Why is he in Max's seat? In Max's clothes? In Max's place?

"Rylee," he begs, "Please help me. Please save me." He sucks in a labored, ragged breath, his fingers relaxing in mine. His voice is barely a whisper. "Rylee, only you can save me. I'm dying. I need you to save me." His head lolls to the side slowly, his mouth parting as the blood at the corner of it thickens, his beautiful emerald eyes expressionless.

I can hear the screaming. It is loud and piercing and heart wrenching. It continues over and over.

"Rylee! Rylee!" I fight off the hands grabbing me. Shaking me. Pulling me away from Colton when he needs me so desperately. "Damn it, Rylee, wake up!"

I hear Haddie's voice. How did she get down this ravine? Has she come to save us?

"Rylee!" I'm jolted back and forth violently. "Rylee, wake up!"

I bolt up in bed, Haddie's arms wrapping around my shoulders. My throat is dry, pained from screaming, and my hair is plastered to my sweat drenched neck. I heave for breath, strangled gasps mingle with Haddie's pants of exertion. My hands are wrapped protectively around my torso, my arms are tired from straining so hard.

Haddie runs her hands down the sides of my cheeks, her face inches from mine. "You okay, Ry? Breathe deep, sweetie. Just breathe," she soothes, her hands running continuously over me, reassuring me, letting me know I'm in the here and now.

I sigh shakily and put my head in my hands for a moment before scrubbing them over my face. Haddie sits down next to me and wraps her arm around me. "Was it the same one?" she asks, referring to the recurring nightmare that stuck with me for well over a year after the accident.

"Yes and no ..." I shake my head. She doesn't ask for more details. Instead she gives me time to push the nightmare back into hiding. "It was all the same except for when I look back after I hear the baby crying. It's Colton, not Max, who dies."

She startles at my comment, her brow furrowing. "You haven't had a nightmare in forever. Are you okay, Ry? You want to talk about it?" she asks, straining her neck to hear the muted music on the speakers I'd forgotten to turn off before falling asleep. Her eyes narrow as she recognizes the song.

"What did he do to you?" she demands, pulling back so that she can sit cross-legged in front of me. Anger burns her eyes.

"I'm just a mess," I confess, shaking my head. "It's just that it's been so long. I feel like I've forgotten what Max's face looks like, and then I see him so clearly in my dream ... and then the suffocating panic hits from being trapped in the car. Maybe I'm just overwhelmed by the emotion of everything." I pick at my comforter, avoiding her questioning gaze. "Maybe it's been so long since I have really *felt* anything that tonight just pushed me over the edge ... just overwhelmed me with ..."

"With what Rylee?" she prompts when I remain silent.

"Guilt." I say the word quietly and let it hang between us. Haddie reaches out and grabs my hand, squeezing it softly to reassure me. "I feel so guilty and hurt and used and so everything," I gush.

"Used? What the hell happened, Rylee? Do I need to go kick the arrogant bastard's ass right now?" she threatens. "Because I'll switch my tune. I mean, I was impressed when he called earlier to make sure that you'd gotten home all right and that—"

146

"He what?"

"He called at like 3:30 … somewhere around there. I answered the phone. Didn't even know you were home. Anyway I came in here to check and told him you were home and asleep. He asked me to have you call him. That he needed to explain—that you took something the wrong way."

"Hmmph," is all I can say, mulling over her words. *He actually called?*

"What happened, Rylee?" she asks yet again, but this time I know she won't be ignored easily.

I relay the entire evening to her, from the point I left her, until she woke me up screaming. I include my feelings about comparing "the after" to Max and how hurt and rejected I felt. "I guess I feel guilty because of the whole Max thing. I loved Max. I loved him with every fiber of my being. But sex with him—making love with him—came nowhere near what it felt like with Colton. I mean, I hardly even know Colton and he just turned on every switch and pushed every button from physical to emotional that …" I search for words, overwhelmed by everything. "I don't know. I guess I feel like sex should have been like that with the guy I loved so much I was going to marry rather than someone that couldn't care less about me." I shrug. "Someone who just thinks of me as another notch on his bedpost."

"Well, I can't tell you that you're wrong to feel, Rylee. If Colton made you feel *alive* after years of being dead, then I don't see what's wrong with it." She squeezes my hand again, sincerity deepening the blue in her eyes. "Max is never coming back, Rylee. Do you think he'd want you be numb forever?"

"No." I shake my head, wiping away a silent tear. "I know that. Really, I do. But it doesn't make the guilt go away that I'm here and he's not."

"I know, Ry. I know." We sit in silence for a few moments before she continues, "I know I wasn't there, but maybe you misread Colton. I mean some of the things he said to you …"

"How is that possible, Had? He was swearing under his breath like he'd just made the biggest mistake. One minute he was kissing me so tenderly and looking into my eyes and the next minute he was swearing and walking away from me."

"Maybe he got scared."

"What?" I look at her like she's crazy. "Mr. I-Don't-Do-Girlfriends gets scared of what? That he thinks I'll become attached to him after one night of sex?"

"One night of mind-blowing sex!" Haddie corrects, making me giggle and blush at the memory. "Well, you do wear your emotions on your sleeve. It seems you don't do *casual sex* well."

"Oh, like it's a class I can take over at the *Y*? I mean, I may be easy to read emotionally, but I'm not in love with him or anything," I defend myself whole-heartedly, despite knowing full well that what I felt between us tonight was more than just full-blown lust. Maybe I did scare him. That final moment between us in the bed, when he held me and stared into my eyes, really got to me. Made me feel hope. Maybe he saw that and had to squelch it before it went any further.

"Of course you're not," Haddie says with a knowing smile, "but that's not what I was talking about. Maybe, just maybe, Mr. I-Don't-Do-Girlfriends … maybe you got to him. Maybe he got scared of what he felt when he was with you?"

"Yeah, right! This isn't a Hollywood romance movie, Haddie. The good girl doesn't get the bad boy to change his ways and fall madly in love with her," I say, sarcasm rich in my voice, as I fall back on my pillow, sighing loudly.

A small part of me relives Colton's words from the night before. *I am his.* I could never be *inconsequential.* He can't control himself around me. That small part knows that maybe Haddie is right. Maybe I scare him on some level. Maybe it's because I am the marrying kind, as I've been told, and he's just not looking for that.

"You're right," Haddie admits. "But that doesn't mean you can't have one hell of a time losing yourself in hours of mindless sex with him." She plops back on the pillow next to me, both of us laughing at the idea. "It could have its merits," she continues. "There's nothing like a good bad boy to make you let go. Remember Dylan?"

"How can I forget?" I reply, remembering the quick fling she had last summer with the gruff and gorgeous Dylan after ending her year-and-a-half-long relationship. "Yum."

"Yum is right!" We both fall silent.

"Maybe Colton is your Dylan. The one to get you over everything that happened with Max."

"Maybe ..." I think. "Oh God," I groan, "What am I supposed to do now?"

"Well, seeing as it's..." she lifts her head to look at my clock "... five in the morning, you should go back to sleep. Maybe give it a day, then call him back. See what he has to say and go from there. Remember our motto. Embrace your inner slut—be reckless with him and try not to think about tomorrow. Just think about the here and now with him. "

"Yeah, maybe." We sit in silence for a few moments. Am I just being an overdramatic female reading into things? I don't think so, but deep down I try to justify his actions to myself. I know that I'll do it again if given the chance, and for my sanity I need to rationalize everything to right the world back on its axis. The feelings and sensations he evoked in me were way too intense. Way too *everything*. Maybe it was just the fall from my alcohol buzz that made everything seem so off. Made him seem so detached. I scold myself. I know this isn't the case, but I'm trying desperately to address my inner slut.

I'm way out of my league here. I just hope I can figure out how to play the game without getting burned in the end.

"Do you want me to stay in here tonight?" Haddie asks, breaking the silence. She used to sleep in my bed on the really rough nights to help me get through them nightmare-free.

"Nah. I think I'm okay. Thanks, though. For everything."

She leans over and kisses the top of my head, "What are friends for?" she says as she heads for the door. "Sleep tight, Ry."

"'Night, Had."

She closes the door and I sigh deeply, staring at the ceiling, thoughts running through my mind until sleep pulls me under.

Chapter Fourteen

I'M SO EXHAUSTED FROM EVERYTHING that I'm able to sleep past my usual six-thirty wake up time. It's nine when I get into my exercise gear and head downstairs.

Haddie is sitting at the little table in the kitchen, bare feet with bright pink painted toes propped on the empty chair across from her. She eyes me cautiously from behind her cup of coffee. "Good morning."

"Morning," I mutter, my normal sunny morning self absent. "I'm gonna go for a run," I tell her as I fasten my audio player to my arm.

"I figured," she says, referring to my attire. "Are you grumpy just because you want to be … or because you are forcing yourself to run after too much alcohol and off-the-charts sex with an Adonis? I'm surprised you can even walk today."

I sneer. "Sounds like someone is a little jealous," I say.

"Damn right I am." She laughs. "I have more cobwebs now than you do." I laugh, my grumpiness subsiding. "Seriously, though … you okay?"

"Yeah." I sigh. "I'm going to take your advice. Try and live in the moment … all that stuff." I shrug.

She nods slowly. "Don't try to sound so convincing!" she says as she stands up, knowing I need to work through things myself. "I'm here if you need me. Have a good run."

"Thanks."

The fresh air, pavement beneath my feet, blaring music in my ears, and moving muscles feel masochistically cathartic as I enter my fifth and final mile. I needed this. Needed to get out, clear my mind, and give myself time to think. My muscles, sore from last night's dancing and great sex, are limber and moving on autopilot. As much as I think I should go for an extra mile, my stupidity in overlooking breakfast before my run has my body telling me that I won't last much longer. Pitbull blasts in my ears, the song's constant beat drives my feet and spins my head back to thoughts of last night.

Oh, Colton. My head is still trying to wrap itself around what happened. He's the chance I have been looking for. To be carefree. To live in the moment. To be alive, not just living. I resolve that I can have sex with Colton with emotion. The emotions just have to be fueled by excitement and anticipation and lust rather than love and devotion and the hope of "more." I need to keep being the sassy, smart-mouthed woman I've been all along because the minute he thinks I want more, he'll be out the door. And it—him, me, us—will be over.

I ponder this my last quarter of a mile, recalling how he made me feel physically last night. I guess there's something to be said for lots of experience as I can attest that the man is skilled in the many facets of sexual dexterity. I blush, steeling my resolve that I can be with Colton without falling in love with him. *I hope.* That I'm going to enjoy every second of it because I know he's not the *staying kind.*

Teagan and Sara's *Closer* fills my ears as I turn the corner onto my street, my footsteps faltering when I see a white Range Rover parked in my driveway. The rhythm has been knocked clear out of my stride at the shock of seeing him here. Colton is leaning up against the front fender of the car, his dark figure haloed by its white. A navy blue shirt fits snugly over his torso, hinting at the corded muscles underneath. Muscles I can still feel on my fingertips. A pair of printed board shorts sit low on his hips and his long, lean legs cross casually at the ankles, and he's wearing a pair of flip-flops. Casual suits Colton very well. It lightens the intensity he naturally exudes. His head is bent, concentrating on the phone in his hands, and his unruly hair is spiked with gel to perfection in stylish, messy disarray. The pang of desire that hits my body is so strong, so overwhelming that I almost have to bring a hand to my torso to stifle it. I force myself to remember to breathe as I push my body to start moving again.

To go home. To go to Colton.

Shit. *I'm in serious trouble.* I admire him from afar, looking so unbelievable and attractive, and I realize that everything I thought about on my run—every stipulation, every rationalization, every justification of why it's okay to sleep with him—doesn't matter. Seeing him right here, right now, I know that I'll do anything it takes, whatever the consequences, to be with him again. To repeat how he made me feel last night.

Almost as if on cue, Colton glances up from his phone and locks eyes with me. A slow, smug grin lights up his face as I run my last few steps, turning up my driveway. I slowly pull out my ear buds, laughing to myself that Christina Aguilera's *Your Body* is blasting. I can feel his eyes run up and down the length of my body, taking in my skin-hugging Capri exercise pants and matching razor-back tank top, a V of sweat down the front of my bust.

"Hi," I say breathlessly, my body still huffing from my exertion.

"Hello, Rylee." The rasp of his voice saying my name is an aphrodisiac sending chills down my spine and eliciting a tingling in my belly.

"What are you doing here?" I look at him with confusion, hiding that my insides are privately jumping for joy, shocked that he is here in front of me.

"Well," he says, pushing himself off of the car as I walk in front of him. He exudes a confidence that most people would kill to have. "According to you, I took the checkered flag last night, Rylee…" a provocative smile forms on his lips "…but I seem to have neglected to collect my trophy."

"Trophy?"

He takes my hand, eyes still locked on mine, sparkling with humor, and tugs on it, pulling me forcibly against his chest. "Yes. You."

Oh. Fucking. My. Thoughts run chaotically through my head.

How do I respond to that? To him? When all I can think about is the feel of his warm, hard body against mine and the fact that he is here for me *again* after I ran out on him last night? I tell myself to breathe, his mere presence stripping me of the ability to perform the most basic functions. I quickly try to regain my composure, telling myself that I need to keep our interactions on my terms—revert to my sarcastic nature—in order to make sure that I can keep my wits about me.

I hear Haddie's voice in my head telling me to channel my inner slut. To go for it.

I breathe in again before I raise my eyes to meet the challenge in his. His pure male scent, soap mixed with cologne, fills my nose and clouds my head. "Well, Ace, I think you've got your eyes on the wrong prize." I pull my hand from his and put it on his chest, playfully pushing him back, distancing his body from mine. Needing the space to keep a clear head. "If all you're looking for is a trophy, you have your bevy of beauties you can pick from. I'm sure that one of them would be more than willing to be a *trophy* on your arm." I skirt past him toward the front door. I turn back to face him, a smile playing at the corners of my mouth. I shrug as I take a step backwards. "You could probably start by calling Raquel, is it? I'm sure she'll forgive you for last night. I mean, you were…" I turn around and take a step for the door, pretending that I'm searching for a word before shrugging and tossing over my shoulder "…*decent*. She's probably thrilled with *decent*."

I wish I could see the look on his face for the sharp intake of breath I hear tells me that I made a direct hit. I don't have to wait long to find out because within a breath, Colton grabs my arm and spins me around to him, pressing my body against his.

"*Decent*, huh?" he questions, his eyes boring into mine. I see anger, humor, defiance, all mixed together with desire. His breath flutters over my face, his lips inches from mine—so close that I clench my fists to resist the temptation to kiss him.

It takes all of my composure to keep up my charade of nonchalance. To hide how much he excites me, ignites my insides and shatters my control with just the sound of his voice, the feel of his touch, and the hint of his dominant nature.

I deliberately bite my bottom lip and look up in thought before bringing my eyes back to his. "Hmmm, a smidgen above average, I'd say." Sarcasm drips from each word as I smirk at him, lying through my teeth and then some.

"Maybe I need to show you again. I assure you that *decent* is not an accurate assessment."

He snorts loudly as I push away from him again and provocatively sashay my way up the front walk. "I need to go stretch," I say, sensing his movement behind me. "Are you gonna come?" I ask innocently with a victorious smirk on my face that he can't see.

"If you keep moving your ass like that, I am," he mutters under his breath as he follows me into the house.

I lead him into the family room hoping Haddie is elsewhere and offer him a seat on the couch before I sit on the floor directly in front of him to stretch. I spread my legs out to either side of me as wide as they can go and lower my chest to the ground, hands out in front of me on the floor. With the help of my sports bra and my chest pressing into the floor, my cleavage is pushed up and hedges over the top of my tank. I can see Colton's eyes wander over my body, stopping at my chest and taking in my flexibility. I can hear his hiss of desire, and I see his throat forcefully swallow.

"So, Colton," I say, stretching out over one prone leg, turning my head to look at him. I stifle a smile as I recognize the lust clouding his eyes. "What can I do for you?"

"Christ, Rylee!" He runs a hand haphazardly through his hair, his eyes moving over the cleavage again, before raising up to meet my eyes. He unintentionally wets his bottom lip with his tongue.

"What?" I respond all doe-eyed, as if I have no idea what he's agitated over. I've never played the femme fatale—never had the courage to—but something about Colton allows me to feel daring and bold. It's a very heady feeling to watch him react to me.

"We need to talk about last night." I see his eyes narrow as I switch positions, now lying on my back. I pull my right leg all the way up, pressing it to my chest, my shin inches from my nose. I lift my head up and look through the open V of my legs to encourage him to go on. He clears his throat noisily before continuing, taking a minute to remember his train of thought. "Why you left? Why you ran away? *Again.*"

I switch legs, taking my time to pull my other leg up, and stretch it over my head, making a low moan at how good it feels to elongate my tightened muscles. "Colton—"

"Can you please stop?" he barks out, shifting restlessly on the couch and adjusting the growing bulge that presses against the seam of his shorts. "Christ," he swears again as I roll over into child's pose, my bent rear in his view. "You in those yoga pants all limber and bending in half—you're making me lose my concentration here."

I look over my shoulder from my stretch and coyly bat my eyelashes at him. "Hmmm?" I feign as if I didn't hear him.

Colton sighs in exasperation. "You're gonna make me forget my apologies and take you right here on the floor. Hard and fast, Rylee."

"Oh," is all I can manage for his threat-laced promise sends shock waves through me, my body more than eager for his skilled touch again. My lips part to remind my lungs to breathe. My nipples harden at the thought. I push myself up to a seated position, cross my legs, and adjust my top to try and hide my body's excitement. "Although I'm sure it's me who should be apologizing, Colton."

He ignores my words, his eyes holding mine, various emotions flickering through them. "Why'd you leave, Rylee?"

The command in his tone has me swallowing quickly, my confidence waning. I shrug. "A number of reasons, Colton. I told you, I'm just not *that* kind of girl. I don't do one-night stands."

"Who said it was a one-night stand?"

A bubble of hope sputters inside of me, but I quickly try to stifle it. Not a one-night stand? Then what the hell was it? What the hell is *this*? I try to figure out what he's looking for. What he might think this is between us. I look at his eyes, searching for a clue, but his expression gives nothing away. "What?" Confusion etches my face. "You lost me. I thought commitment wasn't your thing."

"It isn't." He says with a shrug. "I don't believe you." He crosses his arms across his chest, biceps straining against shirtsleeves, and leans back into the couch. He quirks his eyebrows at me and waits for my answer.

"What?" He's lost me.

"Your excuse for running last night. I don't buy it. Why'd you leave, Rylee?"

I guess that's the end of the no-girlfriend discussion. *But what about the not-a-one-night-stand comment?* As for an answer, how do I explain to him how he made me feel last night after he left the bed? Used and ashamed. How do I tell him he hurt me without sounding like I have feelings for him? Feelings mean drama, and he has let me know he doesn't want or tolerate that in his life.

"I just—" I sigh deeply, pulling my hair tie from my ponytail and letting my hair fall down my back, trying to find the right words. I look him in the eyes, figuring honesty is the easiest route. "You made it clear that you were done with me. With us ..." I can feel the heat of my flush spread over my cheeks. Embarrassed that I am going to sound like a needy, whining female. "Cursing adamantly to demonstrate why my presence was no longer needed."

He eyes me cautiously, his eyes blinking rapidly as he contemplates my words. I try to keep my face unexpressive so he can't see the hurt I feel, and yet I see a myriad of emotions fleet across his face as he struggles to gain his footing. "Sweet Jesus, Rylee!" he mutters closing his eyes momentarily, his mouth opening and closing as if he has more to say. Finally he looks back at me. "Do you have any idea ... you made me—" He stops mid-sentence before standing abruptly and walking to the window. I hear him mutter a curse and I blanch at its severity. "I just want to protect you from—" He stops again, and sighs. He puts a hand to the back of his neck and pulls down on it while he rolls his head. He stands there momentarily, looking out at the front yard, both of us silent.

I made him what? Protect me from what? *Finish the sentences,* I plead silently as I watch his tense body framed by the mid-morning light. I just need an ounce of honesty from him. A sign that what happened meant more than just a quick romp. I'd give anything to see his face at this moment. So I can try to read the emotions he's masking from me.

He turns back around and any emotion that was displayed on his face is gone. "I asked you to stay." He says the words as if they're the only apology he's giving for his actions. "That's all I can give you right now, Rylee. All I'm good for." His voice is gruff and laced with what I think is regret. I feel as if he's trying to tell me so much more but I'm not sure what. The words hang between us for a moment, his jaw clenched, eyes intense.

I snort loudly, uncomfortable with the silence, trying not to read too much into his words. "C'mon Colton, we both know you didn't mean it." I rise from the carpet, grabbing my hair and twisting it quickly into a bun.

He takes a couple of steps toward me, his lips twisting as if that action alone will prevent him from saying more. We stand a few feet apart, staring at each other, and each waiting for the other to make the next move. I shrug before looking down and twisting the ring on my right ring finger. I look back up at him, hoping my explanation will stifle any questions he has about having to manage my expectations of a possible future. Baggage equals drama to him, and he's already admitted to me that he hates drama.

"Let's just say I left last night for reasons you don't want to know about." His eyes remain on mine, silently asking for more. I huff loudly. "I've got lots of excess baggage, Ace."

I wait for the deep exhale from him—the impassive expression to glaze over his face reflecting a man distancing himself from complication, but neither happens. Instead, Colton's mouth widens into a cocky smile and his green eyes fill with humor—both of which ease the severity of his countenance.

"Oh, Rylee," he empathizes with a trace of amusement in his voice, "I know all about baggage, sweetheart. I have enough of it to fill up a 747 and then some." Despite his smiling façade, I see the darkness flicker in his eyes momentarily as some unpleasant thought holds his memory.

Holy shit. What can I say to that? How do I respond to him when he's just hinted at a dark, sordid past? What the hell happened to him? I stare at him, eyes wide and my teeth worrying my bottom lip back and forth. Is this why he doesn't do the girlfriend thing? I mean, talk about going from fun, flirty banter to a serious conversation. And why does this seem to be a common occurrence for us?

Because he matters. Because this matters. The words flicker through my head, and I have to push them away, afraid to believe.

He takes a step closer to me, and I lower my eyes momentarily to the visible beat of his pulse at the base of his jaw. My hands want to reach out and touch him. Console him even. To feel the warmth of his skin beneath my palms. I sigh softly before I look back up at him, a suggestive smile turning up the corners of his mouth.

"This could be interesting," he murmurs as he reaches out to play with an errant curl on the side of my face.

His fingers roam to my haphazard bun and tug the self-sustaining knot. My hair tumbles free, falling down my back in a waterfall of curls. He runs a hand through it, stopping at the nape of my neck where my hair is damp with sweat. I cringe at the thought, but he doesn't seem to mind as he fists his hand in it, holding my curls ransom so I can't look away from him.

"How so?" I ask, a charge jolting through me, arousing me, from the possessive nature of his hold. He mesmerizes me—his eyes, the lines of his face, his sensuous mouth, the way his muscles pulse in his jaw when conflicted.

"Well, it seems that your baggage makes you so scared to feel you constantly pull away. Run from me," his voice rasps as he lazily trails a fingertip down my bare shoulder. I struggle to prevent my body from automatically leaning into his addictive touch. But I can't stop myself. He tilts his head to the side, watching my reaction. "Whereas mine? My baggage? It makes me crave the sensory overload of physicality—the stimulating indulgence of skin on skin. Of you beneath me."

And therein lies the problem—when he refers to me, he speaks of feelings and emotions and when he refers to himself he speaks of physical contact. I try to turn my mind off. I try to tell myself that the physical contact is what I want from him too. The only thing that I can have from him. Acknowledge it's the only part he'll share of himself with me.

It's an easy thing to remember because Colton leans forward and brushes his lips tenderly against mine. All conflicting thoughts disappear with his touch. A soft sigh of a kiss that we slowly sink into. I part my lips for him, his tongue slipping inside to stroke gently and meld with mine. Unhurried, lazy strokes of tongue and fingertips as he runs them over my bare shoulders and up the vertebrae on my neck. I could kiss him like this forever in this hazy state of desire. His earthy scent envelopes me, his heady taste consumes me, and his incendiary touch ignites me. He groans with our kiss, the rumble of it caught within me, vibrating through me.

A warm, soothing ache seeps into my chest and spreads throughout the rest of my body. I turn my mind off and allow myself to just feel. To revel in the sensations that he evokes within me. He is my fire on a cold night, the sun warming my skin on a cool spring morning, the wind caressing my face on an autumn day—he is everything that makes me feel alive, and whole, and beautiful.

And desired.

I slide my hands under the hem of his shirt and splay them wide across his lower back. His taut skin heats beneath my touch. I need this connection with him like I need sunlight. For when we touch like this, when I can feel him like this, I have no doubt that I can do this. That I can be what he needs me to be for however long he'll allow it. Because the chance to be with him, to remain under his spell, means I'll push my needs aside and bury them deeply so that I can be who he wants.

Colton cups my face in his hands, the kiss softening, stopping with a brush of lips so gentle that it sends chills up my spine. I sigh softly into him as he wraps his arms around me, strong muscles pulling me into the comfort of his warmth. I rest my head on his chest, smelling clean linen and fresh soap. I can hear his heart beating, strong and steady against my ear. I close my eyes, wanting this moment to last forever.

He rests his chin atop my head. I can hear him inhale a shaky breath before he speaks. "It's unfathomable how much I want you, Rylee." He pulls me tighter into him. "How much I'm drawn to you."

I bask silently in his admission, a small smile on my lips. Maybe I do affect him. I shake the thought from my head, not wanting to overcomplicate, overanalyze, or over think the simplicity and the sweetness of this moment between us.

"Rylee?"

"Hmmm?"

"Go out with me—on a real date." I can feel his body tense against mine, as if it's painful to ask. To admit he wants this from me. "Go out with me, not because I paid for a date with you but because you want to."

Elation soars through me at the thought of getting to see him again. Of spending time with him again.

"Say yes, Ryles," he murmurs with a quiet desperation as he kisses the top of my head. "It's unimaginable how much I want you to say yes."

I lean back, shocked by the vulnerability I hear in his voice and sense in his body language. Why is he afraid I'll say no when everyone else would say yes? I raise my eyes to his, trying to read the emotions flashing through his. I see passion and humor, desire and challenge, promise and fear. Why does this beautifully tormented man want to spend time with ordinary me? I don't have the answer, but I know in this moment, looking at him, I can see so much more in his eyes than I think he wants me to. And what I see, it scares me on so many levels that I have to tuck it away for later when I'm all alone. I can analyze it then. Replay it then.

Hope then.

I raise a hand to run it against the roughness of his slight stubble, liking its coarseness beneath my fingers. The texture tells me that this moment is real. That he is really here with me. I lean up on my tiptoes and place a soft, closed-mouth kiss on his sculpted lips.

"Yes," I breathe, and with my answer, regardless of all of the psychological propaganda I barrage myself with, I know that Colton Donavan has just put the first fissure in the protective wall around my heart.

He nods his head subtly, a shy smile on his face, no words expressed. He pulls me into him one more time. "Tonight?" he asks.

I still, mentally looking over my calendar, knowing that I have no plans but not wanting to seem too eager.

"I'll be here at six to pick you up, Rylee," he decides for me before I have a chance to answer. He releases me and looks me in the eye to make sure that I hear him. All trace of vulnerability is long gone when I meet his eyes. It's been replaced with his trademark confidence.

I bite my bottom lip and nod in agreement, suddenly feeling shy.

He cups my chin, running the pad of his thumb over my bottom lip. "See you then, sweetheart."

"Bye." I exhale, already missing him.

He walks to the front door, opens it, and then turns back to me, "Hey, Ryles?"

"Hmmm-hmmm."

"No more running away from me," he cautions before flashing a quick grin and closing the door behind him. With his departure, I can suddenly breathe again. His presence is so strong, so overpowering, it overwhelms the room. Infiltrates my senses. With him gone, I feel like I can process what just happened. Finally breathe.

I stand facing the door and close my eyes, absorbing everything that has just transpired. Nothing is solved. None of my questions are answered: Why he doesn't do the girlfriend thing? What is this between us since it's not a one-night stand? What was he really going to say when he said I made him, but never finished? What is he trying to protect me from? What kind of baggage fills his 747?

I sigh heavily. So much has been left unanswered, and yet I feel like so much has been expressed without being said. I sit down on the couch, my head reeling from the last week.

"Is he gone?" I hear Haddie's hushed voice from the other side of the wall.

"Yes, nosy girl." I laugh. "Come out here and give me your two cents."

"Holy crap!" she shouts as she hurries around the wall and flops down on the couch next to me. "Hot date tonight!" she sings loudly, raising her arms up in the air. "Whew, I need to take a cold shower after that."

"You watched?" I blush quickly, embarrassed at the thought of having an audience.

"No, no, no, it wasn't like that," she corrects. "I was in the kitchen when you guys came in the house. If I would've left, you'd have seen me and I didn't want to distract from your floor show," she teases, referring to my stretching routine. "I heard only."

I blush at the thought of her listening to our conversation, but find comfort in the notion that she listened. Now I can get an unbiased opinion about our exchange.

"*Ace?* Does he know what that stands for?"

"Nope!" I smirk.

"*Damn, Ry…*" Haddie shakes her head "…the man's got it bad for you."

I falter. Her statement blindsides me. I pick at the cuticle on the side of my nail for a moment, trying not to jump to conclusions. "Nah, it's more like pure, unadulterated lust."

"Not how I see it," Haddie responds, my eyebrows quirk up in question. "Smitten is the word that comes to mind."

"What do you mean?"

"Oh, c'mon, Rylee! Hard and fast?" she sputters.

"That's just sex." I shrug. "Not commitment."

"It's unfathomable how much he wants you?" she tries.

"Sex again," I correct.

"Unimaginable how much he wanted you to say yes to tonight?"

"Because he thinks it will lead to sex," I reply with a smile on my face.

"How about when he said it wasn't a one-night stand?" she tries again, eyes full of humor. Her heart shaped lips form a smile, thinking she's proven me wrong this time.

"Semantics," I answer. "Maybe he wants a thirty-night stand? I mean he only said it wasn't a one-nighter."

"You're incorrigible." She laughs, grabbing my knee and squeezing it lightly. "But hell, at least it'd be thirty days worth of great sex, Rylee!" she gushes, her excitement for me palpable. "You're going out with him again tonight! On a real date!"

"I know." I sigh, shaking my head at the thought of getting to spend more time with Colton. "At least there might be conversation tonight before we have sex," I joke, although a rational part of me knows the truth.

Haddie bursts out laughing. "Oh, Rylee, my sensible friend…" she pats my leg "…this is going to be so much fun to watch you experience."

I quirk my eyebrow at her and shake my head, filled with so much love for her and so much confusion over the situation with Colton. I sigh deeply, leaning my head back on the comfortable couch and angling it to the side so I can look at her. "Did I handle that right, Haddie? I tried so hard to be what he wants and—"

"You are what he wants, Rylee, or he wouldn't have tracked you down to your house." She is exasperated at having to explain this to me. Again. "C'mon, Ry," she says, oblivious to my train of thought. "What you did was brilliant! You walk out on him after sex last night and the next morning he shows up at our doorstep. I mean…" she shakes her head, a knowing smile on her lips "…that's more than just sex, Ry. The man's got it bad for you."

I feel her words take hold, but I'm afraid to believe them. Afraid to hope that there's a chance at anything with Colton. My head tries to shut out the surge from my heart, but it fails miserably. The hopeless romantic in me allows me a moment to daydream. To hope. I close my eyes, sinking in to the glimmer of possibility.

"Shit!" I scrub my hands over my face as panic makes its way through my thoughts.

"What?" Haddie opens her eyes, narrowing them as she looks over at me.

"What if I can't do it?"

"Which part of it are you referring to?" she questions warily. "Because it's a little late, sister, if the it you're referring to is sex."

"*Very funny.*" I huff. "I meant what if I can't turn off the emotions. *What if I fall for him, Had?*" I sit up and run my fingers through my hair, and the action makes me think of Colton's fingers there earlier. "I mean he's arrogant and overconfident and he warns me away but tells me he's drawn to me, and he's reckless and he's passionate and sexy as hell and … so, so much more." I press my fingers to my eyes and sit there for a minute, Haddie allowing me the moment to absorb everything. "I know without a doubt that it's a good possibility." I look up at her. "Then what?"

"It seems he's not the only one who's smitten," she says softly before I glare at her. She scoots over next to me and lays her head on my shoulder. "No one can fault you for being afraid, Rylee, but life's about taking chances. About having fun and not always playing it safe. So what if he's a little reckless? The fact that he scares you might be a good thing. Life begins at the end of your comfort zone." She leans back and wriggles her eyebrows. "Have some wild, reckless sex with him. He obviously likes you. Who knows, maybe it will turn into something more. Maybe it won't. But at least you took the chance."

Chapter Fifteen

LIFE BEGINS AT THE END of your comfort zone. I think about Haddie's advice as I get ready for my date with Colton. The song in the background makes me smile. It is the song that Colton's earlier text referred to:

Dress casual. Since you still seem to run away rather than talk to me, I'll use your method of communication to relay my message. Taio Cruz, *Fast Car*. See you at six.

Haddie had smiled knowingly when I showed her the text and scrambled for her iPad to play the song for me. We laughed out loud at the song's words. "I want to drive you like a fast car." Perfectly fitting for Colton to send.

We then scrambled to find a song I could send back to him. "Something to make him think about you the rest of the day and knock his socks off," Haddie had said while scrolling through her vast library of music. After several minutes of silence, she yelled, "I've got the perfect song, Rylee!"

"What is it?"

"Just listen," she said as the opening line of the song began. I started laughing out loud, knowing the song and liking the sexiness of it. Before we knew it, Haddie and I were dancing around the living room singing at the top of our lungs. The song was perfect! Sexy, suggestive, and confident—everything I felt but was too shy to be in front of him. So before I lost my nerve, I grabbed my phone and texted Colton back:

Nice song, Ace. It fits you perfectly. Now, I've got one for you that fits me. Mya, *My love is like whoa!* I'll be waiting for you at six.

A few minutes later, I received a response back:

Shit. Now I'm hard. Six o'clock.

I smile at the thought of our earlier exchange, a small thrill running through me that I have such an effect on him. I look in the mirror and scrutinize my outfit, heeding Colton's advice from the text to dress casual. I have my favorite True Religion jeans on with a violet-colored cashmere sweater that has capped sleeves and a sexy but tasteful low V-neckline. I've forgone the Haddie makeover tonight, opting to do my own make-up and hair. My make-up is natural and light: a little blush, some lip-gloss, smudged eyeliner, and thick mascara to highlight my eyes. Despite playing around with my hair for a while, I opt to keep it down, my curls loose on my back. I add simple diamond studs to my ears and some gold bangles to my wrist.

I twist my ring around and around on my finger, contemplating whether I should wear it or not. I take it off and look at it—three thin, wavy, intertwined diamond bands. *Past, present, and future.* I can still hear him whisper those words in my ear as we stared at it on my finger the night he proposed. I close my eyes and smile at the memory, surprised when the tears that usually threaten don't come. I play with it a moment more before hesitantly twisting it off. I stare at it for a beat before I place it in my jewelry box. I pick it back up in indecision, a war of emotions raging inside of me.

Fresh start, I remind myself with a deep, steadying breath, and place it back in the box. I've worn the ring everyday for three years. I feel naked without it, both inside and out. I wiggle my fingers and look at the lighter band of skin that had been protected from the sun. I feel a weight lifting off of me and at the same time a sadness that it's time to move on. I kiss the spot on my finger and say a silent *I love you to Max*, taking a moment to absorb the importance of this moment before turning to do my last minute touch-ups in the mirror.

I'm slipping on my black, heeled boots when the doorbell rings.

I press a hand to my belly, finding it oddly strange that I'm nervous. The man has seen me naked, and yet I still have butterflies. Haddie calls out to me that she'll answer the door. I grab my cropped leather jacket and purse, check myself in the mirror one last time, and make my way down the hallway. I nervously run my hands over my sides and hips, smoothing down my shirt, the clicking from the heels of my boots muted by the runner on the hardwood floor. I hear Colton laugh out loud as I turn the corner near the family room.

His back is to me when I enter the room. I suck in my breath when I see him. A pair of dark blue jeans hang low on his hips, hugging his ass and thighs. *The man can fill out denim*, no question about that. His broad shoulders and strong back stretch the cotton of his plain white T-shirt. The back of his hair curls up at the nape of his neck, and I itch to run my fingers through it. He oozes sex appeal, smolders with rebellion, and radiates confidence. One look at him makes me crave and want and fear all at once. *And he's all mine for the night*.

Before Haddie can acknowledge my entrance, Colton stops mid-sentence. My body tightens at the anticipation, and the deep-seated ache he's awakened in me rises to new heights as he looks over his shoulder, his body sensing my presence. I swear I can feel the air crackle with electricity as our eyes meet, our bodies vibrating.

"Rylee." My name comes out in a breath, the single word laced with so much promise for the night.

"Hi, Ace." It's impossible to mask my pleasure at seeing him again. I smile, hoping he sees how much I want to spend time with him and fearing he might read the emotions simmering beneath the excitement.

We step toward each other as he flashes his megawatt grin at me. I fumble with the strap of my purse anxiously as he simply stares at me. "Gorgeous as ever," he murmurs finally after I feel like all of the air has been sucked out of the room. He reaches out and runs his hand up and down my bare arm, the contact casual but powerful. "You ready?"

Two simple words. That's all they are really, but Colton makes those two simple words sound seductive. I nod my head and murmur, "Hmmm-hmmm," and am caught off guard as he leans in and kisses the tip of my nose. Such a simple gesture but so unexpected from someone like him.

"Let's go, then."

I glance over my shoulder and flash a smile at Haddie, my silent goodbye. I catch the quick thumbs up she flashes me before we leave.

Colton places his hand on the small of my back as he walks me toward the Range Rover, the simple placement of his hand a comfort to my unsettled nerves. Before he reaches for the passenger side door handle, Colton moves the hand from my lower back around to my stomach and pulls me into him so his body ghosts mine. I hold my breath, the unexpected contact with him awakening the smoldering burn he's set fire to. He wraps his other arm around my shoulders and lowers his head to nuzzle his face in the crook of my neck. The warmth of his breath, the sandpaper feel of his shadowed beard, the suggested intimacy of the touch, and the rare glimpse at the affection- ate side of Colton causes me to close my eyes momentarily to steady myself and quiet the mixture of sensations rioting inside of me.

"Thank you for saying yes, Ryles," he murmurs before kissing the hollow spot just below my ear. "Now, let me show you a good time." I angle my head against his cheek and close my eyes enjoying the firm heat of him against me. And all too soon he's released me from his arms and is opening the car door for me, ushering me in.

By the time Colton has reached the driver's side, his brooding silence has returned. He clicks his seatbelt and glances over at me. Despite the apprehension I see flickering in his eyes, he reaches over and places a hand on my knee, squeezing it in reassurance.

We drive in a comfortable silence as I watch the tree lined street of my neighborhood pass by us. The moon is out, full and bright, lighting up the warm January night sky. I look over at Colton, the dash lights casting a glow on his face. A shock of his dark hair has fallen haphazardly over his forehead, and I watch his eyes, framed by thick lashes, scan the road ahead of us. The line of his profile is stunning with his imperfect nose, strong bone structure, and sensually sculpt- ed lips. My gaze trails down to take in his strong arms and competent hands on the wheel. The combination of dark hair, translucent eyes, and bronzed skin mixed with the potency of his indifferent attitude— an attitude that makes you want to be the one who matters and be the one who can break through that tough exterior—that combination, it should be illegal. He really does take one's breath away.

When I look back at his face, Colton glances over at me and his eyes hold my gaze before flicking back to the road. A shy smile forms on his lips, his only acknowledgement of my quiet observation of him. The car revs, gunning forward on the freeway, and I laugh at him.

"What?" he feigns innocently, squeezing my knee.

"You like to go fast don't you, Ace?" I realize the innuendo the minute I say it.

He looks over at me, a wicked grin on his lips, enunciating every word of his answer. "You have no idea, Rylee."

"Actually, I think I do," I reply wryly. Colton throws his head back in a full-bodied laugh and shakes his head at me. "No, seriously. What is it about speed that's so attractive to you?"

He mulls it over momentarily before answering. "Trying to tame …" He stops to reconsider his answer. "No, rather trying to *control the uncontrollable*, I guess."

"That's a fitting metaphor if I've ever heard one." And I can't help but wonder if he's referring to something deeper.

"Whatever do you mean?" He plays along innocently.

"Someone once told me that I should research my dates." I look over at him, his eyebrows rising at my comment. "Quite the wild child, aren't we?"

Colton gives me his brighter than the sun megawatt smile. "No one can ever claim that I'm boring or predictable," he muses, looking over his shoulder to change lanes. "Besides, outrunning your demons has a way of doing that to you." Before I can even process the words, Colton skillfully changes the subject. "Food or fun first?"

I want to ask questions, figure out what he means by his comment, but I bite my tongue and answer. "Fun. Definitely fun!"

"Good choice," he responds, before muttering a curse when his cell phone rings on the car speaker. "Sorry," he apologizes before tapping a button on the steering wheel.

The screen on the dash says the name Tawny, and I immediately bristle at the sight. Researching my date certainly gave me more information than just his run-ins with trouble. I now know what Tawny looks like, that she's been his date to numerous functions over the years, and this is the second out of the last three times I've been with Colton that she's called him. My sudden pang of jealousy surprises me, but it only gets stronger when I hear Colton's familiarity with her.

"Hey, Tawn. You're on speaker," he warns.

"Oh!" I can't help but find a tiny bit of joy when I hear the surprise in her voice. "I thought that you'd called it off with Raq—"

"I have," he responds in a clipped tone. "What do you need, Tawny?" he says with irritation in his tone.

What a bitchy comment from her. What if I had been Raquel in the car with him? I sense her staking a claim on her territory, Colton.

Silence fills the line. "Oh. Um. I was just calling to tell you that the formal letters went out today for the sponsorship." When he doesn't say a word, she continues, "That's it."

What? She works for him? With him? On a daily basis? That's just what I need filling my head as jealousy rears it's bitchy head. *Fucking lovely.*

"Great. Thanks for letting me know." And with that he pushes a button and the line disconnects abruptly. Colton sighs out loud and a part of me is happy at his impatience.

"Sorry," he says again, and I'm sure he's referencing Tawny's mention of Raquel. *So they were an item.* She just wasn't some chick he found at the club. The catty side of me at least revels in the fact it was me he left with that night. The compassionate side of me winces for I know that Colton isn't someone who would be easy to get over.

"No biggie." I shrug as I take notice of our location. We're heading out of the city, the opposite direction from where I would expect to be going.

We ride in a comfortable silence for a couple of minutes then Colton turns a corner and the bright lights of a Ferris wheel light up the sky. I glance over at him, and my heart tumbles slowly upon seeing the boyish grin on his face. Colton drives between the flagged gates and pulls the car slowly down the bumpy, dirt road.

My eyes widen at the scene before me. The dirt field is crammed with every typical carnival ride one can imagine, complete with a flashing sign for a Midway section with games impossible to win and signs advertising horribly fattening food. I'm so excited.

He parks the car and turns to me. "Is this okay?" he asks, and I swear I can hear nerves tinge his voice, but I know that's not possible. Not from the ultra-confident, always-sure-of-himself Colton Donavan. Or is it?

I nod my head, bottom lip between my teeth as he exits the car and comes around my side to open my door. "I'm excited," I tell him as he takes my hand and helps me out. He shuts the door and turns to me, my back against the car. His eyes blaze with desire as he stares at me, brings his hands up to the side of my neck, and brushes his thumbs over my cheeks.

I can see the muscles in his jaw clenching as he shakes his head softly, silently responding to some internal conflict that causes a ghost of a smile to play on his lips. "Sweetheart, I've wanted to do this since I left your house this morning." He leans in, eyes still connected with mine. "Since I got your text." He raises his eyebrows. "You intoxicate me, Rylee." His words surge into my soul as he closes the distance between us.

His mouth captures mine in a dizzying kiss, tempting me with his addictive taste so I'm left fighting to regain my equilibrium. His mouth possesses mine with a quiet demand, yet the kiss is so full of tenderness, so packed with unnamed emotions, that I don't want it to end.

But it does, and I'm left to grip my fingers onto his biceps to steady myself. He kisses my nose softly before murmuring, "You ready to have some fun?"

I don't know how he expects me to respond since he just stole my breath, but after a moment I manage to say, "Definitely!" as he releases me to open the rear door. He pulls out a black baseball hat, well worn with a threadbare spot on the tip of the bill. The logo is a sewn-on patch of a tire with two wings coming out from the hub, and it's curled up at the edges.

Colton tugs it down on his head, using both hands to adjust the brim properly before turning to me with an embarrassed grimace. "Sorry. It's just easier in the long run if I try to go incognito from the start."

"No problem," I say, reaching up to tug on the lip. "I like it!"

"Oh, really?" He grabs my hand and we begin weaving through the parked cars toward the entrance.

"Yeah, I kinda have a thing for baseball players," I tease, looking over at him and keeping my face straight.

"Not race car drivers?" he asks, tugging on my hand.

"Not particularly," I deadpan.

"I guess I'll have to work a little harder to persuade you then," he says suggestively.

"That might take a lot of persuading." I smile playfully at him, his eyes hidden by the shadow cast from the lid of his cap. I swing our hands back and forth. "Do you think you're up for the challenge, Ace?"

"Oh, Rylee …" he chides, "Don't ask for something you can't handle. I told you, *I can be very persuasive.* Don't you remember the last time you dared me?" He tugs me closer and puts his arm around my shoulders.

How can I forget? I'm here right now because of that pseudo-dare.

We approach the ticket booth, and Colton releases his hold on me to buy our tickets as well as a wristband giving us complete access to all rides and games at the carnival. We enter through the gates, Colton tugging his hat down low, covering his eyes, before placing his hand on my lower back. The smell of dirt, frying oil, and barbeque fill my nose while my eyes take in the dazzling, blinking lights. I can hear the rush of the small roller coaster to the right of us, along with the screams of its riders as it plunges downwards. Little kids wander around with dazed looks, clutching balloons in one little hand, holding tightly to a parent with the other. Teenagers walk hand in hand, thinking they're so cool that they're here without their parents. I can't help my smile because despite my age, I'm excited—I haven't been to a carnival like this since I was their age.

"Where to first?" Colton asks as we stroll lazily hand in hand down the Midway, smiling and politely refusing the offers to "win a prize" from the game vendors.

"The rides definitely," I tell him as I look around. "Not sure which one yet, though."

"A girl after my own heart!" He pats his free hand against his chest, smiling at me.

"Adrenaline junkie!" I tell him, bumping my hip up against his thigh.

"Damn straight!" he laughs as we approach what appears to be the center of "Ride Alley" as the sign above us advertises. "So which one, Ryles?"

I look around at the rides, noting several different women staring at us. At first I worry that they recognize Colton, but then realize they are probably just looking at the hot guy standing beside me.

"Hmmmm." I contemplate all of the rides, settling on a long-running favorite. I point toward the ride closest to us. "I used to love this as a kid!"

"Good old Tilt-A-Whirl." Colton laughs, tugging me in its direction. "C'mon, let's go." His enthusiasm is endearing. A man who whirls hundreds of miles an hour around a track, rubs elbows with some of the brightest stars in Hollywood, and could be somewhere upscale right now, is excited about going on a simple carnival ride. *With me.* I have to pinch myself.

We get in line to wait our turn. He bumps me softly with his shoulder. "So tell me more about you, Rylee."

"Is this the job interview part of the date?" I tease playfully. "What do you want to know?"

"What's your story? Where you're from? What's your family like? What are your secret vices?" he suggests, grabbing my hand in his again and raising it to his lips. The simple sign of affection sneaks over the protective wall around my heart.

"All the juicy details, huh?"

"Yep!" His grin lights up his face, and he pulls me toward him so he can casually lay his hand over my shoulder. "Tell me everything."

"Well, I grew up in a typical, middle-class family in San Diego. My mom owns an interior design company and my dad restores vintage memorabilia."

"Very cool," Colton exclaims as I reach my hand up to link it with his that's casually resting over my shoulder. "What are they like?"

"My parents?" He nods his head at me. His question surprises me because it's beyond just the superficial. It's as if he really wants to know me. "My dad's a typical Type A, everything in its order, whereas my mom is very creative. Very much a free spirit. Opposites attract, I guess. We're really close. It killed them when I decided to stay in Los Angeles after college." I shrug. "They're great, just worry too much.

You know, typical parents." We move ahead in the line as the current set of riders vacate their cars and the next set moves on. "I'm very lucky to have them," I tell him, a little pang of homesickness hitting me. I haven't seen them in a couple of weeks.

"Any siblings?" Colton asks, playing with my fingers as he holds my hand.

"I have an older brother. Tanner." The thought of him makes me smile. Colton hears the reverence in my voice when I speak of my brother and smiles softly back at me. "He travels a lot. I never know where he's going to be one week to the next. He's a foreign correspondent for the Associated Press in the Middle East."

He notes my furrowed brow. "Not exactly the safest job these days. Sounds like you worry a lot."

I lean into him. "Yeah, but he's doing what he loves."

"I can definitely understand that." We start to shuffle forward again. "What do you think? Are we going to make it this time?"

I step in front of him and stand on my tippy-toes and gauge the line. A small thrill moves through me as I feel him place his hands on both sides of my torso, where my waist and hips meet. I look a bit longer than I need to, not wanting him to remove his hands. "Hmmm, I think next time," I respond, lowering my heels to the ground.

Rather than remove his hands, Colton wraps his arms around me and sets his chin on my shoulder. I sink into him, my softness against his steel, and close my eyes momentarily so I can absorb the feeling of him.

"So finish telling me about you," he murmurs in my ear, the coarseness of his whiskered jaw rubbing the crook of my neck as he speaks.

"Not much else to tell really," I shrug my shoulders subtly, not wanting him to move. "Played lots of sports through high school. Went to UCLA. Met Haddie as my roommate freshman year. Four years later, I majored in psychology with a minor in social work. Got my job and have been doing it ever since. Pretty boring really."

"Normal's not boring," he corrects. "*Normal is desirable.*"

I am about to ask him what he means when we move forward and are directed onto the uneven surface of the ride. We slide into the car, lower the safety bar, and wait for the rest of the ride to be loaded.

Colton slides his arm around my back before he continues, "So what about vices? *What do you need to have?*"

Besides you? The words almost slip out, but I catch myself before its too late. I look at him, squinting my eyes in thought. "Don't laugh," I warn him.

He laughs loudly. "Now you have me very curious."

"Well, besides the obvious female things, wine, Hershey kisses, mint chocolate chip ice cream." I pause to think, a smile turning up the corners of my mouth. "I'd have to say music." He raises his eyebrows at me. "It's not very scandalous, I know."

"What kind of music?"

I shrug. "All kinds, really. Just depends on my mood."

"When you need it the most, what type do you listen to?"

"I'm embarrassed to say this…" I shield my eyes with my hand in mock shame "…Top 40, cheesy pop music in particular."

"No!" he yells out in mock horror, laughing loudly. "Oh God, please don't tell me you like *boy bands*," he sneers sarcastically. When I just look at him with a smug smile, he starts laughing. "You and my sister will get along just fine. I had to listen to that crap for years growing up."

He plans on me meeting his sister? I quickly wipe the shocked look off of my face and continue. "She must have great taste in music then!" I kid. "Hey, I live in a house full of teenagers, I hear all kinds of Top 40 music, all day long"

"Nice try, but nothing justifies liking boy bands, Rylee."

"Spoken like a true guy!"

"Would you rather I be something else?" he asks, tapping a finger to the tip of my nose as I laugh, shaking my head no. He leans forward and looks around the ride to see when we're going to start. "Here we go."

It's not lost on me that our conversation has been solely about me. I begin to think about this as the ride starts to twist and turn and spin violently in circles. I am thrown against the side of Colton's body, and he clutches his arm around me, holding me tightly to him. He is laughing hysterically at the rush of the ride, and I tell him to close his eyes because it heightens the sensation. I swear I hear him say something about showing me more of that later, but I'm distracted from asking because as soon as it begins, the ride is over.

Colton and I proceed to ride the tea-cups, the swings, sneak a kiss in the Fun House's lover's lane, raise our hands high above our heads as we plummet downward on the roller coaster, and sling back and forth on the dragon ship. We step off of the freefall ride after having our stomachs jolted up into our mouths, and Colton declares his need for a drink.

We stroll over to a food vendor and he buys two drinks and a mammoth funnel of cotton candy. He looks over at me, dead serious. "No carnival is complete without making yourself sick on the pure goodness of spun sugar." He looks at me with the grin of a mischievous little boy, and it melts my heart.

I laugh as we stroll over to a nearby bench. We are almost there when we hear a voice behind us. "Excuse me?"

We both turn to see a middle-aged woman standing behind us. "Yes?" I ask, but it's obvious she couldn't care less about me. Her eyes are completely fixated on Colton.

"Sorry to interrupt, but, my friends and I have a bet going … are you Colton Donavan?"

I can feel Colton's hand tense in mine, but his face remains impassive. A slow smile spreads across his face as he glances over at me and then back to the woman in front of us. "That's flattering of you to think, ma'am, but I'm sorry to disappoint you. I actually get that a lot." The woman's face falls in disappointment. "Thank you for the compliment, though. My name's Ace Thomas," Colton says as he holds out his hands to shake hers. The mixture of my nickname for him and my last name makes me smile softly at the idea that he is thinking of the two of us as being intertwined. Connected.

She shakes his hand reluctantly, muttering, "Nice to meet you," embarrassed at her intrusion, before she turns quickly and walks back to her friends.

"Nice to meet you too, ma'am." Colton calls after her, the rigidity in his shoulders easing as we turn our backs to her and continue to the bench. He lets out a soft sigh. "I hate doing that. Lying like that," he says. "It's just that once one person realizes, then it's nonstop. Out come the camera phones and the Facebook posts and before you know it, we're surrounded, the paparazzi show up, and I've spent the whole evening tending to strangers and ignoring you."

His reasoning takes me by surprise, and I'm flattered that he's put it in these terms. "This is my life," he explains without apology, "for the most part. I grew up by default with a famous family, but I made the choice to be a public person. I accept the fact that I'm going to be followed and photographed and hounded for autographs. I get it," he says, sitting down on the bench beside me, "and I don't mind it, really. I mean I'm not complaining. I'm usually very accommodating, especially when it comes to kids. But sometimes, like tonight, I just …" He tugs his hat down further on his head. "I just don't want to be bugged." He leans forward, angling his head so the brim of his hat clears my forehead, and says, "I just want it to be you and me." He leans in, brushing his lips against mine in a brief but tender kiss, emphasizing his last words.

I pull back and smile tentatively at him, raising my hand to toy lazily with the curls flipping over his cap at the back of his neck. We stare at each other for a moment, exchanging unspoken words: lust, desire, enjoyment, playfulness, and compatibility. My grin spreads wider. "Ace Thomas, huh?"

He grins back at me, the lines at the corners of his eyes crinkling. "It was the first thing that came to mind." He shrugs, raising his eyebrows. "If I'd have hesitated, she would've known I was lying."

"True," I concede, taking a pinch of the cotton candy that Colton offers me. "My God, this stuff is over-the-top sweet!"

"I know. Pure sugar." Colton chuckles, widening his eyes at me. "That's why it's so damn good!" He looks out at the rides. "Man, when I was a kid, after—" He pauses quietly. "After I met my parents, they'd spoil me by taking me to baseball games. I'd get so sick eating this crap." The corners of his mouth turn up in a ghost of a smile at the memory. And I can't help but wonder what life was like for him before he met his parents.

We lapse into an easy silence, watching the rides and the people around us, taking small nibbles of cotton candy. I am really enjoying myself. He is attentive and engaging and seems as if he really is interested in me as a person. I guess I was expecting more of a surface get-to-know-you, so being proved wrong is nice.

Colton moves his hand over to squeeze my knee and points over to the only ride left. "You ready to take on the Zipper, Ryles?"

I blanch at the thought of the small enclosed cage tumbling endlessly through the air. Being jolted and shoved backwards and forwards while being confined. I swallow loudly. "Not really." I shake my head.

"C'mon, be a sport," he pressures jokingly.

I can feel the impending claustrophobia of the ride, and I move my shoulders back and forth to ward the phantom feeling away. "Sorry. I can't," I mutter, feeling the heat of embarrassment flush through my system. "I'm super claustrophobic," I tell him, pushing my hair off my face.

"I've noticed," he says wryly. When I raise an eyebrow at him, he continues, "Remember? Storage closet? Backstage?" he says with a suggestive smirk on his face.

"Oh. Yes." I can feel my cheeks burn red, mortified at my, *then*, actions. "How could I forget?"

"Were you always that way or did your brother lock you in the closet and forget about you as a kid?" he chides, laughing with amusement at the thought.

"Uh-uh." I shake my head and quickly shift my eyes away from his, hoping he misses the tears that fill them momentarily at the memory. Although it has been two years, it still hits me like yesterday when old demons resurface. I reach over to twist my ring around my finger and find the spot empty. I exhale shakily, closing my eyes momentarily to control my emotions. I'm angry with myself for reacting so strongly to the suggestion of a damn carnival ride.

His laugh stops immediately when he notices my agitation, and he places an arm around my shoulder, pulling me into him. "Hey look. I'm sorry, Rylee. I didn't mean—"

"No, it's okay." I say, leaning forward out of his grasp, escaping the heat of him and embarrassed at my reaction, "There's no need to apologize. I'm the one who should be sorry." He nods his head in acceptance to me, his eyes imploring me to say more. "I—um, I was in a pretty bad car accident a couple of years back … I was trapped for a while." I shake my head to clear the vivid memories pressing in on me. "Since then, I can't stand being in small places. Feeling trapped."

He places his hand on my back and reassuringly rubs up and

down. "The scars?" he asks.

"Uh-huh," I answer, still trying to find my voice.

"But you're all healed now?" The genuine concern that fills his voice makes me look back and smile at him.

"Physically, yes," I tell him as I lean back into the comfort of him, resting my back partially on his torso. His arm instinctively goes around me. "Emotionally..." I sigh "...I have my days. I told you, Colton, excess baggage."

He places a kiss to the side of my head, keeping his lips pressed there. I can feel the questions he wants to ask me in our silence. What happened and how bad was it? Why an accident has baggage that makes me run from him? I don't want to mar the night with sadness so I pinch off a piece of cotton candy and turn my body so that I face him, my bent knee resting on his thigh. I wave the piece of cotton candy in front of his face.

"How sweet do you like it, Ace?" I flirt with him before I lick my bottom lip and then provocatively place the fluff of sugar between them.

He leans into me, need darkening his eyes, a salacious grin playing his lips. "Oh, sweetheart, you taste sweet enough already." He bites at the cotton candy hanging between my lips, purposefully nipping my bottom lip, pulling on it. The quick bite of pain is replaced by a quick lick of his tongue. The low moan of pleasure that comes from the back of his throat turns me on. Makes me want to drink him in. Right here. Right now.

"I definitely like the taste of that," he murmurs against my lips. "We just might have to wrap this up and take this with us for later." He lazily brushes his lips against mine. "In case you need a little sweetener after I dirty you up."

I can feel his mouth curve in a smile against my lips. His suggestive words send a tightening pulse deep down in my belly. The promise of more to come with him dampens my sex and turns my soft ache into a smoldering burn.

I sigh against his lips, completely bewitched and totally enchanted by him. I lean my forehead against his, taking the time to steady myself.

"So," Colton says, pulling back and pressing a soft kiss on my forehead before continuing. "We have two things left that must be done before we leave here."

He rises from the bench, tucking the wrapped bag of cotton candy under his arm, a smirk on his face, and grabs my hand, pulling me to my feet. "Oh, really? And what would those be?"

"We have to ride the Ferris wheel," he says, tapping me on the butt playfully, "and I *have* to win you a stuffed animal."

I laugh out loud as we head for the Ferris wheel. The line is short and we chat, surprised at how many things we have in common despite coming from such different backgrounds. How much our likes and dislikes are similar. How our taste in movies and television are alike.

We are ushered to the car and locked in place with the bar across our laps. We start to move slowly, Colton draping his arm around my shoulder. "So you never finished telling me about you."

"What is this?" I laugh. "Don't think I haven't noticed you haven't been put on the spot yet."

"I'm next," he promises, kissing my temple as I snuggle into the warmth and security of his arms as we climb higher. He points at a vendor juggling balls on the ground below. "Tell me, Rylee. What's your future look like? A nice husband, two point five kids, and a white picket fence?"

"Hmmm, maybe. Someday. But the husband has to be *hot and nice*," I kid, laughing out loud. "No kids, though."

I feel his body tense at my words, his silence deafening, before he responds. "That surprises me. You love kids. Work with them all day. You don't want your own?" I can hear the confusion in his voice and can feel his jaw moving as it rests on the crown of my head.

"I'll see what fate deals me," I tell him, hoping he's satisfied with my answer and that he won't pry any further. "Look!" I point out to the skyline where the top part of the full moon is just rising over the hills, glad that I can change the topic. "It's beautiful."

"Hmm-hmmm," he murmurs as we sit watching its ascent. "You know what the rule is when the Ferris wheel reaches the top, right?"

"No, what?" I ask, pulling away from the warmth of his arms to face him.

"This," he says before closing his mouth over mine and fisting a hand in my hair. The hunger in his kiss is so tangible that I lose myself in him and the moment. His tongue slips past my lips, licking seductively at mine. I feel the gentle whir of the ride; the heated warmth of his fingertips whispering over my cheek; the sweet taste of cotton candy on his tongue; the hush of my name on his lips. The feeling of our marked descent has us pulling back, stepping back from the depths of the fire raging between us.

"Sweet Jesus," Colton mutters, amused, adjusting in the seat so he can shift the seam of denim pressing against his arousal. "I react like a damn teenager around you." He shakes his head, his embarrassment clear.

"C'mon, Ace," I say, my ego inflated, "you owe me a stuffed animal."

Thirty minutes later and several games conquered, my sides hurt from laughing at Colton's playful antics, but I'm the proud owner of an oversized and very lopsided-looking stuffed dog. I lean up against the corner of one of the permanent buildings at the fairgrounds, one leg bent at the knee with my foot flat against the building, and my new treasured prize resting on my hip. I watch Colton play one last game, take the small prize he's won, and hand it off to the little boy standing next to him at the booth. He ruffles the little boy's hair and smiles at his mom before sauntering back to me. Taut muscles bunch beneath his T-shirt as he moves, and his body screams that it was made for sin. It's impossible for me to take my eyes off of him. I can see that I'm not the only one as I watch the mom's eyes follow Colton's back as he leaves, an appreciative look on her face.

"Are you having fun?" he asks, approaching me, tugging on the ear of the stuffed dog.

I grin stupidly at him. As if he even has to ask that question. *I'm with him, aren't I?*

He reaches out and runs a fingertip down my cheek. "I love your smile, Rylee. The one you have right now." He cups my neck, the pad of his thumb running over my lower lip. His translucent eyes look into mine and search inside of me. "You look so carefree and lighthearted. So beautiful."

I angle my head, my lips parting at the touch of his thumb. "As opposed to you?" I question. He quirks his eyebrows in question.

"When you smile it screams mischief and trouble." And *heartbreak*, I think. I shake my head when the exact smile I'm talking about graces his lips. I run my free hand up the plane of his chest, liking the hiss of his breath I hear in response to my touch as well as the fire that leaps into his eyes. "And it has '*I'm a stereotypical bad boy*' written all over it."

The grin widens. "*Bad boy*, huh?"

Right now, in this moment, there is no way I'll ever be able to resist him with his tousled hair, emerald eyes, and *that* smile. I look up at him through my lashes, my bottom lip between my teeth.

"Are you one of those girls who like bad boys, Rylee?" he asks, his voice gruff with desire, his lips inches from mine, his eyes glistening with a dare.

"Never," I whisper, barely having enough composure to find my voice.

"Do you know what bad boys like to do?" He takes a hand and places it on my lower back, pressing me forcibly against him. Flash points of pleasure explode every place our bodies connect.

Oh my! His touch. His hard body pressed against mine makes me need things I shouldn't need. Shouldn't need from him. But I don't have the strength to fight it anymore. I suck in a ragged breath, not trusting myself to speak. "No," is all I can manage to say for an answer. Between one breath and the next, Colton crushes his mouth to mine in a heat-searing kiss tinged with near violent desire. He kisses me as if we are in the privacy of his bedroom. His hands run up the length of my torso, flutter over my neck, and cup my face as he slowly eases the intensity of the kiss.

He places his now-signature kiss on the tip of my nose before pulling back, the devilish look still smoldering in his eyes. "Us bad boys?" he continues, while my head still spins. "We like to …" He leans in, his lips at my ear, the warmth of his breath tickling my skin. I think he is going to tell me something erotic. Something naughty he wants to do to me for his pregnant pause leaves me suspended in thought. "Eat dinner!"

I throw my head back and laugh loudly at him, using my hand on his chest to push him away. He laughs with me, taking the stuffed dog from my arm. "Gotcha!" he says as he grabs my hand, saying goodbye to the carnival.

We make our way to the car, chatting idly as we pull out of the parking lot. Colton turns the radio on and I softly sing along as we drive.

"You really do like music, don't you?"

I smile at him, continuing to sing.

"You've known the words to every song that's played."

"It's my little form of therapy," I answer, adjusting my seatbelt so I can turn and face him.

"The date's that bad you need therapy already?" he jokes.

"Stop!" I laugh at him. "I'm serious. It's therapeutic."

"How's that?" he asks, his face scrunched in concentration as we hit traffic on I-10.

"The music, the words, the feeling behind it, what's not being said." I shrug. "I don't know. Sometimes I think music expresses things better than I can. So maybe vicariously, when I'm singing, everything I'm too chicken to say to someone, I can relay in a song. That's the best way to describe it, I guess." A blush creeps over my cheeks, as I feel stupid for not being able to explain better.

"Don't get embarrassed," he tells me as he reaches out and rests a hand on my knee. "I get it. I understand what you're trying to say."

I pick imaginary lint off of my jeans, a nervous habit I have when I'm put on the spot. I laugh softly. "After the accident ..." I swallow loudly, shocked that he makes me comfortable enough that I'm volunteering this information. Pieces of me that I rarely talk about. "It helped me tremendously. When I came home from the hospital, poor Haddie was so sick of hearing the same songs over and over, she threatened to put my iPod in the garbage disposal." I smile at the memory of how fed up she'd been at hearing Matchbox Twenty. "Even now, I use it with the kids. When they first come to us or if they are having a hard time dealing with their situation, if they can't verbalize how they're feeling, we use music to help them." I shrug. "Sounds lame, I know, but it works."

Colton glances over at me, sincerity in his eyes. "You really love them, don't you?"

I answer without hesitation. "With all my heart."

"They are very lucky to have you fighting for them. It's a brutal road for a kid to have to go down. It easily fucks you up." He shakes his head, lapsing into silence.

I can feel the sadness radiate off of him. I reach down and link my fingers with the hand he has resting on my leg and give it a reassuring squeeze. What happened to this beautiful man who one minute is playful and sexy and the next quiet and reflective? What can put that haunted look in those piercing green eyes? What has given him that roughshod drive to get his way, to succeed at all costs?

"Do you want to talk about it?" I ask softly, afraid to pry but wanting him to share what deep, dark secret has a hold on him.

He sighs loudly, the silence thick in the car. I steal a quick glance over at him and see the stress etched around his mouth. The lights of passing cars cast shadows on his face, making him seem even more untouchable. I regret asking the question, afraid I've pushed him further into his memories.

Colton withdraws his hand from mine and takes his baseball hat off, tossing it in the backseat, and shoves his hand through his hair. He clenches and unclenches his jaw in thought. "Shit, Rylee." And I think that is all I'm going to get as the car descends back into silence. Eventually he continues, "I don't …" He stops as he exits the freeway. I can see him grip the steering wheel tightly with both hands. "I don't need to haunt you with my demons, Ry. Fill your head with the shit that's a psychologist's wet dream. Give you ammunition to dissect and throw back in my face at everything I do—everything I say—when I fuck things up."

I immediately hear the *when* not *if* in his statement. The raw emotions behind his words hit me harder than his insensitivity. My years of experience tell me that he's still hurting—still coping with whatever happened long ago.

We stop at a light and Colton scrubs both hands over his face. "Look, I'm sorry. I—"

"No apologies needed, Colton." I reach out and squeeze his bicep. "Absolutely none."

He hangs his head momentarily, closing his eyes before lifting it back up and opening them. He glances over at me, a reserved smile on his face, sorrow in his eyes before mumbling, "Thanks." He looks back at the road and steps on the accelerator as the light changes.

Chapter Sixteen

OUR LATE DINNER IS SINFULLY good. Colton takes me to a small surf-shack type restaurant on Highway One slightly north of Santa Monica. Despite the busy Saturday night crowd, when the hostess sees Colton, she greets him by name and whisks us out to a rather private table on the patio that overlooks the water. The crash of waves serves as soft background music to our evening.

"Come here much?" I ask wryly. "Or do you just use the fact that the hostess is in love with you to get the primo table?"

He flashes a heart-stopping grin at me. "Rachel's a sweet girl. Her dad owns the place. He has a ladder up to the rooftop. Sometimes he and I go up there and throw back a few beers. Shoot the shit. Escape the madness." He leans over and taps the top of my nose with his finger. "I hope this is okay?" he asks.

"Definitely! I like laid back," I tell him. When his grin widens and his eyes darken, I look at him confused, "What?"

He takes a sip of beer from his bottle, amusement filling his face, "I like you laid back too, just not in this environment." His comment causes butterflies in my stomach. I giggle and swat at him playfully. He catches my hand and brings it casually to his lips before setting it on his thigh with his hand closing around it. "No, seriously," he explains, "this is way more my style than the glitz and glamour of my parents' lifestyle and expectations. My sister fits that lifestyle so much better than I do." He rolls his eyes despite the utter adoration on his face when he mentions her.

"How old is she?"

"Quinlan? She's twenty-six and a total pain in the ass!" He laughs.

"She's in graduate school at USC right now. She's pushy and overbearing and protective and—"

"And she loves you to death."

A boyish grin blankets his face as he nods in acceptance. "Yes, she does." He mulls it over thoughtfully. "The feeling is completely mutual."

His ability to express his love for his sister is charming in a man otherwise unwilling to express himself emotionally.

The waitress arrives, halting our conversation, and asks me if I am ready to order, although her eyes are fixated on Colton. I want to tell her I understand, I'm under his spell too. I'm still unsure what I want so I look at Colton. "I'll have whatever you're having."

He looks up at me, surprise on his face, "Their burgers are the best. Does that sound okay?"

"Sounds good to me."

"A girl after my own heart," he teases, squeezing my hand. "Can we get two surf burgers with fries and another round of drinks, please," he tells the waitress, and as I try to hand her my menu, I notice how flustered she is by Colton speaking to her.

"So tell me about your parents."

"Uh-oh. Is this the Colton background portion of the night?" he kids.

"You got it, Ace. Now spill it," I tell him, taking a sip of my wine.

He shrugs. "My dad is larger than life in everything he does. *Everything*. He's supportive and always positive and a good friend to me now. And my mom, she's more reserved. More the rock of our family." He smiles softly at the thought, "but she definitely has a temper and a flair for the dramatic when she deems it necessary."

"Is Quinlan adopted too?"

"No." He drains the remainder of his beer, shaking his head. "She's biological. My mom and dad decided one was enough for them with their busy schedules and all of the traveling to onset locations." He raises his eyebrows. "And then my dad found me." The simplicity in that last statement, the rawness behind the words, is profound.

"Was that hard? Her being biological and you adopted?"

He ponders the question, turning his head to look around the restaurant. "At times I think I used it for all it was worth. But when it comes down to it, I realized that my dad didn't have to bring me home with him that day." He plays with the label on his empty beer bottle. "He could have turned me over to social services, and God knows what would have happened since they're not always the most efficient organization. But he didn't." He shrugs. "In time I grew to realize they really loved me, really wanted me, because, they kept me. They made me a part of their family."

I'm a little taken back by Colton's honesty since I expected him to evade my questions. My heart breaks for the struggles of the little boy he was. I know he is glossing over the turmoil he must have experienced joining an already established family. "How was it growing up with parents in the public eye?"

"I guess it really is my turn for the inquisition," he jokes before stretching his arm out, resting his hand on the back of my chair, idly wrapping one of my curls around his finger as he speaks. "They did the best they could to insulate Quin and me from it all. Back then, the media was nothing like it is today." He shrugs. "We had strict rules and mandatory Sunday night family dinners when my dad wasn't on location. To us, the movie stars who came over for barbeques were just Tom and Russell, like any other people you invite to a family function. We didn't know any differently." He smiles broadly. "Man, they spoiled us rotten though, trying to make up for all I had missed out on in my early years."

He stops talking when the food is served. We both thank the waitress and put condiments on our burgers, deep in our thoughts. I'm surprised when Colton speaks again, continuing to talk about growing up.

"God, I was a handful," he admits. "Always creating a mess of one kind or another for them to have to clean up. Defiant. Rebelling against them—against everything really—every chance I had."

I take a bite of my hamburger, moaning at how good it is. He flashes a smile. "I told you they were the best!"

"Heavenly!" I finish my bite. "Sooo good." I wipe the corner of my mouth with a napkin and continue my quest for information on Colton. "So, why Donavan? Why not Westin?"

"So why Ace?" he counters, flashing me a combative grin. "Why not *stud muffin or lover?*"

It takes everything I have not to burst out laughing. Instead, I angle my head, eyes full of humor, as I purse my lips and stare at him. I was curious how long it'd take for him to ask me that question. "Stud muffin just sounds all kinds of wrong coming from you." I finally laugh, setting my elbows on the table and my head in my hands. "*Are you evading my question Ace?*"

"Nope," he leans back in his chair, eyes never leaving mine. "I'll answer your question when you answer mine."

"That's how you're going to play this?" I arch a brow at him. "*Show me yours and I'll show you mine?*"

Colton's eyes light up with challenge and amusement. "*Baby, I've already seen yours,*" he says, flashing me a lightning fast grin before closing the distance and brushing his lips to mine and then pulling away before I get a chance to really sink into the kiss. My body hums in frustration and arousal. "But I'd be more than happy to see the whole package again."

My thoughts cloud and my thigh muscles tense at the thought, sexual tension colliding between the two of us. When I think I can speak without my voice betraying the effect he has on my body, I continue, "What was the question again?" I tease, batting my eyelashes playfully.

"Ace?" He shrugs, darting his tongue out to wet his bottom lip. "Why do you call me that?"

"It's just something that Haddie and I made up a long time ago when we were in college."

Colton raises his eyebrows at me, a silent attempt at prompting me further, but I just smile shyly. "So it stands for something then? And not just pertaining to me in particular?" he asks, working his jaw back and forth in thought as he waits for an answer I'm not going to give him. "And you're not going to tell me *what* though, are you?"

"Nope." I grin at him before taking a sip of my drink, watching his brow furrow as the wheels in his mind turn in thought.

"Hmmmm," he murmurs, his eyes narrowing at me. "Always Charming and Endearing." He smirks, obviously proud of himself for coming up with what he assumes the acronym stands for.

"*Nope,*" I repeat myself, a grin tugging at the corners of my mouth.

His smile widens further as he tips his beer at me, "I've got it," he says, scrunching up his nose adorably in thought. "Always Colton Everafter."

The smirk on his face and the charming look in his eyes has me laughing out loud. I reach out and place my hand over his and give it a squeeze. "Not even close, *Ace*," I tease. "Now it's your turn to answer the question."

"You're not going to tell me?" he asks incredulously.

"Uh-uh," I tell him, finding his reaction funny. "Now quit avoiding the question. Why Donavan and not Westin?"

He stares at me for a moment, weighing his options. "I'll get the answer out of you one way or another, Thomas," he says suggestively.

"*I'm sure you will*," I acquiesce, knowing he'll probably get so much more than just that from me.

He stares at me for a moment, a mix of emotions flickering though pools of emerald before he shrugs nonchalantly and looks out to the ocean, effectively stopping any chance I have of reading what is in them. "At first my parents used Donavan as a way to protect me as a child. When we traveled or had to use an alias, we would use it. But as I got older..." he takes a sip of his beer "...and as I got into racing, I didn't want to be seen as some spoiled Hollywood kid who was just using his name and daddy's money to make it." He looks up at me, snagging a fry off of my plate despite having a plethora himself. "I wanted to earn it. Really earn it." He flashes that grin at me again. "Now it doesn't really matter. I couldn't care less what anybody writes about me. Thinks about me. But back then, I did."

A silence falls between us. I'm having a hard time reconciling the arrogant, sexy troublemaker the media portrays with the man before me. A man comfortable with himself—and yet a part of me still feels like he is striving to find his place in this world. To prove he is worthy of all of the good and bad he has experienced in his life. I have a feeling that the real Colton is a little bit of both *angel and devil*.

"So Colton, how'd you find this place?" I pick up my glass by the stem and swirl the wine around absently in the glass before I take a sip.

"I found it on the way home from surfing one day when I was in college," he muses, wincing at the small shriek from inside the restaurant as a woman recognizes him and calls out his name.

Ignoring the bystanders starting to gather inside to catch a peek at him, I continue. "I don't picture you in college, Ace."

He finishes the bite of food he's chewing before answering. "Well, neither did I." He laughs, taking another swallow of his beer. "I think I broke my parents' heart when I dropped out after two years at Pepperdine, *sans* degree."

"Why didn't you finish?" I flinch when a flash sparks through the dark night from someone's camera.

He casually shifts his chair in a move so fluid it's obviously well practiced. He now has his back more angled to the center of the restaurant so that less of him can be seen. I don't mind. It moves him closer to me so that now we both face the moonlit ocean off of the deck. "I can give you the bullshit answer about being a free spirit, et cetera ..." He flutters his hand through the air in indifference. "It just wasn't my thing." He shrugs. "Concentrated studies, set formats, deadlines, structure ..." He shivers in pseudo-horror at the last word.

I smirk at him and shake my head, leaning back into my chair where Colton's fingers are now lazily running back and forth between my shoulder blades. "Yeah ... I definitely can't see you twiddling your thumbs in class."

"God, my parents were pissed!" He exhales loudly at the memory. "They had spent all kinds of money on tutors to try and get me up to speed after they adopted me..." he shakes his head, smiling "...and then I went and threw it away by dropping out."

I bite off a piece of french fry. "How old were you when ... I mean how did you meet them?" A shadow passes over his face, and I mentally kick myself for asking the question. "Sorry. I didn't mean to pry."

He stares out at the moonlit ocean in thought for a few moments before answering. "No, there's not much to tell." He wipes his hands on the napkin in his lap. "I was—I met my dad outside his trailer on the Universal lot."

"On the set of *Tinder*?" I ask, referring to the movie that I'd learned about during my Google search. It was the movie his dad had won an Academy Award for.

Colton raises his eyebrows, his beer stopping halfway to his lips. "Somebody was doing their homework," he tells me, and I can't tell if he's perturbed or amused.

I offer him a shy smile, embarrassed. "Somebody once told me that it's not safe to go out with someone you haven't researched first," I explain.

"Is that so?" he quips, leaning back in his chair. He crosses his arms across his chest, a beer in one hand, his biceps pressing against the hem of his sleeves.

"Yes," I toy with him, "but then again, I don't think it matters with you."

"Why's that?" he asks, lifting a bottle to his lips. My eyes are glued to the sight of them pursed over the bottle. His tongue darts out to lick them after his sip. I have to drag my mind out of the gutter from imagining those lips on me. Licking me. Tasting me.

"I don't think it matters how much I learn about you," I tell him, leaning into him so my lips graze against his ear and whisper, "I still think you're dangerous." *To me*, I add silently.

He pulls back, eyes fused to mine as he leans in to brush a gentle kiss on my lips before resting his forehead against mine. "*You have no idea,*" he murmurs against my mouth. His words send a shock wave of confusion through me. One minute playful, the next minute guarded. To say he's mercurial is an understatement.

We finish our meal, continuing to talk comfortably, interrupted only once by a fan asking for a picture and an autograph, which Colton gives. Rachel does a good job keeping the rest of his fans at bay, saying that the patio area is closed for a private party.

I can see why women are so taken with him. Why they try and stake their claim to him as Tawny surely had earlier. He leans back in his chair, stretching his torso up before swallowing the last of his beer. He glances over at me and grins as I slowly look over his torso, over his biceps, and up to his face. My belly tightens at the sight of him and the memory of his body pressing me into the mattress.

"See something you like?" he asks, purposefully pulling up the hem of his shirt to scratch an imaginary itch on his washboard abs just above the waistline of his jeans. I breathe in deeply, his hand lazily scratching down to where his happy trail disappears beneath his button fly. *Damn him!*

I pull my eyes back up to his to see amusement laced with desire in his eyes. *Two can play this game.* I think of Haddie and her advice.

Embrace your inner slut, I repeat like a mantra. Trying to summon my simmering sexuality so that I might somehow fall somewhere in the realm of appeal that Colton has.

I shift in my chair, folding my leg and placing my foot underneath me. I bend forward onto the table, braced on my elbows so my cleavage is on display as I lean into him. I watch Colton's eyes trace over my lips, down the line of my neck, and straight to the curve of my breasts. His tongue darts out and wets his lower lip as they part in concentration. I continue forward until my lips are inches from his.

"*Something I like?*" I reiterate breathlessly as I glance down to his lips and then back up to his eyes. "*Hmmm,*" I whisper as if I'm mulling it over, "I'm still testing the goods to see if they're up to par." My lips are a whisper from his, and when he purses his to kiss mine, I conveniently shift back in my chair, denying him the contact.

Impatience flashes fleetingly in Colton's eyes before the corners of his mouth curl up as he regards me, shaking his head. "That's how you want to play this, Rylee?" His playful question is spoken with a hint of warning. The intensity in his eyes has my body reacting—my pulse, my breath, my nerve endings. "You want to play hard to get, sweetheart?" he asks as he removes his wallet out of his back pocket and pulls a generous amount of bills from it and sets them on the table.

He laughs. The low resonating sound reverberates through me as I continue to watch him silently, a coy smile on my face despite realizing that when it comes to Colton, I'm in way over my head when it comes to playing games. He reaches out and cups the side of my face, running the pad of his thumb over my bottom lip. Desire pools in my belly, aching for him to touch more of me.

Colton leans forward with determination in his eyes. He moves so his mouth is next to my ear. I can feel the warmth of his breath and my skin prickles in anticipation of his touch. "You see, sweetheart, if you want to play hard to get," he whispers, trailing a finger down my neckline, "you've picked the wrong guy to play games with." He closes his lips on my earlobe and sucks on it, the feeling mainlining right down to my sex. I arch my body in response, aware that at our backs is a restaurant full of people. "Didn't your momma ever tell you that playing hard to get is a surefire way to get the man you want?"

His voice is seductive, mesmerizing, and sexy as hell. He continues to trace his finger down my shoulder and arm until it reaches my hip. He smoothes the palm of his hand over my thigh and slides it slowly forward until it reaches the apex. His thumb glances over my cleft, conveniently pressing the hard seam of denim against my throbbing clit. I suck in a breath. "You wanna play hardball, sweetheart? Welcome to the big leagues."

I exhale, his words foreplay to my already thrumming libido. He leans back and brushes a teasing kiss on my lips. He pulls back, triumph on his face. He quirks his eyebrows at me, glancing down to my chest and then back up. "Besides, Rylee, your nipples are betraying your ploy to play hard to get."

What? I glance down to note that the tightened buds of my nipples are pressing tautly against my sweater in an all-out announcement of my arousal. *Damn it!*

Colton stands abruptly, smiling brazenly before reaching out his hand to me. "Come," he says, and all I can think is that I hope to very soon, my body yearning with the desire for him to touch me again.

We exit the restaurant from a rear door that Rachel directs us toward to avoid the paparazzi waiting at the front. We make it to his car unscathed, and Colton quickly maneuvers the car onto Highway One. We drive in silence, the air in the car crackling with the unrequited sexual tension between us.

I'm unsure where we're going but I'm smart enough to know that both of us desire the same thing. No words are needed. I can see it in the way Colton grips the steering wheel. In the invisible waves of anticipation and need rolling off of him.

We eventually exit the highway on the outskirts of Pacific Palisades and turn down a street a couple of blocks from the beach. Colton parks in front of a Tuscan-style townhouse and exits the car without saying a word. His home perhaps? By the glow of a streetlight I can see a stucco façade with wrought iron accents and a courtyard enclosed with a rustic gate. It's comfortably charming and not at all what I think I expected of where Colton lives. I guess I figured him for modern architecture, clean lines, monochromatic. He opens the door behind me and gathers our stuff before opening my door to help me out of the car. He grabs my hand to lead me up the cobblestone walkway without speaking or making eye contact.

I wonder if maybe I'm reading into things because suddenly I feel uncomfortable. Why the sudden change in behavior? Did I miss something? Nerves hit me as I realize that when I walk through this door my previous supposition of what I thought was going to happen has now changed. Shifted for some unknown reason. I stop behind Colton in the cozy courtyard where a small swinging bench seat sits amongst hydrangea and plumeria plants.

I hear keys clinking, him swearing at trying the wrong one, and then Colton is pushing open the distressed front door before placing his hand on the small of my back and ushering me in. He enters the alarm code but it continues beeping as he tries the code two more times before the beeping quiets.

The house is painted in soft browns and tans with a few bold splashes of color in pillows and vases. There are little touches here and there, feminine touches, that make me think maybe he had a female interior designer at some point. *Or a female living with him.* I walk hesitantly into the main room, my hands clasped in front of me, unsure what I should do or say. For the first time tonight, I feel awkward in Colton's company. I hear the door close and then I hear Colton's boots on the hardwood floor as he walks behind me and over to the kitchen area.

All the playfulness of earlier is gone, hidden seamlessly away beneath his masked façade. I watch him open a cupboard looking for something and then mutter a curse when it's not there, before opening two more and then he exhales. "What the fuck?"

My sentiments exactly. I can see the tension in his shoulders. In the lines around his mouth. Uncertainty and anxiety fill me as I take a step toward him. "You have a beautiful home." The words squeak out, betraying my uneasiness.

Colton's eyes flash up at my words, meeting mine, gauging me. "That depends," he mutters as I look on perplexed. He shuts the cupboard door and rounds the counter toward me. His eyes are expressionless. Guarded. "I drove here without thinking …" He shakes his head apologetically. "It was stupid of me to bring you here …"

His words, the sudden rejection, sting like a slap to my face. I look down at the floor in humiliation and wrap my arms around my torso, a useless form of protection against him. I can feel the threatening tears burn in the back of my throat. This is the second time he has led me down this road and then detached without explanation. One minute he makes me feel like I am the only person in the room he has eyes for and then the next it's like he can't stand the sight of me. I shift my feet, telling myself I will not cry in front of him. Will not give him the satisfaction of knowing the effect he already has on me despite the short time we've known each other.

Sighing deeply, I prepare to make my obvious exit now that I'm suddenly unwelcome here. When I know that I can face him, I look up again to see Colton in front of me tugging his shirt over his head. When the collar clears his face, he throws the shirt onto the couch without looking. His eyes are completely focused on me, his jaw set, hands restless as if he's itching to touch me. The intensity in his stare steals my breath.

Now it's my turn to say it. *What the fuck?* I'm thoroughly confused. Dr. Jekyll has turned into Mr. Hyde and is making a repeat performance. One minute I think he's apologizing for bringing me home with him because he wants to back out, and the next he's deliciously naked from the waist up, staring at me as if he's going to devour me without stopping for so much as a breath.

I break from his stare and run my eyes down the length of his body. His torso flexes under my gaze. His jeans hang low on his hips, the V-cut of his muscles dipping beneath the denim. I find myself thinking how I want to taste him there. How I want to run my lips along that ridge of muscles to where it trails down to the end of the inverted triangle. How I want to take him in my mouth, tempt him with my tongue, and make him lose all control. The ache in my body surges, pulses, and itches to be sated.

"Do you have any clue what you do to me?" he asks softly. I lift my eyes from his body to meet his. The unspoken emotions in his eyes shock me, envelop me, and scare me. "You don't, do you?"

I shake my head no, worrying my bottom lip between my teeth. I only know what he does to me. The power he has over me to make me feel again. To make me forget. How his touch alone can quiet the doubts in my head.

He takes a slow step toward me. "You stand there with that innocent look in those stunning violet eyes. With your hair cascading around you like a fairy. And those lips … hmmm, God … those sexy lips that get swollen and so soft after being kissed. I dream about those lips." His words wrap around me, a slow seduction to my ears. He steps closer, reaching out to take my hand in his. "Your face shows vulnerability, Rylee, but your body? Your curves? They scream sin. They make my mouth water to taste you again. They evoke thoughts in me I'm sure would make you blush." He wets his lower lips with his tongue. "The things I want to do to that body of yours, sweetheart."

I suck in a breath, the stark honesty behind his words stripping me bare. Entrancing me. Emboldening me. Creating another crack in the armor protecting my heart.

"You make me *need*, Rylee," he whispers hoarsely as he takes one more step closer.

Goose bumps run up my arms when he reaches out his other hand and runs it up the flank of my torso, stopping casually so that his thumb can brush over the underside of my breast. I respond instantly to his touch, my nipple pebbling in arousal. He leans into me, his face so close to mine that I can see the dark flecks of green floating in his irises. So that I can understand the unspoken words. "*And I don't ever need anything from anybody.*"

His admission is like a match to my gasoline. His incendiary words stroke that small part of me deep down that hopes there might be more here. I look into his eyes, recalling random comments from our time together, and dare to think of possibilities. He has softened me, worn me down, and built me up all in a single space of time.

"Colton?" My voice waivers, riddled with emotion. "I … Colton—"

I never finish my thought because he yanks me into him and crushes his mouth to mine. All the idle flirtation from the night explodes between us in a torrent of seeking lips and groping hands. The urgency is palpable. Our need to feel our skin on each other's is paramount. Colton releases his grip on my hips and grabs the hem of my sweater, pulling it over my head, and only breaking our kiss when it passes over my head. He tosses it on the floor as his mouth crashes back to mine.

Hunger. That is what his kiss tastes like. What his hands feel like on my body. What I feel inside. I want every inch of him and then some. I want to lose myself in him, get lost in the sensation, and become overwhelmed by his touch alone.

"Christ, Rylee ..." he pulls back from me, our chests heaving against each other's, our hearts both beating a frantic rhythm. He cups my face in his hands, the look in his darkened eyes tells me that he understands. He feels the hunger too. "You've stripped me, Rylee. You've teased me all night. *I. Just. Don't. Have. Any. Control. Left.*" He squeezes his eyes shut as I feel his cock pulse against my belly. "I don't think I can be gentle, Rylee—"

"Then don't be," I whisper, my own words surprising me. I don't want to be treated like glass anymore. Like Max treated me. I want to feel that violent passion of his wash over me as he takes me with reckless abandon. I want him to dominate me so that I surge up and crash down without a thought.

His eyes widen at my words, a guttural sigh releases from his throat, and then he is against me, devouring me. Desperation pulses between us. He pushes me backward, our legs shuffling into each other, our hands grabbing at every inch of exposed skin. My backside bumps up against the hard edge of the granite on the kitchen island as Colton's hands fumble with my jeans. He shoves them down over my hips and then easily lifts me onto the countertop.

The chill of the granite slab bites into the bare skin of my heated core, adding a new dimension to the heightened sensation in my sex. Colton tugs my jeans and panties down off of my feet, and then spreads my knees apart. He steps into me, pressing between my legs as he brings his mouth back to mine. His hands run down my chest, cupping my breasts through the thin lace of my bra before continuing their descent to the apex of my thighs. He runs a finger over my cleft before slipping a finger between its seam to find me wet and wanting.

"Oh, Rylee ..." he hisses as he slides a finger up and back, coating me with my own dampness and pleasuring me at the same time. His other hand is fumbling with the button fly of his jeans. He looks down to watch his teasing torment of my sex and then brings his lips to mine. "I want to feel you on me, Rylee. Nothing between us," his mouth murmurs against mine. His words deepening the ache I'm drowning in. "Can you trust me when I tell you that I've been tested?

That I always use protection. Have never had sex without it. That I'm clean." He kisses me again, his tongue slips between my lips, licking, tasting, tempting. "God, I just want to feel you."

"Yes. Me too. Please—" I gasp out as he slips a finger into me, my mind unable to form a coherent sentence. "On the pill … yes … I trust you," I pant as his finger circles inside of me.

"Lie back," he commands as he frees himself from his jeans and grabs my legs just under my bent knees, raising them up.

The cold stone on my back has me arching up the same minute he parts and thrusts into me. I cry out at the overwhelming sensation of his invasion and the sudden fullness of him. He stills, buried completely within me, allowing the pleasure and pain I feel to subside as my body stretches and adjusts to him.

"Oh fuck, Rylee," he rasps as I see his control slipping. His eyes blaze over my body and up to my eyes. I can see the muscles of his torso strain, his jaw clench, and his eyes glaze over wild with need as he tries to rein it back in. "You feel so damn good wrapped around me. Like velvet gripping me."

I gasp as he pulses inside of me, his control depleted. "Yes, Colton, yes," I cry out as he pulls out and slams back into me. Sensation ripples through me as he grabs my hips and pulls me toward him so that my bottom rests off of the edge of the counter. He sets a punishing pace as he thrusts back into me, over and over. Not breaking rhythm, he leans his torso over me and links his hands with mine, pulling them up over my head. He holds them there with one hand while his other hand slides back down to squeeze my breast. His fingers roll my nipple between them, and he swallows the moan he coaxes from me when he captures my mouth again.

The house is filled with nothing but the sounds of our slick flesh hitting each other, our gasping breaths, impassioned pleas between each other, and cries of ecstasy. I can feel the surge building inside of me, my channel tightening around him as he pistons in and out, each iron-hard inch of him hitting every one of my nerves. But I can also see a man on the verge of losing control and finding release as Colton lets go of my hands and braces himself on his elbows, hovering over me. He thrusts one last time before he yells out my name and then suddenly he pulls out of me.

197

My body clenches at the unexpected emptiness as Colton buries his head against my chest. His body convulses with his climax. In his hand? I'm confused. He groans from the violent pleasure that is shooting through his body. I can feel the tension ease out of his body and the warm caress of his lips on my bare flesh. His touch makes my body squirm as my nerves tingle with the loss of my anticipated orgasm.

I can feel his smile press against my abdomen and as if he can hear me thinking, he murmurs, "I want you to come for me, Rylee. I want to see how sweet you taste."

Oh! My mind processes the reason for his sudden withdrawal. His mouth. On me. "Colton…"

"Shh-shh-shh," he whispers in my ear, his lips brushing the sensitive spot just below my lobe. I arch my head back, scraping my nails across his back. He hisses at my touch as he lays a row of kisses down my neck and around to the other ear. "You've teased me all night, Rylee," his voice rasps, hoarse with desire. "Now it's my turn to return the favor."

A chill runs down my back and it has nothing to do with the cold granite that I'm laid out on. Colton's body flanks me but I feel his hand stretch out and hear the crinkling of a bag beyond my head. I turn my head up to see what he is doing and Colton's other hand holds steadfast to my jaw. "Uh-uh-uh," he warns. "Keep your head still. I wouldn't want you ruining the surprise."

"Colton?" I furrow my brow, curious at what he's talking about despite my body being on high alert from his words. I'm not exactly good with surprises, especially not when I'm naked and vulnerable.

He chuckles, deep and sexy. "That's going to be hard for you, isn't it?" When I don't respond, he lifts up on an elbow and regards me momentarily. "I think it's time you stopped thinking, Rylee. Stopped trying to figure what's ten steps ahead when we're only just getting started." He presses a chaste kiss to my lips. "Stay here, Rylee. Don't move. Understood?"

The authoritative tone of his voice turns me on. His reasoning behind it unnerves me. His weight lifts off of me, and I can hear him pad out of the kitchen. A drawer opens and closes. Apprehension fills me. For the carefree girl inside of me dying to get out, the anticipation is thrilling. For the control freak in me, the disquiet is unwelcome. Do I trust him? Yes. *Without a doubt.* Why? I'm unsure, and that scares the crap out of me.

I hear him return to the kitchen, and he leans over me, a lascivious smile curling the corners of his lips. "Do you know how gorgeous you look right now?" I don't respond but rather bite my lip as I feel his fingers suddenly at my cleft. They part me and slowly trail up and down. I arch up to meet his touch. He immediately pulls his hand away.

"Colton—"

"Uh-uh, Rylee," he teases. "I'm in control. Right here and right now." I flutter my eyelids as I look up to meet his eyes. My heart hammers in my chest at his words. My nipples tighten at the thought. Fear tingeing the edges of my Colton-induced haze. Handing my control over to someone else is a disconcerting notion. Submitting without a thought even more so.

"Stop thinking, baby," he whispers as he pulls my hands above my head. "I want to take all control from you so that the only thing your mind can do is feel. You won't be able to think five steps in front when you're not the one making the moves now, will you?"

Oh fuck! What is he— My thoughts are obliterated when he crushes his mouth to mine. I wiggle to move my hands and he laughs as we kiss. "Sorry, sweetheart," he murmurs, "you're going to learn that sometimes, not being in control is extremely liberating." He loops something around my wrists and binds them around the faucet at the other end of the island. As I register what he's done, as I start to realize how practiced that move was and how many times before he's done it, my world goes black as he slips a blindfold over my eyes. I gasp. "Time to take your own advice, Rylee."

What? When did I ever say tie me up and take advantage of me?

"You told me to close my eyes on the Tilt-A-Whirl. That it heightens the sensation." The pad of his thumb traces the outline of my lips.

Oh crap! Me and my big mouth.

Something soft but slightly coarse runs over my stomach and up my torso to circle around my nipples. I suck in a breath as whatever he has strokes me lightly down the tops of my legs and then up one inner thigh and down the other. My sex clenches from its touch, desperate for something to help ease the blistering ache. The only thing that touches my body is this object. The only sound I hear is my own breath. The anticipation that builds within me is profound as he continues his slow, tantalizing torture of my senses.

I've never needed a man's touch in my life as much as I do at this moment. My next thought is only where he'll touch me next. There is nothing to do but focus on the sensations. My nerves are on edge awaiting his contact with my body. He has succeeded in making me forget what step ten will be, but rather revel in the step I'm in. I've lost all sense of my surroundings. Nothing else exists in this moment except for him, my desperation for his touch, and my body's craving for release.

Colton is absolutely silent except for the barely audible rush of air I hear escape his mouth in response to my body's reaction to the delicious torment of his sensual sensory deprivation.

Colton stops at my right breast, and before I can place the sensation, he touches me for the first time by capturing my nipple in his mouth. I buck my hips wildly at the warmth of his mouth on my sensitive bud.

"Colton!" I cry out, tugging my hands against my bindings, wanting to touch him. Wanting to thread my fingers in his hair and hold him against me.

He tugs on my nipple with a gentle pull of his teeth and then the warmth of his mouth is gone only to be felt again on my other breast. I feel the strange object circling around it before his mouth closes over it again. He groans softly. "Tasty," he murmurs against me, and I realize he's teasing me about the cotton candy.

I start to speak and am stopped as his mouth closes over mine, the sweet sugary taste on his tongue. It's a soft, tender kiss. A gradual easing of lips and tongue that lacks urgency yet screams of desperation. His lips travel down my exposed neck and back up, nipping at my earlobe. A slow and welcome torture that is making me want like never before.

I can feel the cotton candy slowly move down my torso to my sex. The confection leaves my skin, and I feel his fingers roaming over me, caressing my folds, and catering to my body's addiction to his touch. I gasp as we kiss and Colton takes in my voracious moan of desire.

He skillfully teases me with his dexterous fingertips, and I push my pelvis against his hand, wanting more. Needing the friction to inch me closer to the edge.

I hiss out a breath as he parts me, very slowly slipping a finger into my core. Heat flashes through me as I feel my muscles tighten around him, clenching as fire burns through my veins. He cups me, leisurely rocking his hand as his thumb finds and stimulates my nub of nerve endings. He withdraws his finger and then slowly tucks two back into me. He curves them, rubbing against the sensitive spot deep inside, his fingers and tongue mimicking each other as he intensifies his pace. I fist my hands inside my bindings, my nails digging into my palms, as he quickens the rhythm.

I am so gloriously close to crashing into the oblivion and then, all of a sudden, I'm not. Colton has withdrawn from me. I cry out his name in frustration. In desperation. I hear a low, rumbling chuckle from him. "Not yet, sweetheart. Turnabout's fair play," he croons in my ear. "I want to drive you crazy like you do me." I feel a softness tickle my lips and I open them, accepting the sweet bite of cotton candy on my tongue. "I want to drive you to the crest, Rylee. Take you to the brink so that your only thought is of me. So that you cry out my name when your body detonates into a million splinters of pleasure."

His hypnotic words entrance me. Seduce me. And without a hint of what's next, Colton's mouth closes over my clit as he slips two fingers back into me. I call out inarticulately at the exquisite pleasure that pulses through me. He sucks, gently teasing me until my legs tighten impatiently. His fingers slowly press in and out of my channel, rubbing, teasing, and urging me higher. I lift my hips to him, reeling from his manipulation, but still wanting more. I pant in need then moan in ecstasy as I feel the quickening start to build again beneath his touch. I am so close. Within a few grazes of my climax, Colton abruptly withdraws his mouth. His fingers remain, yet stay motionless within me.

Damn him! My chest heaves for air as my body stays wound tight, waiting for the slightest movement to set me off. "Greedy little girl," he admonishes, his breath whispering over my slick flesh. "I may have to rectify this." And before he can finish his last word, he withdraws his fingers and slams into me, burying himself to the hilt in my heated depth.

"Oh God, Colton!" The sudden fullness, the unexpected stroke, makes me writhe against the granite slab.

Colton eases out of me slowly before plunging back in. He continues this slow withdrawal followed by his greedy drive back in, setting a delirious pace that pushes me to the edge. "Come for me, Rylee!" he growls at me.

His words are my undoing. My breath quickens. My pulse races. My muscles tense. My hips grind into him, deepening the burning ache until I am pushed over the edge. I explode like a firecracker. A white-hot heat flits though my body. Sensation shatters around me as the first wave of my orgasm explodes. I incoherently yell out as I pulse around him. He stills, allowing me to absorb the intensity of my climax. I release the breath I've been holding, my taut muscles slowly relaxing before another wave shudders through me.

This wave is more than he can bear. My muscles milk his orgasm out of him. He rears back and pushes into me a few more times, my body gripping his. He yells out my name, his own climax tearing through him, and his hips jerking against me until I can feel his warmth erupt within me.

He collapses on top of me, pressing his face into the curve of my neck. Our chests heave in uneven unison, and I can feel his lips form a smile. My breath shudders as I exhale, the frantic tattoo of my heart beginning to ebb. *That was … Wow!* I go to remove the blindfold and remember that my hands are still tied.

I wiggle underneath him. He laughs into my neck, the vibration of it seeping into my chest. "I take it you want your hands back?"

"Hmm-hmmm." I don't think I can speak. My body is still processing what has just happened.

He lifts up and I can feel his hands tugging at my bindings. When one hand is free, I reach down and pull off my blindfold, my eyes easily adjusting to the dimmed light in the kitchen. Colton's face is above me, etched in concentration as he works the other knot free. I see the lines ease as my other hand releases from what appears to be a velvet braided rope.

I reach up to run my hands over his cheeks as he looks down at me, an errant lock of hair falling over his forehead. A shy smile lights up his face. I lift my head and brush a soft kiss against his lips, the only way I can express how I feel, how much what just happened meant to me without having him run for the hills.

I lay my head back down, yet Colton's eyes remain closed, the corners of his mouth still smiling. He shakes his head subtly before opening his eyes and easing his weight off of me. "C'mon," he says, pulling me up by my arms, "This can't be all too comfortable for you."

I hop off of the counter, suddenly feeling modest about my nudity. I look around for my clothes as Colton pulls his jeans up over his naked hips. I put my arms through my bra straps as I watch him button up the first four buttons, leaving the top one undone. I have to stifle a sigh as I stare at him naked from the waist up in appreciation.

I hook my bra together and drag my shirt over my head. I start to run my fingers through my disheveled hair but stop when I catch more than just a glimpse of the tattoos that line the side of his torso. I've never really been able to see the whole of them, so I take a moment to look. Four symbols run vertically down his side, all are similar in style. The first three images are solid, the ink filled in completely while the fourth is just an outline. I angle my head, trying to figure out what exactly they are of when Colton looks up and sees my questioning look.

Chapter Seventeen

"**W**HAT ARE YOUR TATTOOS OF?**"
He turns his body and raises his arm so that I can see the markings. "They're Celtic knots."
"What do they mean?"
"Nothing really," he says gruffly, busying himself by opening the refrigerator, which I notice is almost empty, and grabbing a beer.
"C'mon," I prod, curious about why he is suddenly avoiding the question when he's been so forthcoming all evening. He holds a beer out to me and I shake my head no. "You don't seem like the kind of guy who marks himself permanently without having a reason."
I lean against the counter with my shirt and panties on as he takes a long tug on the beer, his eyes meet mine over the bottom of the bottle. He slides them down the length of my bare legs and back up to my eyes. "The knots mean different things." He lifts his arm again to show me as I move near him. He points to the first one just below his armpit. "This one means to overcome some type of adversity in life." He moves to the next one. "This is the symbol for acceptance. This one is for healing, and the bottom one's for vengeance." He looks up slowly, a darkness in his eyes as they hold mine, waiting for my reaction. Waiting for me to ask why he needs acceptance, healing, and vengeance. We stand silently until he sighs, shaking his head at me, disbelieving that he's said so much.
I step toward him, reach out tentatively, and run my fingers down the four symbols on his body, their meanings resonating in me, telling me somehow, someway they are a marker of his past and where he is in terms of dealing with it. His body shivers at my touch.

"They suit you," I whisper, trying to convey to him that I understand. "Did you get them all at once? Why are three colored in and not the fourth?"

He shrugs away from me, taking another drink from his beer. "No." That's all he gives me, and his tone tells me that that's the end of the conversation.

"You're Irish then?"

"So my Dad tells me."

Mr. Forthcoming. I guess he is done talking about him for the night. The theoretical switch has been flipped, and I'm back trying to catch up to his mercurial mood swings. What now? Does he drive me home? Do I stay the night? Do I get a cab? Unsettled, I pick up my pants and tug them on, struggling to appear coordinated as my ankle gets caught in the cuff. I can feel the heat of his gaze as he watches me although I dare not look up.

"So, Colton …" I look up as I finish buttoning my jeans to see him watching me as I'd thought, an amused smirk on his face and his eyebrows raised. He may be experienced in the protocol of this type of thing, but I sure am not. My cheeks flush. I search for something to talk about, something that will abate my anxiety until he gives me some kind of indication about what I do from here. "The boys are really looking forward to going to the track when you test the car." He snorts, his head bobbing back and forth, before he stifles a laugh. "What?" I ask, confused by his reaction.

"All business now, are we?" I eye him carefully as he walks toward me, wary of the predatory look in his eyes. "How is it that ten minutes ago you were naked and compliant beneath me and now you're nervous and uncomfortable just being in the same space as me?" *Probably because you dominate any space you occupy.* He reaches out to tug one of my curls. His emerald eyes darken as he watches me. "Am I that scary of a guy, Rylee?"

Shit. I have to work harder at not wearing my emotions on my sleeve. "I'm not nervous." My over-emphatic answer a dead give away that I'm lying.

"Oh, Rylee, it's not exactly polite to lie when some of me is still in you."

My blush darkens. Well, when he puts it that way … "I'm not lying. I just wanted to—to—uh get the dates so that I can tell the boys."

He raises his eyebrows, a knowing smile on his lips. I'm a horrible liar, and I know he can see right through mine. "What an apropos time to ask." He smirks. "Well…" he reaches out and cups my neck, laying a tender kiss on my lips "…my day planner's at home. I'll have to text you the dates."

I open my eyes from his kiss as I process his words. *What*? I feel his body tense once he's realized what he said. Did I miss something? I snap my eyes up to his and he takes a cautious step back from me. The look on his face is indiscernible.

"Is this not your house?" I shake my head. "What am I missing here?"

Colton runs a hand through his hair, exhaling loudly. "It's my place. I just don't stay here that often." His expression is guarded, tension in the lines around his mouth. His uneasiness unnerves me.

"Oh. Okay. Where else do you …?" And it hits me. The wrong key in the door. The fumbling with the alarm code. The inability to find something in the kitchen cupboards. The empty refrigerator. Colton saying that he shouldn't have brought me here. How could I be so naïve? I raise my eyes to meet Colton's and he knows that I know. The look on his face says it all. I try to swallow the lump in my throat. "So, this is your place, *but not exactly where you live*." I slowly annunciate every word. "It's where you bring all your dates, escorts, whatever you call them, *to fuck*." I choke on the last word. "Right?"

"That's not what this is." His voice is reticent. Rueful.

I snort at his response. "Then what the fuck is this, Colton? I think I need a little clarity here seeing as I still have *some of you in me*, as you so kindly pointed out. Are you referring to the house or as a definition of you and me?"

He just stares at me, green eyes glistening like a hurt puppy dog. "You and me," he breathes.

I walk out of the kitchen, rolling my shoulders, needing some space from him. From that look in his eyes. Why the fuck am I feeling guilty about the look in his eyes when I've done nothing wrong? Ugh! This is bullshit. I walk out into the family room, not wanting him to see the tears of hurt that flood my eyes. I quickly wipe them away with the back of my hand as I focus on the painting, a wash of colors over his fireplace.

"That's not what this is? Then tell me what I'm supposed to think. You tell me you don't do girlfriends, you only *do casual*. Is this where you bring them for a no strings attached good time?"

"Rylee." My name is a one-word plea on his lips. And he is right behind me. I hadn't heard him follow me, my thoughts too loud in my own head. "I keep screwing this up with you," he mumbles to himself.

"You're damn right you do." I turn around to face him. "What? You like me enough to fuck me but not enough to stick around or bring me to your *real house*? Unbelievable!" I huff at him, my confidence at an all time low. Does he really think that I'd be okay with this? Just when I think that I can move on from Max, he makes me jump back as if a rattlesnake has bitten me. *Bastard*! "Maybe you should explain to me a little bit more about your setup here. Make me understand the shit that's in your head." Why am I even asking? It's not like I really want to know the details about his sordid affairs. *To know about what else goes on here on the kitchen counter.* "I mean if that's all I am to you, then I at least deserve to know what's expected of me. *My protocol*." My words drip with anger laced sarcasm. I cross my arms over my chest, a useless form of protection from him.

"Ry? I—uh ..." I can see the regret in his eyes. He regards me silently for several moments, an internal struggle warring behind his façade. "Rylee, this is not what I'd planned for me. For us." He pauses, his eyes flooding with emotion. "*You. What you are? What we are? It scares the shit out of me.*"

Whoa! What? Haddie's words come back to me in a rush. I want to melt at his words, at the knowledge that I affect him that much, but a part of me feels like I'm being played here. An easy out for him as an excuse for his actions. Tell me what I want to hear to get me back in his bed, crisis averted, and then drop me at the first chance he gets. He hates drama and I've just caused some. I'm not going to let myself be played by the master player.

"*I scare you?* Shit, Colton, I just let you tie me up, blindfold me, and have your way with me on the kitchen counter. A man I've only known for two weeks when I've only been with one other person before! *And. I. Scare. You?*" His eyes widen, startled by my admission. I raise my hands up, exasperated, wanting to move on before I have to address that little fact about myself. "You told me at the beach that night that you set guidelines, mitigate promises for the future or some bullshit like that … tell me, Colton, do you do that before or after you bring them to this—to here?" I'm on a roll here, anger and humiliation fueling my fire. He just stares at me, eyes wide, arms hanging limply at his sides. "C'mon. Since you didn't have the courtesy to let me know what I was getting in to, I think you should at least tell me now."

"Rylee, that's not what this—"

"I'm waiting, Colton." I lower myself to the edge of the camel-colored leather couch, crossing my arms across my chest. I think I'm going to need to be seated for this one. "How do you set up your *mutual, I'm-only-giving-you-sex-and-nothing-else-arrangements*?"

He sighs loudly, running his hand over his jaw, scrubbing it back and forth before looking back at me. He finally speaks, his voice is soft and hesitant as if he's scared to tell me. "Usually, I hit it off with someone. We figure out we like each other." He shrugs apologetically. "And then I tell her that I enjoy her company, that I would love to spend more time with her, but all I can give her is a few nights a week … to meet me here…" he gestures at the room we're in "…and have some fun."

I'm not sure if I want to hear this answer. "Go on …"

He cocks his head to the side and regards me intently, the timid person I'd seen moments before slowly morphing back into the confident man I expect him to be. "The first time we meet here …" He eyes me cautiously, knowing that I'm thinking this is my first time here. Was this the imminent plan he had laid out for me after screwing me on the counter? I purse my lips, trying hard to keep my face enigmatic. I nod at him to continue, anger unfurling in my belly. "Well, I sit her down and explain that I want to spend time with her, but that there is no happily ever after. Never will be. And if she can accept my terms, my requirements, then I would love to spend time with her here, have her accompany me to functions if need be, and allow her the notoriety and perks of being with me, until our mutual agreement has run its course."

Wow. It takes me a minute to process his words. Talk about taking emotion out of the picture. It sounds more like a business transaction. He stares at me, unashamed.

I look at him wide eyed. "This really works for you?" I sputter, taken aback. "Why not just hire an escort? I mean that's what you're really doing." My head is reeling with this information and yet the masochistic part of me wants to know all the gory details. Wants to hear the words so I heed the warning and walk away unscathed. "Someone to look pretty on your arm and for you *to use* when it suits you."

"I beg to differ," Colton says vehemently. "It's not like that. I never exchange money for sex, Rylee. Never. I've already told you that once. I won't tell you that again."

Like he has any room to be pissy. He just told me he expects me to be his compliant little woman, happy with any scraps he throws my way. Too many thoughts are running through my head to form a coherent, intelligent response. "What—" I finally ask, stumbling for the right words. "You say your arrangement has rules. Do you mind if I ask what exactly those are?"

I'm curious. I'm horrified. I'm floored that this is the path he has chosen when he could obviously have anyone he wants.

I can sense that he's uncomfortable, embarrassed even to respond and this fact gives me a tiny bit of hope. Hope for what though, I'm not exactly sure.

"I know it sounds cold, but I've found that if I lay it all out on the table beforehand, it minimizes complications and lessens expectations further down the line. That way they walk into this willingly after they know the stipulations."

"Not me!" I shout at him. "You didn't tell me!" He starts to speak, and I raise my hand to shut him up. I need a moment to think. I need a minute to wrap my head around his screwy ideals. I lower my head, swallowing loudly. Is this what I am to him? A complication? *God, too much information is sometimes a bad thing.* I chew the inside of my lip in thought. "Why not just say friends with benefits or fuck buddies?"

Irritation flashes through his eyes, and he shifts restlessly, running his fingers through his hair, blatantly ignoring my comment. "You really want to know this, Rylee? The stipulations?" he asks.

I nod, biting down on my bottom lip, worrying it back and forth. "I'm curious," I say, in the back of my head thinking that a psychiatrist would have a field day with this conversation. "I guess I'm just trying to understand this. Trying to understand you. Trying to understand what exactly you *would have* expected from me." His eyebrows shoot up at my comment, and I know that he's heard me. My statement in past tense. That now he knows in no way will I be accepting his self-serving arrangement.

He sits down across from me, his eyes on mine. "What I *would have* expected from you?"

"Yes, your *requirements*," I say sarcastically.

He sighs tentatively, and I nod my head for him to get on with it. "I require monogamy. I require confidentiality, as my reputation as well as my family's is very important to me." He pauses, looking deeply at me, gauging to see if he should continue. "What else?" He breathes in deeply. "I require good hygiene, that she is healthy, drug free, and STD free. Birth control is a deal breaker since as I've told you, children are not now, nor will they ever be an option for me or my future."

He stops and I'm not sure if he's really done, or just thinking of more of his requirements. Ironically enough, I don't think his demands are all that odd. I mean it seems a little much to hammer out on a first date, but if I were to be in a committed relationship with someone, these are things I'd want to know. But then again, to me a committed relationship has the promise of a future, give and take, and the potential for love.

"So...wow!" I say, taking a moment, "that's quite a laundry list of requirements. Are there any more?"

"A few," he admits, "but I think we've exhausted this topic, don't you?"

I silently agree, but I've already delved this far, I might as well get the answers I want from him so I continue. "Oh, you must want to bypass the part where you have your *Pretty Woman* moment and leave the money on the nightstand after you've had your way with her." His eyes whip back up to mine, and I know that I've hit the nail on the head. "I mean, this is all on your terms. Let me guess, you don't actually sleep with her because it's too intimate? Or you buy her clothes and show her off in between bedding her and little do you know, she's using you to further her fledgling modeling career? What exactly is she getting out of this, Ace, besides a quick fuck with a guaranteed prick? And I'm not talking about the one in your pants." My stomach is a bit queasy all of the sudden, and I realize that I don't want to know these details. I don't want to hear what rules and regulations some floozy agrees to so that she can sleep with him and be seen on his arm.

I'm flustered. I'm in way over my head and way out of my element here. I understand that with his usual arrangements, they both use each other. I get that. He gets a companion and she gets the media buzz that might further her career. What I think hurts the most is that I have no intention of using him. I'm not a model or struggling actress. I worry that he dangled the rhetorical carrot in my face with the money for Corporate Cares. That way he can justify using me if he thinks I am using him.

I can feel the tears burn in the back of my throat. I'm so mad right now and oddly it's not at Colton. I'm mad at myself for believing—despite my false bravado that I didn't want anything to progress with Colton—deep down, I still had a touch of hope. Now I know way more than I want to and enough to know that what he's offering is not enough.

"But why, Colton? Why is this all that you'll allow yourself when you deserve so much more?" The look in his eyes tells me that the honesty behind my words affects him.

He puts his head in his hands, his shoulders moving as he sighs. He looks back up at me, a myriad of emotions on his face. "I hate the drama of it, Rylee. The points system of who is contributing how much, the jealousy over my lifestyle and the media surrounding it, the expectation of the next step to take. So many things." He pauses, eyeing me, his tone indifferent. "Relationships are just way too much shit to handle in my crazy life."

I stare into the depths of his eyes and can see right through the bullshit lies he's just tried to feed me. There is something more here. Why is he afraid to get too close to somebody? What happened to get him to this point? "That's a bullshit answer and you know it." He flinches. "I expected more from you."

"Rylee, I'm not one of your troubled kids that needs fixing. I've been fucked up for way too long to be fixed now, so don't get that look in your eye that you know different. Some of the best shrinks in L.A.

couldn't do it, so I doubt you'd be able to."

His words sting. The hurt from them sits heavy on my chest as he just sits staring at me. I can see him emotionally pulling away. The cold, detached look on his face tells me he is shutting down. Shutting me out when I'm still fighting for him. But for what?

I rise from the couch, pacing the living room as I try to process everything. The more I think, the angrier I get. "Tell me something, Colton?" I whirl back around. I'm a mix of random emotion. I want to go, to have him leave me alone, and yet I can't stop staring at the train wreck in front of me. Can't stop the part of me that wants to help him. "Is this what I am to you? Is this the type of *relationship*—and I use that term loosely—that you were hoping for between you and me?" I ask him, my voice wavering.

"Rylee, that's not what I—" He shakes his head, running both hands over his face, his emotional struggle being played out before my eyes. "At first, yes," he says, "but after this past week—after to-night—I'm just not sure anymore."

"What? Now I'm not good enough for you?" What the hell am I doing? One minute I'm mad that he thinks of me as a mutual agreement and the next I'm pissed that now he doesn't. *Get your head straight, Rylee!*

"Christ, Rylee!" he hisses as he stands abruptly, shoving a hand through his hair and stalking toward me. He reaches out to touch me, but thinks better of it when I shrug my shoulder back. "I don't know what I want." The muscle in his jaw twitches, and I can see the strain in his neck. He clenches and unclenches his fists, closing his eyes and sighing deeply before opening them up to meet my gaze again. I catch a fleeting glimpse of fear and then resolve before he reins it in. "But whatever this is, *I know I want it with you, Rylee.*"

I have to control the rush of feelings that flood through me from his words. He wants it with me. *What with me, though?* He is so close that I want to reach out and touch him. Calm that fear that I see in his eyes. But I know if I touch him, skin to skin, I will acquiesce to his ridiculous demands. And I know deep down, as much as I want him, I don't think I can be what he wants me to be.

"My way? My *arrangement* as you call it…" he shakes his head "… is all I know how to do, Rylee. Is all I know how to be." He reaches out to grab my hand, and I have to steel myself to not react to his touch. "It's all I can give you right now." The solemnity in his voice touches me deep down and twists in my heart.

I turn from him and walk the length of the room, grabbing his beer without thinking and taking a long swallow. I hate the flavor of beer but I don't even taste it. I'm tired. I'm hurt. And I can't fight the tears anymore. My eyes pool and a single tear falls over and runs down my cheek. My back is to him so I can't see the look on his face when I say, "I don't know if I can do this, Colton." I shake my head, sighing deeply.

"Rylee, don't be ridiculous."

"Ridiculous?" I sputter. "No, ridiculous is me thinking for a second that I *could* do this, Colton." I shrug my shoulders in sadness and resignation. "I walked into this—whatever we have here—telling myself that all you want is a quick fuck from me." I turn back to him as I speak and see him wince at my words. "Maybe a little fling ... and I thought I could give that to you. Take that from you. But now that you're actually offering it to me, I don't think I can." Another wayward tear falls, and I see him watch it before bringing his eyes back up to mine.

"What do you mean, Rylee?" His mask slips momentarily, and I see vulnerability and panic flutter over his face. "Why not?"

A small part of me relishes the idea that my threat can make him panic but staying is not going to fix things. I press my fingers to my eyes. I'm sure I look like hell right now: hair frizzed, eyeliner smudged, lipstick gone, but I really don't care. My insides are ten times more devastated than what my outside looks like. "When I tell myself that this is all I am to you—sex without feelings or the possibility of a future—it's one thing."

Without thinking I give into my addiction. I can't resist. I reach out and brush my fingers over his cheek. He starts to turn his cheek into my hand and catches himself before he does. I let my hand fall at his subtle rejection. "But when I hear the words from your lips. When I hear you tell me your *rules and regulations*, it's a whole different thing." I close my eyes momentarily, trying to stop the small tremor in my voice. "*I will not be inconsequential, Colton. To you or anyone else.*"

Colton runs a hand through his hair and scrubs his hands over his eyes. "That's not what you are to me, Rylee," he breathes, raising his eyes to me.

I stare at him. I want to believe him. I really do. But I can't sell myself short. I deserve more than this. I want more than what he's offering. "That may be true, Colton, but that admission, it's not enough for me." It breaks my heart to say these words to him.

"Rylee, just try it," he urges. "Try it my way."

"Oh save it, Colton!" I bite at him, throwing my hands up in the air. "I'm not one of your little floozies who's going to do whatever you say just because you say to. I'm sure you have those lining up waiting to be your plaything. Catch one of them and toss her back when you're tired of her. Not me, Ace. I don't work that way." My anger has resurfaced, despite my exhaustion and aching heart.

Colton just stares at me. We stand within a foot of each other, eyes locked, and yet I feel so far away from him. It's hard to believe it's been less than an hour since we were intimate.

"Rylee," he pleas.

"What, Colton?" I snap, immediately wincing from my tone.

"That first night …" he begins softly and then stops turning from me and walking toward the kitchen.

"What about it, Colton?" I follow him partway, leaning against the back of his couch. "I should have seen it then. You sleeping with me and then humiliating me by jumping out of bed like I'd burned you."

"You did, Rylee."

"What? What in the hell are you talking about?"

"That first night," he continues, ignoring my comment. "After the second time," he says, blowing out a loud breath. He continues to look at his bare feet, his hips resting against the counter, hands shoved in his pockets and discomfort rolling off him in waves. "I kissed you and asked you if you were all right." I nod my head acknowledging him, remembering the raw honesty in that simple moment between us. "I swear to God, Rylee … I felt like you saw me. *Really saw me.*" He raises his eyes to meet mine and they're swimming with emotion. "And you were sitting there, your dark hair falling all around you with that white sheet pooled around your waist…" he shakes his head before continuing "…your lips were swollen, your eyes were so wide and trusting … and I realized in that second that it meant more to me." His voice is hoarse with emotion. "That you meant more to me, Rylee, than anything I can remember. *Ever*."

I stare at him, so many things running through my head, but more than anything, his words resonate in every dark part of me that craves to be wanted, needed, and desired. At least I know why he reacted how he did. Why he showed up this morning. Hope starts to soar in me. Maybe I can do this. Maybe with time, I can prove to him that there can be more. I wring my hands to try and stifle my sudden enthusiasm.

"You scared the shit out of me, Rylee. *You burned me*." He runs his hand through his hair, his eyes darkening, "And then I realized, as I do right now, that in the end I'm going to break you apart."

"What?" I snap my head up to meet his eyes, my hopes crashing down around me. *Did I just hear him correctly?*

"I can't do that to you, Rylee." I see his fists clench as he fights his emotions. "I tried to warn you, but I'm so frickin' drawn to you. I just can't stay away."

I feel schizophrenic trying to keep up with his moods. "You tell me you can't do this, that you'll destroy me, but then you tell me you can't stay away even though you are the one warning me. You push me away then show up at my doorstep and give me tonight." I walk toward him in the kitchen until I stand in front of him. "Which way is up, Colton?"

Without a word, he grabs me and pulls me against his chest, wraps his arms tightly around me, and buries his nose in my hair. I press my hands against his back and absorb his warmth, surprised by his unexpected show of emotion. His need for me is palpable. It oozes off of him and wraps its way into my soul. It takes everything I have to not tell him yes. Tell him I'll do anything just to have a piece of him. That is how much he means to me. But my thoughts are louder than my heart. I wish that I could just quiet my head and sink into the reassuring feeling of his arms. Block out everything else.

"I'm going to hurt you, Rylee. And you already mean too much to me to do that to you." I stiffen at his words. But despite them, he holds me tighter. I try to push away from him but his arms will not release me. I relent eventually and lay my face against his chest, inhale the smell of us mingled together, feel the coarseness of the hair on his chest, and hear the strong, steady beat of his heart. "It's a first for me to care enough about someone to stop. But knowing it ahead of time isn't going to stop me from doing it. And I just can't do that to you, Rylee." His chest heaves a long breath. "And that's why I can't do this anymore with you. Why we can't …"

"But why, Colton? Why can't you? Why can't we?" I'm panicked now. Now that I want him, he's telling me no. Or maybe that's exactly why. I'm grasping at straws now.

"Look, let's not get this confused here. I'm not and never have been the boy you bring home to mom, Ry. I'm the one you throw in her face to piss her off and show her you are asserting your independence. Let's not make me out to be better than I am."

I'm still not buying it. Why does he think so horribly of himself? He can repeat this crappy answer ad nauseam and I still won't believe it. "Who did this to you?"

We're quiet for a few moments as he mulls over my questions. Eventually he sighs. "I told you, Rylee, I've got a 747 of baggage."

I push against his chest. I need to see his eyes. Need to look into them. When I do, I can see he's hurting too. But he's also shutting down. Putting me at arm's distance emotionally so that it prevents further hurt in him. *But what about me?* I want to scream at him. What about my hurt? Why does this have to be so complicated? Why can't I just let it be and enjoy the ride? Hope that he'll see the real me and fall in love? Because I know that if he doesn't face whatever trauma has made him this way, he'll never get over it. He'll never be able to have a normal relationship. He's right. His 747 of baggage is going to ruin whatever chance we may have. "I'm not buying it, Colton."

With my words, he removes his hands from my arms, now physically distancing himself from me. "I can't give you any more, Rylee." He looks down and then looks back up, the mask effectively in place. "This is who I am."

Tears pool in my eyes, my voice a whisper. "*And this is who I am, Colton.*" When I speak those words I know. I have already started to fall for him. Warts and all. Somehow, someway, despite the short amount of time I've spent with him, he has penetrated that protective wall around my heart, and I've started the slow descent toward love.

And that's why I know I can't do this. I can't walk knowingly into heartbreak. I've been devastated once. I don't think I can survive that again. And I know without a doubt that loving Colton and not getting love in return would devastate me.

"I guess we're at an impasse." His voice is gruff and he stuffs his hands in his pockets. The weight of his hands causes his jeans to hang lower on his hips. I have to physically stop myself from looking at the sexy inverted triangle of muscles that peeks over his waistband. I don't need a reminder of what is no longer mine.

"Then I guess it's time for you to take me home." I avert my eyes, unable to meet his as I choke the words out.

"Rylee …" he says.

"I deserve more than this, Colton," I whisper, raising my eyes to meet his, "and so do you."

I can see his hands grip the kitchen counter as he digests my words, his knuckles white, and his face twisted in anguish. "Please, Rylee. Stay the night."

I hear the desperation in his voice, know that he really means it, but I know he is asking for the wrong reasons. He is asking to ease the hurt he knows he is causing me, not because he wants to make this more than the arrangement he desires.

"We both know that's not how this story goes." A tear slides down my cheek. "I'm sorry I can't be what you want me to be. Please take me home, Colton."

The ride home is silent. Adele's velvety voice sings softly on the radio about never finding someone like you, and deep down I feel the same way. It would be hard to compare anyone to Colton. I glance at him occasionally, watching the shadows and lights of the night play over the angles of his face. I know I am doing the right thing, self-preservation at its best, but my heart still aches at the thought of walking away from this mesmerizing man.

We arrive at my house with fewer than ten words spoken between us. Oddly, I'm still comfortable with Colton's presence despite my inner-turmoil.

He opens my door and escorts me out with a sad half-smile on his lips. He places his hand on my lower back as we walk up the walk-way. At the front door, lit by a lone porch light, I turn to him. We both say each other's names at the same time and then smile softly at each other. The smiles never reach our eyes though. They reflect a weary sadness.

"You first," I tell him.

He sighs and just stares at me. I want so much for him to be able to express to me the emotions I can see swimming in his eyes, but I know that he'll never get the chance to tell me. He reaches out and brushes his knuckles over my cheek with the back of his hand. I close my eyes at the sensation. When he stops, I open them back up, tears pooling in them, to meet his. "I'm sorry," he whispers.

I know that his apology is for so many things. For what can never be. For what should be. For hurting me. For not being the person I need him to be. For not being able to confront whatever is in his past.

"I know." I reach up and run my fingers over his unshaven jaw and up through his wavy hair before returning back to his face. It's almost as if I am committing his lines and his features to memory. Something I can hold on to. For despite still having to work with him, I know that this will be the last time I'll allow myself to touch him. Touching him will be too dangerous for my weakened heart.

I step up on my tiptoes and brush my lips gently against his. Within moments, Colton has his arms around me and is lifting me up to his level. Our eyes lock on each other. He leans into me to resume our kiss. I feel something different in it. I realize that we are saying an unspoken goodbye. All of the hurt and unspoken possibilities are thrown into the unyielding softness of our exchange. The desperation and carnal need of earlier has been replaced with a poignant resigna-tion. We slowly end the kiss, Colton gently lowers me, my body slid-ing down the familiar length of his. Once my feet are on the ground, he rests his forehead against mine. Our eyes remain closed as we take in this last moment with each other.

I move my hand between our bodies and place it over his heart, our foreheads still touching. "I wish you'd explain to me why you don't do relationships, Colton." My voice is barely a whisper, the threat of tears evident. "Maybe I could understand you—this—better then."

"I know," he breathes in response. He shifts and places his trademark kiss on the tip of my nose.

This action is my undoing. Tears silently coarse down my cheeks as Colton whispers, "Goodbye," before turning without looking back at me and hurrying down the pathway.

I can't bear to watch him leave. I fumble clumsily with the lock before shoving the door open and slamming it shut. I lean against the door and slide down it to sit on the floor, my silent tears turning into uncontrollable sobs.

This is how Haddie finds me moments later after being woken by my less-than-graceful entrance.

Chapter Eighteen

THE WEEK HAS SUCKED. My applicants for the new staff position at The House have been horrible. Unqualified. Underwhelming. Unexciting.

It might not help that my mind is not all here. I'm tired because sleep comes in short bouts interrupted by confusing nightmares of Colton and Max. My subconscious is obviously having a field day with my emotions.

I'm cranky because I'm eating everything in sight, and yet I have no desire to go run and work off all of the excess calories that I'm stuffing in my mouth to abate my misery.

I'm irritable because Haddie is watching me like a hawk, calling me every hour to check up on me, and turning off Matchbox Twenty anytime she catches me listening to it.

I'm petulant because Teddy just forwarded me an email from Tawny listing all of the events that CD Enterprises is requesting my presence at to promote our new partnership. And that means that I will have to stand side by side with Colton, the sole cause of my miserable state. Because despite the four days that have passed, nothing has helped to ease the ache radiating through my heart and soul from my last moments with Colton. I want to tell myself to get a grip, that we only knew each other a short time, but nothing works.

I still want him. I still feel him.

I'm pathetic.

The only personal contact I've had with him came via email the day after he dropped me off. He sent me a text saying:

***Whataya Want From Me* by Adam Lambert.**

I listened to the song, confused by the lyrics. He's telling me that we're not going to happen and yet he sends me a song asking me not to give up while he works his shit out. A part of me is pleased that he's still communicating, while another part of me is sad that he just won't let me lick my wounds by myself. I wasn't even going to respond until I heard the song playing on Shane's radio. I texted back:

***Numb* by Usher**

I was trying to tell him that until he confronts his same old modus operandi, nothing's ever going to change, and he's going to remain numb. He never replied, and I didn't expect him to.

I sigh loudly, alone at the kitchen counter at The House. Zander is at a counseling session with Jackson, and the rest of the boys are at school for another two hours. I'm on my last stack of resumes . One applicant is coming for an interview, but besides her, I've come across no one else even close to qualified.

The muffled sound of my cell phone ringing breaks me out of my trance. I scramble frantically to pick it up, my heart racing, hoping that it might be Colton even though we have not talked since Sunday night. My mind tells me it's not going to be him while my heart still hopes that it is.

My screen says *private caller* and I answer it with a breathless "Hello."

"Rylee?"

My heart swells at the rasp of his voice. Shock has me hesitating to respond. Pride has me wanting to make sure that the hitch in my voice is absent when I finally speak. "Ace?"

"*Hi, Rylee.*" The warmth mixed with relief in his voice has me shaking with an undercurrent of emotions.

"*Hi, Colton.*" I reply, my tone matching his.

He chuckles softly at my response before silence fills the phone line. He clears his throat. "I was just calling to let you know a car will pick you up at The House on Sunday at nine-thirty." His voice, so full of warmth moments before, is now disembodied and official sounding.

"Oh. Okay." I sag in my chair, overcome by disappointment that he's just calling to reiterate the email one of his staff members sent two days ago. I can hear him breathing on the line and can hear voices in the distance.

"You still have a total of ten, right? Seven boys and three counselors?"

"Yes." My tone is clipped, business-like. My only form of protection against him. "They are extremely excited about it."

"Cool."

Silence hangs in the air. I need to think of something to say so he doesn't hang up. Despite the tension between us, knowing he is on the other end of the line is better than him not being there at all. I know my line of thinking screams "desperate," but I don't care. My brain scrambles to form a sentence, and right when I say his name, Colton says mine. We laugh.

"Sorry, you go first, Colton." I try to rid my voice of the nerves that creep their way into my tone.

"How are you, Rylee?"

Miserable. Missing you. I infuse happiness into my next words, glad he's not in front of me to read through my lie. "Good. Fine. Just busy. You know."

"Oh. I'm sorry. I'll let you go."

No! Not yet! My mind grasps to think of something to keep him on the phone. "Are-are you … ready for Sunday?"

"We're getting there." I think I hear a tinge of relief in his voice but chock it up to my imagination. "The car seems to be working great. We've made some adjustments to the lift/drag ratio, which seems to be working better." I can hear the enthusiasm in his voice. "We'll dial it in more on Sunday. And Beckett, my crew chief, thinks we need to adjust the camber, and you asked me why I don't do relationships."

What? Whoa! Direction change. I don't know what to say so I just murmur, "Hmm-hmmm," afraid that if I speak, it might reveal to him just how much I want to know, and at the same time, afraid to find out.

I can hear him sigh on the other end of the phone, and I imagine him running his hands through his hair. His voice is hushed when he finally speaks. "Let's just say my early childhood … those years were … more fucked up than not." I can sense his apprehension.

"Before you were adopted?" I know the answer, but it's the only thing I can think to say without him thinking I feel pity for him. And silence would be even worse.

"Yes, before I was adopted. As a result … I … how do I …?" He struggles to find the right words. I hear another exhaled breath before he continues. "I sabotage anything that resembles a relationship. If things are going too well … depending on which shrink you talk to, I purposely, unknowingly, or subconsciously ruin it. Screw it up. Hurt the other person." It all comes out in a quick jumble of words. "Just ask my poor parents." A self-deprecating laugh slips out. "Growing up, I fucked them over more times than I care to count."

"Oh … I … Colton—"

"I'm hardwired this way, Rylee. I'll purposely do something to hurt you to prove that I can. To prove that you won't stick around regardless of the consequences. To prove that I can control the situation. To avoid getting hurt."

So many things run through my mind. Most of them are about the unspoken words he's saying. That his history makes him test the limits of the person he's with to prove he's not worthy of their love. To prove they'll leave him too. My heart aches for him and for whatever unknown thing that happened to him as a child. On the other hand, he has opened up to me some, partially answering the question I asked against his lips on my front porch.

"I told you, a 747 of baggage sweetheart."

"It doesn't matter, Colton."

"Yes it does, Rylee." He laughs nervously. "I won't commit to anyone. It's just easier on everyone in the long run."

"Ace, you're not the first guy I've known with commitment issues," I joke, trying to add some levity to our conversation. But deep down I know that his inability to commit stems from something way deeper than just typical male reluctance.

I hear his nervous laugh again. "Rylee?"

"Yes?"

"I respect you and your need for the commitment and the emotion that comes with a relationship." He pauses, silence stretching between us as he finds his next words. "I really do. I'm just not built that way … so don't feel bad. This would've never worked."

My hope, which has been rising despite my trying to control it, crashes back down. "I don't understand. I just—"

"What?" Colton says distracted, talking to a voice I hear in the background. "Saved by the bell! I'm needed on the track right now. More fine tuning." I can hear the relief in his voice.

"Oh. Okay." Disappointment fills me. I want to finish this conversation.

"No hard feelings then? I'll see you at the track on Sunday?"

I momentarily close my eyes, fortifying my voice with false nonchalance. "Sure. No hard feelings. See you on Sunday."

"See ya, Ryles."

The phone clicks and the dial tone fills my ear. I sit there not hearing it. Does he realize that he used his defense mechanism right now? Hurt me to keep me away? Put me in my place so that he can have all the control.

I'm unsettled. I want to finish our conversation. Tell him that it doesn't have to be this way. I want to comfort him. Ease the panic that laces his voice. Tell him that he makes me feel again after being numb for so very long. Confess that I want to be with him despite knowing deep down I will be destroyed in the end.

I pick up my phone, pondering what I'm going to say. In the end, all I text is:

Be safe on the track Ace!

He responds quickly.

Always. You know I've got great hands.

I smile sadly. My heart wanting so much that my head knows I'll never get.

Chapter Nineteen

THE LIMO BUS PULLS THROUGH the gates of Auto Club Speedway in Fontana. The boys are buzzing with excitement, eyes wide as saucers taking in the sheer size of the complex. They have put on their shirts and all access lanyards that Colton's staff has left aboard the bus for them. Their wide smiles and their constant *oohs and aahs* fill the air and fill my heart with joy. Zander bounces unexpectedly on the seat, vibrating with an obvious energy that takes me by surprise. I look at Jackson and Dane, my fellow counselors, and note that they see it too.

For the first time in almost a week, I feel like I can smile, and ironically, it's Colton that has made me feel this way. I'm thankful to him for the little touches he has added for the boys: a personalized letter, the shirts, the lanyards, and glossy magazines with his car on the cover. Things that make them feel special. Important.

Our bus is directed down a tunnel under the stands before driving onto the infield. I didn't think it possible, but the boys' hooting and hollering becomes even louder. We come to a stop and the doors open. Within moments, a man hops on the bus, bounding with enthusiasm. He directs us off of the bus and has us follow him to a meeting room where he tells us we will meet up with Colton.

I feel small walking through this large arena. To the south of us, a large grandstand juts up to towering heights while the banked oval of the track encompasses the entire field around us. I can hear engines revving and see people scurrying to and fro in a garage on my right. With each step we take, my anxiety about seeing Colton again increases. How is he going to react after his telephone confession to me? Will it be business as usual or will there still be that magnetic pull between us? Despite my anxiety, I'm also excited to see Colton in action. To watch him in his element.

We arrive at a brick building and our facilitator, who we've learned on our walk is named Davis, leads us into a room with a red door. We heed his advice to gather around, the boys chattering excitedly. They call out random questions to Davis who patiently answers them.

When they settle down a bit, Davis explains the reason for testing. "When we're testing, a lot of time goes into tweaking the car. Little adjustments here and there that makes the car go faster or handle better. These changes are essential to the overall performance of the car when the season starts in late March. Along with these tweaks, Colton meets with his crew chief, Beckett Daniels, and reviews what they are working on. That is where Colton currently is now, discussing—"

"Not anymore." Chills dance up my spine as I hear the rumble of Colton's voice. Whoops go up as the boys greet him. I look down at Zander and the wide, genuine grin on his face causes my heart to lodge in my throat.

"Hey, guys!" he throws back at them. "So glad you're here! Are you guys ready for a fun day?"

The cheers go up again as I inhale deeply, preparing myself to turn around and face him. When I do, my heart squeezes tightly. Colton is on his haunches, eye level with the little guys of our group, and ruffling the hair on their heads playfully. He laughs sincerely at something Scooter says and then stands slowly, lifting his eyes, locking them with mine.

All thoughts leave my head as I drink him in. He's wearing a red fire safety suit, the top portion unzipped and tied around his waist to reveal a snug-fitting white t-shirt with a faded logo across the chest and a small hole in the left shoulder. His hair is a spiked mess and his jaw sports the shadow of a day's missed shave. My thoughts immediately focus on how much I'd love to run my tongue over his lips and fist my hands in his hair.

I bite my bottom lip, the quick pain a reminder that this is not going to happen—we're not going to happen—and to help me resist any urges that I might have of thinking otherwise. Colton's eyes stay locked on mine as the boys I love surround him. A slow, lazy grin spreads on his face.

All thoughts of resistance vanish. Shit! I'm in so over my head.

"Hello, Rylee." So much is behind those two words. All of the hurt and confusion and over-analyzing from the past couple of days disintegrates. In case I didn't know it before, it's obvious now that his proximity clouds both my judgment and my common sense.

"Hi." My nervous response is all I can manage as we continue to hold each other's gazes, as if we are the only two people in the room. I fidget with my hands, trying to ignore the desire blooming in my core. Kyle tugs on his hand, and after a beat, he drags his gaze away from me to focus back on the boys.

I slowly exhale the breath I didn't know I was holding. Dane scoots near me and leans in. "Damn, Rylee! What the hell's going on here?" I give him a bemused look, as if I don't know what he's talking about. "If I didn't know any better, that stare said he wanted to eat you for dessert." I laugh at him, nudging him playfully, trying to avoid having to answer. And to hide the blush crawling into my cheeks, remembering Colton's version of cotton candy dessert. "The man obviously wants you, girl!"

"Oh, whatever! You read the tabloids, Dane. He's a total player. I'm sure he gives that look to every woman." I'm grateful for the distraction when Zander sidles up next to me, and I place my hand on his shoulder. Colton notices and looks up from the other boys to meet Zander's eyes. He moves from the crowd of boys and walks over to kneel in front of us.

"Hiya, Zander. I'm so glad you could come today." Colton remains still, watching and waiting for an indication from Zander about how he should proceed.

I suck in a breath as I hear a hoarse sound from Zander's mouth. A croaked, "Hi," comes out and the cautious smile on Colton's face spreads to a megawatt grin. A tear trickles down my cheek, and I quickly dash it away, looking over to Dane and Jackson to see relief and pride on their faces as well.

Zander spoke his first word!

Colton clears his throat, and I think the moment may have gotten to him too. "So I'm going to need special help from you later, if that's okay?" When Zander nods, Colton slowly reaches out, showing Zander the intention of his actions, and when he doesn't flinch, Colton gently tousles his hair.

Colton glances up to me as he stands, and the tears swimming in my eyes are for both Zander's reaction and because of the man before me. Over everything that can't be with him. He gives me a resigned, knowing smile before turning his focus back on the other six boys. "So guys, are you ready to head down to the pits, check out the car, and get ready to test it all out?" Colton staggers back playfully at the roar of the boys' consent. "I take that as a yes!" He laughs.

Out of the corner of my eye, I notice a statuesque blonde enter the room with a clipboard in one hand, a worn baseball cap in the other, and an official-looking pass around her neck. She leans against the doorjamb watching Colton and must feel my stare on her because she turns, slowly eying me up and down. Her eyes finally meet mine, a small smirk on her lips and a less than friendly look in her eyes. And then it dawns on me who she is. She's Tawny Taylor: sometimes escort, CD Enterprises employee, and who knows what else to Colton. I bristle at the realization; her lengthy legs, sample size figure, long blonde hair, and stunning face making me feel beyond insecure. Why would Colton chase someone like me when he could have someone like her?

Colton looks over at her as she says his name in her throaty voice, interrupting his answer to Shane's question. "Just a minute, boys." He excuses himself and walks over to where she stands.

She holds out the battered baseball cap, and he runs a hand through his hair before placing it on his head. I hear their quiet voices and make out a few words in between the yells of my boys. Colton holds his hands on his hips, broad shoulders filling out the faded T-shirt, as he nods his head at Tawny. Her smile is wide, knowing, and when she reaches a hand out to place it on Colton's upper arm, I hate her immediately. My ears perk as I hear my name. *What?* Tawny glances over at me quickly before returning to Colton. It seems as if they are wrapping things up, so I busy myself by paying attention to the posters hanging on the walls. I hear Colton say, "Thanks," before returning to his audience. Tawny turns for the door and notices me studying her. She flashes me an insincere, catty smile as she walks out the door. Her smile says it all. Colton's her territory, and I'm just an intruder.

Well, game on, sweetheart!

With Tawny gone and at least one adversary known, I turn my attention back to Colton, who is telling the boys what to expect from testing. He patiently and simply answers their questions. Zander stands closely to Colton, engaged in watching the conversation, his eyes never leaving his face. When he finishes, Davis glances at his watch and pipes up, "Okay, guys, I'm going to lead you down to the pits. You guys can sit in the seats right above so you can see everything. We're also going to get you outfitted with headsets so that you can hear us talking back and forth with Colton." He grabs his clipboard and turns toward the door, "So if you'll follow me, we'll get you all set!"

The boys fidget animatedly as they fall into line behind Davis. I grab my bag and start to follow, anxiety rising at the possibility of being alone with Colton. I usually have strong will power but when it comes to Colton, it's nonexistent. I take my first step when I hear his voice behind me. "Can I have a sec, Ry?"

I ignore the raised eyebrows that Dane gives me before turning and following the boys out the door. Not trusting my voice, I figure that my lack of forward movement is enough of an answer for Colton.

"It's good to see you." His voice is gruff.

I take a deep breath and close my eyes momentarily, trying to clear the emotion from my face and remove my heart from my sleeve. I slowly turn around, a falsely calm smile on my lips as I remind myself of his words from the other day. The full force of the devastating effect he has on me hits me when I meet his eyes.

This would've never worked. "You too, Ace."

He's sitting on the edge of a table, one foot resting on the seat of the chair in front of him, his hands twirling his sunglasses. My heart twists at the sight of him, knowing I can have some of him but not the whole I need. I walk toward him, our chemistry irrefutable and his pull on me magnetic. I smile shyly at him, trying to keep my emotions under wraps. I stop in front of him, my fingers itching to touch. His eyes watch my hand as I reach out and wipe off an imaginary piece of lint from his shirt. "You look so official!" I laugh anxiously, saying the only thing that comes to my mind.

He cocks his head and raises an eyebrow at me. "What? You think I'm faking it and this is all for show?" he says dryly, rising from the table. When he unfolds himself and stands to his full height, his body is mere inches from mine. His scent envelops me and I take a step back to prevent myself from reaching out to touch him again. Any measure to try and preserve my dignity.

"No. That's not what I meant." I shake my head flustered, stepping back again to create some space. "Being here just makes it all so real— the track, seeing you in your suit, the grandstands … the enormity of it all." I shrug. "Thank you so much, Colton." With these words I look down at my hands where I instinctively go to worry the ring that's no longer on my finger. Instead, I lace my fingers together and try to hide the emotion swarming in my eyes.

"For what?"

"You went over and above. The stuff in the bus for the kids. Having them here today. Everything." I look back up at him, tears of happiness swimming in my eyes, and say softly, "Zander's first word."

"A breakthrough is so important to healing invisible wounds." I know he understands these words more than most. He reaches out and wipes the lone tear that spills over. That simple act of compassion leaves me shaken. His eyes meet mine, and I can see the feelings he has for me. I just wish he could see them himself. He slips his sunglasses on his face, shielding my ability to read more, and holds his hand out to me. "Come walk me to the pits?"

When I just stand there staring at him, confused, he answers for me by grabbing my hand. We walk in silence, both occupied by our thoughts. So many questions I want to ask remain unspoken, for this is not the right time or place for them. I place a hand on my stomach to settle the nerves fluttering there.

"Why do you seem so nervous when I'm the one that's going to be hurling myself around the track at two hundred miles an hour?"

I stop and look at him and am unable to see through his dark lenses, wondering if he really doesn't get that spending time with him, being with him when I can't have him, does this to me. Has me walking on eggshells and thinking of what ifs. I decide to take the easy way out. "I'm nervous for you. Aren't you ever afraid that you are going to crash?"

"Oh, I've crashed plenty of times, Ryles." He lifts his sunglasses so that our eyes meet. "Sometimes you need to crash a couple of times to learn your mistakes, and then when the smoke clears, sometimes you're better off in the end. Lesson learned in case there is a next time." He shrugs, squeezing my hand and smiling shyly. "Besides, sometimes the dents just add more character in the long run. Looking pretty can only last so long." Our eyes hold each other's, and I know he is talking about more than racing. My eyes beseech his, silently asking the questions I'm afraid to voice, but he slips his glasses back on, pretending he didn't see them. He tugs on my hand again to start walking.

I try to think of something to say to add some levity to our walk. "Aren't you supposed to have a pre-race face on or something indicating you're *in the zone*?"

"Something like that." He laughs at me. "But it's not a race today. Besides, I usually get that way once I walk onto pit row. It pisses my sister off to no end."

"Why's that?"

"Because I can just tune everything and everyone out instantly," he says wryly, a small smile on his beautiful lips.

"Typical male." I laugh shaking my head. "Thanks for the warning, Ace."

"And she says I look mean. I try and tell her it's just part of my job but she doesn't buy it." We walk for a bit more in silence, a smile on my lips. I can hear an engine revving to my left and hear the clatter of a wrench on concrete somewhere to my right. "I wasn't sure if you were going to come today." His words surprise me. I think I do a pretty good job of hiding it on my face. "I thought you might send another counselor in your place instead."

"No," I murmur as we stop at the corner of a building, and I look up at him. Doesn't he realize that even when he pushes me away I am irrefutably drawn to him? That I couldn't stay away even if I wanted to? "I wanted to see you in your element. Watch the boys experience it."

He watches me for a moment, nodding at someone who walks past before returning his eyes to mine. "I'm glad you're here."

"Me too," I mouth back to him, fighting the urge to avert my eyes from the intensity of his.

"This is as far as I go," he tells me, leaning back against the wall, propping one foot back behind him.

"Oh." He runs his thumb over my knuckles on the hand he is holding.

A slow mischievous smile spreads across his lips. "Don't I get a good luck kiss, Rylee?" He tugs on my hand and has me falling against him. He splays his free hand against my back, holding me up against him.

His warnings, his mixed signals, the hurt he's caused all vanish when my eyes flutter up to see his sensual lips inches from mine. Every muscle beneath my waist clenches in desire. I close my eyes momentarily, wetting my lips with my tongue, before opening them back up to meet the clear green of Colton's. *Why the hell not?* It's not like the term levelheaded has been in my vocabulary the past few weeks when it comes to him anyway. Sensibility slips through my fingers like sand when I am near him.

"It's the least I can do," I murmur as he removes his baseball cap.

All sense of reason and modesty at our surroundings vanish the minute his lips capture mine. I pour all of the pent up hurt and emotion and need from the past few days into our kiss, and I know that I can taste the same from him. The pressure of his hand on my back urges me on, tempts me to run my hands up his chest, skim fingers on his neckline, and tangle in his hair curling at the back of his neck. Our hearts pound against each other as we each take what we need, regardless of the impasse we find ourselves at.

Our surroundings slowly seep into my consciousness as I hear someone shout out, "Get a room, Donavan!"

I feel Colton's smile against my lips as he breaks the kiss and turns his head to the right and yells laughing, "Fuck off, Tyler! You're just jealous!"

I hear a loud chuckle as Colton turns his head back to me, and I run my hands down to frame his face. "Good luck, Ace!"

We stare at each other a beat before he leans back down and brushes a tender kiss on my lips. A silent goodbye and now I am more confused then ever. "Remind me to bring you to my next race?"

"What? Why?"

"Because if that's how you kiss me good luck when I'm just test-ing, I can't wait to see what it's like when I'm really racing!" He raises his eyebrows, a playful smile turning the corners of his mouth, and he squeezes his hands around my waist. I laugh out loud.

"Colton?"

I turn to look into the startled eyes of a stunning woman a few feet to our left. She has a classic beauty that reminds me a lot of Had-die. She has tendrils of blonde hair that cascade around her shoulders, her caramel colored eyes regard me pensively, and her full, painted lips purse as she takes me in. I feel a punch in the stomach. Despite being pressed against Colton, in the split second I have to size her up, I can see true adoration and love in her eyes toward him. Something about her is different though, and the feelings I see in her eyes are much more intense than Tawny's or Raquel's.

Will the endless barrage of women in love with Colton ever end?

"Impeccable timing as usual," Colton says through gritted teeth without even looking at her. I look back at him, slightly confused as he kisses the tip of my nose and pulls back. "Rylee, meet my annoying little sister, Quinlan."

"Oh!" This makes sense now! I extricate myself from Colton's arms, the interruption not allowing me to even think about our inti-mate exchange. I hold out my hand in greeting, my cheeks blushing at the thought of the first impression she must have of me. "Hi. I'm Rylee Thomas."

Quinlan looks me up and down and then to my outstretched hand before eyeing Colton, an incredulous expression on her face. She shakes her head at him, a warning look in her eye as she com-pletely disregards my hand. I let it fall as Colton sighs a warning to her. "Quin?" She just looks at him like a mother does when scorning her child. He glares back at her. "Q, quit being rude. I'll be right there. I'm a little busy right now."

She snorts rudely, surveying me again before turning on her heel and stalking off the way she came. "Sorry," he mutters, "she can be an annoying little punk sometimes, regardless of how old she is." And with those words, for some reason, I think I get it. She thinks I'm one of Colton's little disposable playthings. And she acted how I probably would act if it were my brother. Disgusted. Fed up.

"It's okay." I step back from him. "You need to get going."

"That I do." He nods, running his fingers through his hair.

"Be safe, Colton. I'll see you at the finish line."

"Always," he says before flashing a quick, roguish smile at me and then turning to walk toward the pits. I watch his sexy swagger as he tugs his baseball hat on his head and adjusts it. He turns back to look at me, the bill of his hat shadowing his eyes and a wayward grin on his lips, *dangerous* written all over him. If nothing else, he is the definition of sexy. I sigh, shaking my head as I instinctively smile at him. He turns back around, and I watch him until I can't see him any more.

How do I even begin to process the last fifteen minutes?

Chapter Twenty

"OKAY, BOYS, I THINK THAT last wing adjustment dialed it in. Great job! I'm going full throttle for the last twenty starting next time I hit the line," Colton's disembodied voice comes over the headset as we watch him on the stretch of track behind us.

"Don't push too hard, Colt. We'll need to make a couple more adjustments for next time out. I don't want you burning up the motor before we can mess with it."

"Relax, Becks." Colton laughs. "I'm not gonna break your baby." I can hear the engine rev up on the backstretch as Colton heads out of turn two. "Davis? You on?"

"What do you need, Wood?" Davis' voice fills my ears. *Wood? What's that all about?*

On the open mic, I can hear the car downshift as he heads into turn three. "Get Zander in the flag stand." I can hear the vibration of the car in Colton's voice as he increases his speed. "Let him wave. Then the rest of the boys."

"Ten-four."

The boys are all listening on their headsets and they turn to look at me with eyes big and grins wide. Davis climbs up the stairs to the little box where we sit above pit row and motions for the boys to follow him. Dane descends and then Jax looks back at me, eyebrows raised in question. "Go ahead, Jax," I motion for him to go as I remain seated. "I'll stay here."

I watch the boys make their way to pit row, heads turned to the right as Colton comes flying out of turn four toward the start-finish line. The rumble of the engine fills my ears and vibrates through my body, reverberating in my chest as he whips past us. Once gone, Davis leads them across the track and they disappear as they head to the flag stand. Moments later, Davis climbs into the little white boxed in platform with Zander at his side, and they wait for Colton to come back around the track again. I can hear the pitch of the motor heighten as Colton hits the accelerator down the backstretch. Before I know it, he is completing the two-mile circuit and tearing down the front straight away before me. Zander's hands are on the flag, and Davis cautiously helps his little arms wave it as Colton approaches and quickly zips past. I capture his smile with my camera before he heads back down the stairs for Aiden to have his turn.

It has been an incredible day. The boys have gotten a once-in-a-lifetime experience, thanks to Colton and his team. I've been interviewed by reporters from the Los Angeles Times and the Orange County Register about the fundraising collaboration of CD Enterprises on behalf of Corporate Cares. A photographer took pictures of us while we were watching the test laps. The boys have been filled with sugary treats as well as great food that Colton's team brought in for us. We've been treated better than I ever could've imagined, especially considering this was not a race or official engagement.

I snap a shot of Shane as he waves the flag when Colton passes by, pleased that I perfectly captured the look of joy in his face. When I look up from the digital image on my camera, Tawny is standing in front of me, a cool, calculating look in her frosty blue eyes. I give her a cautious but courteous smile.

When she continues to stand there and stare at me, I decide to make the first move. Her attempt at intimidation is ineffective. I just pray that for once in my life I can have that quick wit I always think about after the fact because I think I'm going to need it. "Can I help you?"

She crosses her arms across her ample bosom and leans a hip against the railing, her eyes never leaving mine. "You know you're not his typical type, right?"

Oh, so that's how this is going to be. I watch Colton come down the straightaway and wait for the deafening sound to pass us before pulling my headphones off. I lean back in my seat and allow the knowing smirk I feel to ghost my lips—the ones that Colton's lips had been on earlier. "And your point is what? That you are?" I cringe inwardly at my last comment, because I know that she actually does fit the Colton pre-approved mold. *So much for being witty.*

She laughs snidely. "*Oh, doll,* your innocent little self has no clue what you're getting yourself into, do you?"

Condescending bitch! "And what? If I had all of the experience that you do, I would?" My voice drips with sarcasm. "Let's get something straight, what's between Colton and me is none of your business. And I'm more than capable of taking care of myself, Tawny. Thanks for your misguided concern, though."

She stares at me through the slits of her eyelids, her face twisting in amusement. "Oh, Rylee, *everything Colton does is my business.* I make sure of it."

I stare at her momentarily, stunned by her impudence and wondering if there is any truth behind her words. I try to hide the bewilderment in my voice with cynicism. "I wasn't aware he needed a keeper. He seems quite capable of making decisions for himself." I cross my arms over my chest, mirroring her.

"You don't know anything, do you?" She laughs cattily, her patronizing tone grating on my nerves. "Every man needs a woman whispering in his ear, telling him what's best for him." She smirks. "And, *Rylee, doll,* I'm that person to Colton. Have been…" she arches an eyebrow "…and will continue to be."

I plug my ears as Colton comes back around again, thankful for the brief moment to let her comments sink in. "I'm pretty sure Colton doesn't let anyone tell him what to do, Tawny. Nice try, though."

If she laughs that annoying know-it-all laugh one more time, I'm going to strangle her. "You just keep thinking that, doll." She taps an acrylic nail to her perfectly white teeth. "And before you know it, you'll think you've reeled him in. And despite his little spiel about not wanting a girlfriend, you'll think he actually wants more with you. That you can change him and his ways. You'll think that you've tamed that rebellion and topped him and his domineering ways." She turns to watch him fly down the backstretch of the track before turning back to me and taking a step closer. "And just when that happens, you'll be over quicker than that lap he just clocked. You don't have what it takes to keep him. He gets bored quickly." Her eyebrows rise as she studies me. "Oh, my God!" She gasps, putting a hand over her mouth to hide her smarmy smile. "You've already fucked him, haven't you?"

I just stare at her, trying to hide the truth, silence my only answer. I don't want to let her know that she's getting to me. That her little bitchy comments are starting to get under my skin and feed the insecurities that I have in regards to why Colton likes me.

"Well, it won't be long now, then."

"'Til what?" I ask, already assuming what she's going to say.

I can see her move her tongue around the inside of her mouth as she thinks of how to best phrase her next piece of venom. "I've seen enough of his *hussies* come and go to say that I'll give you two months tops, doll. You'll be out of his bed and his life before the first race of the season." She squints her eyes, glaring at me, waiting for the reaction I won't give her. She takes a step closer. "Just know that it'll be me he turns to then. It'll be me telling him he's too good for someone like you. I told you. *I'm. The. Voice. In. His. Ear,*" she whispers the last words to me.

"And let me guess, it'll be you he finds happily ever after with, right?" I retort, my voice sugary sweet despite the ire bubbling beneath my surface.

"Eventually, once he's done biding his time with bimbos like you." She chuckles, eying me up and down. "You're smart. I'll give you that. But I've known him longer than anyone, and I've put in the time. His parents love me. I'm the only one he needs. He may not realize it yet, but he does love me—"

"*Looks like you need to find something better to do with your time, doll,*" I say, rising from my seat and taking a step closer, fed up with her egocentric diatribe. "Waiting around to be second best must be really frustrating."

"A little testy are we? Don't shoot the messenger," she says, holding up her hands, "I just thought I'd save you the inevitable heartbreak."

I manage a single laugh. "Yeah, I can see the sincerity oozing out of your pores." I roll my eyes. "Your compassion is just overwhelming."

She purses her lips. "Us girls have to look out for one another."

Now I really laugh. What a bitch! "Yeah, I'm sure you have my back!" *With a knife pointing into it.* "I appreciate the heads up, but I'm a big girl, Tawny. I can take care of myself just fine."

She throws her head back and laughs loudly before eying me up and down again, a look of disdain on her face. "Oh, he is going to eat you alive and then spit you out, and I am so going to enjoy watching it!"

I see Colton complete his last lap and swing the car into the pits to the right of us. The boys will come looking for me any moment to go down and see the car, and frankly, I've had enough of Tawny's little "let me put you in your place" speech. I've tried to take the high road. I've tried to not be the catty bitch she's being. But enough's enough.

I take one step closer to her, my voice a spiteful whisper. "You better get used to watching, Tawny, because that's all you'll be doing. When he cries out a name, it'll be mine, sweetheart." The corners of my mouth turn up, my voice implacable. "Not yours."

"*That's what they've all thought!*" She snorts derisively.

How I'd love to throttle her right now. Wipe that sarcastic smirk off her face and show her she has no clue what she's talking about. But I can't. In the end, she may be right. *And that kills me.* Reminds me I need to keep my guard up. I give her the same, slow appraisal that she's given me, and I shake my head in disinterest. "This conversation has been stimulating, Tawny, but I'm going to go spend time with people that are worth my breath."

I rush down the stairs quickly, wanting to make sure that I get the last word in. At the bottom of the stairs, I walk toward where I can hear the engine of Colton's car. As I turn the corner, I see my boys following Davis down to the garage area of the speedway. I hurry to catch up, trying to let the anger and irritation from Tawny's words dissipate.

I shrug it off and tell myself that she's just a catty bitch trying to hold on to something that's not hers. A drop-dead-gorgeous catty bitch, but a catty bitch nonetheless. I think the combination of her being his type and my fear that there is some truth to her words, keeps the anger running through my system.

I catch up to the group as we approach the garage where Colton's crew has set up. The purr of the engine stops, and I see Colton hand the now-detached steering wheel to a crewmember before slowly pushing himself up from his seat. He lifts one leg over the side and then the other to stand on the ground. He takes a moment to settle on his legs before removing his helmet and the white fireproof balaclava from his face. He accepts the Gatorade that someone hands him and takes a long pull on it before running a hand back and forth through his sweat-soaked hair. Colton gives the man who approaches him a huge grin, and it takes me a moment to place him. He is the rakish gentleman who was at the Merit Rum party with him.

I stand back with the boys away from the flurry of activity in the garage. Several people are talking to Colton, who is motioning with his hands to demonstrate what he is saying. Other crewmembers are tending to the car, using instruments to measure things. Colton is completely in his element. It's not hard to sense his enthusiasm and respect for his sport.

His smile is wide and authentic, and I feel a pang in my heart when I see it. If he is this passionate about the sport that he obviously loves, I can't help but wonder what he'll be like when he finally accepts love from someone. My heart twists at the thought that it won't be me. I push the thought from my head, but it stays at the edge of my mind as I watch him.

The flurry dies down as several of the people who Colton is speaking to back off and attend to the engine in the back of the car. Now Colton is just speaking to the man from the club, and I observe an easy camaraderie between the two.

Davis motions for the boys to enter the garage, and they quietly follow in line, trying to stay out of the way. I remain rooted, choosing to watch from afar. Colton notices them and looks up from his conversation, giving the boys a wide smile. He waits until they approach before speaking. "So what did you think, guys?"

All of them shout out words at once ranging from "awesome" to "cool" to "unbelievable." He unzips his fire suit and pulls his arms out of the sleeves, letting them fall and hang below his waist. His shirt, darkened with sweat, clings to the defined muscles of his chest. The sight of him, sexy as hell, pulls at every part of me.

"I'm so glad you guys liked it! Now, this here," he says, putting his arm around the man from the club, "is one of the most important people out here. More important than me," he kids. "None of this…" he gestures to the garage around them "…would run so smoothly if it weren't for him. This is Beckett Daniels, my crew chief."

The boys say hello to him and he smiles back at them. Ricky throws out a question and Beckett smiles broadly, motioning the boys over to the car to look at something. Colton stays where he is and watches the boys follow. He rolls his shoulders and takes another long drink before looking up and around the garage. I feel that sudden crackle of electricity when his eyes meet mine, and that slow lazy grin turns up the corners of his mouth, his dimple deepening. He looks like sex: hot, sweaty, disheveled, and mouthwateringly irresistible. He looks back at Beckett to make sure that things are okay before sauntering over to me.

"Well, hello there." I can't help the smile that forms on my lips when I speak to him.

"Still think I'm faking it?"

"No." I laugh as he stops in front of me.

"Well, as long as you're not, then I'm doing my job correctly," he quips, reaching out a hand to tug on a curl.

I shake my head at him with a soft smile before taking a deep breath. *Faking it is definitely not a necessity when it comes to Colton in the bedroom.* We stare at each other, the activity of the garage buzzing around us, as we become entranced by one another.

"You looked good out there, Ace," I finally manage to say, breaking our silence.

He takes another drink of his Gatorade. "You know nothing about racing, do you?" He laughs as I shake my head, laughing with him. "Didn't think so, but thanks for the compliment."

"But I have watched it with my brother before, and the boys obviously were Googling all about it to make sure they knew as much as possible." I shrug, glancing over his shoulder to check on the kids. "So, Wood, huh?"

He smiles shyly at me. "It's not what you're thinking. It's an old nickname." I raise my eyebrows at him, amused. "When I first started racing, someone called me Hollywood. The name stuck. Has been shortened to Wood over time. Anyone who calls me that has been around a long time." He looks back at Beckett for a beat. "Is someone I trust."

"Don't let the press get a hold of that or they'll have a field day with it."

"Believe me, I know." He laughs.

We both turn our heads as Shane's laughter fills the garage. Beckett has his arm around his shoulder and is laughing with him while Davis is lifting Ricky into the seat of the car to sit for a picture. "Thank you so much, Colton. For making them feel special for a day." He turns from watching the boys to look back at me. "For everything. I can't begin to tell you how much it means to the boys."

A dark look flashes across his face. "It's not a big deal." He shrugs it off, picking at the label on the Gatorade bottle. "I understand that need more than most." He shifts his attention back to the boys who are each getting their chance to sit in the car and get their picture taken. We watch them for a few moments, Colton taking his hat off of his head and running his hands through his hair. I watch him out of the corner of my eye as he looks at his watch and then turns his attention back to the boys.

Tawny's words ring in my ears. Two months, tops. What if she's right? Even if whatever we have lasts three or four months, I know it won't be enough. I don't think any amount of time will be enough to love someone like Colton. He is one of those guys who consumes every part of you. Makes you whole when you never thought you were incomplete. Gives you strength and makes you weak all at the same time. I know I am capable of loving him like that—like he deserves— but I know I will never get the chance. Tawny may be a catty bitch, but she knows him way better than I do. Between her words, Colton's own admissions, my research, and my intuition, I know that I will end up being destroyed if I allow myself to fall in love with Colton. And I can't allow that to happen. The rise might be more than fun, but the devastation after the fall will break me.

Colton breaks through my thoughts. "We have a meeting in ten minutes," he says, turning to look at me. "Can you stay and then I'll drive you home when it's over?"

I twist the ring I'd put back on this morning—a source of comfort to me. I desperately want to say yes. "It's probably not a good idea,

Colton," I shake my head, avoiding his gaze.

"For who?" he says, turning and taking a step closer to me. His scent envelops me—the outdoorsy, clean scent of his cologne mixed with the scent of a man who has put in a hard day's work.

I eye him warily, trying to keep him at an emotional distance. "For both of us, Colton. You said so yourself the other night." He takes a step closer to me and I can feel my pulse surge.

"But maybe I think something different today ..."

I sigh deeply, telling myself that nothing's changed since Saturday night. He is who he is, and he's not going to change. That a few days away from each other has just made him horny, and he wants some relief. That's all this is. I push his last comment out of my head and try to carry on like he never said it. "Besides, I have to get the boys home. They're my responsibility."

He takes another step toward me, and I put my hands up on his chest to prevent him from getting any closer. I don't think I'd be able to bear the feeling of his body pressed against mine. My hands pressing against the firm muscles of his chest makes it hard enough for me to resist him as it is.

Colton takes a hand and lifts my chin up. "What's wrong, Ry?" His eyes search mine, trying to understand my hesitancy. How can he understand why his idea of a relationship is unacceptable to me? How do I explain that him pushing me away one minute and then kissing me senseless the next is making me question what I might concede in order to have him in my life?

"You," I whisper.

"Me?" he mouths.

"You confuse me at every turn, Colton." I shake my head softly and despite telling myself that touching him will only make walking away that much harder, I lift my finger and trace the hem of the neckline on his damp shirt. "One minute you tell me you can't stay away and the next you tell me you have to keep me at arm's length because you're going to hurt me. On Saturday you told me whatever is between us will never work unless I agree to your terms and then today you kiss me breathless." I step back from him and look over at the boys getting a tour of the garage, to avoid meeting his gaze. "I can't give you what you want and you can't give me what I need. That's all I know. All I understand, Colton."

He steps toward me again and tugs on my ponytail, forcing my head to lift and my eyes to meet his. And despite the chaos around us—the boys laughter, the clang of metal on metal, the sound of an air compressor in the distance—when his eyes hold mine, it all disappears. It's just he and I. A guy way too irresistible for his own good and a girl in way over her head.

"As much as I keep telling myself that this needs to be—should be—over, Rylee, for both our sakes ... I still want you." He cups the side of my face with his free hand and traces the pad of his thumb over my bottom lip. "Desperately," he whispers. His words resonate in my heart. "I think about how soft your skin is. The feeling of your body against mine. Of it under mine. How you tighten around me when I'm buried in you ..." His words, mixed with the intensity in his eyes, leave me breathless. Has my body vibrating with a deep-seated need for him that I'm not sure will ever be sated. "Christ, Rylee, it ... you ... are consuming me." He leans in and brushes a soft, brief kiss on my lips. The innocence and vulnerability behind it beguiles me. "And I intend to have you again."

I breathe in a sharp, audible gasp. I step back from him, holding his gaze for a second longer, before looking around the garage to check on the boys. I notice more people have joined us since we started talking. I notice a perplexed look pass between Beckett and Quinlan. I see Davis rounding the boys up, and I know our time here is ending.

"I'm sure you'll feel that way until you find someone else who fits your requirements," I quip, fearing my words speak the truth. I turn back to Colton, still trying to recover from the impact of his confession and yet needing to show him that I have some self-control when it comes to him. "Why waste your time on me when you can have any other girl willing to give you exactly what you want?"

"But. I. Want. You. Rylee. No. One. Else." He smirks.

The man is relentless, but I still think he's after the challenge when it comes to me. I shake my head. "You have a habit of telling me what you want, Ace, without asking me what I want."

Colton takes the baseball hat in his hands and tugs it down over my head, a Cheshire cat grin spreading across his face and a sinful gleam in his eyes. "Oh, sweetheart…" he emits a low rumbling chuckle as he takes two steps back from me "…I know exactly what you want." He holds his hand up to motion to Beckett that he's coming when his name is called. His grin widens into one of the wickedest and most carnal smiles I have ever seen. My core coils and I tense to stifle my desire. "*And I have just the right tools to give it to you.*" And with those parting words, he turns on his heel and walks over to Beckett, his laughter reverberating in the garage. Beckett eyes him up and down, a bemused look on his face as Colton says goodbye to the boys.

When Colton finishes, he turns back toward me and smirks. "All consuming experience!"

He laughs at my confused expression. "*What*?"

"*What it stands for.*" He grins and I finally get it. He's still guessing what Ace means.

"Nope," I say, fighting the smile that tugs at the corners of my mouth.

He takes a step backwards, biting his bottom lip in concentration. I can see the minute he thinks of another one as his eyes light up, the corners around them crinkling. "The amazing Colton experience," he shouts over to me, garnering an eye roll from Beckett.

"Oh geez!" I laugh at his lack of humility and mimic Beckett with an eye roll of my own. "Nope," I yell back, suppressing a laugh.

Colton takes another step backwards, his face filled with humor, and shakes his head at me. "Later, Ryles."

"Later, Ace," I mutter, begrudgingly accepting the fact that in so many ways Colton is right. That no matter how intelligent I am or how rational I try to be, his pull on me is just too strong.

I tug his hat down on my head, adjusting my now-wrecked ponytail, and watch him throw a playful arm around Beckett's shoulder as they walk down the pathway. I shake my head, overwhelmed by the day's events, and head over to collect my excited but very tired boys for the long ride home.

Chapter Twenty-One

"CHECK IT OUT!" DANE THROWS a newspaper proof onto my desk as he walks by my office at Corporate Cares. "Your cleavage is going to be in the newspaper and we're going to get some good press."

I whip my head up to look at him, confused, before glancing down at the paper. On the lower half of the cover of the sports section is a side-by-side picture of our outing at the track and the accompanying article. The picture on the left is a picture of Colton's car with all of the boys kneeling in front of it with Colton in the middle. The picture to the right is a close up of Zander, Ricky, and myself. I am in between the two, and unfortunately, the way my arms are positioned, my cleavage is on display in the V of my snug T-shirt. "Lovely! Oh my God, that's embarrassing!"

"C'mon, Ry, you look hot. And the girls look great!"

I throw my pencil at him, laughing. "When does this go to print? Can we ask him to change the picture?"

"Yeah, right! You know they picked it so that the guys that open up the sports page will read the article and not flip past it." I roll my eyes, feeling the flush of embarrassment creep into my cheeks. "Just think of it as taking one for the team—"

"What?"

"It's a really good article that's going to give us good press." He laughs out loud. "Hell, if I was into playing for your team, I'd keep the picture for late night fun!"

"Oh, shut up!" I shout at him, unable to keep my laughter from bubbling up.

"C'mon, Ry—read it. You're gonna like what it says."

"Really?" I raise an eyebrow as I skim through it, pleased with what I see.

"Seriously. It is," he tells me, taking a seat in front of my desk. "A lot of good info about The House and about corporate and the new facilities."

"When's it running?"

"This Sunday, and the *OC Register* most likely will run then too, but I haven't seen their proof yet."

"Hmmm, not bad." I set it down on the side of my desk where I can read it more thoroughly later.

"How was your interview?" he asks, referring to the one good candidate I had for the open counselor position. I interviewed her earlier in the day and was quite impressed.

"She was actually really good. Almost too good to be true really, but her references check out, and I think I'm going to make her an offer. I think the boys will really take to her. I'll need you to help me train her but—" The ringing of my cell phone interrupts me. I glance down to see who is calling. "It's Teddy," I tell him.

Dane rises from the chair and mouths he'll come back later as I answer. "Hey, Teddy!"

"Rylee! Heard we got a good article from the *LA Times*. Great job!"

"You're breaking up on me, Teddy." The phone line crackles.

"I need to talk to you—" The call drops and the line goes dead.

I wait a second for my phone to ring again and when it doesn't, I go back to looking at the budgetary numbers I was working on before Dane interrupted. After a few minutes, my cell rings again.

"Hello?"

"Rylee Thomas, please," a monotone male voice says over the phone.

"This is she."

"Hi, Ms. Thomas, this is Abel Baldwin."

Oh, crap! What boy is it this time? "Good afternoon, Principal Baldwin. What can I do for you today?"

"Well, it seems to me that Aiden can't seem to keep his hands to himself lately. He was in yet another fight last period, Ms. Thomas."

Disdain fills his voice at having to deal with this again.

This is Aiden's third fight in as many months that has been caught by school authorities. I have a feeling that there have actually been a couple more that have gone unnoticed as well. Oh, Aiden. "What happened?"

"Not quite sure. He won't really talk with me about it." *And I really don't think you care, either.*

"What about the other kid?" A question that I ask every time and always get a less than satisfactory answer to.

"They said it was a simple misunderstanding."

"They?" There's more than one? "I hope that they are in your office as well, Mr. Baldwin."

He clears his throat. "Not exactly. They are in class and—"

"What?" I shout at him, perplexed by his obvious bias.

"And I think it's better if you come and pick up Aiden—"

"He's suspended?" I ask through gritted teeth.

"No, he's not." I can hear the irritation in his voice at having me question him. "If you'd let me finish Ms. Thomas—"

"He's not suspended, but you want me to come get him while the other boys get to stay in class?" My rising frustration is more than evident in my voice. "Surely you can understand why I'm upset at what seems to be favoritism here."

He stays quiet for a moment as I gather up my things as best as possible with one hand so I can go pick him up. "Ms. Thomas, your accusation is unfounded and serves no purpose here. Now I would appreciate if you could come collect Aiden so we can let the two parties simmer down. This in no way indicates that Aiden is at fault in this matter. In addition, Aiden has blood on his clothing and seeing as it's against school policy for him to walk around with it there, I think it's in the school's best interest to send him home for the afternoon."

I sigh loudly, biting my tongue from telling this less-than-stellar principal exactly what I think of him. "I'll be right there."

Aiden is silent all the way home from school. My shift at The House doesn't start for another three hours, but I think that Aiden and I need to have a little alone time to talk about what happened. I haven't pushed him to tell me, but I need to know. Is he being bullied? Is he looking for attention that he's not getting? Is he releasing frustration from his past? I need to know so that I can figure out how to help.

Before we walk into the house, I motion for him to sit down on the front porch step next to me. He rolls his eyes but obeys. He stares at me as I take in the swollen lip with dried blood at the corner, the dark red mark on his right cheek and the start of bruising on the left eye. His cheeks flush deeply under my scrutiny.

"I know you don't want to talk about it, buddy, but you have to tell me what happened." I reach out and grab his hand while he lowers his head and watches an ant crawl slowly on the step beneath us. We sit in silence, and I allow it for a bit but finally squeeze his hand, letting him know he needs to talk.

"They were just being jerks," he grumbles.

"Who started it, Aiden?" When he doesn't respond, I prompt again. "Aiden? Who threw the first punch?"

"I did." His voice is so soft, so sad with shame that it breaks my heart. I see a fat tear slide down his swollen cheek, and I know that something is off.

"Talk to me, Aiden. Who was it and what did they do to make you want to hit them?"

He reaches up to dash away the fallen tear with the back of his hand and leaves a smear of dirt in its path. "They called me a liar," he mumbles, his bottom lip quivering. "Ashton Smitty and Grant Montgomery."

Little punks! The know-it-all, privileged, popular kids from his grade whose parents never seem to be around. I wrap my arm around his shoulder and pull him to my side, kissing the top of his head. "What did they say you were lying about?"

His voice is barely audible. "They told me I lied about going to the track on Sunday. That I didn't really meet Colton or know him ..."

My heart squeezes. He was so excited to go to school and tell all his friends about his experience. So excited to be cool for once and have something that the other kids didn't. I sigh loudly, squeezing him again. I want to tell him that the little punks deserved it and that he did the right thing, but that's obviously not the most responsible way to react. "Oh, Aiden ... I'm sorry, buddy. Sorry they didn't believe you. Sorry they pushed you ... but Aiden, fighting somebody with your fists is not the way to solve things. It only ends up making it worse."

He reluctantly nods his head. "I know, but—"

"Aiden," I scold sternly, "there are no buts here ... you can't use your fists to fix problems."

"I know, but I tried to tell Ms. McAdams when they started pushing and shoving and she wouldn't listen."

I can see another tear threaten to fall from his thick lashes. "Well then, I'm going to make an appointment to speak with her and Baldwin about this." His head whips up and his eyes open widely in fear. "I'm not going to make it worse, Aiden. I'm just going to ask them to keep their eyes open a little more. To make sure that they do not let this happen again. And I'll make sure that the other kids don't know."

He nods his head, releasing a noncommittal grunt. "Am I in trouble?" He looks up at me with fear in eyes.

I wrap both my arms around him and squeeze his little body that's known so much hurt and abandonment. I hold him to me, trying to reassure him and let him know that it's okay. That getting in trouble doesn't mean a severe beating and food withheld for days. "Yeah, bud, you are ... but I think that icky feeling you have might just be the worst of it." I feel his shoulders sag in relief as a plan forms in my head.

"I knew you couldn't stay away from me for long." Colton's voice fills the other end of the telephone line, arrogance redefined. His sexy voice alone makes my pulse race, but I have to put how I feel aside as I put my plan to help restore Aiden's self-confidence at school into motion.

"I'm not calling for me, Ace."

"Ooooh, I love it when you're all business and straight to the point. It's such a turn on, Ryles."

"Whatever!" I say, but I can't help the slow smile that creeps over my face.

"No, seriously, what's up, sweetheart?"

Why do I love when he calls me that? Why does it make me feel like I'm special to him?

"It's Aiden," I tell him filling in the details as he listens attentively, despite the voices I hear in the background. "Is it possible that I can get some kind of signed picture of you or something he can bring to school tomorrow to prove that he's met you and actually was there on Sunday?"

Colton laughs loudly, and I'm confused by his reaction. "That's only going to get his teeth knocked in, Rylee. That's something only a geek would do … those brats would eat him alive."

"Oh … um … I had no idea."

"You wouldn't." Colton chuckles, slightly offending me.

"What's that supposed to mean?"

"And please don't go have a conference with the teacher or principal," he groans. "Inevitably someone will see you and then it will only make things harder for Aiden."

"I wasn't—"

"Oh yes, you were," he kids, and I'm shocked he has me pegged so well. "I just know you were one of those preppy kids who had their homework done before it was due, helped the teacher in class, and was part of the 'in' crowd. No offense, Rylee, but you have no idea what it is to be a misfit on the verge of puberty who gets the crap beat out of him *just because.*"

I'm flustered that he has such a good read on me, but more than that, his words about understanding the misfit crowd gives me more insight to him as a child. When I don't respond, he laughs again. "You were like that, weren't you?"

"Maybe," I answer slowly, heat flushing my cheeks.

"It's nothing to be embarrassed about, Rylee … it's just different for kids like Aiden."

And like you were. "What do you suggest I do then, since I obviously don't understand?" I try to hide the hurt in my voice.

"Are you on shift there tomorrow?"

"Yeah … what does that have to do with anything?" When he remains silent, I prompt him. "Colton?"

"Give me a second to think," he snips at me and I blanch at his tone. I hear someone call his name in the background. Of course it's a female. "What time do you leave for school in the morning?"

"At eight. Why?"

"I'm tied up right now," he says innocently, but my mind drifts to braided velvet ropes and cold counters. I jolt my mind from my thoughts, chastising myself. "Okay. I'll have something for him at The House before you leave."

"What are you—"

"Relax, control freak." He sighs, "I have something in mind. I just have to move some things around to make it happen."

"Oh, but—" I protest, wanting to know what he's bringing.

"Rylee," he interrupts, "this is the part where you let someone else handle the details. All you have to say is 'Thank you, Colton. I owe you one,' and hang up."

I pause momentarily, knowing he is right but wanting to know anyway. "Thank you, Colton," I comply.

"And?" he prompts.

I remain silent for a few moments. I can almost hear his smirk. "And I owe you one."

"And you can bet I'll collect on it." His seductive laugh fills the phone until I hear the dial tone on the other end.

Chapter Twenty-Two

*D*AMN IT! I KNEW I shouldn't have said anything to Aiden. I shouldn't have told him that I had something to fix what had happened yesterday. I shouldn't have depended on someone like Colton to come through when I am so used to relying on myself. He hasn't even answered my texts or calls this morning.

I glance at the clock and another minute has ticked by. It's seven fifty-two and I need to get the boys into action in order to get them to school on time. Mike's already left to take Shane and Connor to high school. Bailey has already come and left to take Zander to his therapist's appointment and Kyle to the eye doctor before dropping him back off at school. I'm left with the remaining three elementary school kids, and I know that getting them in the car should have started ten minutes ago.

I glance at the clock again and it's seven fifty-three now. *Shit!* "Rylee, are you going to tell me what it is yet?" Aiden begs again with hope in his eyes.

"Not yet, Aiden. It's a surprise." Now I have to scramble to think of something to do to make up for an empty promise.

I could strangle Colton right now. What did I expect from a careless playboy? I guess if there isn't a promise of getting laid at the end of the deal then he's not going to follow through. I pound a fist on the table, the silverware on it rattling, knowing I'm overreacting after how much he did for the boys. But at the same time, he's letting down one of my boys and he's letting me down too.

I start stuffing lunches into the backpacks that Aiden is handing me, concentration etched on his face as he tries to figure out what I can possibly have to help him. "C'mon, guys. It's time to go!" I shout. Aiden, my little helper, leaves the kitchen to go see what they are up to.

When after a few minutes I don't hear the usual scurry of feet, I sigh in frustration and head out toward the hallway. "Ricky, Scooter ... C'mon, guys, its time to go!" I turn the corner to the hallway and do a double take when I see Colton standing in the foyer with the door open behind him. The sun is at his back, casting his body and dark features in a halo. Three little boys stand in front of him, their backs to me, but I can see all of their heads angled up to look at him. He steps further into the room smiling briefly at me, before turning his attention to Aiden.

"So, Aiden," Colton says, and I can see his subtle appraisal of the bruises on Aiden's sweet little face, "are you ready for school today?"

"What?" he asks bemused before looking back at me, a mix of anticipation and realization on his face. I look back at Colton, wondering what he's brought to help the situation.

Colton cocks his head to the side, realizing that no one gets what he's doing here. "I'm taking you guys to school," he says as silence fills the house before the boys start whooping and jumping around like loons. Their excitement is contagious and I feel my smile widen to match Colton's. He steps forward and kneels down in front of Aiden. "Hey, buddy, what do you say we go show those bullies that they're wrong and they can take a hike?" Aiden's eyes widen, moisture pooling at the corners, as he nods excitedly. "Go get your backpacks then," Colton instructs them as he stands back up.

My eyes follow him, and it is in this moment—with his dark features haloed by the bright light of the sun, when he's come to stand up for children that no one else cares to stand up for anymore—that I know I've fallen for Colton. That he has penetrated my heart's protective exterior and made me love him. I lift my hand and press the heel of it against my breastbone, trying to rub at the sudden ache there. Trying to will his self-professed, ending-filled devastation and hurt away. Trying to tell myself that I cannot let this come to fruition.

Colton looks questioningly at me. "Rylee?"

I shake my head. "Sorry." I shake my head again and smile at him as the three boys come barreling back down the hallway toward the front door.

"I guess they're ready." He laughs as he ushers the boys out of the house.

Colton purposefully revs the engine of the Aston Martin as I direct him into the school parking lot. I'm sitting in the front and the three boys are squeezed tightly together in the backseat, grins on their faces and bodies bristling with excitement. I glance over at Colton and he has a half-smile on his lips as if he is remembering a grade-school memory of his own. I'm about to tell him he can take the shortcut to the drop-off section in front of the school but I bite my tongue. I realize that he is taking a long, slow cruise through the parking lot, gunning the sexy purr of the motor every chance he gets, so that he draws the attention of everyone around us.

We finally make it to the drop-off line where Colton swerves around the long line of cars and carefully cruises down a narrow passage between the line and the sidewalk, despite the dirty looks shot at him. I know he'd love to floor the gas pedal and make a grand entrance, but he refrains. He pulls up right in front of the school's entrance, angling the car so that the passenger door faces the large crowd of students out front. He revs the engine a couple more times, its sound purring in the peacefully quiet morning air, before sliding out of the driver's seat.

He unfolds his long limbs gracefully and stands a moment by the opened car door. I can see him raising his arms over his head, stretching with a loud groan, making sure that all available eyes are on us. I glance around and notice the moms near us staring openly. I laugh as I watch them try to fix their bed-ridden hair.

Colton shuts the door and struts slowly around the front of the car toward my side. He opens the door for me and I exit, catching the amusement in his eyes and the gratified smirk on his lips. He squats down and flips the seat forward so the boys can exit one at a time.

The looks on their faces are priceless as they take in the crowd.

Out of the corner of my eye, I see Principal Baldwin approach from the far side and his stern face startles at seeing a car parked improperly in his strictly rule enforced parking zone. I can hear whispers of Colton's name and my smile widens. Colton shuts the door and places himself with Aiden on one side and Ricky and Scooter on the other. He leans over and I hear him say to Aiden, "Do you see the bullies, buddy?" Aiden looks around the sea of faces, and I see him stiffen when he sees the boys. I follow his line of sight, as does Colton, to see the stunned expressions of Ashton and Grant. "Well, champ, it's time to go prove a point."

We move as a unit toward the two boys, their eyes widening with each step. I'm curious what Colton plans on doing once we reach them. I glance over to see his face relaxed in a huge, approachable grin as we come to a stop in front of Ashton and Grant. In the periphery of my vision, I notice Principal Baldwin scurrying over to us to stop any confrontation before it starts.

"Hey, guys!" Colton says enthusiastically, and I get the feeling he is going the kill-them-with-kindness route. Both boys just stand there gawking at Colton. He turns to Aiden. "Hey, Aid, are these the boys that didn't believe you're my buddy?"

I wish I had a camera to take a picture of the reverence on Aiden's face as he looks up toward Colton. His eyes are alive with disbelief, and I can see the pride brimming in them. "Yeah …" Aiden's voice comes out in a croak. The crowd around us has grown.

"Oh, man," Colton says to Aston and Grant, "you should've seen Aiden on Sunday. I let him bring six of his friends, including Ricky and Scooter here, with him to the track to test out the car…" he shakes his head "…and boy, were they the biggest help to me! We had so much fun!"

I see Ricky and Scooter bristle with pride now as well, and I wonder if Colton has any idea what he is doing, not only to their self-esteem but also to their status here at school. "Too bad you guys aren't friends of his," Colton said, shaking his head, "or maybe you could've gone too!"

The school bell buzzes. Principal Baldwin reaches us, slightly out of breath, and tries to disperse the crowd by ushering everyone to the doors. He looks down at the boys who are still staring at Colton before giving them a stern look and clearing his throat, making them snap out of it. Colton flashes his megawatt, no-holds-barred smile and winks at them. "Bye, boys! Make sure you say 'hi' to my man Aiden here when you see him in class!" They just nod their heads at Principal Baldwin, forcing themselves to take their eyes off of Colton, or they'll walk into a wall.

With their children safely inside, the mothers remain outside for no apparent reason—trying to look busy by retying their shoes or foraging in their oversize purses for something that they will never see because their eyes are locked on Colton.

"Boys, you too," Principal Baldwin tells my three.

Colton looks over at me questioningly and I nod subtly, letting him know this is the dipshit I told him about who favors everyone who fights Aiden. Colton flashes the same megawatt smile at him and says, "One moment please, sir. I just need to say bye to my boys." I didn't think it was possible for the grins to get wider on the boys' faces, but they do. Colton turns to talk to the boys and then turns back, in second thought, to address Principal Baldwin again. "Next time, sir, it'd be best to remember that Aiden is telling the truth. It's the bullies that need to be sent home, not good kids like Aiden here. He may not be perfect, but just because he doesn't come from a traditional home, doesn't mean that he's at fault." He holds his gaze and then turns his back on the wide-eyed principal, effectively dismissing him. The flustered look on Principal Baldwin's face is priceless.

Colton kneels down, bringing Ricky, Aiden, and Scooter around in front of him. He raises his eyebrows and grins at them. "I don't think they'll be bugging you anymore, Aiden." He reaches out and ruffles his hair. "In fact, I don't think anyone will be bugging any of you any more. If so, you let me know, okay?"

All three nod eagerly as Colton rises. "Time to get to class," I tell them, gratitude evident in my voice. They usually grumble at these words, but today they all obey and seem actually eager to enter the building.

Colton and I stand side by side as the boys walk through the door that Principal Baldwin is holding open for them. Nosy bystanders scurry by, pretending they are not watching. Aiden stops in the doorway and turns around, awe still on his face and says, "Thanks,

Colton," before disappearing inside the building.

When we turn back to the car, I catch a look of accomplishment and pride on Colton's face. I have a feeling mine looks the same way.

"Why did you agree to come here if you don't like coffee?"

Against my better judgment, I've agreed to go get some coffee with Colton after leaving the school. I'm still floored by Colton's actions, and feel I at least owe him my time in return for what he's just done. I can still see the look on Aiden's face in my head. I don't think I will ever forget it.

"I may not like the coffee part, but Starbucks has some damn good food that is oh-so-bad for you." I laugh as he shakes his head at me. *Kind of like you, Colton.*

We place our order amid glances from the other patrons who recognize Colton. He's sans baseball hat and not incognito. We shuffle over to a corner that luckily has an empty table with two deep, comfortable-looking chairs on either side of it. We sit down and Colton pulls our muffins out of the bag and sets mine before me.

"You know that after what you did today, you've most likely reached idol status with the boys now."

He rolls his eyes at me and picks a piece of his muffin off and places it in his mouth. I watch it clear his lips and see his tongue dart out to lick a crumb. A flash of desire sears through me. I see the corner of his mouth twist up, and I force myself to look up to his eyes, which have noticed where my attention is focused. We stare at each other, unspoken words igniting the heat between us.

The barista at the counter calls out, "Ace," and Colton smirks at me before rising from the table to get the drinks. I watch him walk, his long, lean legs covered in denim with a forest green Henley shirt covering his broad shoulders and narrow waist, the long sleeves pushed halfway up his strong forearms. I watch the barista blush as she hands him our drinks and continues to stare as he turns to prepare his coffee.

I stare at him, confusion running through my head. We are so comfortable together. So drawn together. And yet we can't give each other what the other needs. Maybe I'm being selfish, but I know I won't be satisfied with just bits and pieces of him. Scraps he'll throw my way when he deigns to. But that notion confuses me even more since I've yet to see him act that way with me thus far. He tells me one thing about how his arrangements operate, but then acts another way with me.

Is he worth it? Colton sinks down into the chair across from me, a soft smile on his lips as he meets my eyes. *Yes. He definitely is.* But what do I want to do about that? He sighs after swallowing his first sip. "Now I can think clearly." *At least someone can, because it sure isn't me.*

"It seems to me like you were doing okay before your coffee," I kid as I swallow a bite of muffin. He smirks. "I have to tell you again, Colton, thank you so much for showing up and doing that. It was … you were … what you did for Aiden was above and beyond, and I really appreciate it."

"It wasn't anything, Rylee." He can see that I'm about to argue with him. "But you're welcome."

I nod my head and smile shyly at him, glad he has accepted my gratitude. "The looks on those brats' faces were priceless when you walked up!"

He laughs out loud. "No, I think the principal's face was even better," he counters, shaking his head at the memory. "Maybe next time he'll think twice before taking sides."

"Hopefully," I murmur, taking a tentative sip of my hot chocolate and trying not to burn my tongue. *You burned me.* Colton's words pick this moment to flash through my head. I push them to the back of my mind as I take a sip of my drink. The damn man clutters my mind, overwhelms my senses, and clouds my heart in one fell swoop.

We sit in an easy silence, watching store patrons and sipping our drinks. I put my hot chocolate down and absently fold the corners of my napkin, deciding if I should say the next comment that pops in my head or let it go. Typical me has to get it out. "Colton?" His eyebrows quirk up at the gravity of my tone. "You're so good with the boys, I mean way better than most people, and yet you tell me you'll never have any. I don't understand why."

"Having a child and being good with one are two completely different things." The muscle in his jaw tics as his eyes watch something outside in the parking lot.

"Colton, what you did today," I tell him, reaching out to put my hand on top of his. My touch draws his eyes back to mine. "You showed a little boy that he was worth something. That he was worthy enough to stand up for." Emotion fills my voice. My eyes try and tell him that I understand. That he did what should have been done for him as a child. Even though I don't know his circumstances, I know enough in my line of work to see that no one stood up for him or made him feel like he mattered, until he met his Andy Westin.

"Don't you do that every day, Rylee? Stand up for them?"

I mull over his words as I finish chewing my bite. "I suppose so, but not with your dramatic flair." I smile. "I guess I'm more behind the scenes. Not nearly as public and self-confidence boosting as you are."

"What can I say?" He picks at the cardboard guard on his coffee cup. "I know what it's like to be in Aiden's shoes. To be the odd kid out who doesn't fit in due to circumstances beyond your control. To be bullied and made fun of *just because.*" He squeezes my hand. "You get the picture."

Sympathy engulfs me as I think of a raven-haired little boy with haunted green eyes. Of the pain he experienced and the memories that will forever be etched in his mind. Of the things he missed out on like comforting lips expressing unconditional love, warm arms to cuddle him tight, and fingers to tickle him into fits of deep belly giggles.

"Don't look at me like that, Rylee," he warns, pulling his hand away from mine and leaning back in his chair. "I don't want your pity or sympathy."

"I'm just trying to understand you better, Colton." My words the only apology that I'll give him.

"Delving into my dark and dirty past isn't going to help you understand me any better. That shit..." he waves a hand through the air "...it's not something I want to haunt you with."

"Colton—"

"I told you before, Rylee..." his stern voice silencing me "...I'm not one of your kids. My shit can't be fixed. I've been broken for way too long for that miracle to happen." The look in his eyes—a mix of anger, shame, and exasperation—tells me that this conversation is now over.

An uncomfortable silence hangs between us and I can't help but wonder what happened to him as a child. What is he so afraid to confront? Why does he think that he's so broken?

His voice pulls me from my thoughts, turning the focus of our conversation from him to me. "What about you, Rylee? You treat these kids like they're your own. What's going to happen when one day you meet Mr. Right and have kids of your own? How are you going to balance that?"

Even after two years, the pang that hits me still knocks me to my knees. I swallow purposely, trying to wash the acrid taste in my mouth. I pick at the corner of my napkin, watching my fingers rip tiny pieces off as I answer him. "I can't … after the accident I was told that getting pregnant, that the chance of having a child is…" I shake my head sadly "…a very slim possibility. Like basically being on the pill for life. Most likely never going to happen." *Again.* I lift my eyes to his, rocking my head subtly from side to side. "So it's not something I put much thought into."

I hear him draw in a breath and can feel the pity roll off him. There is nothing worse than someone giving you *that look*. The pity look.

"I'm sorry," he whispers.

"It is what it is." I shrug, not wanting to dwell on what can never be. "I've come to terms with it for the most part," I lie, and in true Colton Donavan fashion I change the subject to something other than me. "So, Ace…" I wriggle my eyebrows "…you looked kind of hot in your race suit!"

He laughs, "Nice change of topic!"

"I learned from you," I reply, sucking a crumb off of my thumb. When I look up, Colton is watching me draw my finger from my mouth. Intensity and desire mingle in the depths of his eyes as he studies me. The sexual tension between us mounts. Our draw to each other is undeniable.

"Hot, huh?" he says.

I tilt my head and purse my lips as I study him back. "I wanted …" My voice is quiet, unsure, when I speak. The small smile playing at the corners of Colton's lips gives me the surge of confidence I need to continue. Knowing that he desires me and wants more of whatever this is, emboldens me. It empowers me to finish my thought. "I wanted you to take me right there on the hood of your car." I can feel my cheeks flush as I look up at him through my eyelashes.

He takes in a sharp breath, his lips parting, eyes clouding with desire. "Why, Ms. Thomas…" he darts his tongue out to lick at his bottom lip "…we might just have to rectify that situation."

"Rectify?" Desire blooms in my belly at the thought.

He leans in across the table, his face inches from mine. "It's always been a fantasy of mine."

I think he's going to lean in and kiss me. My chin trembles in anticipation, synapses misfiring as I try to tell my brain to be the voice of reason here. To pull me back from the brink of Colton insanity. And then the alarm on my cell phone goes off. It startles us both and we jump back. "Oh crap! I have a meeting I have to get to," I tell him as I start gathering our trash and stuffing it inside my empty muffin bag.

Colton reaches out and grabs my hand, stopping my flurry of movement. He waits until my eyes meet his to speak. "This conversation isn't over, Rylee. You keep sending me so many damned mixed messages that—"

"What?" I screech, dumbfounded, trying to pull my hand back from his, but his grip holds my hand still. "What are you talking about? You're the one sending mixed messages. Whispering sweet nothings one minute and then pushing me away the next!" Are we experiencing the same thing here? How am I being confusing?

"I swear to God," he murmurs softly to himself, releasing my hand as he leans back in his chair shaking his head, amusement on his face. I can barely make out his next words when he speaks. "We haven't really even started this yet, and you're already topping me from the bottom." I can sense his exasperation as he runs a hand through his hair.

I look at him, unsure what exactly he means, but not really having the time to ask him to explain. I stand up and Colton grabs my hand again, pulling me up against him so I am forced to tilt my head up to see his face. He closes his eyes momentarily, as if he is resigning himself to something, before opening them again to lock onto mine. "I want you, Rylee. Any way I can have you."

His words create a vacuum of air, and I feel like I can't breathe. We're standing in a packed Starbucks with orders being called and people talking on cell phones and espresso machines steaming milk, but I hear none of it. It is just Colton and me and his deafening words.

I swallow loudly, trying to process them. Unable to speak, time passes until I find my voice. "Any–any way you can have me?" I stutter breathlessly, eyes wide with optimism. "Does that mean that you're willing to … to try more than an *arrangement*? Try to compromise with me?"

I feel his body tense from my words and when I see the look in his eyes, I realize I misunderstand what he's saying. My chest deflates and my hopes sputter when he speaks, unable to look me in the eyes. "That's not what I meant, Rylee. All I know is how I operate. By my rules. They allow me that deep-seated desire for control that I so desperately need to be able to function. I have to have it on my terms." I feel his body shift before bringing his eyes to mine. I glimpse an unexpected vulnerability in them. "Rylee, this is all I can give you. *For now* … Will you at least *try* my way? *For me?*"

For now? Try for me? What the fuck is that supposed to mean? That there is the possibility of a future? I try to stop my mind from reading into that comment. Colton's proximity and the words he just dropped like bombs on my rationality leave me stuttering as I try to respond coherently. "I thought you told me this wouldn't work. That we have two different sets of needs. That you … I think your words were, that you're going to *break me apart*?" My words may sound strong and decided, but I'm anything but that.

He grimaces when I throw his words back at him and hangs his head, his voice soft. "Yeah, I know. I can't prevent the inevitable. But I still want you to try."

Blinded by my feelings for him, I ignore his admission of inevitable hurt because my head is still wrapping itself around that word: try. He's asked me to try. Am I willing to do that? For him? For a chance at us? To hope for the opportunity to show him that it's okay to want more. That he deserves more. My train of thought derails when Tawny's words flitter through my mind. *You'll think you can change him and his ways. And just when that happens, you'll be over quicker than that last lap he just took.* I shake my head, trying to rid her words from my head.

"Don't answer yet, Rylee." Colton's voice is a plea, mistaking the shake of my head as a denial to his request. "Have dinner with me first before you tell me no." I step back from him, needing the distance despite knowing I'm already going to tell him yes. "I have to have at least one more night with you. I need to." His eyes search mine for an answer. "I'll pick you up at three o'clock tomorrow."

I stare at him. "I can drive, Colton," I say, exasperated that once again he's made the decision for me. If I'm willing to try for him, shouldn't he try for me as well?

"Nope." He smiles, holding the door open for me as we leave. "I'm driving. That way you can't run away."

Chapter Twenty-Three

"WE DON'T HAVE TO FIX *each other. Come over. We don't have to say forever. Come over."* I hum along with the Kenny Chesney song that is playing softly on the speakers of the Range Rover as we drive north along on the Pacific Coast Highway. I smile at the coincidence that Colton texted me this song earlier, and now it is playing on the radio as a member of his security staff, Sammy, drives me to wherever he is.

I reach beside me at my bag, rifling through the change of clothes and miscellaneous toiletries I packed. I pull out my compact mirror to check my reflection. My hair is piled on the top of my head in a stylish yet effortless disarray of curls with several wisps hanging loosely around my face and onto my nape. I set down my compact and bring my hands back to check the tie on my neck where the straps of my blue maxi dress meet, leaving my back bare until just below my shoulder blades. I say a silent thank you to Haddie for her suggestion to wear the dress. *Cute, casual, and just enough cleavage to keep him sneaking a peek* she told me over our second glass of wine.

As we drive north, the lush hills on my right give way to the ocean on our left. I place a hand over my stomach to try and settle the butterflies. I shouldn't be nervous to see Colton, but I am. I feel that tonight is going to be a turning point for whatever "we" are. I lean my head back and look out the window at the endless sea and hope that I can handle the repercussions of whatever that turning point may be. I close my eyes momentarily and wonder how an intelligent woman like me can knowingly walk into foreseeable devastation.

Taylor Swift's *Red* is playing when we start driving through Malibu. I listen to the words, relating to them. "Loving him is like driving a new Maserati down a dead end street." I shake my head, feeling like that dead end is going to come so much quicker than I want it to.

Sammy turns left onto Broadbeach Road, and I am pulled from my thoughts. Expensive houses line my left, bordering the coveted Malibu shoreline. Houses range from modern to Cape Cod to old world, with perfectly manicured landscaping and gated walls.

Within moments, we turn up to a driveway where large wooden gates are swinging open for us. We pull through the gates onto a cobblestone and grass driveway and come to a stop. Sammy escorts me from the car, and I look up at the two-story structure in front of me. It has an impenetrable-looking ledge stone façade, the top portion shaped like a stretched letter 'U' where an open-air deck sits between two sections of the house. There are no windows on the walls that face me, and I assume that the opposing walls are solely glass to showcase the Pacific. At ground level below the deck is a massive arched wooden door, and my eyes are drawn to it as it slowly opens.

Colton stands in the doorway, stopping me in my tracks when a slow, lazy smile lifts one corner of his mouth. The sight of him is like a sucker punch to my abdomen. I struggle to breathe as I drink him in. He is all kinds of sexy, wearing a pair of worn blue jeans, a faded black T-shirt, and bare feet. I'm not sure why the sight of his bare feet peeking out from beneath his pant legs is so attractive to me, but it's worth another glance. I regain my wits despite the humming of nerves and start moving toward him again as his eyes languorously appraise my body. I reach the doorway and stop in front of him, my smile matching his.

"I told you I'd hurt you and yet here you are," he murmurs captivated, astonishment flickering through his green eyes. Before I have a chance to process his words, he reaches out and takes my hand, pulling me against him. My hands land on his chest feeling every bit of muscle beneath the incredibly soft cotton of his shirt.

"Hi," he breathes, a shy smile on his lips and eyes steadfast on mine.

"Hi," is all I can manage before he leans in and brushes a slow, tantalizing kiss on my lips that speaks of the possibilities this evening holds. When he pulls away, every nerve in my body is humming.

"Beautiful as always, Rylee," he praises, taking my hand and ushering me in the door. "Welcome to my home."

The significance of his statement is not lost on me. This is his home. Not a place he brings his *sometimes girl*. I can't help wondering if he has invited me here to prove a point. To demonstrate that he is trying.

All thoughts leave my head as we enter the great room of the house. I am met with an unhindered view of a beautiful terrace and the ocean. Glass pocket doors have been slid aside, leaving the house open to the subtle breeze blowing in off of the water. My gasp is audible as I step past him without invitation and out onto the deck to admire the sight for several moments.

"It's beautiful. I—" I murmur, turning my head back to him. He is leaning against the back of a chocolate leather couch, his hands shoved casually in his pockets, and the look in his eyes as he connects with mine is so intense that I suddenly feel shy. I feel as if he can see everything deep within me: my hopes, my fears, and the fact that I've fallen in love with him. Uncomfortable that my every thought feels like it is on display, I try to break up the intense atmosphere. "Thank you for having me here, Colton."

He pushes off of the couch and saunters toward me, every part of my body aching for his touch. "I'm glad you're here. Would you like a tour or a drink out on the patio?"

"Patio," I tell him immediately, wanting to soak up the sun and the beautiful view with him. I wander out onto the sprawling deck complete with an infinity edge pool, built-in barbeque island, and the most comfortable looking patio furniture I have ever seen.

"Take a seat," he tells me. "I'm going to get us a couple of drinks. Is wine okay?"

"Sounds great." I ignore his request to sit and walk to the edge of the railing to take in the unobstructed view of the beach that stretches to the left and right of us. My thoughts turn to what it would be like to wake up every day to this spectacular view. *Beside Colton watching this spectacular view, to be exact.*

"I could sit here all day." I'm startled by his voice behind me.

"It's very soothing." He sidles up next to me and places a glass of wine on the railing beside me. "Thank you. I imagine it could be very distracting when you have other things to do."

Colton places a soft kiss on my bare shoulder and keeps his lips there as he murmurs, "Nothing could be more distracting than you standing here right now with the wind in your hair and your dress billowing around you, revealing those sexy legs of yours."

His words are like an electric pulse to my system, stoking my ever-present burn for him. Despite the warmth of him behind me, I have goose bumps on my arms. "Are you trying to sweet talk me, Ace, so that you can get laid tonight?"

"If it's working, then yes I am."

How will I ever be able to say no to him?

"I told you," I say, feigning disinterest, "I'm not really into race car drivers."

"Ah … yes." He laughs, moving to the side of me, resting his hip on the rail but keeping a hand on my lower back. "I forgot, only baseball players do it for you." He takes a long sip from his bottle of beer, watching me. "I'm sure you could be persuaded, though."

I raise an eyebrow and tilt my head, trying to hide my smile. "Might take an awful lot of persuading …"

He moves quickly so my back is to the railing now and his arms box me in on either side. His warm, hard body presses up against mine and a mischievous grin plays at the curves of his mouth. "You know I can be awfully convincing, Rylee."

In a flash, his lips are on my mouth and his tongue is pushing through my parted lips to meld with mine, attacking my mouth with purpose. I wrap my arms through his, hooking them up so I can press my hands against his shoulders. He deepens the kiss, demanding more, taking more, and igniting little licks of desire deep in my belly. One of his hands palms my butt and presses me against him while the other leaves whisper-soft touches on my bare back. I moan softly from the multitude of sensations his touch alone creates.

I hear a thumping sound and I screech suddenly, breaking away from our kiss as I feel something insistently trying to force itself between his hips and mine. I laugh loudly as I look down at the oversized ball of black, white, and tan fur. A beautiful and rather large dog wriggles against us, tail beating against the railing, wet nose pushing and prodding.

I take the dog's head in my hands. "Baxter!" Colton groans at him. "I apologize. He's a little out of control."

I coo to the gentle giant, and when I begin scratching behind his ears, he plops his bottom down on the ground complacently, tail thumping, and groans in pleasure.

"Holy shit! How'd you do that?"

"What?" I ask him over my shoulder as I squat down, continuing to rub the dog.

"He's never that calm with anybody except for me."

"I'm a dog person." I shrug casually, as if that explains everything, and move my hands to rub the dog's chest so that his back leg kicks out in pleasure.

"Obviously," Colton says, bending over to kiss the dog on the head and scratch the fur on his neck. The sight makes me smile. "You're supposed to help me *get* the girls, big guy, not come in between us when we're kissing."

I laugh as Baxter groans on cue. "He's beautiful, Colton."

"Yeah, he's a keeper," he tells me as he takes my hand and pulls me up. "I haven't taken him for his walk yet today so he's mad at me."

"Then let's go take him," I offer up, a walk on the beach sounds like a perfect idea. Colton cocks his head and furrows his brow at me. Did I say something wrong? "What?"

"You just surprise me sometimes," he says, shaking his head at me.

"Good surprise or bad surprise?" I ask him over the rim of my glass of wine.

"Good," he says softly, reaching out and touching a loose curl on my neck. "You're just so different than what I'm used to."

Oh! Yes. I forgot to bleach my hair blonde before I came over. I fidget nervously under his gaze.

"Shall we?" he asks, nodding toward the steps that lead off the patio and on to the beach. I smile at him as he places a hand on the small of my back and ushers me down the stairway, pulling me quickly aside as Baxter bounds down the steps in excitement.

Barefoot, we walk side by side along the path where the wet sand meets the dry sand. Colton throws a ball for Baxter while we chat.

"You know, my sister was surprised to see you at the track the other day."

"Really? I couldn't tell. She seemed so warm and inviting when I met her."

Colton smiles ruefully. "I apologize. She's usually not like that."

"Hmm-hmm," I murmur, my expression telling him I find it hard to believe. "It's okay though because I thought she was another of the BBB."

"BBB?"

"Your Bevy of Blonde Beauties club."

"Oh, come on." He laughs. "I'm not that bad!"

"C'mon, Ace, have you Googled yourself lately?" He goes quiet and for the first time I think I see embarrassment wash through his cheeks.

"No, I don't Google myself," he says finally, "but it's kind of hot knowing that you're looking at me when you're not with me." I turn my head from him and look at the houses on our right, hiding my blush from him.

We walk a bit further, each lost in our own thoughts until I stop to absently dig up a shell with my big toe that is lying partially in the sand. Colton breaks the silence. "I lied to you the other day."

My foot stops digging at his words, curious where he is going with this. I look over at him. "Go on," I prompt.

"Well you asked me if I ever fear crashing." *Oh. Okay. Nothing bad.* "And I thought about it the other night when I was lying in bed. I mean we all fear crashing, but we try to push it out of our minds or it will affect our driving. I guess it's a knee-jerk reaction to say that I don't."

"Have you ever had a bad crash?" I envision him in a mangled car, and I don't like the feelings it evokes.

"Once or twice where it's shaken me up," he admits as he stops and stares out at Baxter biting at the tiny waves in the water. "So yeah, it scares the shit out of me. All it takes is that one time, but the minute I start driving like I have that fear … the minute I start letting up be-cause of it … is the day that I need to quit."

"That makes sense," I say, although I can't fathom hurling myself around a track that fast. Can't comprehend experiencing that horri-ble disoriented and dizzying tumbling feeling more than once in my lifetime.

"Besides, I've feared much worse things in my life." He shrugs, still looking out toward the shoreline. "At least on the track, it's me that puts myself in danger … no one else. My whole team has got my back."

And you're not used to that. Not used to depending on others or needing anything from any body.

I hear a distant voice off to the right of us shout in a feeble voice. "Hi, dear!"

Colton looks over and a huge grin fills his face as he sees a figure standing in the second story window of the clapboard house we are passing. "Hi, Bette!" he responds, waving to her as we pass by before grabbing my hand. "That's Bette Steiner. Her husband was some software tycoon. He died last year so she calls me sometimes if she needs help with anything." He stoops down to scratch a wiggling Baxter before picking up the ball and throwing it toward the water again.

So the rebellious bad boy takes care of his elderly neighbors. Isn't he full of unexpected surprises?

We walk for a little while longer in comfortable silence, our fingers intertwined, hands swinging playfully. The houses are beautiful and the mixture of sun on my face, sand on my feet, and Colton beside me warms my heart. We follow a bend in the beach where the bluffs start to rise so that the houses are raised a bit rather than sitting right on the sand, and Colton pulls me toward a little alcove. A rather large rock with a flat top sits at the base of a small hill layered in various types of greenery that looks out at the ocean.

"I'll let you in on a little secret," he tells me as he helps me up onto the rock, before hopping up so that he can sit beside me.

"Oh?"

"This spot, right here, is my little slice of heaven. My place to go and sit when I need a break from everything."

I lean my head on his shoulder, watching Baxter crash into the waves, pleased that he's shared something with me. "Your happy place," I murmur, looking up at him. God, he looks gorgeous with his wind-blown hair and yet still a little aloof with his eyes hidden behind his sunglasses. He smiles at me and places a soft kiss on my forehead.

He is silent for a moment before speaking. "When I was little, I always had this image in my head, my *happy place* to use your term, where I'd go to when …"

With his silence, I can feel his body tense up at some memory. I reach out and put a hand on his knee, drawing lazy lines with my fingernails. I know I shouldn't, but "the fixer" in me prevails. "When what, Colton?" I can feel him shake his head back and forth. "Do you want to talk about it?"

"Babe, it's old news," he says, shrugging his shoulders, effectively pushing me away before hopping abruptly off the rock. "I'm not the only kid who's had a rough go of things." Emotion clouds his voice as he walks a couple of feet away from me. I start to speak when he talks over me. "Don't bother, Rylee." He chuckles a self-deprecating laugh. "I've been picked apart and put back together by the best of them. A waste of my parents' money if you ask me, seeing as none of them fixed or erased anything." His next words are barely audible above the sound of the surf, and I'm not sure if he means for me to hear them anyway, but they bring a chill to my skin when he speaks. "I'm damaged goods."

I want to reach out to him. To tell him that a person who is damaged goods doesn't help elderly women with chores and make neglected boys feel special by standing up for them. I want to tell him that he is worthy of love and a real relationship. To tell him that what happened as a child—whatever horrible, unimaginable thing it was—does not define who he is today or where he is going. But I say nothing. Instead, I trace the lines of his body with my eyes, wanting to reach out, but unsure how he'd take it.

I am so focused on Colton, that I don't see Baxter bound up in my periphery until he decides to shake his wet fur all over me. I screech out loud at the bite of the cold water hitting my skin. Colton whirls around to see what happened and lifts his head up to the sky laughing at me. A deep, sincere laughter that lights up his face and eases the tension in his shoulders.

"Baxter!" I shout as Colton walks back to me, removing his sunglasses and hooking them onto his T-shirt's neckline. I look up to him, a false pout on my lips. "I'm all wet now."

Colton presses his thighs between mine so he stands in front of me while I stay seated. The rock's height brings us to almost eye level with each other. A slow, salacious grin spreads across his lips and he raises an eyebrow at me.

"All wet, huh?" he asks as he places his hands on my hips and pulls me into him, his hips between the apex of my thighs. "I like it when you're all wet, Ryles."

I swallow loudly, the clouded look in his eyes hinting at passion and desire and so much more. He leans forward, bringing his hands up to my shoulders, his thumbs rubbing back and forth at the hollow dip where my collarbones meet, before brushing a kiss on my lips. I bring my hands up to skim my fingernails up his chest and then around to the back of his neck and play in his hair before tugging his head forward, deepening the kiss. The low groan in the back of his throat excites me and ignites me, sending licks of white-hot pleasure to every nerve. Despite the barrage of sensation his lips evoke on mine, he keeps the kiss slow and soft. Soft sips, slow licks of tongue, slight changes in angle, and soft murmurs of sweet nothings that seep into my soul and wind around my heart. Colton backs away with a shaky sigh after placing a kiss on the tip of my nose.

Oh my, the man sure knows how to kiss a woman senseless. If I was standing right now, I think I'd need someone to help me because he's made my knees weak.

He tilts my head up so that my eyes are forced to look at him. I feel shy under the intensity of his gaze. He just smiles softly at me and shakes his head as if he can't believe something. Baxter nudges at him, jealous of the lack of attention, and Colton laughs, reaching his hand down to pet his head. "Okay, Bax, I don't mean to neglect you!" He takes the ball out of Baxter's mouth and turns around to chuck it down the beach.

I hop down off the rock and watch Baxter take off, kicking up sand as he goes. "He's fast!" I exclaim as I feel Colton's hands slide around my waist, pulling me back into him.

He wraps his arms around me, my back to his front, and he rests his chin on my shoulder. My body relaxes and yet perks up with awareness at the feel and warmth of his body pressed against mine. I close my eyes momentarily, drinking in the uncensored affection that Colton rarely displays.

"Hmmm, you always smell so good." He nuzzles my neck, and I

can feel the vibration of his words against the sensitive skin beneath my ear where his lips press. "It's scary how easily I can get lost in you."

I still at his words. As much as I want and need to hear these words, my mind chooses this time for insecurity and disbelief to rear its ugly head. Images flash through my head. Page upon page of Google images with Colton and his BBB. He is so smooth. So practiced. How many women has he uttered these words to?

"What is it, Rylee?" *What? How does he know?* "I just felt your entire body tense up. What's going on in that beautiful and intriguing head of yours?"

I shake my head, feeling silly for my thoughts and yet afraid of the answers. When I try to pull away from him, his arms tighten around me. "It's nothing, Colton." I sigh.

"Tell me."

I take a deep breath and steel myself to ask the two simple words swimming around in my head. "Why me?"

"Why you what?" he asks, confusion in his voice as he releases his hold on me.

Despite being let go, I take a step away and keep my back to Colton, lacking the courage to ask him to his face. "Why me, Colton? Why am I here?" I can hear him take a deep breath behind me. "Why not one of the score of women before me? There are so many others that are so much prettier, sexier, skinnier ... why am I here and not one of them?"

"For someone so sure of yourself, your question astonishes me." His voice is closer than I had expected. We stand in silence and when I do not turn around to face him, he puts his hands on my arms and does it for me.

"Look at me," he commands, squeezing my biceps until I comply. He shakes his head at me, disbelief and, I think, a little bit of surprise etched in his features. "First of all, Rylee, you are an extremely beautiful, tremendously sensual woman. And that ass of yours," he pauses, the guttural sound in the back of his throat is one of pure appreciation, "is something men fantasize about." He snorts. "I could sit and admire you all day."

His eyes lock on mine and I can see the honesty in his eyes. A part of me wants to believe him. Wants to accept that I am enough for him. He moves his hands from my arms to the sides of my ribcage and then slowly runs them down to my hips and back up.

"As for these, I have to admit, sweetheart, that I've dated mostly waifs in my years, but damn, Rylee, your curves are so incredibly sexy. They turn me on like you wouldn't believe. I get hard just watching you walk in front of me." He leans into me, his arousal pushing against me, and kisses me softly on my parted lips. He rests his forehead against mine, his fingers playing idly with the tie at my neck. "As to why they are no longer here?" he murmurs, the words fanning over my face before pulling back so that his green eyes burn into mine. "It's simple. Our time was over."

I pull back from him, trying to wrap my head around that last part. "They just up and left?" I try to hide the desperation in my voice, as I suddenly need to know what I'm in for. "I mean, why was it over?"

He looks at me momentarily before answering. "Some found others that could give them more, some caused too much drama for my liking, and some wanted the white picket fence and two point five kids," he answers indifferently.

"And—and I assume that you ended things with them then?" He nods cautiously, the cogs in his head turning as he tries to figure out why I want to know. "Did you love any of them?"

"Jesus, Rylee!" he barks, running his hand through his hair, "What the fuck is this, fifty questions?" He walks a couple of feet away from me, exasperation emanating off him, but I've asked this much, I might as well find out what I really want to know.

I sit down in the sand, aware that Baxter is a ways down the beach, and hug my knees to my chest, twisting my ring around and around on my finger. "No, I need to know what I'm getting myself into." Colton's eyes snap up to mine, an indiscernible look on his face. "What I'm already into." I sigh more to myself than him, but I know he hears because I see the muscle in his jaw tic at the words. "You told me that you sabotage anything good. I need to know if you loved any of them."

He steps next to me and runs a hand through his hair. I have to crane my head up to meet his eyes. "I'm not capable of love, Rylee," he deadpans, his voice a haunted whisper, before staring out to sea and shoving his hands in his pockets. "I learned a long time ago that the more you want someone, the more you covet them, and need and love them ... it doesn't matter. In the end they're going to leave you anyway." He picks up a shell and tosses it. "Besides, someone can tell you they love you, but words can lie and actions can fake something that's not."

A shudder runs through me. What a sad, horrible way to go through life. To always want, but to never have, because you think it will be taken away without notice. To be so hurt that you think it's the words and actions that hurt rather than the person behind them. My heart is wrenched for the poor little boy who lived a life without unconditional love. It aches for the man before me. A man so full of passion and life and possibility but denying himself the one piece that can help make him whole.

Oblivious to my line of thinking and my overwhelming pity for the lonely boy within him, Colton continues. "Did I think I might have loved any of them? I'm not sure, Rylee. I know how they wanted me to feel. How they wanted me to demonstrate and reciprocate, but I told you, I'm just not capable of it." He shrugs his shoulders as if this is just a simple fact of life. He turns and looks at me, a ghost of a smile on his lips. "What about you, Rylee?" he asks playfully. "Have you ever been in love?"

I look at him for a beat and then back out to the waves, searching for the memories that are there but slowly fading. A wistful smile plays on my lips as they come back to me. "Yes. I have."

"Baxter, come!" Colton yells before holding his hand out to help pull me up from my seat in the sand. "Let's head back," he says as he keeps my hand in his, and it's not lost on me that he has not responded. We walk in silence for a while, and I can sense he wants to ask more but is unsure how.

He sighs. "I have no right to even feel this way," he says, running his hand through his hair, "seeing as how my past is so ..." He drifts off without finishing when he meets my eyes. "Why does it bug me? Why does the thought of you with someone else drive me absolutely crazy?"

A part of me likes the fact that it bugs him. "You surely can't think that I've been waiting around my whole life to be your plaything, Ace." I laugh, shrugging away the unease I feel about the next question I know he is going to ask. I rarely talk about what happened. I never speak of the after effects. Of the indescribable loss that can never be forgotten. Of the horrid, callous words his family said to me. Their accusations that still haunt me to this day.

Despite the passage of time, I still feel that sharp pang of grief when talking about it. Time has dulled it some in the two years since the accident, but the images burned into my mind will never fade. The guilt still weighs so heavily on me at times that I can't breathe or function. In the past it has prevented me from living again. Taking risks and putting myself out there. From taking a chance like the one I am taking with Colton. I try to hide the shiver that runs through me at the memories and prepare myself for how much I to want to reveal.

Colton looks at me, a ghost of a smile on his sculpted lips. "Spill it, sweetheart. What happened?"

I take a deep breath. "There's not much to tell," I begin, staring at the sand in front of us as we walked casually. "We were high school sweethearts, followed each other to college, got engaged, were planning our wedding …" I feel him stiffen beside me at my last words, his fingers tensing in mine. "And he died a little over two years ago. End of story." I glance over to find him looking at me. I'm glad the tears that usually fill my eyes don't come. How embarrassing to be in love with one man and crying about another.

He stops, tugging on my hand until I falter. Sympathy fills his eyes as they search mine. "I'm sorry," he says gently, pulling me into his chest and wrapping his arms around me. I bury my face in his neck, finding comfort in the steady beat of his pulse beneath my lips. I wrap my arms around him, inhaling his delicious scent—so new yet so comforting. He brushes a soft kiss to my temple, and his tenderness is so unexpected that tears burn in the back of my throat.

"Thank you," I whisper, leaning back to look at him and smiling softly.

"You want to tell me about it?" he prompts as he runs a hand down my arm and grabs my hand, bringing it up to his mouth and placing a kiss on it.

Do I want to talk about it? Not really, but he deserves to know. Most of it anyway. He pulls me to his side and puts an arm around me as we start to walk again. "There's not much to tell, really. Max and I had pre-calc together. He was a senior and I was a junior. Typical high school romance. Football games, prom, each other's firsts." I shrug. "I followed him to UCLA, stayed with him throughout, and then we got engaged my last year of college." I watch Baxter bite at the waves again, and it offers a welcome diversion from what I'm going to say next.

"One weekend, Max decided to surprise me with a road trip. He said it was just what the doctor ordered before …" I falter, wondering how I should continue. Colton squeezes my hand in encouragement. "Before life got more hectic; new jobs, marriage … everything. We had no set destination, so we just drove. No one knew that we were going anywhere, so there was no one to expect us back home. We headed north and ended up by Mammoth, passing the town, but veering off a two-lane road not too far from June Lake. Thankfully it had been a dry winter, so there wasn't much snow on the ground. Just a few patches here and there. It was early afternoon and I was starving, so we decided to explore and find the perfect spot for a picnic. Stupid us." I shake my head. "We had cell phones with us, but without any service, we turned them off to not waste the batteries." I stop now, needing a minute to remember those last carefree moments before life changed forever. I release Colton's hand and wrap my arms around myself to stifle the shivers that race through me.

Colton senses my anguish and wraps his arms around me, his body ghosting mine. "You guys were young, Rylee. You did nothing wrong. Don't put whatever happened on yourself," he says as if he already knows that the guilt eats at me like a disease on a daily basis.

I take in his words, grateful that he's said them but still not believing them. "We came around a corner on this winding road we were driving on. There was an elk in the road and Max swerved the car to avoid him." I can hear Colton suck in an audible breath, knowing where this is going. "We veered into the oncoming lane and the tires grabbed the edge of the road because Max had overcorrected too much. I don't know. It all happened so fast." I shudder again and Colton holds me, his arms squeezing tighter around me as if their strength can ward off the inevitable. "I remember seeing the first trees as we went over the edge and started down the ravine. I remember Max swearing and it struck me as odd because he rarely swore." My stomach lodges in my throat as I remember the weightless feeling as the car lifted from the ground and the centrifugal force that tossed me around like a rag doll as the car tumbled down. I reach up and wipe the single tear that has slid out of the corner of my eye. I shake my head. "I'm sure you don't want to hear all of this, Colton. I don't want to put a damper on our evening."

I can feel him shake his head as it's resting on my shoulder. His arms are wrapped across the top part of my chest, from shoulder to shoulder, and I bring my hands up to hook onto them. "No, please continue, Rylee. I appreciate you sharing with me. Letting me get to know and understand you better."

Maybe if I open up to him, he'll feel comfortable enough to explain his past to me as well. I think about this for a couple of seconds and realize that as much as I can hope this might happen, the reality is that I feel relieved to be talking about it for the first time in a long time.

I draw in a shaky breath before I continue. "The next thing I remember is coming to. It was getting dark. The sun was already past the crest of the mountain so we were in the shadows of the deep ravine we were in. The smells—oh, my God—they were something I will never forget and will always associate with that day. The mixture of fuel and blood and destruction. We were at the bottom of a ravine. The car was sitting on an angle and I was on the high side while Max was on the low. The car was mangled. We had rolled so many times that the car had crushed into itself, making the interior almost half the size it should have been.

"I could hear Max. The sounds he made trying to breathe—trying to stay alive—were horrifying." I shudder at those sounds that I can still hear in my dreams. "But the best part about those sounds were that he was still alive. And at some point in those first moments of waking up, he reached over and held my hand, trying to take away my fear from regaining consciousness in the hell we were embroiled in."

"Do you need a minute?" he asks sweetly before pressing a kiss to my bare shoulder.

I shake my head. "No, I'd rather just finish."

"Okay. Take your time," he murmurs as we start to walk again.

"I panicked. I had to get help. It was only when I went to release my seatbelt that I felt the pain. My right arm wouldn't work. It was visibly broken in several places. I let go of Max's hand with my left hand and tried to undo the belt, but it was jammed—some freak thing the manufacturer studied after the fact. It was the result of metal jamming in the mechanism from the crash. I remember looking down and feeling like it was a dream, when I realized I was covered in blood. My head and arm and midsection and pelvis were screaming with pain so intense I think I would rather die than ever feel that again. It hurt to breathe. To move my head. I can recall Max mumbling my name, and I reached over groping for his hand. I told him that I was going to get us help and that he needed to hold on. That I loved him. I grabbed a shard of glass. Tried to use it to cut through my seatbelt but only ended up slicing my hand some and stabbing myself in the abdomen. It was brutal. I kept blacking out from the pain. Each time I would come to, the blinding panic would hit me again."

We reach the steps up to his house, and I watch Baxter bound up with endless energy. Colton sits on the bottom step and pulls me down to sit beside him. I use my toes to make mindless imprints in the sand. "The night was freezing and dark and terrifying. By the time the sun started to lighten the sky, Max's breaths were shallow and thready. He didn't have much time. All I could do was hold his hand, pray for him, talk to him, and tell him it was okay to go. Tell him that I loved him. He died several hours later."

I run the back of my hand over my cheek to wipe away the tears that have fallen and try to erase the memory in my mind of the last time I saw Max. "I was beside myself. I was losing my strength from all my blood loss, and I knew I was getting weaker and worse off by the hour. That was when the panic set in. I was trapped, and the longer I stayed in the car, the more I felt like it was closing in on me.

"When night fell near the end of the second day, the claustrophobia was smothering me, and I completely lost it. I couldn't deal anymore with the pain and the feeling of defeat so I thrashed around in fear, in anger, and in defiance that I didn't want to die yet. All of my movement somehow dislodged my cell phone that had gotten stuck up under the dash amidst the tumbling down the hill. It fell to the floor beneath me."

I take a deep breath remembering how it took every ounce of determination and strength that I'd had left to get that phone. My lifeline. "It took what felt like hours to reach it and when I turned it on there wasn't any service. I was devastated. I started yelling at everything and nothing until something clicked in the back of my mind about a story I had heard on the news. About how they'd found some missing hiker by following the pings on their cell phone despite a lack of service.

"I knew that when I didn't show up for work in the morning, someone would call Haddie and that would get the wheels in motion. She's a worrier and knew I was preparing for a big meeting I had that morning that I would've never missed. I figured that maybe they'd be able to track my cell phone to our location. It was a long shot, but it was the only hope I had." I touch the ring on my finger with my thumb. "I clung to it and willed every thought I had that it would work."

"I don't even know what to say," Colton says before clearing his throat. I'm sure that he never expected this to be my story. Nonetheless, I am impressed by his compassion.

"There's nothing you can say." I shrug, reaching over to place a hand gently on his cheek. A silent thank you for letting me talk and for listening without interjecting. Without telling me what I should have done as most people do. "It almost took another day and a half for them to find me. I was hallucinating by then. Freezing cold and trying to escape the confines of the car in my own head. I thought the rescuer was an angel. He looked in the window and the sun was behind him, lighting him up like he had a halo. Later he told me I screamed at him." I laugh softly at the memory. "Called him an SOB and that he couldn't have me yet. That I wasn't ready to die."

Colton pulls me onto his lap so that my body is cradled between his knees and softly kisses the tracks left by my tears. "Why does it not surprise me that you'd tell off an angel?" He laughs, his lips pressed to my temple. "You're very good at telling people off," he teases.

I lean into him, accepting and being grateful for his comfort. I close my eyes and let the heat of the sun's rays and the warmth of Colton against me melt away the chill deep in my soul. "I told you, Ace. *Baggage.*"

"No," he says, his chin resting on the top of my head, "that's just a fucked up situation in circumstances way out of your control."

I wish everybody saw it that way. I shrug the errant thought away. "Too many sad thoughts for such a beautiful evening." I sigh, leaning back and looking at Colton.

He smiles wistfully at me. "Thank you for telling me. I'm sure it's not the easiest thing to talk about."

"What do you want to do now?"

Colton grins wickedly at me and grabs my waist, lifting me off of him as he stands up. He doesn't release me and continues to lift me up, ignoring my growing shrieks as I realize his intentions, and places me over his shoulder.

"I'm too heavy! Put me down!" I squeal as he starts to trot up the stairs. I smack him on the butt, but he continues.

"Quit wiggling." He laughs as he reciprocates the spank. By the time we reach the top, my sides hurt from laughing so hard and Baxter is barking loudly at us. Colton continues to carry me despite reaching the patio, and I swat at him again.

"Put me down!"

"It's taking everything I have to not toss you in the pool right now," he warns.

"No!" I screech, kicking wildly as he swings me so that I can see how close we are to the edge.

He hovers there momentarily as I cry out, but then steps away and I sag in relief. He stops and pulls my legs down, and my body slowly slides down the length of him. When our faces are even, he tightens his arms around me so I am standing on air, acutely aware of my chest pressed against his. "Now, there's that smile I like," he murmurs, his breath brushing over my face.

"Very funny, Ace!" I chastise. "You—" My next words are smothered as he captures his mouth with mine. Soft, tender, and seeking, I yield to him. Needing the virile man against me to make me forget my story earlier and to remind me why it's okay to move on. We sink into the kiss as he lets me slowly slide the rest of the way down his body, my hands holding his face. The calluses of his hands rasp across the bare skin of my back as he slides them down to hold my hips.

I mewl in protest as he pulls back from me. Emotions flicker through his eyes that are impossible to read. "You hungry?" he asks.

Yes, for you. I bite my bottom lip between my teeth and nod to keep the words from slipping out. "Sure," I say, stepping back from him to turn and find a table set up to the left of us, complete with food. "What? How?"

Colton smiles. "I have my ways." He laughs as he leads me over and pulls a chair out for me. "Thank you, Grace," he says toward the open doors into the house, and I hear a faint reply from inside.

"Your secret weapon?"

"Always!" He pours us wine. "Grace is the best. She takes care of me."

Lucky woman. "It smells delicious," I say, taking a sip of my wine as Colton dishes out what appears to be chicken with artichokes and angel hair pasta.

"It's one of my favorites," he muses, taking a bite. He watches me as I taste it, and I can see him visibly relax when I hum with approval.

Dinner is light and relaxed. The food is excellent, and I despise Colton telling me that Grace does not divulge her recipes. I tell him I'll talk her out of it somehow, someway.

We talk about our jobs, and Colton asks how Zander is doing. I tell him that he hasn't spoken any more words yet, but that he seems to be responding more. I tell him that hero status has been definitely bestowed on him by the boys, and that they can't stop reliving how he pulled up to the school. I explain what needs to be done next to get permits for some of the new facilities when Corporate Cares gets the green light.

He tells me that he's been busy with the media side of the upcoming season along with everyday operations at CD Enterprises. In the past week, he's filmed a commercial for Merit Rum, did a photo shoot for a new marketing campaign, and attended an IRL function.

We sink into a relaxed rhythm, mutually sharing with each other, and it feels normal in what is otherwise a surreal setting for me. When we finish dinner, he offers a quick tour of the rest of the house, which I have secretly been wishing for. Colton tops off our glasses and grabs my hand. He shows me a state-of-the-art kitchen with warm-hued granite accompanied by top-of-the-line stainless steel appliances.

"Do you cook, Ace?" I ask, running my fingers over the enormous island as my thoughts flash back to a different kitchen island. When he doesn't answer, I look up to meet his eyes and I flush, knowing that he is remembering the same thing.

He shakes his head and smirks. "I can throw a little something together when I need to."

"Good to know," I murmur as he leads me to the next room, a sunken family room that the kitchen overlooks. Deep, chocolate leather couches that look like you could sink into oblivion in are shaped in a semicircle facing a media unit. He takes me into an office oozing of masculinity in rich leather and dark wood. A broad desk takes up a large portion of the space, the walls are lined with bookshelves, and a lone acoustic guitar propped up against the far wall.

"You play?" I ask, nodding my head toward the guitar.

"For myself." His answer mixed with the unexpected softness in his voice has me turning to look at him. He shrugs. "It's what I do to help me think … to work though stuff in my head." As he talks, I step back further into the office and run my fingers across bookshelves, looking at the scattered pictures of his family. "I don't play for others."

I nod my head, understanding the need to have something to help when your head is troubled. I continue perusing the bookshelves and one photo causes me to do a double take. A younger Colton looks exhausted, yet jubilant, in his race suit standing in front of his car, arms raised in victory, smile wide with accomplishment, and confetti raining down. The only thing detracting from the picture is a woman wrapped around his torso. She stares up at him, love, adoration, and reverence plastered on her face. I'd know her anywhere.

"What's this picture of?" I ask casually as I turn to where he's relaxed against the doorjamb, watching me.

"What's that?" he asks, tilting his head and walking toward me. I lean back and point toward the photograph.

A smile graces his lips and his eyes light up. "That was my first win in the Indy Lights circuit." He shakes his head in remembrance. "God, that was a year."

"Tell me about it." He arches an eyebrow at me as if wondering whether I really want to hear about it. "I want to know," I prompt.

"It was my second year and I thought I was going to lose my ride if I didn't pull a win. I had come close so many times and something always prevented it." He reaches out and takes the picture off of the shelf. "Looking back, I know now that I made a lot of rookie mistakes. But back then I was just frustrated and scared I was going to lose the one thing I really loved—too much ego, too little listening. Some things never change, huh?" He glances up and I smile at him. "Anyway, everything seemed to be going bad this race. We couldn't get the car adjusted right because the weather was erratic. But with five laps left I made a run at the lead. I passed the leader in a stupid risk that I never should have taken, but it paid off and we won."

"First of many victories, right?" I ask as I take the picture from his hand and study it again.

"Right." He smirks. "And hopefully more this season."

"Who's this?" I ask, pointing to Tawny, getting to my real question.

"You didn't meet Tawny at the track the other day?"

"Oh." I play stupid. "Is that who you were speaking with before you tested?"

"Yeah. I apologize. I thought you'd been introduced."

"Uh-uh." I place the frame back on the shelf and follow him as he steps out of the office. "Did she work for you way back then?"

"No." He chuckles, showing me into a den filled with racing memorabilia, a huge flat screen television, and a pool table. "She's a family friend and we kinda grew up together. We, uh, actually dated a while in college, and it was a long-running joke between our families that we would end up married someday."

Whoa! Did I just hear that right? Only a guy would think nothing of making that comment to the woman he is currently doing whatever we are doing together with. Their families think they'll end up married some day? Fuck! I swallow loudly as he takes me into a guest suite. "Why'd you guys break up?"

"Good question." He sighs, giving me an odd look, and I wonder if I am being too pushy. "I don't know. She was just too familiar. I thought of her like a little sister. It just didn't work for me." He shrugs. "When that picture was taken we were still dating. In the end, we remained good friends. She's one of the few people I can really trust and depend on. When she graduated from college with a degree in marketing and I started CDE, she helped me out. She was good at what she did, so when the company became a reality, I hired her."

Well, he might want a platonic relationship but she sure wants more than that. I turn from looking out at the ocean and look at him. He holds his hand out to me, "C'mon, let me show you upstairs."

We ascend the wider-than-normal freestanding staircase, and I find myself impressed with the lived-in feeling of his stone fortress. I tell him I assumed it was going to be cold and uninviting but it's the exact opposite. He tells me he opted for the stone exterior to limit the maintenance required from being exposed to the harsh beach conditions.

When we reach the top of the stairs, we come to an open room that is the patio I saw from the front of the house. "I think I found heaven," I murmur as I take in the indoor/outdoor space. Lights wrap around an overhead trellis covered in a growing vine, twinkling in the darkening sky. Four chaise lounges I could get lost in are arranged around the space.

Colton laughs at me as he tugs my arm. "We can enjoy that space later," he says, wiggling his eyebrows.

"Man with a one-track mind," I tease, but my words soon falter when he brings me into his bedroom. "Wow." I breathe.

"Now this is my favorite place in the house," he says, and I can see why. An oversized bed is facing the ocean. The room is covered in soft browns and blues and greens. A love seat sits on an angled wall and a coffee table is in front of it, where magazines and books are thrown. A large dog bed sits in another corner beneath a fireplace with chewed toys and a rumpled, blue blanket. The focal point of the bedroom is a wall of windows, and I can feel the breeze blowing in off the ocean.

I watch the distant lights of boats making their way home. I can see the silhouettes of surfers waiting to catch one last set before paddling in. "Your place really is magnificent."

Colton takes me by surprise when I feel his arms slide around my waist and pull me into him, his front to my back, and nuzzles his nose into my neck. "Thank you," he murmurs as he lays a trail of feather-light kisses down to my shoulder and back up.

My body shudders and a soft sigh escapes from my lips. His hand splays over my stomach and presses me against him, my curves mold to his firm lines. His mouth is at my ear again, kissing that sensitive spot just underneath.

"Can I tell you how much I enjoy having you here?" he whispers, licks of his breath tickling my ear.

I sigh into him, leaning my head back to rest on his shoulder. "Thank you for tonight, Colton."

He chuckles. "I sure hope you're not implying it's over yet, because I'm just getting started." His hands run up and down the side of my torso, fingertips skimming the edges of my breasts. Tiny hints at what's to come. I arch against him, my body humming with desire, my heart reveling in his tenderness.

I tilt my head up and he captures my mouth with his. His tongue delves past my lips and licks at mine. Teasing. Entwining. Tasting. Worshipping. I turn into him, needing more to feed my insatiable craving. He backs me up against the wall of glass. His forearms press against it, framing my head while his body pushes into mine.

A strangled sigh escapes him as I nip at his lower lip and run a tongue down the line of his unshaven jaw. I reach his ear and tug on his ear lobe with my teeth.

"No." I breathe into his ear. "The night is most definitely not over, Ace." I make my way down the line of his throat and back up to lay a kiss at the pulse in his throat. "It's just beginning."

"Rylee," he moans, a sound of pure appreciation.

I feel empowered by his unbidden reaction. I want to show him how he makes me feel. Tell him with actions since I am unable to with words. I dip my tongue in the indent of his collarbone, his coarse hair tickling my lips, his scent enveloping me, and then trail a row of soft kisses back up to his other ear. "I want to taste you, Colton."

I hear him suck in a breath, and suddenly his hands are on the sides of my cheeks, cupping them. He pulls my face back from his, his thumbs rubbing over my swollen lips. His eyes search mine, for what I don't know, but the depth of emotion that I see is all I need. We stare at each other for what feels like an eternity, trapped in our hazy state of desire.

Our silent interlude lasts until he groans, "God, yes, Rylee," before crushing his mouth to mine.

His kiss is a bombardment of what I see in his eyes: greed, passion, blazing need, and an unexpected urgency. I have no chance to offer anything for Colton just takes, and I submit willingly to his unspoken commands. I hand myself over to him, mind, body, heart, and soul.

I ease back from the kiss, a salacious look in my eyes that stops Colton from pulling me back to him. Our chests heave with anticipation. I bite my lower lip as my mouth spreads into a wicked grin. My thoughts turn to how I want to run my tongue down his body and feel him shudder in response to my touch.

I reach out, surprised by my reaction. Max's passive, shy girl who thought having sex with the lights on was adventurous is no more. Colton makes me need things I never knew I wanted. He makes me feel sexy. Desirable. Wanted.

I bunch the hem of Colton's shirt up until my hands graze his abdomen. I run a fingernail across his stomach just above the waistline of his jeans, and I smirk as his lips part and eyes darken with need from just my touch.

I start to pull his shirt up and off of him. "Let me," he rasps as he reaches up and grabs the back of the neck of his shirt and pulls it off in one fell swoop, as only a man who has no worries of messing up hair or make-up can.

"Just how I like you," I murmur, taking in his sculpted shoulders and lean torso all the way down to the trail of hair in the middle of the sexy V of muscle that disappears beneath his waistband.

"My body is yours to take advantage of." He breathes with a sexy smirk, hinting at the dirty things he wants me to do to him. He holds his hands out to his sides, offering himself up to me.

I reach out and cup his neck, bringing his face to mine. I press my lips to his and dart my tongue in his mouth, pulling back every time he tries to control the kiss. "I. Want. You," I whisper.

I skim my fingers down the plains of his torso, nails scratching softly so his body twitches in reaction. My mouth follows the same path but at a much more leisurely pace. Colton lets his head fall back and groans when I stop to lick the flat disks of his nipples. His hands trail down my arms, up and over my shoulders, and fiddle with the ties at the back of my neck.

"Uh, uh, uh," I chastise. I look up at him from beneath my eyelashes as I lace openmouthed kisses down the skin-gloved muscles of his abdomen. "My turn, Colton."

I step back from him, never breaking eye contact, raise my hands to the back of my neck, and slowly untie my dress. "It's a little hot in here, don't you think, Ace?" I toy with him as I take in a fortifying breath and let the material slowly slide down the curves of my body. I see the fire leap into Colton's eyes as he takes in what's underneath. I've worn my Agent Provocateur strapless bra and panty set in a rich, dark purple lace that hides little but highlights my figure perfectly.

"Sweet Jesus, woman! The sight of you is enough to drive a sane man crazy," he drawls as his eyes drag their way back up and down my body.

He rubs his thumb over his other fingers as if they are itching to touch me. I step toward him again, my body hyperaware of everything around us and between us. I reach out and lay my palms on his chest, his body quivering in anticipation.

I pull them down and undo the top two buttons of his jeans, relieving some of the tension. My hands slide around the inside of his jeans and boxer briefs and grasp the solid muscles of his very fine ass. I skim my fingers back up and over his lower back while I trace my tongue down the trickle of hair below his belly button. I look up at him as I sink to my knees and very slowly undo the last three buttons of his jeans.

He stares at me beneath eyelids heavy with desire, his lips parted, and need palpable. I lower his jeans and boxer briefs, his iron length springing free. I run my fingers down the dark smattering of hair and grip the base of his shaft. I lean forward and Colton sucks in an audible breath as I circle my tongue lightly around the bell-shaped tip and then flutter it slowly down to the root and back up. My hand moves slowly up and down the veined length while my other hand comes up to cup his balls beneath, gently grazing them with my fingernails.

I look up at Colton and I'm swallowed up by the look in his eyes as he watches me. His jaw flexes in expectancy as my fingers tease him, and when I take him very slowly into my mouth, he winces in pleasure before throwing his head back and hissing "Fuccckkk, Ryleeee!"

I tease him gently at first, only taking the tip of him into the warmth of my mouth, rubbing my tongue with pressure on the sensitive underside just beneath the rim of his crest. I twist my hand around his shaft, stimulating him with friction and wet heat.

When I've tormented him enough and can feel the tension in his thighs from anticipation, I sheath my teeth with my lips and take him all the way in until I can feel him hit the back of my throat. The guttural groan that comes from Colton's lips fills the room as the musky taste of his arousal and evidence of his desire for me churns an exquisite ache that invades the depths of my very core.

I bob my head down his length again, my throat convulsing when I reach maximum depth, and slowly press my tongue on the underside as I pull it back out. I feel Colton's fingers tangle into my hair as the blissful need for release starts building within him. The harsh exhale of words and beseeching calls of my name urge me to move faster. Quicker. I take him deeper and stroke him harder. He suddenly swells and I can taste him.

"Rylee," he grates out between clenched teeth, "I'm gonna come, baby. I want to be buried in you when I do."

With his length still hard in my mouth, I look up at him to see his face pulled tight with pleasure. A man on the razor thin edge of losing control. He convulses as I hollow my cheeks and pull tightly on him one last time.

My mind doesn't have enough time to register Colton hauling me to my feet and crushing his mouth to mine with near violent desire. Spirals of sensation whirl through me as he urges my back up against the windowed wall. The anticipation of what's to come causes the ache in my groin to intensify.

Raw need ricochets through my body and straight to my core when his calloused fingers find their way beneath my dampened panties. He parts me gently and finds my clit waiting and throbbing for his attention. I grow dizzy wanting more as his fingers work their magic, stimulating my nerve endings. His mouth plunders mine, filling me with his addictive taste.

"I want you in me, Colton," I pant out when I break from our kiss. He lifts me and pulls my legs around his hips. The delicate strap of fabric holding the two triangles of my lace panties together snaps as Colton rips them from me.

I'm no longer in control. The notion sends an unexpected thrill through me but the thought is short lived as Colton spans his hands across my sides and lifts me up, pressing me against the wall for leverage. He lowers me down while his hips thrust up, burying into me. I cry out, overcome by the feeling of fullness as he stills so I can adjust to him.

"Christ, Rylee," he gasps brokenly, his face buried in my throat. The gentle draw of his mouth on my skin causes me to dig my fingers into his solid shoulders and slowly flex my hips into him. "Oh, sweetheart," he pants as he rocks his hips out and then strokes back into my quivering softness.

His body slides against mine, his hands trapped between the glass and my hips, pressing me into him and pushing himself as deeply as possible. I draw a shuttered breath through parted lips as my body softens and heats up. "Colton," I mewl as I'm pushed toward the precipice. Filling me until I can hold no more. Connecting us in every way possible. Blood pounds in my ears and sensation rockets through my body as we find each other's rhythm.

"Hold on, Ry. Not yet!" he commands as he quickens his tempo and brings me closer to the brink. Our lungs pant in short, sharp breaths, hands grip sweat-slickened flesh, and mouths claim any part of the other we can taste.

I can feel my body quickening at the same time Colton stiffens inside me. "Colton," I warn, my body tensing around him.

"Yes, baby, yes," he shouts at the same time I'm unable to deny myself another single second. My thighs turn to steel as I crash over the edge, lost in the explosion. The intense contraction grabs hold of Colton and drags him over with me. A litany of pleasure-induced words falls from his lips, his face buried in the curve of my shoulder as his body shudders with his release. We stay like this, connected as one and locked around each other momentarily, until we slowly slide down the wall to the floor. We sit entwined, my face is nuzzled against his throat, and his arms encircle me.

And in this moment, I am completely and utterly his. Swallowed by him. Lost to him and the moment so much so that I am frightened by the power of my feelings.

We sit like this, tangled around each other in a spellbound state without speaking. The lazy tracing of fingers on cooling skin and the reverberation of our hearts against each other is the only communication we need. Our labored breaths finally even out as the sky falls dark, leaving us bathed in moonlight.

I'm afraid to speak. Afraid to ruin the moment.

"You okay, Ace?" I ask finally, my foot slowly falling asleep and needing to move. Colton grunts, and I laugh at him, pleased that I reduced him to incoherence. I try to pull away from him and lean my back against the glass behind me, but he shifts with me so his face is now in the crook of my neck. He moans a sigh of satisfied contentment that spears straight into my heart.

My eye catches my torn underwear on the floor and I snicker. "What is it with you and tearing my panties off, huh? I would have gladly stepped out of them for you." I scratch my nails languorously over his back.

"Takes too long." He snorts, his unshaven jaw tickling my skin.

"Those were one of my favorite pairs. Now I don't have any to match this bra," I pout.

Colton pulls away from me, a smirk on his lips and humor in his eyes. "Tell me where they're from and I'll buy you a hundred sets so long as you stand before me like you did tonight." Colton leans forward placing a slow kiss on my lips. "Better yet," he says, pulling back and tracing a finger along the line where my breast meets the lace of my bra. "Since that is such a mighty fine bra, maybe you should just wear that and nothing else under your clothes. Talk about sexy," he grunts. "No one would even have to know."

"You'd know," I counter, arching an eyebrow.

"Yes, I would." He grins wickedly, "And I'd walk around hard all fucking day thinking about it."

I laugh. A deep, soul-baring laugh because I am so overcome with emotions that I'm bubbling over.

"Shall we get off the floor?" he asks as he shifts and unfolds himself from me. He rises, reaching out for my hand, and helping me up to my feet. "The bathroom's through there…" he points to the wide opening to the left of the bed "…if you want to get cleaned up."

"Thanks," I murmur, suddenly self conscious about my nudity. I gather my dress, pressing it to my front and look for what's left of my panties. "What—?" I ask when I can't find them. I look up to see Colton watching me as he pulls his jeans up over his naked hips, the remnants of my underwear haphazardly stuffed in his front pocket. He stops when my eyes remain on his.

Leaving his fly unbuttoned, he walks to me and reaches out to tug my dress out of my hand. I try to pull it away but I realize his intentions a moment too late. "For God's sake, Rylee, there's no need to be shy. After you just stood before me like that?" He shakes his head at me. "You're hot as hell and having confidence about it is even sexier, sweetheart." He senses my unease and leans in to brush a kiss on my lips. "It's not like I haven't seen you naked before." He smirks and holds my dress out.

I stare at him, naked except for my bra, trying not to fidget. His compliment eases my insecurities a tad. I am plain old me and Colton frickin' Donavan is in front of me. Telling me I am sexy. That he loves my curves. I feel like I need to pinch myself. Instead, I push back my lack of self-confidence and tell myself I can do this. A slow smile quirks at one corner of my mouth as I glance at my dress in his hand before I very deliberately walk past him.

I can feel his smile when I turn the corner into the oversized bathroom, filled with granite and tumbled stone. I release the breath I was holding, proud of myself for having the courage to do that. I glance up at my reflection in the mirror and am pleasantly surprised to see that my bag is sitting on the countertop. Grace must have brought it up.

"Feel free to grab one of my shirts off of the stacks in my closet," Colton calls to me from the bedroom.

"Um–Okay. Thanks."

"I'm going to run and get us a drink. Let Baxter out. I'll be right back. Take your time."

"Uh-huh," I reply as I wander around the ridiculously large space. I walk into an open doorway to find a closet that would make Haddie the Clotheshorse cry. I peruse his vast selection of T-shirts and settle on a heather gray one. I press my nose into the fabric and can smell the detergent that makes up part of Colton's scent that I love so much.

I clean up, freshen up my make-up, pull on a pair of boyshort panties I brought—because yes, I knew this was a forgone conclusion—and slip Colton's shirt over my head.

Chapter Twenty-Four

WITH COLTON STILL GONE, I wander down the hallway and out the open door onto the second story terrace. I walk to the railing that overlooks the lower patio and the ocean beyond and lean against it, enjoying the nighttime breeze and the moonlight on the dancing waves.

I am so overwhelmed by what's happened recently that I can't even begin to process it. One minute I am lonely, afraid, and feeling too guilty to live again and a few weeks later I am here with a man who's complicated and wonderful and so incredibly alive. I've gone from empty and aching and raw, to happy and sated and feeling like I am having an out-of-body experience.

"Just when I thought you couldn't get any sexier, I find you wearing one of my favorite shirts." His words startle me, and I turn to find him beside me, holding out a glass of wine.

"Thank you," I murmur, taking a sip and reaching a hand out to rub Baxter's head, as he tries to squeeze between us again.

Colton edges a hip up on the railing and turns to face me as I look out at the water. "I like seeing you here," he admits, his voice soft with reflection as he tilts his head and watches me. "I like seeing you in my surroundings, in my shirt, with my dog … more than I ever could've imagined." I transfer my gaze from the water to meet his, trying to read the emotions swimming beneath the surface. "That's a first for me, Rylee." He confesses in a soft whisper, and I can barely make out the words above the noise of the waves. But his admission speaks volumes to me. Holy shit! Does this mean that he means there is a possibility of more? That whatever we are is more than just one of his stupid arrangements? I can sense his unease so I try to lighten the mood.

"What? You don't drag all of your wenches to this hideous lair of yours?"

He reaches out, a quiet smile on his lips, and cups my neck, his thumb brushing over my cheekbone. "Just the one," he replies. I smile back at him, adoring the tender side of Colton as much as I love the stubborn, feisty one. He lifts his beer bottle to his lips and takes a long pull on it. "I brought up some dessert," he offers.

"Really? I thought that's what we just had." He smiles and a carefree laugh escapes his lips.

"C'mon." He tugs on my arm and pulls me down to sink into one of the chaise lounges. Colton walks over to a console hidden in the wall, and within seconds, I hear Ne-Yo's soft voice. Baxter groans in satisfaction as he plops his large body down in the open doorway.

"So," he says as he scoots a table next to me, "I have two options for you. Mint chocolate chip ice cream or chocolate kisses."

"You remembered!" I gasp.

"Well when it comes to you and sweets, I have a hard time forgetting." He smirks as he puts a hand on my back, urging me to sit up, and then slides himself behind me.

A smile he can't see spreads on my face as I think of Colton and his imaginative ways of eating a certain confection. I lean back into his bare chest, fitting myself to him, and reach out at the tray to grab a Hershey's kiss. I unwrap it and pop it in my mouth, laying my head back onto his shoulder and groan at its heavenly taste.

"If that's all it takes to hear you make that sound, I'm buying you a truckload of them," he breathes in my ear as he moves behind me, adjusting himself.

"Want one?" I tease as I bring it to his lips and then take it away and put it in my mouth, moaning intentionally this time. He laughs and I give him a Hershey's kiss for real this time. "A girl could get used to this," I murmur, liking the warmth of him against me.

We sit for a while and talk about families, travels, experiences, and work. I avoid the topic that I really want to delve into, knowing that his past is off limits. He is funny and witty and attentive, and I can feel myself falling deeper for him, entangling myself further in his tantalizing web.

"Awesome, charismatic, and exciting," Colton says, breaking the silence between us.

I can't help but laugh out loud. "Nope," I say again, leaning back further into the warmth and comfort of his chest.

"You're never going to tell me are you?" he asks lifting a hand to brush hair off the side of my neck, exposing my bare skin so that his mouth can place a kiss there.

"Nope," I repeat, fighting the shiver that runs through me as he nuzzles his nose down to my ear.

"How about addictive cock experience?" he murmurs, his breath tickling my skin.

The laugh that bubbles in my throat falls to a sigh as he nips at my earlobe and sucks gently on the hollow spot just beneath it. "Hm-mmm, that could work," I manage as he wraps his arms around my chest, and I begin to run my fingers up and down the parts of his arms that I can reach. I angle my head further to the side, giving him more access to my sensitive skin as my nails cross a jagged line on his right forearm.

"That's a nasty scar," I murmur. "What super-masculine thing were you doing to acquire that?" I cringe at the thought of how much it must have hurt.

He's quiet for a beat, kissing my temple and pressing his face to the side of mine so I can feel him swallow. "Nothing of significance," he says then falls quiet again. "Do you surf, Rylee?" he asks, changing the subject.

"Nope. Do you, Ace?" I take a sip of wine as he murmurs in assent.

"Ever tried?" he asks, the rasp of his voice in my ear.

"Uh-uh."

"I should teach you sometime," he says.

"Probably not the best thing to do for someone like me who's scared of sharks."

"You're kidding, right?" When I don't respond, he continues, "Oh come on, it'd be fun. There aren't any sharks out there that'll bug you."

"Tell that to the people who've been chomped on," I challenge, and despite the fact that he's behind me, I cover my face in embarrassment when I say, "When I was little I was so scared of them that I never swam in our pool because I used to think they'd come out of the drain and eat me."

Colton laughs. "Oh, Rylee, didn't anyone ever tell you that there are much more dangerous things on dry land?"

Yes. You.

As I try to think of a witty retort, my ear catches the song playing over the speakers and I murmur, "Great song."

Colton stills as he listens to the music, and I can feel his head nod against the side of mine. "Pink, right?"

"Hmm-hmm. *Glitter in the Air*," I respond, distracted as I listen to the words of one of Haddie's and my all-time favorite songs. Colton runs his hands up my arms and starts to knead my shoulders. His hands are powerful and add just the right amount of pressure. "That feels like heaven," I breathe as my already relaxed body turns to gel beneath his skillful fingertips.

"Good," he whispers. "Just relax."

I close my eyes and hand myself over to him, humming softly to the song. Colton runs his fingers down the line of my spine and rubs my lower back, my head lolling to the side at the sublime feeling.

"Here comes the best part," I say. I sing along as the words wash over me, moving me as they always do. *"There you are, sitting in the garden, clutching my coffee, calling me sugar. You called me sugar."*

"I don't get it," Colton says, "Why is that the best part?"

"Because it's the moment she realizes that he loves her," I say, a soft smile on my face.

"Why, Rylee, you're a hopeless romantic, aren't you?" he teases.

"Oh, shut up." I shift to swat him, but Colton grabs my wrist before I can, and pulls me into him. His lips slant over mine and make a languid sweeping pass before licking mine. He tastes of chocolate and beer and everything that is uniquely Colton. He cradles my head with one hand while the other runs aimlessly over my bare thighs. Fingertips graze softly, without urgency, or attention to any one spot. I could sit in this moment forever, his actions unraveling me.

Colton brushes a kiss on the tip of my nose before resting his forehead to mine, his hand still cupping the back of my head, fingers still knotted in my hair, his breath fluttering over my lips. "Rylee?"

"Hmm-hmm, Ace?"

He flexes the hand in my hair. "Stay the night with me." He says quietly.

I still, holding my breath. *Oh. My.* I can feel the emotion behind his request and can sense a change from the last time he said it to me. He's not saying it out of obligation but because this is what he wants..

"I've never said that before and truly meant it, Rylee." His voice is a hushed plea that tugs at my heart. He wraps his arms around me, cradling me in his lap, and pulls me with him as he leans back in the chaise, fingers playing in my hair. I remain silent, trying to clear the emotion from my voice before I speak.

"Hmmm, I don't think I could move even if I tried," I murmur.

"You'll stay?" The eagerness in his voice surprises me.

"Yes."

"In that case," he muses, "I might have to take advantage of you again."

"Again?" I laugh. His response is to grab my hips, lift me up, and place me astride him. He situates me on him so that our bodies fit together perfectly, each movement from him traveling through my thin panties and hitting me in just the right spot.

He sits up and kisses me forcefully, his tongue plunging between my parted lips, his hands pressing my body to him possessively. I grow dizzy wanting more of everything from him.

"I. Want. You. So. Much. Rylee." He pants between kisses down my neck. I bring my hands to his face, fingers touching coarse whiskers, and draw his head up to meet my eyes. "You're addictive."

"I know," I whisper, telling him with my eyes that I feel addicted to him too. The muscle in his jaw tenses momentarily before he crushes his mouth to mine, the connection between us a necessity like air.

"Ride me," he pants. Such a simple command, but the way he says it—as if the sun won't rise in the morning if I don't—has me pulling back. I stare into his eyes, so hypnotizing, so intense and so full of desire I wouldn't deny him even if I could.

So I begin to move, surrendering myself to him. Again.

Chapter Twenty-Five

THE COOL AIR THAT WISPS over my skin is a stark contrast to the radiating heat pressing against me. My sleep-induced haze slowly clears from my mind as my eyes flutter open, startled by the natural light filtering in through the open windows.

I start to shift in the sinfully comfortable bed, wanting to stretch my muscles that oddly feel sore, until I realize why. Sex, sex, and more sex. A smug smile crosses my lips.

Colton is wrapped around me like a vine. He is on his side, one leg bent and slung over mine, and his hand splays possessively over my bare chest with his palm cupping my breast. I turn to find his head half on my pillow, half on his.

I study his face: the angles, the fan of thick, dark lashes against his golden skin, the curve of his nose. I reach over and brush an errant lock of hair off his forehead, careful not to disturb him. In sleep, Colton's dark and dangerous aura is softened by his disheveled hair, the absence of the intensity he carries around like a badge of protection, and the lack of tension in his jaw. I enjoy catching this rare glimpse of him—vulnerable and relaxed.

Staring at him, my mind drifts back to last night. I recall his complete and unyielding attentiveness to me and my every need. I think of the new experiences he introduced me to, and the pleasure he's induced in me. My thoughts stray to leather restraints, vibrating eggs, and ice cubes inserted to melt as we became one, evoking that walk down the fine line of pleasure edged by pain. I think of how he showed me slow and soft before pushing me to the brink of oblivion with hard and fast. How, by the light of the moon, in this expanse of a bed, he hovered over me, eyes intense, voice beseeching, and asked me to submit to him. Asked that I trust him to know what my body can handle and which threshold to push it to. And in that moment, I was so captivated with him, I handed myself over to him without question, or second thought. I agreed, knowing he already dominated my mind, heart, and body.

Afterward, as I drifted off to sleep, his warm body pressed against my back and his mouth pressed softly in my hair, I questioned my judgment. Before drifting off to sleep, I wondered what the hell I was getting myself into by accepting his seemingly innocent request, for what is simple under a blanket of moonlight never seems to be when the next morning dawns.

Colton shifts beside me, rolling over so his back is toward me, and pulls the covers with him and off me. I shiver from the chill but am happy that I can now stretch out my overused muscles. I wince as I flex my feet and extend my legs. I definitely wasn't treated like glass last night, but my body quite liked it too.

I'm starting to get cold. I look over at the artfully sculpted lines of Colton's back and I turn into him, tucking my body around him so I can enjoy the feeling of my bare skin against his. My chin rests on his shoulder and my breasts press up against his back as I curl my arms around him. I absently run my fingers across his chest, as I slowly sink back into sleep.

I'm in the first stages of sleep when Colton suddenly emits the most gut-wrenching, feral cry I've ever heard. I would've remained frozen in shock but he bucks his body violently back against me, connecting his elbow against my shoulder. "No!" falls from his mouth in a strangled shout. He jumps from the bed and turns around, legs spread, knees bowed, arms bent, and hands fisted in front of his face. His face is the picture of terror: eyes wild and haunted, flickering, teeth clenched, and tendons straining in his neck. His chest heaves shallow breaths, body tense and vibrating with acute awareness as sweat beads on his forehead.

I instinctively grab my shoulder where it is smarting with pain. The shock of what just happened is sinking in, my adrenaline is pumping, causing my body to shake. If I hadn't witnessed this reaction from a nightmare before, from my kids, I would have been more startled than I am right now. If Colton didn't have such a look of complete fear in his eyes, I would have laughed at him standing nude, looking like he's ready to throw down. But I know this isn't a joke. I understand that Colton has had a dream dredging up the past that silently chases him and continues to traumatize him on a daily basis.

I roll my shoulder, pain still shooting through it. "Colton," I say evenly, not wanting to startle him.

I see his eyes slowly come into focus and the tension in his stance slowly abate. He turns his head and looks at me, a plethora of emotions in his eyes: embarrassment, shame, relief, fear, and apprehension. "Oh, fuck!" He shudders a breath, bringing his hands up to rub the fear from his face. The only sounds in the room are his heaving breaths, hand chafing over his stubble, and the ocean outside.

"Fuuuccckkk!" he repeats again, his eyes narrowing on my hand rubbing my shoulder. I can see him clench and unclench his fists as he realizes he's hurt me. I remain still as his eyes lower and his shoulders slouch. "Rylee—I—" he turns abruptly and grabs the back of his neck with his hand, pulling down. "Give me a fucking minute," he mutters as he quickly strides into the bathroom.

I gather the sheets up to my chest and watch him leave, wanting to reach out to him and tell him things he doesn't believe or want to hear. I sit in indecision when I hear the unmistakable sound of Colton vomiting. A knife twists deep down in my gut, and I squeeze my eyes shut, wanting desperately to comfort him.

The toilet flushes followed by a muttered curse, and then I hear the faucet turn on and the brushing of teeth. I rise from the bed, sliding Colton's shirt on when I hear him sigh again. I enter the bathroom, needing to make sure he is okay. We stand frozen, as he focuses on the water running from the faucet. His angst is palpable and hangs in the air between us. Colton scrubs the towel over his face and turns toward me.

When he drops the towel from his face, the eyes that stare back at me are not his. The ones I've come to love. They are dead. Cold. Devoid of emotion. The muscle in his jaw pulses and the cords in his neck strain as he works his throat.

"Colton..." His glazed green eyes glare intently on mine causing my words to falter on my lips.

"Don't, Rylee," he warns. "You need to leave." His command is flat. As lifeless as his eyes.

My heart lurches into my chest. What happened to him? What memory has reduced this vibrant, passionate man to nothing? "Colton," I plead.

"Go, Rylee. I don't want you here."

My bottom lip trembles at his words, for he can't possibly mean them after the evening we've just shared. I saw the emotion in his eyes last night. Felt from his actions how he feels about me. But now … all I can do is stare at him, the man before me is unrecognizable.

I'm not quite sure what to do. I take a step forward and I hear his teeth grind. I've worked with traumatized children but I am way out of my element here. I look down at my clasped hands and whisper brokenly, "I just want to help."

"Get out!" he roars, causing my head to snap up in time to see his dead eyes spark to life with unfiltered anger. "Get the fuck out, Rylee! I don't want you here! Don't need you here!"

I stand there frozen, his unprovoked anger immobilizing me. "You don't mean that," I stutter.

"Like hell I don't!" he yells, the sound echoing off of the stone tiles and reverberating. Our eyes hold in silence as I process his words. Colton takes a threatening step toward me and I just stare at him, shaking my head. He throws the towel with a curse, the clatter of bottles it knocks over ricocheting around the pin-drop quiet bathroom. His eyes angle back toward mine as he clenches and unclenches his jaw. When he speaks, his voice is chillingly cruel. "I've fucked you, Rylee, and now I'm done with you! *I told you that's all I was good for, sweetheart …*"

His brow creases momentarily as the tears that burn the back of my throat well in my eyes and spill over. His callous words turn my stomach and wring my heart. My head tells my legs to move—to leave—but my body doesn't listen. When I just stand there, dumbfounded and shell-shocked, he grabs my bag from the bathroom counter and shoves it forcefully against my chest, propelling me through the door. "Out!" he grates through gritted teeth. His bare chest heaving. His pulse pounding in his temple. His fists clenched. "I'm bored with you already. Can't you see that? You've served your purpose. A quick amusement to bide my time. Now I'm done. Get out!"

Blinded by tears, I fumble with my bag and run blindly down the stairs. I can feel the weight of his stare on my back as I descend. I race through the house, my heart lodged in my throat and my head an absolute mess. My chest hurts so bad that pain radiates in it as I drag in each labored breath. Thoughts elude me. Hurt engulfs me. Regret fills me, for I thought what we had meant so much more.

I burst through the front door into the bright early morning sun, but all I feel is darkness. I stagger, drop my purse, and fall to my knees. I sit like that, staring at a beautiful morning, but seeing none of it.

Letting the tears wash over me.

Allowing the humiliation to consume me.

Feeling my heart break in two.

Colton and Rylee's journey continues in Book #2 of
The Driven Trilogy

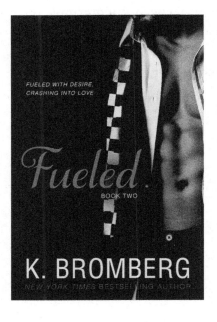

keep reading for an excerpt

Excerpt from

Fueled

Book 2 of the Driven Trilogy

"Y OU REALLY SAID THAT TO him?" Haddie asks incredulously, the look on her face over-exaggerated and hilariously funny.

"I swear!" I told her, holding up my hand in testament. I look down at my phone where a text just pinged. It's from Colton, and all it says is: *Get this Party Started – Pink.*

Haddie doesn't notice the odd look on my face when I read it because she is concentrating on filing her nails. What the hell? First the text about Matchbox Twenty today, which threw me for a loop, and now this? He's a little all over the place and a lot confusing.

"Shit! I'd have loved to see his face when you shut that door."

"I know." I laugh. "It felt kind of good to leave him stunned for once rather than the other way around."

"See, I told you!" she says, pushing on my knee.

"Besides the testosterone fest with Colton, did you and Tanner have a nice visit?"

"Yeah." I smile softly. "It was so good to see him. I don't realize how much I miss him until—" a knock on the door interrupts me. I look over at Haddie, my eyes asking her who could be knocking on our door at seven o'clock on a Friday night.

"No clue." She shrugs, getting up to answer it since I have a slew of work papers strewn across my lap and on the couch beside me.

Moments later I hear laughter and voices and Haddie exclaiming,

"Well look what the cat dragged in!"

Curious, I start to clear my papers when Haddie enters the family room, a broad smile on her face. "Someone's here to see you," she says, a knowing look in her eyes.

Before I can ask her who it is, Colton comes barreling into the room in a less than graceful stride with a laughing Beckett right behind him. Something's amiss with Colton, and I'm not sure what it is until he sees me. A goofy grin spreads across his face and it looks out of place against the intensity of his features. Luckily, I'm shuffling up my papers because he unceremoniously plops down right beside me.

"Rylee!" he exclaims enthusiastically as if he hasn't seen me in weeks. He reaches out, calloused fingers rasping against my bare skin, grabs me, and pulls me onto his lap. All I can do is laugh because I realize that Mr. Cool and Always in Control is a tad bit drunk. No, make that well on his way to being drunk. And before I can even respond to his sudden appearance, Colton's mouth closes over mine.

I resist at first, but once his tongue delves into my mouth and I taste him, I'm a goner. I groan in acceptance and lick my tongue against his. It's only been a few days but God, I missed this. Missed him. I forget that other people are in the room when Colton tangles his hand in my hair and takes possession of me, holding me so all I can do is react. All I can do is absorb the feeling of him against me. He tastes of beer and mints and everything I want. Everything I crave. Everything I need. I bow my back so my chest presses to his, my nipples tingling as they brush against the firm warmth of his chest. Colton swallows the moan he's coaxed from me when his arousal pushes up through my thin pajama pants and rubs against me.

"Should we clear the room?" I hear Haddie say before she clears her throat loudly, shocking me back to reality.

I pull my head back slightly from Colton's, but his hand remains fisted in my hair holding my curls hostage. He rests his forehead to mine as we both draw in ragged breaths of need.

After a beat, he throws his head back on the couch and laughs loudly, his whole body shaking from its force, before choking out, "Shit, I needed that!"

I start to scramble off his lap, suddenly aware that I'm wearing a very thin camisole tank with some very aroused nipples sans bra, and

Beckett—whom I've only met once—is sitting across from me, studying us with a quiet yet amused intensity. Before I can even cross my arms over my chest, Colton's hands grip me from behind, wrapping his arms around me and pulling me back against him.

"Hey!" I shout.

"I got it!" he shouts playfully in response. "And Colton's inebriated."

What? I shift in his lap, trying to turn and look at him. "Huh?"

He chuckles and it's such a carefree boyish laugh—so at odds with the intensity he exudes—that my heart swells at the sound. "Ace," he states confidently. "And Colton's inebriated."

He busts out laughing again, and I can't help but laugh along with him. "Nope." And before I can say anything else, Beckett jumps in.

"You're drunker than I thought. Inebriated starts with an 'I,' you douchebag. Spell much?"

Colton flips him the bird, his boyish laugh returning again. "Whatever, Becks. You know you love me!" he says pulling me back against him. "Now, back to business," Colton announces loudly. "You're coming with us."

Haddie raises her eyebrows, amusement on her face at my flustered expression. "Colton, let me go!" I sputter loudly in between laughs, trying to wriggle out of his iron tight grip on me. He simply holds me tighter, resting his chin on my shoulder.

"Nope! Not until you agree that you're going with us. You and Haddie are going on a little road trip with Becks and me." I start to wiggle again, and I feel Colton's free hand slip up to cup my breast through my shirt, his thumb brushing over my nipple. I suck in a breath at his touch and embarrassment floods my cheeks.

"Uh-uh-uh," he teases, his breath feathering over my cheek. "Every time you fight me, baby, I'm gonna cop a feel." He nips at the skin between my shoulder and my neck, his arousal thickening beneath my lap. "So please, Rylee," he begs, "please, fight me."

I roll my eyes despite the shock wave of need that's reverberating through me at the sound of his bedroom voice, and I can't help the laughter that bubbles out, Haddie and Beckett joining in. Drunken Colton equals a very playful Colton. I like this side of him.

"Typical male," I tease. "Always misguided and thinking with the head in your pants."

He pulls me tighter against him, one arm around my shoulders while the other is around my waist. "Well then, don't be afraid to blow my mind," he murmurs, a low, seductive growl in my ear that has me laughing from the corniness of the line all the while tensing at the suggestion of it.

"So get your asses up, pretty ladies, and get ready!" he suddenly orders, breaking our connection, pushing me to my feet, and swatting my backside.

"What are you talking about?" I ask at the same time Haddie pipes up asking, "Where are we going?"

Beckett laughs out loud at Haddie's all-in reaction before bringing a bottle of beer to his lips. "Hey!" Colton shouts. "Don't be drinking my beer you bastard or I'll take you down."

"Chill out, Wood." He chuckles. "You left yours on the table by the front door."

"Shit!" he grumbles. "I'm a man in need of a beer and of women to get their asses moving. Time's a wasting!"

"What in the hell are you talking about?" I turn to him, arms across my chest.

A slow, roguish grin spreads across his lips as he stares at me. "Vegas, baby!"

Mysterious text solved.

"What?" Haddie and I shout, but both with different meanings. There is no possible way I am going to Las Vegas right now. What in the hell?

Colton holds up his phone, biting his lip as he tries to concentrate on its screen, and I realize he's trying to tell the time with his alcohol-warped mind. "We'll be back in the morning, but wheels up in one hour, Rylee, so you better get that fine ass of yours moving!"

What? We're flying? What am I even thinking? I'm not going anywhere. "Colton, you can't possibly be serious!"

He pushes himself up from the couch, and looks a little wobbly before getting control. He looks down at me, an errant lock of hair falling over his forehead with his shirt untucked on the right side. "Do I need to pick you up over my shoulder and haul you to your bedroom to show you just how serious I am, sweetheart?"

I look over at Beckett for some kind of help. He just shrugs his shoulders, silently laughing at our banter. "I'd just give in, Rylee," he drawls, winking at me. "He doesn't give up when he's in this mood. I suggest you go get changed."

I open my mouth to speak but nothing comes out. I look over at Haddie who has excitement dancing in her eyes. "C'mon, Ry," she prompts. "It couldn't hurt to escape with everything that's going on tomorrow." She shrugs. "Have some fun and forget a little." I nod at her and her smile widens. She whoops loudly. "We're going to Vegas, baby!"

Beckett stands from the chair asking for the bathroom. Haddie offers to show him on the way to her room to get ready. I turn to face Colton but am caught off guard as he swoops me up and over his shoulder, swatting my butt as he carries me rather unsteadily toward the hallway.

"Colton, stop!" I shriek, smacking his ass in turn.

His only response is a laugh. "Which room is yours?" I squeal as he tickles my feet. "Tell me, woman, or I'll be forced to torture you some more!"

Oh, I definitely like drunk and playful Colton!

"Last door on the right," I screech as he tickles me some more before throwing me unceremoniously onto my bed. I'm out of breath from laughing, and before I can even speak, Colton's body is flanking mine. The feeling of his weight on me, pressing intimately against me, creates a crack in my resolve. So much for being aloof. That card was thrown out the window the minute he wobbled into the family room with that playful and captivating grin on his face.

His mouth slants over mine and his tongue plunges into my mouth. I slide my hands up and under the hem of his shirt and run them up the planes of his back. The kiss is full of greed, angst, and passion, and I know I'm losing myself in it. To him. His hands roam, touching every inch of my bare skin he can find as if he needs this connection to tell him everything is alright between us. That our union is reassuring him, confirming that whatever's between us is still there.

I freeze when I hear a knock on the doorjamb. "C'mon, loverboy." Beckett chuckles uncomfortably. "Rein it in. You can do that later. Right now we've got a plane to catch."

Colton rolls off of me, groaning as he adjusts his arousal in his jeans. "You're such a buzz kill, Becks!"

"That's why you love me, brother!" He laughs as he retreats down the hall, giving me some privacy to get ready.

Colton props his hands behind his head and crosses his feet at the ankles as I scoot off of the bed. "God, you look sexy right now," Colton murmurs, his eyes focused on my nipples pressing against the thin cotton of my tank.

"She'll look sexier in about twenty minutes, Donavan, if you get the hell out of here and let her do her thing," Haddie says unabashedly as she breezes in my room holding a handful of barely-there dresses on hangers for me to try on.

"Well shit," Colton says, pushing himself up off of the mattress, "I guess I've been told. Beckett?" he bellows down the hall, "Time for another beer."

Acknowledgements

I have to start by thanking my husband, friend, and partner in crime, J.P. When Rylee and Colton started buzzing around in my head, he looked at me and said, "What are you waiting for, write the book already. Quit talking about it and just do it!" So thank you for pushing me to take the chance. And then when I started dragging my feet with nerves whether the story was good enough, thank you for telling me to press the "go" button repeatedly. Thank you for keeping the kids happy and entertained so that Mommy had time to write. And for trying to understand that even when a scene was stressing me out, the chance to write allowed me to relax. Thank you for understanding and not being upset the many times when you went to bed alone and I stayed up with Colton for a little while longer. And more important than anything, thank you for telling me endlessly how beautiful I am, inside and out, even when I felt/feel ugly. Your words have given me confidence and a sense of self that I've lacked for so long.

To my three wonderful, beautiful, demanding, headstrong, passionate, loving, and very active children for letting Mommy sit at the computer a minute longer than she should have when you needed a re-filled glass or help with something so that I wouldn't lose that thought in my head. You've taught me what true, unconditional love is and that a bad day truly can be erased with the grace of your smile, the sound of your giggle, or the squeeze of your hug. You are my world, my life, my happiness. I love you.

To my parents, who have probably read every horrible and not so horrible story I have written throughout my life, thank you for always being my number one fan and believing in me. For always surrounding me with positivity and encouragement. For taking chances in life to show me that most times the risk is worth it. For showing me humility, that sometimes less is definitely more, and for demonstrating what true love looks like. Thank you for always wanting more for me than you ever had.

To my sister, for always being great at everything so that I always had a bar to hold my accomplishments against. Thank you for being my friend and an ear to use when I needed it the most.

To the rest of my family (MC, SB, RK, BB) and everyone else I'm not mentioning, thank you for your support. To AK, for sharing my love of reading as well as helping promote my book—and for being the only person I can ask what the rating is on a book and knowing exactly what I'm talking about. Thank you to all my other friends that didn't look at me like I was crazy when I told them I wrote a book and for being supportive (even if it's not their type of book) – you know who you are, so thank you.

Thank you to Maxanne Dobson of the Polished Pen for cleaning up my grammar and making things flow a little smoother for you guys with her editing experience. Thank you to Deborah at Tugboat Designs for not telling me "What?" when I said I don't know what I wanted but that I definitely didn't want a person on the cover. And then when she gave me mock images, for not getting whiplash when all of the sudden I knew exactly what I wanted and it was definitely the image of the woman's hip that we ended up using.

Thank you to all of the BLOGGERS out there! If you didn't do what you do on your sites, there would never be a chance for independent authors such as myself to succeed. So thank you for reading my emails, accepting my ARC's, offering to give me space on their blogs, and for taking the time to read a debut novel and offer a review—especially during a crazy month with so many other great releases. Thank you for being patient with me as I figured out the correct protocol in going about all of this. Thank you for taking the chance on me. A special thank you to Emily of the SubClub—you were the first person to finish the ARCs I sent out and your comments allowed me to own the confidence I felt in the story I'd written. Thank you to Jess from Fab, Fun, and Tantalizing Reads for commenting on Goodreads as she read her ARC and starting a buzz about Driven on that site.

And thank you to you—the reader—for taking a chance on an unknown author with a debut novel. I hope that you fell in love/hate with Rylee and Colton as much as I have. Sorry about the cliffhanger, but I promise the story only gets better and more intense in **Fueled**

If you enjoyed Driven, please take a moment to give it a rating as those ratings are so very important to us independent authors. I'd love to hear what you thought of **Driven** as well. Feel free to visit:

my webpage: www.kbromberg.com

Facebook page: facebook.com/authorkbromberg

Goodreads: goodreads.com/Kbromberg

or just plain drop me an email at kbrombergwrites@gmail.com

About the Author

New York Times Bestselling author K. Bromberg writes contemporary romance novels that contain a mixture of sweet, emotional, a whole lot of sexy, and a little bit of real. She likes to write strong heroines and damaged heroes who we love to hate but can't help to love.

A mom of three, she plots her novels in between school runs and soccer practices, more often than not with her laptop in tow and her mind scattered in too many different directions.

Since publishing her first book on a whim in 2013, Kristy has sold over one and a half million copies of her books across eighteen different countries and has landed on the *New York Times, USA Today,* and *Wall Street Journal* Bestsellers lists over thirty times. Her Driven trilogy (*Driven, Fueled,* and *Crashed)* is currently being adapted for film by the streaming platform, Passionflix, with the first movie (Driven) out now.

With her imagination always in overdrive, she is currently scheming, plotting, and swooning over her latest hero. You can find out more about him or chat with Kristy on any of her social media accounts. The easiest way to stay up to date on new releases and upcoming novels is to sign up for her newsletter (http://bit.ly/254MWtI) or text KBromberg to 77948 to receive text alerts when a new book releases.

Connect with K. Bromberg

Website: www.kbromberg.com
Facebook: www.facebook.com/AuthorKBromberg
Instagram: www.instagram.com/kbromberg13
Twitter: www.twitter.com/KBrombergDriven
Goodreads: bit.ly/1koZIkL

Made in the USA
Monee, IL
07 September 2020